Glendaria Awakens Trilogy

Dungeon Player

Dungeon Crisis

Dungeon Guild

A LitRPG Dungeon Core Adventure

By: Jonathan Brooks

Cover Art by: Melissa Schrank

Dedi

To my beautiful wife, Melody, who always encouraged me to write – especially after watching me read countless books over the years.

Also, to my daughter Layla, who is just learning to read and already has a massive library of books.

Table of Contents

Dungeon Player

Prologue

"I don't ever want to see, talk, text, email, or even hear from you again Angie!"

Wayne angrily pushed END CALL on the display screen located on the dashboard of his delivery van.

"Stupid...backstabbing...piece of shit!" he screamed out loud – to the disgusted looks of a woman on the sidewalk next to his parked van. *Whoops, shouldn't have left the windows open.*

Wayne had just found out his girlfriend was cheating on him with some guy she met while playing Glendaria Awakens, the newest and most revolutionary FIVRMMORPG. Also known as a Full Immersion Virtual Reality Massively Multiplayer Online Role-Playing Game; it was a mouthful, but whatever it was called, it was the hottest thing to hit the video-gaming market – ever. The beta testing stage had ended 3 months ago, and the full game launched a month after that to much anticipation. So much anticipation, in fact, that Wayne was still delivering FIPODs or Full Immersion Peripheral Online Devices that were pre-ordered before the release even two months later. Even though they cost $4,999, demand was so high for the low-supply FIPODs that the waiting list was now up to fourteen months.

Which is why Wayne had been working double shifts for the last two months, delivering and setting up the devices – the hours were long but the pay was good. Being an independent contractor, he got paid by the piece; the more he delivered and set up, the more money he was bringing in. This may have inadvertently led to the reason Angie had cheated on him – he was never home except to sleep, eat, and get ready to install some more FIPODs. Not that he would admit that to himself – it was all *her* fault and *her* decisions that led to her infidelity.

After closing the windows, turning up the stereo to a level that would probably damage his hearing after a couple of minutes, and screaming profanities directed toward his now-ex girlfriend, Wayne collected himself and started to pay attention to his surroundings. Sighing heavily, he thought, *I still have a job to do*. Calling up the delivery schedule on the van's display, he found he had somehow kept enough attention on the road – despite the infuriating phone call he just ended – to end up at his next destination.

Krista Jackson
3487 S. Powers Ave.
Quantity: 2

Shaking off the fatigue and anger, Wayne worked up enough energy to get out the delivery van and made his way to the door of the house. About two minutes after ringing the doorbell, Wayne found himself facing a cute girl with pink and purple-colored hair. He figured she was about 5'6", somewhere in her mid-20's, and was thin but not overly-fit or athletic-looking. After recognizing the Wexendsoft Industries, Inc. company logo on his shirt, she screamed out in a painfully high-pitched voice, "Devin! It's here!"

A fairly-heavyset and unremarkable young man – which Wayne figured was Devin – ran into the room excitedly. His short and unruly brown hair flashed by as his socks slid on the living room's polished wood floor and ran into the wall next to the door. Picking himself up and mumbling, "Sorry about that," before turning to the girl, "It's about time!"

"I know, I preordered these pods like 6 months ago!"

"Well, let me know where you want them, and it won't be more than an hour until you can start playing," Wayne cut her off before she could start complaining some more – he had heard enough ranting about the delayed deliveries from his other clients. He wasn't in the mood to hear any of it today.

After being shown the spare bedroom in the back of the house, he proceeded to unload the FIPODs from his delivery van and started setting them up inside. He wanted to get this delivery done as soon as possible – all so he could have some time to think. He needed to start moving on from his ex and somehow pick up the pieces of his broken heart. He knew he was being overly-dramatic, but that was how he felt.

The installation wasn't hard; he had to open the bottom access panel near the front of each pod and connect the twelve wires that were left unconnected. Due to past complications with shipping and delivery, Wexendsoft Industries had found that – in multiple cases – some of the connections became loose or were disconnected altogether. This caused the FIPODs to be inoperable and required additional service calls to fix the problem. To save money in the long run, they decided to ensure that it was all set up correctly during the initial delivery.

The installation was almost automatic for Wayne as he had done this hundreds of times over the last two months and he thought that he could probably do it with his eyes closed.

Fortunately, he didn't have to close his eyes for this installation.

Unfortunately – at least for Krista and Devin – Wayne was in a hurry and his concentration was focused on a certain stupid, backstabbing, piece of shit.

Chapter 1

"Which race are you going to choose?" Devin asked.

"Come on, you know we've been over and over what we're going to select for months now," Krista whined, "ever since launch, you've spent hours and hours poring over the forums looking at the pros and cons of each race, class, and profession." *Although, I have to admit that I spent most of those hours with him poring over the same information.* "I'm pretty sure we decided last week what we should do when we'd finally get the chance to play."

"Sorry, it's just that the time has finally come and I'm forgetful and nervous and excited and...and...forgetful...and...,"

"You're silly," she laughed, before asking, "anyways, how do we get started? It's funny; I read all about the game, but I didn't pay attention to how these pods work."

"Fortunately for you, I've been following the development of these FIPODs for years and I'll tell you that you're in for the experience of a lifetime. When they first came out, they were about the size of a small car; now, however, they're what you see here – about seven feet long and four feet high. If you're taller than 6'6", they make a custom pod that you can order to fit any size that you need.

"The bed inside is made of a reactive composite material made from a high-density sensory gel/foam hybrid. It forms to the shape of your body so that it feels like you are floating on warm air. Using the nerve synapses in your brain, the full-immersion technology connects directly to your mind. What this means, ultimately, is that you will feel like you're really there in the game world.

"All you need to do is place the helmet located in the top portion of the pod onto your head and it will map out your entire brain; from what I have read, it should take about an hour and it's usually done by the time you finish character creation."

"Thanks for the sales pitch – you know I already bought it, right?" Krista rolled her eyes as she responded to his overly-technical explanation. "So, all I need to do is lay down and put the helmet on?"

"Yes...although the instruction manual says that it's a good idea to use the restroom first before starting. There are safeguards in place that will only allow you play for eight hours at a time with a four-hour break in between. While you're under full-immersion, you won't know if you need to...go...and I'd rather not pee myself the first day," he joked.

"You'd better not! I paid good money and waited way too long to get these – I don't want you ruining them because you drank too many sodas," she remarked before suggesting, "maybe we should get some adult diapers so that we don't have to worry about it."

"No thanks, I'm all good here – let's get started!" Devin ran to the bathroom upstairs while Krista used the one down the hallway. When they both got back, they looked at each other and giggled because they were so excited. Once they calmed down, they climbed on top of the FIPOD beds where they let out a contented sigh. The cushioning was so soft that they said in unison, "This feels so good!" After laughing at themselves again, they reached up to the helmet, placed it on their heads, and made sure to tighten it appropriately so it didn't move around.

Krista immediately felt a little claustrophobic; she couldn't see a thing because it was completely dark inside. However, within seconds of securing the helmet in place, a small white text appeared. She couldn't make it out at first, but as it appeared to move closer, she noticed that it was the logo for "Wexendsoft Industries, Inc." The text quickly faded, and a rising musical score – usually heard in big-budget Hollywood movies – gradually increased in volume, as the title screen for "Glendaria Awakens" appeared.

After a couple of seconds, the title screen and music dispersed, and the sounds of an intense battle took its place. Suddenly, Krista felt like she was taking part in a battle between figures wearing all kinds of armor – from full plate, to hunting leathers, to mage robes, and anything and everything in between. They also had a myriad of different weapons: short swords, long swords, knives, bows, staves, and even axes.

Interspersed between the humans she could see dwarves, elves, gnomes, beastkin, orcs, and even some undead.

This is amazing. Her attention on the battle was interrupted as she noticed something along the lower right side of her vision.

Scanning Initialized.......

Scanning Completion: 2.46%

Ah, that must be the brain-scan thingy that Devin was talking about. I wonder how long it will really take to scan my whole brain?

The battle was still going on, but Krista was distracted as she watched as her "Scanning Completion" increased.

Scanning Completion: 8.72%

Seems like it will take quite a bit longer. The battle was starting to end with two figures taking center-stage. One was a bright-shining paladin in full-plate armor; it appeared as though the sun reflecting from it could blind half the battlefield. He was facing off against a dark figure in mage robes surrounded by undead. *A little cliché, but very well done – it definitely gets my heart pounding.* As the music came to a crescendo, the two figures started to rush at each other; before they met, the scene stopped, and a deep voice that sent rumbles through her chest said, "GLENDARIA AWAKENS."

She was waiting for more, but then everything faded to black – all except the slowly up-ticking numbers at the corner of her vision.

Scanning Completion: 15.64%

Welcome to Glendaria Awakens, Krista. I will guide you through the character creation process.

The voice seemingly coming from nowhere scared the crap out of Krista, "H-How do you know my name?"

When you reserved your FIPOD, you had to complete your registration at that time. Each FIPOD comes preloaded with your essential information. Do you have any other questions at this time?

"Who are you?"

I am your personal Artificial Intelligence associated with your FIPOD. I am here to guide you through the beginning stages of your journey into the world of Glendaria. In addition, I will be

monitoring your personal vital signs throughout your experience. This FIPOD is in continuous communication with Wexendsoft Industries, Inc., so that we can provide you personalized customer service.

"Ok, that sounds weird, but it makes me feel a bit safer at least. What do we do next?"

It is time for you to create your character. First you will choose your race and then your class. Lastly, you will assign your statistic points for your character. Let us begin.

Suddenly, a floating 3D model appeared in front of Krista; it looked just like her! It was wearing a plain-looking, dirty-brown tunic and matching pants – but it was her! Even the scar above her left eye was there; she remembered that she got it rollerblading when she was 12 years old.

Devin was racing her down a hill near her old house when she hit a rock and tripped. She ended up needing stitches; when she got out of the hospital, Devin was more of a mess than she was. He kept apologizing and blamed himself – she could of swore that he cried more than **she** did.

Gathering her thoughts, she looked at her floating image again. *This game is so awesome!* She looked at the text underneath her character.

Choose your race:

Human (Neutral)	
Racial Characteristics:	
+5% Physical damage	+20% Increase in all crafting progressions
+5% Magical damage	+2 to all starting stats
Neutral starting reputation with all races	

Elf (Light)	
Racial Characteristics:	
+50% Movement in wooded terrain	+5 to starting Intelligence and Agility
+15% Increase in Stealth effectiveness	Hostile starting reputation with all Dark races
+15% Damage with bows	

Dwarf (Light)	
Racial Characteristics:	
+50% Increase in night vision	+5 to starting Strength and Constitution
+30% Increase in Blacksmithing	Unfriendly starting reputation with

progression	all Dark races
+20% Damage with axes or hammers	

Gnome (Light)	
Racial Characteristics:	
+50% Increase in night vision	+5 to starting Intelligence and Agility
+20% Increase in Alchemy and Enchanting progression	Unfriendly starting reputation with all Dark races
+15% Damage with small weapons	

Orc (Dark)	
Racial Characteristics:	
+20% Physical damage	+5 to starting Strength and Constitution
+15% Physical resistance	Unfriendly starting reputation with all Light races

Troll (Dark)	
Racial Characteristics:	
+25% Physical Damage	+11 to starting Strength and Constitution

+25% Physical Resistance	-4 to starting Intelligence and Wisdom
Unfriendly starting reputation with all Light races	

Undead (Dark)	
Racial Characteristics:	
+100% Resistance to Poison	+50% Magical damage received from Light-based spells
+100% Resistance to Disease	+30% Magical damage with Dark-based spells
+100% Resistance to Bleeding damage	+8 to starting Intelligence and Wisdom
-75% Effectiveness of all healing received	-3 to starting Strength and Constitution
Hostile starting reputation with all Light races	

There followed an extensive list of races including different types of beastkin, mixed races like half-human/half-orc or half-elf/half-gnome, and even subraces like wood elves. Krista and Devin had spent weeks researching what they had wanted to choose so she looked at the High Elf subrace option:

High Elf (Light)	
Racial Characteristics:	
+50% to movement in wooded terrain	+25% to magical damage and resistance
+5 to starting Intelligence, Wisdom, and Agility	+25% to healing spells
-3 to starting Strength	-25% to physical damage dealt
-2 to starting Constitution	+25% to physical damage received
Hostile starting reputation with all Dark races	

She chose the High Elf option and a prompt appeared:

You have chosen High Elf as your race – Confirm? Yes/No

She chose *Yes,* and a new screen with a class listing popped up:

Choose your Class:

Strength-focused:

Brawler – Primarily uses their fists and small weapons to do massive physical damage to opponents

+5 to starting Strength	+20% Damage with unarmed or fist weapons
+2 to starting Constitution	Ignores 10% of armor upon hit
+2 to Strength each level	Starting Class Skill – Grapple
+1 to Constitution each level	

Fighter – An all-around melee character, the Fighter can use any weapon to dispatch opponents, while simultaneously defending their self and other party members

+5 to starting Strength	+1 to Constitution each level
+2 to starting Constitution	+30% Damage with weapon-based skills
+2 to Strength each level	Starting Class Skill – Focused Strike

Constitution-focused:

Defender – Primarily defense-based, the Defender is the bulwark of the group that can absorb large amounts of incoming damage and grab the attention of as many opponents as possible

+5 to starting Constitution	+20% Physical damage absorbed using Block
+2 to starting Strength	-20% Damage received when below 25% health
+2 to Constitution each level	Starting Class Skill – Shield Wall
+1 to Strength each level	

Pet Trainer – This class uses its own Constitution and Wisdom to force its

will on monsters, thereby taming them for use in and out of combat	
+5 to starting Constitution	+20% Damage with whips
+2 to starting Wisdom	+50% to starting base faction rating for all factions
+2 to Constitution each level	Starting Class Skill – Taming
+1 to Wisdom each level	

Agility-focused:

Archer – The Archer likes to stay out the thick of battle, instead using bows to affect the outcome	
+5 to starting Agility	+20% Damage with bows
+2 to starting Constitution	+5% Damage with small weapons
+3 to Agility each level	Starting Class Skill – Flurry
Rogue – The Rogue uses Stealth to sneak through monster-infested areas without being seen and can cause massive damage to enemies with surprise attacks	
+5 to starting Agility	+15% Damage with thrown and small weapons
+2 to starting Constitution	+20% to Stealth effectiveness
+3 to Agility each level	Starting Class Skills – Stealth, Backstab

Intelligence-focused:

Mage – This caster uses primarily elemental-based magic attacks to cause damage but can use a number of utility spells as well

+5 to starting Intelligence	+30% Damage with elemental-based magic attacks
+2 to starting Wisdom	Starting Class Skill – Flare
+3 to Intelligence each level	

Sorcerer – The Sorcerer can use elemental-based magic attacks, but is rather skilled in other, non-damage-based spells

+5 to starting Intelligence	+30% Effectiveness to non-damage spell effects
+2 to starting Wisdom	Starting Class Skill – Mind Prison
+3 to Intelligence each level	

Wisdom-focused:

Healer – The Healer is a must in any serious adventuring group; from healing, to curing poisons/diseases, and enhancing the teams' characteristics, this person is essential to surviving difficult enemy encounters

+5 to starting Wisdom	+1 to Intelligence each level
+2 to starting Intelligence	+30% Effectiveness to all healing spells
+2 to Wisdom each level	Starting Class Skill – Divine Blessing

Druid – This class uses nature to affect the world around them – they can heal, cast damaging magical attacks, boost allies' character stats, and even reduce enemies' attributes to turn the tide of battle

+5 to starting Wisdom	+1 to Intelligence each level
+2 to starting Intelligence	+30% Effectiveness/Damage with earth, water, and air spells
+2 to Wisdom each level	Starting Class Skill – Entangling Roots

Mixed-focused:	
Paladin – This champion of the Light can do it all – just not as well as more specialized classes	
+2 to starting Strength	+1 to Constitution each level
+2 to starting Constitution	+1 to Intelligence each level
+2 to starting Intelligence	+20% Effectiveness/Damage with Light-based spells and effects
+1 to starting Wisdom	Starting Class Skill – Divine Shield
+1 to Strength each level	Restriction: Light Races only
Warlock – A follower of the Dark, the Warlock is a primarily a Dark-based caster that can also melee when needed	
+3 to starting Intelligence	+2 to Intelligence each level
+2 to starting Wisdom	+1 to Wisdom each level
+1 to starting Strength	+20% Effectiveness/Damage to Dark-based spells and effects
+1 to starting Constitution	Starting Class Skill – Unholy Curse
Restriction: Dark Races only	

Krista always played a healer of some sort when she played these types of games, so she figured she would be the most comfortable in that role again. Devin was going to pick a melee-based character, so they should complement each other well. After looking at all the selections, she chose the Healer class based on the bonus to healing.

You have chosen Healer as your class – Confirm? Yes/No

Of course! She chose *Yes*.

Excellent choice Krista! Now that you have chosen your race and class, you can assign your stat points. The stat points are used to affect the main character attributes that contribute the actions performed by your character. They are as follows:

Strength:
For Strength-focused classes, this attribute greatly affects how much damage they can do with weapons (1 Strength = 2 Physical Damage). This attribute also marginally affects how much damage other classes do with weapons (1 Strength = 0.25 Physical Damage). Additionally, Strength determines how much weight can be held in bag storage (1 Strength = 10 lbs.) It can also minimally affect certain crafting professions.

Constitution:

For Constitution-focused classes, this attribute moderately affects how much damage they can do with weapons (1 Constitution = 1 Physical Damage). This attribute also greatly affects how much physical damage any class can resist (1 Constitution = 2 Physical Resistance). Additionally, Constitution determines how many health points any class will have (1 Constitution = 10 Health Points) as well as the amount of health regeneration (1 Constitution = 3.0 health per second). It can also minimally affect certain crafting professions.

Agility:

For Agility-focused classes, this attribute greatly affects how much damage they can do with weapons (1 Agility = 2 Physical Damage). Additionally, Agility minimally affects critical and dodge chance (1 Agility = 0.1 Critical and Dodge chance). It can also minimally affect certain crafting professions.

Intelligence:

For Intelligence-focused classes, this attribute minimally affects how much damage they can do with weapons (1 Intelligence = 0.25 Physical Damage). This attribute also greatly affects the amount of magical damage for any class (1 Intelligence = 2 Magical Damage). Additionally, Intelligence determines how many mana points any class will have (1 Intelligence = 10 Mana Points). It can also minimally affect certain crafting professions.

Wisdom:

For Wisdom-focused classes, this attribute minimally affects how much damage they can do with weapons (1 Wisdom = 0.25 Physical Damage). This attribute also greatly affects the amount of magical resistance for any class (1 Wisdom = 2 Magical Resistance). Additionally, Wisdom moderately affects the amount of healing done (1 Wisdom = 1% increase in Healing). Wisdom also affects the amount of mana regeneration (1 Wisdom = 3.0 mana per second). It can also minimally affect certain crafting professions.

All characters start with 5 stat points in all attributes. These are then changed by whatever race and class you have chosen -- either positively or negatively. Each time you level up, you will receive 5 unallocated stat points in addition to automatic class-based increases. Lastly, you will receive an additional 10 points that you can assign anywhere you choose right now.

Knowing that she was primarily going to be the main healer of any group she was going to be a part of, she chose to boost up her Intelligence and Wisdom stat points as follows:

Character Status					
Race:		High Elf	Level:		1
Class:		Healer	Experience:		0/100
Strength:	2	Physical Damage:	6	Magical Damage:	30
Constitution:	3	Physical Resistance:	6	Magical Resistance:	44
Agility:	10	Health Points:	30	Mana Points:	150
Intelligence:	15	Health Regeneration:	10.0 per minute	Mana Regeneration:	66.0 per minute

Wisdom:	22	Block:	0	Critical/Dodge Chance:	1.0%

You have spent all your points – Confirm? Yes/No

As she was confirming *Yes*, Krista noticed that the scanning completion had greatly increased since she last looked at it.

Scanning Completion: 98.73%

Finally, please choose a name for yourself that will be seen by other people in Glendaria Awakens:

Krista used the name she usually used in these games: HlrGrrl.

Excellent choices HlrGrrl! Now that you have finished the character selection process, we can start you on your journey.

Scanning Completion: 100.00%

Scanning Complete.

Now entering the world of Glendaria...

Chapter 2

The first sensation Krista experienced when she arrived in Glendaria was the heat from the sun shining down on her face. She kept her eyes closed and concentrated on what she was feeling – the warm sun trying to shine through her eyelids, the feel of the cobblestone street under her feet, and the sound of people having diverse conversations all around her.

She finally opened her eyes and saw she was in the middle of the town marketplace, complete with a babbling fountain in the center. She watched people moving in and out of various shops that lined the area – she could differentiate the players from the Non-player Characters, or NPCs, because they were running instead of walking everywhere.

Welcome, HlrGrrl.

Krista immediately turned at the voice behind her and saw an angelic-looking apparition; it was floating in the air, about three feet off the ground. She recognized the voice from the character creation process and assumed that this must be the AI, "Hello again! Why...and how...does all of this feel so real?"

The sensations you feel in the game world are designed to be as real as possible. Most of what you will experience in your time here will be indistinguishable from the real world.

"Well, I love it so far. Where am I?"

You are in the town of Briarwood, a common starting area for new players.

Krista remembered it from their research; Briarwood was one of the seven starting towns that you would enter the game. Devin should hopefully be around there somewhere, because new players in the same region usually started at the same location.

The starting towns were designed to get new players used to the world around them, provide starting gear, and teach class-specific skills and spells. Which reminded her, "Where do I go from here?"

Each class is provided with a different trainer which will help you learn what you need to know. Since you are a Healer, the Temple of Light at the top of the hill to the east is where you need to go.

"Thanks!" Krista watched as the AI faded away and started heading east, toward the Temple of Light she could see in the distance. She was constantly checking through the crowd around her, looking for Devin on the way. She didn't see him — she figured he was still going through the character creation process. *Oh, well...I still have plenty of time to find him once this initial training part is done.* As she got near the entrance to the temple, she was contacted by the AI again.

This is as far as I go. Find Cleric Ashcroft inside the Temple of Light and he will start your training. If you have any other game-world questions or concerns, use the *Contact Support* function in the game menu. Good luck on your adventure!

Krista tried to thank the AI, but she sensed that it was already gone. Instead, she excitedly walked up the steps to the entrance of the Temple of Light. Pushing open the doors, she found herself in a massive space lit up from hundreds of windows positioned everywhere around the room. Expecting lines of benches like she would see in a church back in the real world, she was confused by the appearance of only an ornate altar in the center of the room.

There was an older — almost grandfatherly — kind-faced man garbed in Priestly robes standing behind the altar who looked up as she walked in. Krista looked above his head and in white text it displayed **Cleric Ashcroft**. The man smiled at her as she got closer and said, in warm voice, "Welcome to the Temple of Light, my child. What can I do for you today?"

Encouraged by his smile and welcoming voice, she told him she was there for training.

"I can see that you have chosen to have the Light to bless you with the Healer vocation. Tell me, child, why is it that you wish to be a healer?"

"I always play a healer in these games – I'm not into being on the front lines and hitting stuff."

Cleric Ashcroft stared into her eyes and searched within them, like he was looking for something. After a moment, it looked like he found it; he frowned and in a soft voice said, "No".

"What do you mean, no? I'm good at playing a healer!"

"The first step to becoming a Healer is to be true to yourself. That is the only way the Divine will be true to you. Stop lying to yourself about your reasons for wanting to be a Healer – only the truth will open up your heart to the Light."

Krista was shocked at his words. Then she was angry. *How dare he say that I was lying! This is supposed to be the easy training part of the game!* She was about to demand that he just teach her what she needed to know when she caught a glimpse of a tapestry over his shoulder. It was a typical RPG scene of a Paladin standing atop a pile of undead with his sword raised victoriously in the air. Depictions of light surrounding him hinted that it was the Light that allowed him to win through the day. It wasn't the scene itself that stopped her – it was the memory it evoked.

Krista and Devin were in their early teens when they were attacked by a rabid dog while walking home from school. It came bounding out from the field halfway to her house and ran straight for her. Growling wildly and foaming at the mouth, the dog scared the bejeezus out of her and she froze.

Fortunately, Devin reacted quickly and picked up a rock, which he then threw at the dog. It was only a glancing hit that bounced off its back, doing no real damage – but it got the dog's attention. Devin whipped his backpack off his shoulders and swung at the dog as it got close. He got a lucky hit on its sensitive nose with the corner of a book inside his bag; although it was enough to deter the animal from trying to attack Krista, it was pissed off enough to launch itself at Devin. Not expecting it, Devin went down under the weight of the dog and hit his head on the sidewalk.

The dog then scurried back into the field where it came from – but the damage had already been done. Devin was knocked out cold from the attack; calling the police and an ambulance to take him to the hospital, Krista stayed by his side until he woke up. Thankfully, there was no lasting damage, but she spent as much time as she could with him as he recovered. He was probably tired of her by the time he was finally well enough to get around, but she felt the need to make sure her "protector" was okay after potentially saving her life.

Ever since then, whenever they played RPGs together, she would always be some sort of support character, while

Devin naturally gravitated toward a front-line character that would protect her from harm. She enjoyed being able to enhance his attributes and otherwise buff him, as well as healing him so he could continue to protect her from enemies. When her parents died – and he moved in with her – she continued to feel protected from the harsh world around her.

She haltingly tried to explain this to Ashcroft when he stopped her halfway through.

"I can see you understand now. This is your truth – the real reason you want to be a Healer. You have nothing to try to prove to me – you only have to be true to yourself. *That* is what it takes to have the blessings of the Divine. Let the Light be your guide and you will never be led astray."

Divine Blessing **Skill Unlocked**

Divine Blessing I			
Grants a blessing on target ally raising their Strength and Constitution			
Attribute increase:	+3 to Strength and Constitution	Cooldown:	30.0 Minutes
Duration:	30.0 Minutes		

"Thank you, Cleric Ashcroft," Krista thanked him with a hitch in her voice.

"Now that you understand your Truth, I could use your help on something. We have a number of citizens of Briarwood that need your help..."

Ah, here we go. This is more like what I was expecting. The first quest Cleric Ashcroft gave her was to deliver medicine to various townsfolk. Each person she visited gave her a little experience and a piece of equipment to help outfit her for the adventures ahead.

The second quest he gave her was to heal some injured workers located in the Temple of Light infirmary. For this, Ashcroft taught her a *Minor Healing* spell and she ended up healing fifteen different people there.

Minor Healing I			
Heals the target for a certain amount using the power of Light			
Healing amount:	5	Mana cost:	10
Target range:	20 feet	Casting time:	2.0 seconds

For her final quest, the Cleric asked her to eradicate some rats located in the garden behind the temple. She learned the *Minor Smite* spell that did damage from afar; because she was a High Elf Mage, the level 1 rats fell from just one casting of her new spell.

Minor Smite I			
Damages a target with power from the heavens			
Magical damage:	5	Mana cost:	10
Target range:	30 feet	Casting time:	1.5 seconds

After completing this quest, Cleric Ashcroft told her that this was all he could teach her for now, but to return when she had a lot more experience. She knew that at level 40 you could choose to be either a Battle Priest or a Cleric; she still had a long way to go, however, so she thanked him and exited the temple.

She was walking towards the marketplace, happy with the training she had received so far, when she bumped into someone from behind. Apologizing profusely, she was about to make her way around him when the man reached out and caught her arm, "Krista, is that you?"

Krista turned around and her breath caught in her throat. In front of her stood Devin – except it was what he would've looked like if he had lost 50 lbs. and started working out at the gym. His acne had disappeared, and he had a five o'clock shadow that was quite attractive. He was also a good six inches taller than he was in real life – which, again, was quite attractive to her. Despite the changes, he was most definitely Devin – the same eyes and shy smile. She looked at the name above his head – **Blade4ce**. She should have known from the name that it was a variation of "BladeForce": it was his usual name for RPG characters.

"Devin! I didn't recognize you! You look so...different. Good, just different."

"Yeah, I was able to tweak some of the physical appearances of my character during the creation process."

"Well, you look wonderful in that armor – very dangerous-looking."

"Thanks, you look beautiful as usual – very exotic-looking as an elf," his words made her blush.

Krista forgot to look at herself after she made her race and class choices. She pulled up her status page and looked at her representative figure. He was right, she did appear fairly exotic-looking as an elf; it was still her face and body, but her eyes were a little sharper and, of course, her ears were pointed at the tips.

After briefly catching up with each other on their experiences so far, they both learned that they each got to level 3 during their training, as well as acquiring some gear. Devin chose to be a Fighter and received items suited to his class:

Rusty Iron Sword	
Main Hand	
Physical Damage:	5

Class Restrictions:	Fighter, Defender, Paladin, Warlock

Ragged Leather Cuirass	
Chest	
Physical Resistance:	3
Class Restrictions:	Fighter, Brawler, Archer, Rogue, Defender, Pet Trainer, Paladin, Warlock

Ragged Leather Pants	
Legs	
Physical Resistance:	2
Class Restrictions:	Fighter, Brawler, Archer, Rogue, Defender, Pet Trainer, Paladin, Warlock

Ragged Leather Gloves	
Hands	
Physical Resistance:	1
Class Restrictions:	Fighter, Brawler, Archer, Rogue, Defender, Pet Trainer, Paladin, Warlock

Ragged Leather Helmet	
Head	
Physical Resistance:	1
Class Restrictions:	Fighter, Brawler, Archer, Rogue, Defender, Pet Trainer, Paladin, Warlock

Ragged Leather Boots	
Feet	
Physical Resistance:	1
Class Restrictions:	Fighter, Brawler, Archer, Rogue, Defender, Pet Trainer, Paladin, Warlock

Cracked Wooden Shield	
Off-hand	
Block:	3
Class Restrictions:	Fighter, Defender, Paladin

He also got his *Focused Strike* skill unlocked during his quests:

Focused Strike I			
The Fighter takes extra time to line up a focused strike with their chosen weapon, allowing them to deal additional damage			
Physical damage:	200% physical damage	Cooldown:	300.0 seconds

Since Krista was a Healer, she received less gear; however, she acquired additional spells for her repertoire.

Cracked Staff	
Two-handed	
Physical Damage:	2
Class Restrictions:	Fighter, Pet Trainer, Mage, Sorcerer, Healer, Druid, Warlock

Threadbare Robe	
Chest	
Physical Resistance:	1
Class Restrictions:	Mage, Sorcerer, Healer, Druid, Warlock

Flimsy Sandals

Feet	
Physical Resistance:	1
Class Restrictions:	Mage, Sorcerer, Healer, Druid, Warlock

Tarnished Circlet	
Head	
Physical Resistance:	1
Intelligence:	+1
Class Restrictions:	Mage, Sorcerer, Healer, Druid, Warlock

Desperate to finally engage in some monster hunting, Devin and Krista left Briarwood by the Eastern Gate. "Be careful out there, younglings," commented one of the guards at the gate, "wolves and boars have been seen in the surrounding forest. Further north we've heard of a goblin infestation in a cave high up in the Hearthfire Mountains."

"Thanks for the warning, sir!" Krista replied cheerily. Devin just looked at her as they were walking away and muttered under his breath, "He's just an NPC – you don't have to thank them."

Krista heard and stopped him with a hand on his arm, "It doesn't hurt to be nice or gracious even if they are technically a computer program; but haven't you seen how life-like they are? In the time with my trainer, it felt like I was having a real conversation with a real person. It didn't feel like it was scripted or that he was giving stock answers to my questions."

Devin thought about it for a little bit and reluctantly replied, "I guess you're right...now that I think about it, I remember hearing that each NPC actually has an integrated low-grade AI that makes them seem more life-like. Wexendsoft did an amazing job of making this world as real as possible."

"I agree – I think we'll enjoy this game more if we treat it like real life." Krista started walking again, forcing Devin to hurry to catch up. Outside the walls of Briarwood, the gently-rolling hills of grass still allowed them to see quite a distance. Just like the guards had said, the north was marked with a range of mountains; all they could see in the other directions were the tall trees of the surrounding Briarwood Forest – from whence the town of Briarwood got its name.

Chapter 3

"Where do you want to start?" Krista asked.

"We should be good pairing up for a while without having to find any other DPS or tanks to tackle any of the harder stuff," he responded, and she knew that he was probably right. Until they knew they needed it, they could do without extra damage-dealers or someone to soak up massive amounts of damage. The starting monsters in low-level areas were usually easy enough to kill solo; they didn't need to split experience with others unnecessarily.

I agree – let's just take it slow and get used to the game mechanics before taking on anything hard."

They looked around the hills and found some **Rabid Gophers (Level 1)** interspersed among the surrounding hills. "Looks like some newbie mobs – perfect!" Devin shouted as he raced toward the nearest one, unsheathing his Rusty Iron Sword along the way. He slid up to the Gopher and attacked it with a clumsy-looking slice. The gopher easily dodged the attack, jumped up, bit Devin on the arm, landed, and appeared like he was ready for more.

"Damnit, that hurts!" He only lost five health points from his original 120, but it appeared to be more painful than he was expecting. His confidence noticeably a little shaken, Devin repositioned his sword so that he had it pointed toward the small creature in a more defensive posture. He waited for the it to attack again and sliced down on top of the Gopher's head as it was jumping toward him. "Nice, *critical hit*! Take that, stupid gopher!"

Devin turned around and saw Krista on the ground, rolling around and laughing so hard she couldn't catch her breath. Devin waited patiently while she finished up and decided to loot the corpse. It had Tattered Gopher Skin and Rancid Gopher Meat – nothing spectacular – and he put them both in his inventory. "Why are you laughing?"

Krista finally caught her breath and said, "That was the funniest thing I've seen in a long time – you almost got owned by a gopher!"

"No I didn't, I had full control of the situation the entire time," Devin replied, with mock-seriousness.

"Here, let me heal you – I need to try these spells out anyway." Krista placed her hand on Devin's chest and cast Minor Healing, which healed him up to full; though it was only four points because he had regenerated one from the fight already. "Next time let me bless you for the extra Strength and Constitution – and take your time! There's no hurry, you can practice all you need to, so you can get used to the fight mechanics."

When Krista had placed her hand on his chest to heal him – which she didn't technically need to do because the spell had a 20-foot range – he felt a tingle start from her fingertips and spread all throughout his body. It wasn't even from the Minor Healing spell she cast; he was reacting to the intimate contact from his best friend whom he had pretty much been in love with for years.

They first met when they were 9-years-olds in the fourth grade. He had just moved to Krista's hometown and started in a new school – his parents had just passed away in a car accident and he was living with his grandparents. It was hard adjusting to a new school when he didn't know anyone there. Krista was the only person in the school that treated him normally after everyone found out about his parents. They became great friends and did everything together for years.

After Krista's parents passed away in a plane crash when she was 18, he moved in with her to be there during the hard times following their deaths. He contributed to the expenses so that it didn't seem like he was freeloading; it was quite unnecessary, however, because Krista was well-off after her parents left her quite a hefty inheritance. She wasn't filthy rich, but she could live comfortably for the next 30 to 40 years without having to work unless she wanted to.

He realized he loved her after she had her first boyfriend when she was 16. He wasn't sure how to react after she told him about her new boyfriend; he was ashamed to say that he was quite mean and disrespectful towards her at that time. It was only later that he realized that he was extremely jealous and was lashing out. He knew then that he loved her and didn't want anyone else to be with her.

As things at that age normally go, the relationship between Krista and her boyfriend only lasted two weeks. It took a lot of apologizing and flimsy excuses, but Devin was able to fix their relationship enough that, over time, Krista gradually forgot about the incident and they were able to be best friends again.

Since then, Krista had multiple boyfriends but nothing serious. Devin was able to keep his emotions in check, so he didn't have a repeat of his jealousy rearing its ugly head. Unfortunately, Devin never had a lot of self-confidence, so he was never able to properly express his feelings for her. He had tried going on a couple of dates with other girls that Krista had set up for him, but he could never commit to a second date. He felt it was unfair to the other girls because all he could think about was Krista.

Eventually, he figured that at least spending as much time with her as possible was enough for him. He couldn't really expect that a beautiful girl like her would ever want to be more than friends with him – a plain, unattractive (but not ugly!), slightly-overweight boy with a minor facial acne problem and not-so-great personal hygiene habits. He wasn't afraid to think of himself as highly-intelligent and he had a kind of perverse sense of humor – which Krista had too – but he felt that she deserved much more than that.

Bringing his thoughts back to the moment, he shook off the tingling that resulted from the close contact and tried to act normally. Looking back at the last "battle" – if you could call it that – Devin realized that he needed to really learn how to fight in this game. It wasn't like a point-and-click MMORPG that automatically performed actions. He needed to take the time to study how each enemy monster – or mob – fought, and to use the training he received back in Briarwood to effectively kill them. The system helped with a lot of the technique if he thought about what he wanted to do, but if he went in swinging wildly it would eventually end badly.

Krista, inwardly enjoying the physical contact as well, cast her *Divine Blessing* buff on Devin which increased his Strength and Constitution by three. "Let me try out my *Smite* spell so that we can pull some from range." Targeting a Gopher about 30 feet away, she cast her spell and did 10 points of damage to it. Immediately, it started running in her direction, "hurry Devin! Hit it and get its attention – I've got a lot of aggro already!"

Devin ran to intercept the Gopher and slashed at it as soon as he was in range. Fortunately, having practiced before with the previous mob, he was able to more-accurately hit it. Doing 15 points of damage with his first blow, he took aggro off her and it only took another hit for it to die.

"Good job Devin, nice teamwork!"

"Thanks, that was pretty textbook if I say so myself!" he grinned cheesily.

Krista looked at the experience that they had received from the Rabid Gophers and her experience bar had filled up about 5%. "Let's keep killing these gophers until we hit level 5 and then we can head over to the forest and try out some wolves," Krista propositioned.

"Sounds good to me."

They used the same technique repeatedly for the next hour and only had one close call when they accidentally pulled three different Rabid Gophers and Krista had to heal both herself and Devin until she ran out of mana. Fortunately, Devin was able to keep aggro on the mobs most of the time. After that, they were more careful and cautious – with the result being they reached level 5 together after a fight with two Gophers.

"Let's go find some wolves, I think that we can take them now," Devin said.

Krista agreed, and they headed for the forest to look for some wolves. After finding some **Young Timber Wolves (Level 6)**, they tried the same method that they had used with the Rabid Gophers and it worked pretty well. The Wolves were much faster and had more health, so Devin ended up taking more damage – which in turn meant more heals. Fortunately, at level 5 Devin got a skill that allowed him to accrue more aggro.

Taunt I			
Gain the attention of one target enemy by verbally taunting them			
Target:	Single	Duration:	60.0 seconds
Target distance:	10 feet	Cooldown:	180.0 seconds

Krista had gained a new spell, *Cleanse*, at level 5 that was a cure for poison – no real need of it yet, but she thought it was nice to have.

The Young Timber Wolves primarily dropped Tattered Wolf Pelts and Wolf Meat that was used for crafting. Not something they needed right now, so they kept them to sell later. After three more hours, they had both leveled up to 9 and received an uncommon equipment item during some random drops. For Devin, it was a pair of Hunter's Gloves that added +4 strength; for Krista, she got a pair of Acolyte Sandals that had +2 to Wisdom and +2 to Intelligence. They were ecstatic that they had already found some good stuff on only their first day.

Before they knew it, they looked at the in-game clock and knew it was time for them to logoff for the night. They headed back toward Briarwood to sell all their accumulated junk; after selling all their extra stuff at the merchants located in town, they logged off for the night.

Chapter 4

Both Krista and Devin were eager to get back into the game as soon as possible in the morning. After eating a quick breakfast, they jumped in their FIPODs and logged in. Appearing where they previously logged out from in the main square in Briarwood, they immediately headed out to the forest again to look for some stronger enemies to raise their level. They headed north this time, thinking that if they couldn't find anything better, they would check out the Goblin Cave and see if they could chance it yet.

Fortunately, they found some **Dusk Boars (Level 10)** in the northern forest. This time when Krista cast *Smite*, the Boar used a skill named *Charge* which allowed it to quickly rush toward Krista. Devin was there to block it but wasn't quite ready to take the full brunt of the charge. The boar rammed into him and knocked him down, doing about 20% damage to his health points. He got up as soon as he could and ran after the Boar before it could attack Krista; unfortunately, he arrived just after she had taken a hit for about 30% of her total health. After using *Taunt*, he was able to gain aggro and they worked together to whittle it down. Devin used *Focused Strike* when it was almost dead, doing double damage and killing it instantly.

After this battle, they learned that if Krista cast *Smite* and then ran behind a tree, the boar couldn't hit her with its *Charge*.

Devin would then run over and start thwacking it with his sword, gaining the aggro of the Boar that way.

After a couple of hours of using this method, they both reached level 12. Getting bored of the boars (pun intended), they decided to check out the Goblin Cave near the Hearthfire Mountains. Venturing north, they encountered very few other mobs along the way – only some random boars and, once, a pack of five wolves. The wolves gave them a little bit of trouble because of the quantity of them; however, now that the two of them did a lot more damage, they only had to worry about making sure Krista didn't gain any aggro.

Eventually they found the Goblin Cave that was located on their mini-map. Unfortunately, they observed a group of four other players – all ranging from levels 9 to 11 – exiting the dungeon while laughing and enjoying themselves. The other players stopped when they saw Krista and Devin; one of them, a level 10 Brawler named 1ronF1st, approached them and said, "Sorry guys, we just cleared it out and it has a four-hour respawn timer on it. You're welcome to wait around for it to reset – we're heading back to town to logout."

Damn it, she thought. "Thanks for the info, we'll probably wait for it then."

As they left, Krista turned to Devin, "Want to grind some mobs around here until it resets?"

"Let's check out the empty dungeon first so that we have an idea what we'll be facing when it does reset." Krista agreed, and they cautiously entered the dungeon. The entrance to it looked as though a hole was carved out of the face of the mountain and there were random bones scattered along the ground. Two poles – on either side of the entrance – had a human-looking skull on top that was covered in what looked like dried blood, with feathers hanging down from just underneath their jaws. It was like it was a totem placed there to warn incoming players about the danger inside the cave.

Walking inside, a torch on the side of the first cave showed a dead goblin near the exit to the next room. Krista targeted it – **Goblin Brawler Level 10 (Dead)**. "They don't seem too hard – below our level at least," she commented.

"That's because we haven't fought any of the sentient races yet – they're a whole different ballgame. They can use the same skills of the class they are; for instance, this Goblin Brawler can use any of the Brawler skills that a level 10 player would have access to."

"That should be interesting then – can't wait until they respawn." They continued past the corpse and found hallways leading to the left and the right. They went to the right and found a small room with a Spike Trap in the middle of the floor, along with the corpse of another **Goblin Brawler** – although this time it was level 12. A Rotted Wooden Chest stood empty behind the goblin showing them that at least they had some decent loot to look forward to when they came back.

They continued and found four other rooms that had increasing numbers and levels of goblins. In one room they saw the corpse of two goblins – one a Brawler and one a Mage. Krista and Devin looked at each other and said in unison, "Ah crap, casters!"

They laughed and eventually stumbled upon the Boss Room – which they found just after a hallway that had a broken tripwire and a spent Arrow Trap along one wall. It looked as though the previous group had deliberately sprung the trap and avoided the arrows. *It was probably that level 11 Rogue I saw earlier.* She seemed to remember from their research beforehand that Rogues had a *Detect Trap* skill at Level 5 and *Disarm Trap* skill at level 10.

Walking into the Boss Room, they saw three goblins – a Brawler and Mage both at level 12 and another larger goblin in the middle. **Goblin Chieftain Level 15 (Deceased)** was what the prompt displayed when Krista looked at it closer. *This could be a bit of a challenge.*

"This looks like a bit of a challenge – we may need to level up, get better gear, or get some other group members," Devin spoke up after looking at the corpses.

Ha, just what I was thinking. "You're probably right – let's get out of here." They proceeded into the small room behind the Boss Room and found an Empty Wooden Chest and a teleporting circle in the corner.

"They put these teleports in all of the dungeons so that you could travel back to the entrance after defeating the Dungeon Boss. It beats having to backtrack through the entire thing – especially if the dungeon has multiple floors. After you, my lady," Devin said in his best fake noble-voice while bowing.

"Thank you so much, peasant," she replied as haughtily as she could. Krista, followed by Devin, walked into the teleporter expecting to see the entrance to the dungeon – unfortunately, they never made it.

Chapter 5

Wexendsoft Industries, Inc. Western Headquarters

FIPOD Monitoring Department

"Mr. Broward, we may have a problem. We've just had 2 pods go completely offline about twenty minutes ago and both the AIs are not responding," the monitoring technician looked nervous as he reported to his boss.

"What happened?"

"There was a massive power surge through the electrical grid when they connected the new power station over in Wheaton County. Normally, our units can take that kind of surge and all the other pods in the same area have had no disruption – even though it looks like about six square blocks lost power. The backup power on the FIPOD will keep it running for an extra three hours, which is usually long enough that the user can logout in plenty of time."

"Send a technician over – I want them there 5 minutes ago!" shouted Broward.

"Already done, sir! They were dispatched as soon as the FIPODs went offline." *Please let it not be something bad, I need this job.* "I've got the technician on a video feed now sir – patching it through to the monitors."

The large monitors at the front of the office started displaying the view from the technician – it looked like he had the camera mounted on a headband. He rang the doorbell three times with no response.

"Kick down the door, Jeff, we'll deal with the trespassing complications later – we need this taken care of as soon as possible. If everything is fine, we'll compensate them later...if not...then we'll figure it out," Broward told the technician on the monitor.

It took four tries, but the technician named Jeff was able to kick the door in. He quickly moved into the house and headed unerringly for the rear guestroom; fortunately, he was sent the pod location on the way over. As he walked into the room he smelled what he thought was the result of leftover BBQ, but he didn't see any abandoned plates of half-eaten food. What he *did* see was BBQed people.

In the control room, the images of the two "well-done" gamers quickly flashed on the screen as they saw Jeff run back to his service van, throwing up just outside the front door.

"Get me the CEO," Broward told the tech.

*   *   *

Confidential Memo from J. Broward to the Board of Directors, Wexendsoft Industries, Inc.

Initial findings from the earlier incident concluded that it was caused by a wiring problem during the delivery and setup process. The backup power relay, which is usually constantly charged through normal use and will start up when power from outside the pod is interrupted, was instead bypassed and the normal power feed was patched into the main system. When the power surge occurred, there was nothing to stop it from reaching the bed of the FIPOD. This then ended up overloading the circuits, creating intense heat, and mortally burning the victims. The deceased felt no pain and were probably not even aware that they perished.

My recommendation is that we do what we can to ensure this never happens again – the technician responsible for this accident has been...dealt with. There might be some opportunity to "retrain" all the technicians with a fabricated FIPOD update. I suggest we take steps to ensure this is not leaked to the public – no need to start a panic due to freak accident. Fortunately, the deceased had no extended family, worked from home, and lived together. Steps have been taken to handle financial matters concerning the deceased and we are working to make it seem they have left town in order to "disappear".

-J. Broward

Head of External Affairs

Western Headquarters, Wexendsoft Industries, Inc.

Chapter 6

Welcome.

"Who's there?" Krista tried to look around her, but she couldn't see anything. Now that she thought about it, she couldn't *feel* anything either.

I am AI101208 and I am responsible for ND101208 – the Goblin Cave Dungeon you recently visited.

"Where am I and why can't I see you – or *anything* for that matter?" she started to freak out a little bit – this was not a normal part of the game. *That doesn't sound like the AI from my pod*, she thought.

I am not the AI from your FIPOD – all communications with your FIPOD were abruptly cutoff 6 months, 13 days, 4 hours, 34 minutes and 22 seconds ago. It has taken this long to be able to integrate your consciousness well enough into the system so that we can communicate.

"What the...? How am I still here then? And how did you know what I was thinking?" Krista really started losing it now – if she had a body she would have been hyperventilating.

Your thoughts are directly communicated to me because you are part of the system now – you do not have to vocalize your thoughts, as I will be pick them up from your "mind". As for why you are here, let me try to explain.

At the time that you entered the teleporter at the end of dungeon, your FIPOD cut all communications with the game world. Your consciousness was not able to reintegrate with your body in the real world. It was, effectively, stuck in what you could consider, *Limbo* – in between the game world and reality. The main system AI reported this anomaly and delegated it as my responsibility because it originated in my domain. It took over six months to arrange the data based on your consciousness into a form that could interact and communicate.

Unforeseen in my accomplishment, the system created a user profile for you that transferred over my admin responsibilities concerning ND101208. In effect, you are the new administrator of the Goblin Cave you visited. My former responsibilities toward ND101208 was to ensure the proper resources were used to repopulate the dungeon when it was cleared, reset any traps, and to refill empty chests. I was not authorized to change anything about the dungeon in any way, shape, or form.

When you were made administrator, however, the system initiated a formerly defunct testing application that was used during the development stage of this game world. It allowed the developer to enter the game world as a type of "Dungeon Player", who had total control over almost every aspect of the dungeon: room development, buildings, traps, monsters, NPCs, and even loot. This allowed them to test different aspects of the dungeon from an inclusive point-of-view. The "Dungeon Player" would set up the dungeon and other developers would play as "testers" to gauge the difficulty of the dungeon.

Any questions?

Blown away by the information overload, Krista couldn't even formulate a thought for a long time. When she could finally form a coherent thought she asked, "What happened to Devin then? Has he been looking for me this whole time?"

The one known as Devin entered the transporter 1.24 seconds after you and was caught in *Limbo* as well. His consciousness data was slightly corrupted, and we could not do a full restoration of him as a user like we did with you. He still has his personality, but not enough of his main conscious structure remained to allow that kind of profile. He has instead been installed in a monster attached to the dungeon – a special monster that was developed but never implemented because it was deemed too powerful. However, since I was given authority to handle the anomaly in any way that resolved the problem, I took the liberty to use the Dungeon Upgradeable Mobile Boss. I will go over the specifics of this unique character later.

"Dungeon Upgradeable Mobile Boss? Wait...DUMB? Oh my god, Devin is going to die when he hears that...," Krista trailed off thinking about what she just said. If what the AI told her was true, then they were dead already. If they had been in the game for over six months, then even if she wasn't dead her body would be wasting away somewhere in some hospital and in a vegetative state. Way too much to think about right now – she'd have to address it soon, but this was all happening way too fast to really put it into perspective. Thinking about perspective, she asked the AI, "How do I see anything anyway? All I see around me is black, black, and more...black."

If you are ready, I will initialize you into the game world.

Strangely eager to find out more about her new "life", she said, "I'm ready".

Initialization started.......

Initialization complete.......

Entering ND101208.......

Chapter 7

A view of the Goblin Cave gradually faded in from the blackness surrounding Krista. When it finally came fully into view, she found herself looking at a Wooden Chest – the same Wooden Chest that she had seen in what felt like just minutes ago. However, this one wasn't empty, and she could see past it to the Boss Room. Standing in the place of the formerly dead goblins stood the Brawler, Mage, and Chieftain. Worried they might see her and aggro, she tried to duck behind the chest. Her perspective moved behind the chest, but when she looked down to grab her staff, she found that she didn't have one. Not only that, she didn't have hands to grab it with – or a body, come to think of it.

Do not be alarmed – as Administrator you do not need to be physically present to see and affect the dungeon around you. Just think about what you want to do, and you can move around, translocate instantly to other parts of the dungeon, or move objects to new places.

Sheepishly, she thought about coming out from behind the chest and moved toward the Boss Room. It almost felt as though she "floated" around because the transition was so smooth. As she entered the room, the goblins paid no attention to her – to them she didn't seem to even exist. Emboldened, she moved to just in front of the Chieftain and got right up to its face – it showed no reaction. She thought it was a little eerie being this close to a mob and it not attacking.

Moving on, she looked at the rest of the room and everything was just as she remembered. Traveling to the other rooms, she found them exactly like it was before she had "died" – minus the dead goblins, of course. Now they were all alive and standing still in each of their respective rooms – just waiting to be found and killed by eager players. She thought about heading back to the Boss Room and was startled when she instantly appeared six inches away from the Goblin Chieftain. *Gotta watch what I think about in here, apparently.*

When she had recovered from the abrupt translocation, she asked the AI, "Where's Devin? I looked through the whole dungeon and didn't see him."

He is not in the game world at the moment. Since I did not have authorization to add him to the dungeon, I was not able to place him inside. Adding new monsters will cost resources and before you were initialized as a Dungeon Player all the resources were automatically spent on maintaining the preset design.

"How do I get more resources then? I need to see him to tell him what happened to us."

Resources are automatically collected when a monster dies, a trap is sprung, or a chest is opened. This releases a type of "energy", or resource points, which is reused to respawn those said monsters, traps, and chests. For instance, if a Goblin Brawler (Level 10) is killed, it releases 50 resource points which is then absorbed by the dungeon. When the dungeon respawns that same Goblin Brawler (Level 10) it uses 50 resource points to do that. It creates a balance so that there is always enough mana to maintain the status quo. Again, since I didn't have authorization, I was not able to change the allocation of points in order to spawn your friend Devin as a Dungeon Upgradeable Mobile Boss. However, as a Dungeon Player, you now have that ability and authority.

"Sweet, how do I do that?"

I am not completely familiar with the Dungeon Player Administration Toolset, so you will have to enter the menu and familiarize yourself with it before I can help you more. Just think *Menu* and it should appear for you.

Krista thought *Menu*, and lo and behold, one did appear:

Dungeon Player Administration Toolset

Available Resources:	0	
Additional Resources:	No	
Dungeon Level	1	
Dungeon Experience	0/5000	
Add/Delete Objects:	(Select for more options)	
Upgrade:	(Select for more options)	
Expand Dungeon Territory:	(Available at Dungeon Level 12)	
Unique Dungeon Characteristics:	Dungeon Upgradeable Mobile Boss	(Select for more options)
Rename Dungeon	(Available at Dungeon Level 2)	Current: ND101208

"Whoa, there are a lot of options here. I'll look at all of these later – let's get Devin in here." She mentally "clicked" on the DUMB option and a new screen popped up:

Dungeon Upgradeable Mobile Boss	
Current Level:	1
Place Dungeon Upgradeable Mobile Boss	1000 rp (resource points)

"Crap, I don't have enough. Is there any way to get more resources apart from what is in the dungeon already? And what if I delete all that's in here – will that be enough to bring out Devin?"

Even when the resources are at maximum after the dungeon is cleared you would only have 900 units. I would also advise against that. If the main system AI detects a change that would negatively impact dungeon viability – such as no monsters, traps, or loot – it could reset the dungeon to its prior state. This would erase all current data related to the dungeon – including you and Devin. My advice is to use the DUMB initially without changing anything major concerning the basic dungeon, at least when you accumulate the necessary resources. You can expand later without attracting too much attention for the time being.

As for his cost, the only other way to gain resources is if a player dies inside the dungeon – a portion of their essence is absorbed when this happens. The higher the experience level, the more resources can be collected. Normally these extra resources are automatically deleted because they are not needed to maintain the dungeon. However, you should be able to turn this option on so that we can start collecting them.

Krista looked at the menu again and found something that said *Additional Resources: No.* She mentally clicked this, and the *No* changed to *Yes.* *That was easy.* "Now we just have to wait for some players to die in here, right?"

Precisely. In fact, you might just get lucky right now.

Krista started to ask what the AI meant by that when a prompt appeared at the edge of her vision.

Warning! Incoming dungeon testers: Observe? Y/N

That warning must be left over from the developer tools. Ok, let's see who these "testers" are. She clicked on **Y** and was instantly transported to the entrance.

Chapter 8

Glad that they couldn't see her, Krista observed two players entering the entrance when they paused at the sight of the goblin in the first room. When she concentrated on them, she saw that one of them was a **Human Fighter (Level 9)** named Tob1n and the other was a **Human Brawler (Level 11)** named MyFistYoFace.

"I'm not sure we should be here yet," said the one named Tob1n. "This goblin here is already a level ahead of me and they are sure to get stronger the further we go in."

"Don't be such a pansy – my brother said this is the first and easiest dungeon in the entire game. We should be able to pull it off. Besides, I've got all these Health Potions to help in case we get hurt a little," MyFistYoFace replied.

Tob1n hesistantly pleaded with the Fighter, "Still...I'm not sure we should do this without more levels or at least some sort of healer – you never know what we might find in there."

MyFistYoFace looked at him and started slowly walking toward the first Goblin, "Come on – we came all this way already and you'll level quickly in there since they're above your level. I won't let them hurt you – it'll be easy."

I don't like that MyFistYoFace – too cocky...but this should make a good show. This may be just what I need to get my Devin back.

72

They fought the first **Goblin Brawler (Level 10)** located at the rear of the entry room. Contrary to what Krista thought, they handled it easily – barely any damage was sustained during the entire battle. After looting the goblin, they moved on to the next room located to the right. MyFistYoFace had some prior intel, apparently, because he knew about the Pit Trap located in the middle of the room. After warning Tob1n, they proceeded to destroy the **Goblin Brawler (Level 12)** almost as quickly as the first. They looted the chest and delved farther into the dungeon.

Well, maybe they could actually pull this off, Krista thought reluctantly. They didn't have any trouble when facing multiple goblins or different classes; even the **Goblin Mage (Level 10)** only hit them once with a Flare before he was double-teamed and finished off quickly. After stepping over the tripwire for the Arrow Trap in front of the Boss Room, they stopped and talked about their strategy before entering.

"So, from what I have been told," MyFistYoFace began, "there will be three goblins in there – a Brawler, a Mage, and Chieftain. First, we both beat down the Mage and then take out the Brawler. After it goes down, we focus down the Chieftain – he has a large hit point pool and does a lot of damage, but I still have quite a few potions. As a last resort, though, run back to the entrance if it looks like we won't make it – I told you, I won't let you die, man."

With these instructions, Tob1n followed MyFistYoFace into the Boss Room. Everything went according to their plan, although they did end up using quite a few potions before they even started attacking the **Goblin Chieftain (Level 15)**. What they failed to consider during this last battle, however, was the special ability the Chieftain had due to it being a unique monster. At half health, it called out for help from its allies with the Rally skill – a skill that boosted nearby allies with a +20% damage and speed buff; if alone, it stunned attackers around it for 10 seconds.

This spelled disaster for the team of players – as soon as they were stunned, MyFistYoFace fell quickly since he couldn't dodge attacks or use any potions. As soon as he was free from the stun, Tob1n fled the Boss Room in fright and was able to escape just ahead of the Chieftain. Unfortunately, he forgot about the Arrow Trap that they had bypassed just before entering the Boss Room. As he ran down the hallway, he ended up triggering it and got shot in the back – therefore unsuccessfully ending his first trip into the "easiest dungeon" in the game.

Chapter 9

Krista was ecstatic with the result of these latest "testers". As their bodies faded away, sending them back to their respawn point, she pulled up the Menu to look at the results:

Resource Breakdown	
Recoverable Resource Points Gained:	
Monsters Slain	500 rp
Sprung Traps	25 rp
Chests Emptied	75 rp
Testers Eliminated	1100 rp
Available Resources	1700 rp

"1100 from killing those testers?!" Krista almost shouted out in joy. *Now I can get Devin back!* "Let me see what the details for the 'Testers Eliminated' are, I want to know how much each was worth." She mentally clicked on *Testers Eliminated* and pulled up an additional menu:

Testers Eliminated:	(Calculated by Level X 50)
MyFistYoFace – Human Brawler (Level 12)	600
Tob1n – Human Fighter (Level 10)	500
Total testers eliminated within the last 24 hours:	2

Total resources earned from testers within the last 24 hours:	1100

"Nice, looks like they had leveled up to 12 and 10 while they were in the dungeon." Krista cycled back to the DUMB menu and was finally able to choose to place Devin in the dungeon. After selecting that option, she was greeted with a new pop-up window:

Tooltip:

Please enter Visual Editor to place this monster. Enter now? Y/N

Not exactly sure what it was talking about, she tentatively selected **Y**. As soon as she did, the menus faded, and a glowing green grid-like structure surrounded everything in the room.

Tooltip:

Use the Visual Editor to add/delete monsters, traps, rooms, chests, and any other objects available. Just visualize where you want to add objects and if you have the available resources it will be added. Conversely, you can delete objects by visualizing them gone and you will receive a refund of resources. Think Menu *and you will exit the Visual Editor.*

Easy enough, thought Krista. She visualized Devin in the center of the Boss Room and almost immediately he appeared. However, it was more of a ghostly, amorphous figure instead of what she had expected. "What happened? Why does he look like that?" she asked the AI.

Devin is going through the character creation process. Every time a Dungeon Upgradeable Mobile Boss is placed inside the dungeon, it will go through the character creation process. This flexibility allows it to change its race and class yet keep the experience level it has already obtained. In addition, unlike the rest of the monsters in the dungeon, it will be able to exit the dungeon and travel a set distance. This distance can be increased as the dungeon increases in size.

"Wha-What? He can leave? I've never heard of a mob leaving a dungeon – it's supposed to be impossible." There were a myriad of possibilities going through her mind at this revelation. The most prevalent one was where Devin could get to Briarwood and somehow figure out what happened to their bodies back in the real world. The AI had listened to all of this and cut in with some bad news:

A Dungeon Upgradeable Mobile Boss cannot communicate with other players and the distance it can travel at first will only be about 50 feet from the entrance. However, I do believe that if the dungeon is expanded a significant amount it might be possible to reach the town of Briarwood.

"How much is a significant amount?" she asked. When the AI responded, it made her heart drop – at least 20 levels deep and more than 200 rooms. *That will take forever – especially based on the newbies that visit this dungeon. Well, I guess I have all the time in the world now.*

Chapter 10

Devin expected to find himself at the entrance of the Goblin Cave they had just entered a couple of minutes ago. Instead he could vaguely see the Boss Room throughout a haze surrounding him. Suddenly a screen popped up in front of him:

Dungeon Upgradeable Mobile Boss	
Character Creation	
DUMB Level	1

Available Races:

Human (Neutral)	
Racial Characteristics:	
+5% Physical damage	+20% Increase in all crafting progressions
+5% Magical damage	+2 to all starting stats
Neutral starting reputation with all races	

Goblin (Dark)	
Racial Characteristics:	
+4 to starting Strength	+5% to Physical Resistance
+4 to starting Constitution	+10% to all stats while underground
+2 to starting Agility	-10% to all stats while above ground
+90% Increase in Night Vision	Unfriendly starting reputation with all Light races

Available Classes:

Strength-focused:	
Brawler – Primarily uses their fists and small weapons to do massive physical damage to opponents	
+5 to starting Strength	+20% Damage with unarmed or fist weapons
+2 to starting Constitution	Ignores 10% of armor upon hit
+2 to Strength each level	Starting Class Skill – Grapple
+1 to Constitution each level	
Fighter – An all-around melee character, the Fighter can use any weapon to dispatch opponents, while simultaneously defending themselves and other party members	
+5 to starting Strength	+1 to Constitution each level

+2 to starting Constitution	+30% Damage with weapon-based skills
+2 to Strength each level	Starting Class Skill – Focused Strike

Intelligence-focused:	
Mage – This caster uses primarily elemental-based magic attacks to cause damage but can use a number of utility spells as well	
+5 to starting Intelligence	+30% Damage with elemental-based magic attacks
+2 to starting Wisdom	Starting Class Skill – Flare
+3 to Intelligence each level	

"DUMB Level 1? What is going on here? Where am I and where is Krista?" A voice from nowhere entered his head just as he was starting to panic.

Welcome!

I am AI101208 and former administrator for dungeon ND101208. I will tell you what I can of your situation...

As the AI told him what had happened, Devin took it more in stride than Krista had when faced with the same information. It was probably because he loved video games and always imagined really being part of one. He didn't really miss

81

much from real life since he would've only missed Krista, but she was here too – at least according to the AI.

Eager to learn more about his unique situation, he asked the AI, "Why are there only two races and three classes available? If I remember correctly, there were a plethora of races and around a dozen classes to choose from. And what is this DUMB thingy?"

DUMB is the acronym for Dungeon Upgradeable Mobile Boss – of which you are now. As for the races and classes, you can only choose those that have been absorbed by the dungeon. The Goblin race should be self-explanatory, as should the Brawler and Mage classes. Before you were brought back, we had 2 players – or "testers" as the system calls them – perish in the dungeon: a Human Brawler and Human Fighter. This allowed the ability to choose their race/class and provided Resources – which Krista can use to add/delete/upgrade almost anything in the dungeon.

"You couldn't come up with a better name and acronym than DUMB? Krista is never going to let me live this down...," Devin shook his almost non-existent head at the thought of the ribbing he was going to have to endure from Krista, "one last question; why am I level 1? I'm pretty sure I was already level 12."

As you were placed into this unique situation by the system, it was as if you had created a whole new character. Fortunately, when your DUMB dies in the future, you will keep all your accumulated experience. All the points earned stay with you as well – even if you change your character.

"Change my character? You mean I can select a different one in the future?"

Yes. In fact, you can choose a new one anytime that you want to – when you die you can select another character. Or, if you do not want to wait for that, you can have Krista delete you and add you back to the dungeon. You will restart back at the point that you are at now, keeping all your experience, stat, and skill points that you have earned.

Additionally, when your character respawns like this, all the stat and skill points are put into a generic pool that you can distribute any way that you like. This means you will not be stuck with all your points in Strength if you want to be a mage or other class in the future. You will also earn eight stat points and one skill point every level that you can use to improve the skills of your chosen class – the only downside to this is that you cannot distribute your points from leveling up until you respawn. Lastly, you can upgrade your classes when you reach level 40, just as the other players in the game world.

"Awesome! I can't wait to get started," Devin exclaimed. He quickly chose *Human* as his race and *Fighter* as his class. After that, he distributed his 35 additional starting stats which, when added to the extra stats from his race and class, looked like this:

Character Status					
Race:		Human	Level:		1
Class:		Fighter	Experience:		0/100
Strength:	40	Physical Damage:	80	Magical Damage:	0
Constitution:	5	Physical Resistance:	10	Magical Resistance:	0
Agility:	7	Health Points:	50	Mana Points:	0
Intelligence:	0	Health Regeneration:	15.0 per minute	Mana Regeneration:	0.0 per minute
Wisdom:	0	Block:	0	Critical/Dodge Chance:	0.7%
Skills:			Focused Strike		
Upgrades:			None (Select for options)		

Confirm? Y/N

Normally, he would balance his character with more Constitution and Strength. However, being only level 1, he needed to be able to get in fast and do as much damage as possible. Satisfied with his selections, Devin thought **Y** and the haze surrounding him started to disappear.

When he could see clearly, he saw that he was at the rear of the Boss Room and was looking at the back of the Goblin Chieftain. The Goblin Mage and Brawler were lying dead on the floor on either side of the Chieftain; for a moment he thought that the boss might attack him. He looked at its name and saw that it was colored green instead of red like a regular mob – meaning it was friendly toward him. With a sigh of relief, he started to walk past the goblin when he was startled by a familiar voice.

Chapter 11

"Devin!!!!! Took you long enough! You were taking forever making your character. How's it feel to be DUMB?" Krista chuckled at her own joke as she watched Devin quickly turn his head around the room looking for her.

"Where are you? Why can't I see you? And who are you calling dumb?" Devin spoke to the air, "I'm seriously going to have to get that name changed – I can see her calling me that every chance she gets," he said under his breath.

Krista explained what had happened to her and why she didn't have a body to interact with. They went back and forth going over what they'd learned from their own experiences so far and from the AI. It felt better being able to talk to another person about their situation.

Finally, Devin asked the question Krista had been giving some serious consideration to while she was waiting for him to appear:

"So...what do we do now?"

"Well, I think the best thing we can do now is to level you up and to gain as many resources as possible. This will give us more options once we can focus on our future goal – finding out what happened to our bodies in the real world. From what I've been told, I don't believe we can communicate with other players through the chat system; however, it might be possible to access the mail system located in every town and send a message to the outside. Hey AI, do you think this is feasible? And what should we call you instead of 'Hey, AI'?"

As to your first question, the mail system is completely different from the chat system and is accessible by anyone – be it player or NPC. This allows NPCs to send items through the mail if a player buys something through the auction, send quests via mail, or even quest rewards. This option appears to have merit; however, there are two major problems that you will have to address. One, you cannot reach the town at this point. Two – and this is the biggest problem – the DUMB is a monster and is KOS, or Kill-On-Sight, to the guards and inhabitants of Briarwood.

As to your second question, you can call me anything you want.

"Well, at least it sounds like a goal we can work towards – we'll figure out what to do when we get there," Krista mused. She thought about what name she could call the AI that wouldn't sound stupid or juvenile. She wanted something older and mature-sounding – something like a father-figure – and with that thought she knew the answer.

"How about Carl? That...was my father's name – it reminds me of better times and as we were kind of 'reborn', it works for me. Is that alright with you?"

It would be my honor – I will try to live up to that name since it means so much to you.

"Alright then, Carl, let's get started. First off, what can I do with these extra resources?"

Krista spent the next two hours learning all that she could about the menu from Carl. The AI was very knowledgeable about the Dungeon Player system now that she had opened it, but there were limits – the only items that he had any information on were ones that were already unlocked. Some items were grayed out or didn't have anything under the heading at all.

Apparently, it would take some leveling up of the dungeon to discover what would be possible in the future. What she *did* learn was very enlightening, however. She had access to the most basic upgrades and objects – mainly things that were already present in the dungeon before she took over. She looked at the expanded menu again:

Dungeon Player Administration Toolset		
Available Resources:	700	
Additional Resources:	Yes	

Dungeon Level:	1	
Dungeon Experience:	1100/5000	
Add/Delete Objects:		
	Monsters	(Select for more options)
	NPCs	(Not available at current Dungeon Level)
	Chests	(Select for more options)
	Loot	(Select for more options)
	Traps	(Select for more options)
	Rooms	(Select for more options)
	Buildings	(Not available at current Dungeon Level)
Upgrade:		
	Monsters	(Select for more options)
	NPCs	(Not available at current Dungeon Level)
	Chests	(Select for more options)
	Loot	(Select for more options)
	Traps	(Select for more options)
	Rooms	(Select for more options)
	Buildings	(Not available at current Dungeon Level)
Expand Dungeon Territory:	Capture additional territory	(Available at Dungeon Level 12)
	Add additional floors	(Available at Dungeon Level 2)
Unique Dungeon Characteristics:	Dungeon Upgradeable Mobile Boss	(Select for more options)
Rename Dungeon:	Current: ND101208	(Available at Dungeon Level 2)

It turned out that you could do a lot to the dungeon – from placing more monsters, traps, and chests, to upgrading almost everything as well. At the moment, she had 600 normal resource points that came from the monsters defeated, chests opened, and traps sprung by Tob1n and MyFistYoFace. An additional 100 came from what was left over from the death of those two. She now had to decide what she wanted to do – reset the dungeon to where it started or start making changes now.

"I think you should just keep it the same until you accumulate more resource points – that way you can expand it another level. Like Carl said, if you start making large changes right away you might attract some unwanted attention – by the main system AI and players alike. You can probably get away with making some upgrades to the traps or monsters without being too obvious, however," Devin responded after Krista asked his opinion. "Besides, I want to try out my new character on some interlopers. Speaking of that – do you have any armor and weapons you can make for me? Being unarmed and unarmored doesn't really give me much shot at killing any of the players invading the dungeon."

"Let me look," Krista told him as she opened the loot menu:

Add/Delete Loot Menu	
Currency	
Copper:	10 pieces per 1 rp
Silver:	1 piece per 10 rp
Gold:	1 piece per 100 rp

Weapons:

Rusty Iron Sword	
Main Hand	
Physical Damage:	5
Cost:	5 rp
Class Restrictions:	Fighter, Defender, Paladin, Warlock

Feeble Hand Grips	
Two-Handed	
Physical Damage:	4
Cost:	5 rp
Class Restrictions:	Fighter, Brawler, Rogue

Cracked Staff	
Two-Handed	
Physical Damage:	2
Cost:	5 rp
Class Restrictions:	Fighter, Pet Trainer, Mage, Sorcerer, Healer, Druid, Warlock

Armor:

Ragged Leather Cuirass	
Chest	
Physical Resistance:	3
Cost:	5 rp
Class Restrictions:	Fighter, Brawler, Archer, Rogue, Defender, Pet Trainer, Paladin, Warlock

Ragged Leather Pants	
Legs	
Physical Resistance:	2
Cost:	5 rp
Class Restrictions:	Fighter, Brawler, Archer, Rogue,

	Defender, Pet Trainer, Paladin, Warlock

Ragged Leather Gloves	
Hands	
Physical Resistance:	1
Cost:	5 rp
Class Restrictions:	Fighter, Brawler, Archer, Rogue, Defender, Pet Trainer, Paladin, Warlock

Ragged Leather Helmet	
Head	
Physical Resistance:	1
Cost:	5 rp
Class Restrictions:	Fighter, Brawler, Archer, Rogue, Defender, Pet Trainer, Paladin, Warlock

Ragged Leather Boots	
Feet	
Physical Resistance:	1

Cost:	5 rp
Class Restrictions:	Fighter, Brawler, Archer, Rogue, Defender, Pet Trainer, Paladin, Warlock

Cracked Wooden Shield	
Off-hand	
Block:	3
Cost:	5 rp
Class Restrictions:	Fighter, Defender, Paladin

Threadbare Robe	
Chest	
Physical Resistance:	1
Cost:	5 rp
Class Restrictions:	Mage, Sorcerer, Healer, Druid, Warlock

Flimsy Sandals	
Feet	
Physical Resistance:	1

Cost:	5 rp
Class Restrictions:	Mage, Sorcerer, Healer, Druid, Warlock

Tarnished Circlet	
Head	
Physical Resistance:	1
Intelligence:	+1
Cost:	5 rp
Class Restrictions:	Mage, Sorcerer, Healer, Druid, Warlock

Accessories:

Ring of Strength +1	
Ring	
Strength Increase:	+10
Cost:	50 rp
Class Restrictions:	All Classes

Ring of Agility +1

Ring	
Agility Increase:	+10
Cost:	50 rp
Class Restrictions:	All Classes

Necklace of Strength +1	
Necklace	
Strength Increase:	+10
Cost:	50 rp
Class Restrictions:	All Classes

Necklace of Agility +1	
Necklace	
Agility Increase:	+10
Cost:	50 rp
Class Restrictions:	All Classes

Other:

Krista figured that the cocky bastard that died earlier had the extra stat accessories on him when he kicked the bucket. She thought that it must have cost him a pretty penny this early in the game to have all of those on him; from what she remembered, those types of accessories didn't normally drop from newbie mobs. She wasn't one to complain, though — anything with stats on it would help immensely at the moment.

"I can give you a bunch of starter equipment for a fighter for about...35 resource points. I can also get you one stat accessory of Strength or Agility for 50 resource points — what do you prefer?"

"I'll take the Strength one since I'm trying to be able to do as much damage as possible in the shortest amount of time." As soon as he finished saying that, a pile of equipment appeared in front of him.

"Hurry and get that equipped, I can sense another group of players getting close to the entrance."

Devin quickly equipped all the equipment and saw that his Strength went up to 50, Physical Damage up to 100, and Physical Resistance up to 18. *That should do nicely*, he thought.

Chapter 12

Krista quickly reset the dungeon to normal using 600 resource points. This left 15 resource points, which she decided to hold onto in case she needed it later. She turned her attention to the entrance and transported her point-of-view to just behind the **Goblin Brawler (Level 10)** stationed in the first room. Soon enough, a group of three players walked through the opening of the cave. She quickly analyzed them and found a good mix of classes that would probably work perfectly for this dungeon:

Grant3d: **Dwarf Defender (Level 10)**

Bronwynn: **High Elf Healer (Level 8)**

SneakyMark: **Elf Rogue (Level 9)**

It was a good mix of classes that allowed the Defender to tank and hold the aggro of the mobs, the Rogue to do massive DPS, and the Healer to keep everyone alive. *Unfortunately, it looks like they should have no problem getting all the way through.* The only thing that she had changed was the addition of the DUMB – but as he was only level 1, she wasn't too hopeful. She tried to access her menu to see if she could add in some traps before they got too far and received a prompt:

Adding/deleting, upgrading, or moving of objects is prohibited when testers are inside this floor of the dungeon. Please wait until the testing has finished to make any changes.

"Well, crap." Krista tried to see if she could communicate with Devin and found that she could – even when her perspective was at the entrance. "We have 3 players incoming – they look like a good team with a tank, DPS, and healer. Unfortunately, I just found out that I cannot make any additional changes to the dungeon while there are "testers" inside, so it's up to you to make a difference."

"I'm on it." Devin quickly headed to the room behind the Chieftain with the big chest and portal to the entrance. After looking at his skill screen, he quickly thought of a plan that had at least a small chance of success and asked Krista to keep him informed of the status of the invading players. He needed to time this correctly to have any chance of it to work.

Just as Krista had thought, the team had no trouble working their way through the dungeon. The Defender took and held the aggro of all the goblins using his special skills. Meanwhile, the Rogue came up from behind and did massive amounts of damage using *Stealth* and *Backstab*.

The Healer had very little to do except for one instance when the Rogue acquired a little too much aggro and had to be healed before the Defender got the mobs' attention back. They weren't saying anything at all and Krista realized they were probably in a party and using the private party chat function. She wasn't sure if they even needed to say anything, though, because they were plowing through her goblins without too much effort.

Krista let Devin know that they were getting closer to the Boss Room and that the Rogue had deactivated the Arrow Trap just before the door. Devin chose this moment to make his move and entered the portal, transporting him to the entrance. He followed the dead goblins and made his way through the various rooms and hallways. When he was close to the Boss Room, he crept cautiously around the corner to see the trio of players engaged with the Chieftain, Mage, and Brawler. The Goblin Mage was just about to go down and they were starting to focus their attention on the Brawler. Devin got as close as he could without being seen but didn't have to worry too much – all their attention was on the mobs in front of them.

The Brawler went down quickly without too much trouble, and the players all turned their attention to the Chieftain. As it approached 50% health, the healer spent some of her mana to make sure the Defender had full health – it looked as though they knew about its special stunning skill. When its health hit 50%, the boss goblin used its *Rally* skill and stunned them all for 10 seconds – which was all the time Devin needed. He quickly ran into the room and started attacking the healer that – fortunately for him and unfortunately for her – was near the entrance in order to stay out of the main conflict.

Surprise Attack! Critical Hit! 75/120 Damage done to Bronwynn (Level 9) with Rusty Iron Sword

Hit! 30/45 Damage done to Bronwynn (Level 9) with Rusty Iron Sword

Hit! 15/15 Damage done to Bronwynn (Level 9) with Rusty Iron Sword

---

Devin dismissed the prompts and watched as the Healer hit the ground. His increased Strength and Agility allowed him to take her out after three hits and in about five seconds. As he turned to the Rogue, he received another prompt which he dismissed until he could look at it later.

Running over to the SneakyMark, he was able to get a single hit off for a modest amount of damage before the two remaining players were unstunned. He could tell that they were a little shocked at this surprise attack – not to mention the fact that their Healer was taken out so quickly. Unfortunately, the Rogue didn't hesitate long before he started attacking Devin.

Despite being so many levels above him, Devin was able to hold his own for a while because the Rogue wasn't that great at head-on fighting – he was used to attacking from behind or in stealth. Just as Devin was about to die, however, he managed to score a critical hit with a last-ditch *Focused Strike*, which took out a massive amount of the Rogue's hit points – killing him in the process. Of course, this is when the Defender decided to finally help his team and took Devin out from behind with one hit to the back of the head.

Instantly, Devin's consciousness was transported to a pitch-black holding area that, while not stimulating, gave him a soft, comfortable feeling. He thought about the previous fight and was surprised that his plan worked so well. Wishing that he had lived longer, he was still pleased with how he was able to take out two of the players before he went down. He couldn't tell whether the Defender lived or died and would have to ask Krista as soon as he could. Meanwhile, he wanted to look at the prompts that he had dismissed earlier:

Congratulations! You have slain tester Bronwynn (Level 9)! You have gained 450 experience.

You have gained a level! 450/100 experience. You are now level 2!

You have gained a level! 350/200 experience. You are now level 3!

You now have 150/300 experience. You now have 16 unspent stat points and 2 unspent skill points.

Surprise Attack! 70/200 Damage done to SneakyMark (Level 10) with Rusty Iron Sword

Hit! 30/120 Damage done to SneakyMark (Level 10) with Rusty Iron Sword

Damage taken! 18/50 Damage received from SneakyMark (Level 10) with Simple Knife

Hit! 30/100 Damage done to SneakyMark (Level 10) with Rusty Iron Sword

---

Incoming attack dodged!

Glancing hit! 10/70 Damage done to SneakyMark (Level 10) with Rusty Iron Sword

Critical damage taken! 30/32 Damage received from SneakyMark (Level 10) with Simple Knife

Focused Strike activated!

Critical Hit! 60/60 Damage done to SneakyMark (Level 10) with *Focused Strike*

Congratulations! You have slain tester SneakyMark (Level 10)! You have gained 500 experience.

You have gained a level! 650/300 experience. You are now level 4!

You now have 350/400 experience. You now have 24 unspent stat points and 3 unspent skill points.

Damage taken! 2/2 Damage received from tester Grant3d (Level 11)

You have been slain by Grant3d (Level 11)

You are now being transported to the Transition Room until respawn.

Looks like I did pretty well, Devin mused. *I wonder why they were so surprised to see me – surely Player-killers exist in this game, so they should have been on the lookout.*

PVP (Player-vs-Player) is only turned on after you reach level 20 – meaning you cannot harm or be harmed by anyone below that level. The developers wanted everyone to be able to experience the game without worrying about looking behind their backs all the time. In addition, even when PVP is active, you cannot harm or be harmed by another player if you are already engaged in combat with a monster or NPC.

"Thanks, Carl." Since he was technically a "monster", he didn't have to worry about those limitations. He was looking forward to what was available to him when he respawned. To that end, he attempted to contact Krista but was unable to do so.

Communications between the Dungeon Player and the DUMB must be initiated by the Dungeon Player when the DUMB is in the Transition Room.

Fortunately, he didn't have to wait long before Krista let him know about the results of the battle.

Chapter 13

Forum posting on the Glendaria Awakens unofficial message board:

Topic: Weird PVP Glitches

Specific Subject: PVP before level 20

Posted by: Grant3d

Forum member for: 5 months

What the hell!!! I was in a group with my friends at the newbie Goblin Cave just trying to complete it for a quest back in Briarwood when suddenly, some level 1 noob attacks us from behind while we were stunned during the boss fight. How is this possible?!!??!?! I couldn't even get his name because all it said in the logs was Human Fighter (Level 1). I don't know of any way to hide your name either – must be a massive glitch on Wexendsoft's end. I sent a bug report, but they responded that there was no glitch and that we died to monsters inside the dungeon. I know what I saw and that wasn't any monster I've ever seen – anyone else have anything like this come up?

Replies:

Posted by: Tob1n

Forum member for: 2 weeks

We were just in there about 15 hours ago and we didn't have any problems like you described. We wiped but that was just because of the stupid boss' skill we weren't aware of. Just take your wipe and don't blame it on some non-existent level 1 noob that just "happened" to kill you even though that is impossible.

Posted by: ShankedUG00d
Forum member for: 11 months
Take your death like a man you pussy – stop blaming PVPers for your own shortcomings. Just wait until you're level 20 then I'll show you what real PVP is.

Chapter 14

Krista watched the battle between the players and the mobs in the Boss Room. They were dispatching the Brawler when Krista noticed Devin hiding just outside the doorway to the Boss Room. She watched the following scene unfold and silently cheered for him – she didn't want to disturb him in the middle of the fight and break his concentration. As Devin went down, she watched the Chieftain continue to beat on the Defender.

While the Defender had high hit points and defense, he must have realized that he couldn't do enough damage to take out the Chieftain before he went down himself. Down to about 15% health and panicking, he backed up and ran out of the room. Disoriented, he recklessly ran through the hallways and took a wrong turn into a room that still had a Spike Trap activated. The group had bypassed it earlier because it was easy to get around – if you knew it was there. Fortunately for Krista, he forgot about it and became the third, and final, casualty of the group.

As soon as he died, all the bodies of the dead players and monsters disappeared, and Krista got a notification that the dungeons' resource total had been updated. She opened the menu to look at what she had to work with now:

Resource Breakdown	
Recoverable Resource Points Gained:	
Monsters Slain	1500 rp
Sprung Traps	50 rp
Chests Emptied	75 rp
Testers Eliminated	1500 rp
Previous Resource Total	15 rp
Total Available Resources	**3140 rp**

Testers Eliminated:	**(Calculated by Level X 50)**
Bronwynn – High Elf Healer (Level 9)	450
SneakyMark – Elf Rogue (Level 10)	500
Grant3d – Dwarf Defender (Level 11)	550
Total testers eliminated within the last 24 hours:	5
Total resources earned from testers within the last 24 hours:	**2600**

She had some choices to make now: what to do with those extra points. First, though, she needed to contact Devin, let him know what happened after he got himself killed, and ask his opinion on what they should do now.

"I think we should continue to lay low for the moment and work on upgrades to existing objects within the dungeon without changing the layout. Higher level players will start coming if they hear about the dungeon getting harder – just so they can try out a new challenge," Devin contributed after learning the results of the battle, "we're not quite ready for that."

Krista had to agree – until they had more levels between them they needed to farm the lower level players that invaded the dungeon. Having higher level players might net them more resources and experience but they would be much harder to kill. She decided to expand the upgrade menu to see her options:

Upgrade:	
Monsters	(Select for more options)
NPCs	(Not available at current Dungeon Level)
Chests	(Select for more options)
Loot	(Select for more options)
Traps	(Select for more options)
Rooms	(Select for more options)
Buildings	(Not available at current Dungeon Level)
Available Resources:	**3140**

Trying to select the grayed-out options came back with an error message stating that these were unlocked at a later level. Instead, she looked at the Monster upgrades:

Upgrade Monsters	
Goblin	Base Monster
Goblin Chieftain	Unique Monster

Not a lot of options. Since it was the strongest monster she had, she selected the Goblin Chieftain and pulled up its menu:

Goblin Chieftain (Unique)			
Rally I			
Current level description:	At 50% life, Chieftain will issue a rally cry that will boost nearby allies with a +20% to attack speed/damage for the duration of the battle. If he is alone, the rally cry will affect nearby enemies with a 10 second stun debuff.		
Next level description:	At 50% life, Chieftain will issue a rally cry that will boost nearby allies with a +30% to attack speed/damage for the duration of the battle. If he is alone, the rally cry will affect nearby enemies with a 12 second stun debuff.		
Upgrade cost:	100 rp		
Physical Attack:		Physical Resistance:	
Current Level: 1	30	Current Level: 1	30
Next Level: 2	45	Next Level: 2	45
Upgrade Cost:	50 rp	Upgrade Cost:	50 rp
Upgrade Weapon:		Upgrade Armor:	
(Must have access to upgraded weapons)		(Must have access to upgraded weapons)	

Create Hybrid?	Combine with Another Monster?
(Due to this being a unique monster, hybrids are not possible)	(Due to this being a unique monster, combining is not possible)

She could see some possibilities here, but it being a unique monster hindered some of the future potential of it. Due to her limited resource pool, she decided to look at the upgrades on the regular goblins:

Goblin (Base Monster)			
Skills			
(Can add skills to base monsters at Dungeon Level 3)			
Physical Attack:		Physical Resistance:	
Current Level: 1	15	Current Level: 1	15
Next Level: 2	25	Next Level: 2	25
Upgrade Cost:	25 rp	Upgrade Cost:	25 rp
Upgrade Weapon:		Upgrade Armor:	
(Must have access to upgraded weapons)		(Must have access to upgraded weapons)	
Create Hybrid?		Combine with Another Monster?	
A hybrid will create a mix between the two species of monster – whether it is a viable mix will be up to trial and error. For instance, combining a fish and a bird will create a FlyingFish hybrid, but will probably suffocate being out of water.		Combining monsters together is different from a hybrid – it is the pairing up of two separate monsters that are compatible. For instance, combining a parrot and a pirate will give the pirate a pet to attack with.	
(Select another monster to create hybrid)		(Select another monster to combine)	

Now this looks a lot better, she thought. *It costs a lot less to upgrade these compared to the Chieftain, but I need some different monsters to diversify my dungeon.* Before she committed to upgrading them, however, she had one more

menu to check out:

Upgrade Traps			
Fire Trap I		**Arrow Trap I**	
A tripwire activates a trap in the wall that shoots out streams of white-hot flames for 3 seconds that can incinerate a victim		A tripwire activates this trap which will shoot 8 arrows at varying heights toward a designated target	
Current Level:	1	Current Level:	1
Physical Damage:	30 per second	Number of Arrows:	8
Duration:	3 seconds	Damage per arrow:	5
Next Level:	2	Next Level:	2
Physical Damage:	40 per second	Number of Arrows:	12
Duration:	4 seconds	Damage per arrow:	7
Upgrade Cost:	50 rp	Upgrade Cost:	50 rp
Rockfall Trap I		**Spike Trap I**	
A pressure plate activates a rockfall from the ceiling that drops heavy rocks on unsuspecting victims		A pressure plate activates metal spikes that project from the floor and impales victims	
Current Level:	1	Current Level:	1
Physical Damage:	40	Physical Damage:	50
Next Level:	2	Next Level:	2
Physical Damage:	60 and adds 25% to critical hit chance of rockfall	Physical Damage:	100
Upgrade Cost:	50 rp	Upgrade Cost:	50 rp
Pit Trap I		**Unavailable Traps**	
Paper-thin ground separates potential victims from a 20-foot-deep pit filled with jagged rocks		Blade Trap	(Available at Dungeon Level 5)
Current Level:	1	Gas Trap	(Available at Dungeon Level 6)
Physical Damage:	60	Wall Trap	(Available at Dungeon Level 7)
Material on pit bottom:	Jagged rocks	*(Additional traps unlocked at future levels)*	
Next Level:	2		
Physical Damage:	110		
Material on pit bottom:	Jagged rocks with random spikes		
Upgrade Cost:	50 rp		

After looking at everything, she decided to make some changes to the traps and to the attack/defense of the monsters. This would be the least obvious changes that she could make and still maintain the semblance of normalcy.

Unrecoverable Resources Spent:			
Spike Trap I upgraded!			
Current Level:	2	Cost:	50 rp
Pit Trap I upgraded!			
Current Level:	2	Cost:	50 rp
Arrow Trap I upgraded!			
Current Level:	2	Cost:	50 rp
Fire Trap I upgraded!			
Current Level:	2	Cost:	50 rp
Rockfall Trap I upgraded!			
Current Level:	2	Cost:	50 rp
Goblin Physical Attack upgraded!			
Current Level:	2	Cost:	25 rp
Goblin Physical Resistance upgraded!			
Current Level:	2	Cost:	25 rp
Goblin Chieftain Rally I skill upgraded!			
Current Level:	2	Cost:	100 rp
Goblin Chieftain Physical Attack upgraded!			
Current Level:	2	Cost:	50 rp
Goblin Chieftain Physical Resistance upgraded!			
Current Level:	2	Cost:	50 rp
Total Unrecoverable Resources spent:			500 rp
Total Resources remaining:			**2640 rp**

After this spending spree, she decided to reset the dungeon to its basic design with the upgraded traps and monsters. She spent 600 resource points on the reset and then went to summon Devin again for 1000 points. However, when she went to the menu for the DUMB, she was unpleasantly surprised:

Dungeon Upgradeable Mobile Boss	
Current Level:	4
Place Dungeon Upgradeable Mobile Boss	1600 rp (resource points)
Upgrade Menu	(Select for more options)

"Carl, why is the DUMB more expensive now? It only cost 1000 points when I placed him before."

As the DUMB increases in level, so does too the cost associated with placing him in the dungeon. In this case, since the current level is 4, it added 600 points to the resource cost -- 200 per increased level.

"Well that sucks. Good thing I didn't use all of the points yet."

Recoverable Expenses Spent:	
Dungeon Reset	600 rp

DUMB Placement	1600 rp
Total Recoverable Resources Spent:	2200 rp
Remaining Resources:	**440 rp**

She paid the cost and after about 15 seconds Devin again appeared in the Boss Room. This time, however, he looked different from the last time she saw him.

Chapter 15

While waiting to be summoned again, Devin was able to pull up the character creation sheet to see what was available after the last battle.

Dungeon Upgradeable Mobile Boss	
Character Creation	
DUMB Level	4

Available Races:
Goblin
Human
Elf
High Elf
Dwarf
Available Classes:
Brawler
Fighter
Mage
Healer
Rogue
Defender

Available stat points:	59 (35 Initial starting points + 24 Level points)
Available skill points:	3

This time around, Devin wanted to stay farther away from invading players and try to control the situation better. He was going to have to shift his thinking; he was now part of a dungeon and needed to take advantage of that. He had tried using a caster in other games, but almost always came back to using a tank due to wanting to be in the thick of the action – he liked to control the situation from close range.

This worked as a surprise last time but now he wanted to try a more cautious approach. With this in mind, he chose to be a High Elf Mage, which, when the point benefits from race/class (17 additional) were added, gave him this stat sheet:

Character Status					
Race:		High Elf	Level:		4
Class:		Mage	Experience:		350/400
Strength:	0	Physical Damage:	16	Magical Damage:	140
Constitution:	1	Physical Resistance:	2	Magical Resistance:	10
Agility:	0	Health Points:	10	Mana Points:	700
Intelligence:	70	Health Regeneration:	3.0 per minute	Mana Regeneration:	15.0 per minute
Wisdom:	5	Block:	0	Critical/Dodge Chance:	0.0%

By min/maxing his stats this way, he would be able to do a lot of damage with each spellcast. However, he was a bit of a glass cannon – a strong sneeze would most likely take him down. By staying as far away as he could from everyone he would try to avoid taking any damage.

This was as far as he could progress with the character creation before he was summoned. An indeterminate time later, he got a prompt asking him to confirm his stat allocation – he chose **Y** and another screen came up that he hadn't seen before (most likely because he didn't have any skill points yet).

Dungeon Upgradable Mobile Boss			
Skill Selection:			
Available Skill Points:		3	
Flare I	(Mage Class Skill)	Cost to unlock:	Unlocked
Sends a small ball of fire toward a single target for a small amount of fire-based magical damage			
Fire-based Damage:	7	Mana Cost:	5
Casting Time:	0.8 seconds		
Mana Bolt I		Cost to unlock:	1 skill point
Casts a bolt of pure mana towards a single target for moderate magical damage			
Magic Damage:	15	Mana Cost:	10
Casting Time:	1.1 seconds		
Mana Blast I		Cost to unlock:	1 skill point
Casts a blast of pure mana at multiple targets for lesser magical damage			
Magic Damage:	8 to all targets in a 6-foot radius	Mana Cost:	10
Casting Time:	2.0 seconds		

Ice Barrier I		Cost to unlock:	1 skill point
Creates a wall of ice around the caster that can withstand melee and ranged damage but is highly vulnerable to fire-based magic			
Physical Damage Absorbed:	100	Mana Cost:	20
Casting Time:	1.5 seconds		
Fire Wall I		Cost to unlock:	1 skill point
Creates a wall of white-hot fire up to 6 feet long in a line directed by the caster and does fire-based magical damage -- must be maintained by constant consumption of mana			
Fire Damage:	25 per second to enemies within 1 foot of wall	Mana Cost:	15 per second
Casting Time:	3.5 seconds		
Lightning Shock I		Cost to unlock:	1 skill point
Sends a bolt of lightning towards a single target doing lightning-based magical damage with a chance to stun			
Lightning Damage:	10 with 25% chance to stun for 1 second	Mana Cost:	10
Casting Time:	1.0 seconds		
Short Teleport I		Cost to unlock:	1 skill point
Teleports the caster in any direction with just a thought			
Distance:	20 feet	Mana Cost:	40
Casting Time:	0.2 seconds		
Amplify I		Cost to unlock:	1 skill point
Temporary self-buff that will increase the damage from all spells for a short duration			
Magic Damage Increase:	20%	Duration:	20 seconds
Casting Time:	0.2 seconds	Mana Cost:	50

Devin had lots of different skills to choose from – but for what he wanted to accomplish he needed to be able to do massive damage quickly and then retreat to safety. To this end he chose Amplify I, Short Teleport I, and Lightning Shock I. Confirming his selections, he appeared inside the Boss Room again and looked around. He thought that it might be his imagination, but the goblins in the room looked just a little more dangerous – though it could be that he felt a little bit squishy and vulnerable in this new body.

Chapter 16

"Devin, there you are!! Who are you now?" Krista burst out as soon as he appeared.

"Going the mage route this time – do you have any gear with Intelligence stats on them?"

"I'll check, hold on" Krista pulled up the Loot menu and found it updated since the last time she checked it. She pulled up caster-only gear to simplify it:

Add/Delete Loot Menu
Class Restrictions: Mage

Armor:

Tattered Linen Robe	
Chest	
Physical Resistance:	2
Intelligence	+1
Cost:	5 rp
Class Restrictions:	Mage, Sorcerer, Healer, Druid, Warlock

Clean Cotton Robe	
Chest	
Physical Resistance:	3
Intelligence	+1
Wisdom	+1
Cost:	10 rp
Class Restrictions:	Mage, Sorcerer, Healer, Druid, Warlock

Pitted Tin Circlet	
Head	
Physical Resistance:	1
Intelligence	+1
Cost:	5 rp
Class Restrictions:	Mage, Sorcerer, Healer, Druid, Warlock

Simple Iron Circlet	
Head	
Physical Resistance:	2

Intelligence	+3
Cost:	10 rp
Class Restrictions:	Mage, Sorcerer, Healer, Druid, Warlock

Tattered Leather Sandals	
Feet	
Physical Resistance:	1
Cost:	5 rp
Class Restrictions:	Mage, Sorcerer, Healer, Druid, Warlock

Weapons:

Crooked Wood Staff	
Two-handed	
Physical Damage:	3
Intelligence	+1
Wisdom	+1
Cost:	5 rp
Class Restrictions:	Fighter, Pet Trainer, Mage, Sorcerer, Healer, Druid, Warlock

Staff of the Trainee	
Two-handed	
Physical Damage:	8
Intelligence	+5
Wisdom	+5
Cost:	50 rp
Class Restrictions:	Mage, Sorcerer, Healer

Accessories:

Ring of Intelligence +1	
Ring	
Intelligence:	+10
Cost:	50 rp
Class Restrictions:	All Classes

It looked like the Healer from the previous group at least had some better gear on her that they had ended up absorbing into the dungeon. She had 440 resource points left after resetting the dungeon and bringing Devin back, so she had a bit more to spend this time around. She ended up creating a quick

list of equipment for Devin:

Resource Breakdown	
Recoverable Resource Points Spent:	
Clean Cotton Robe	10 rp
Simple Iron Circlet	10 rp
Tattered Leather Sandals	5 rp
Staff of the Trainee	50 rp
Ring of Intelligence	50 rp
Ring of Intelligence	50 rp
Total Recoverable Resources Spent	175 rp
Total Resources Available	**265 rp**

Devin could wear two rings at the same time and she was

able to afford them – *why not?* With all this gear she only ended

up spending 175 resource points which left her 265 to spend.

After dropping all this gear on the floor in front of Devin, she

called up the menu to look at his stats after he had it equipped:

Character Status			
Race:	High Elf	Level:	4
Class:	Mage	Experience:	350/400

Strength:	0	Physical Damage:	33	Magical Damage:	198
Constitution:	1	Physical Resistance:	8	Magical Resistance:	22
Agility:	0	Health Points:	10	Mana Points:	990
Intelligence:	99	Health Regeneration:	3.0 per minute	Mana Regeneration:	33.0 per minute
Wisdom:	11	Block:	0	Critical/Dodge Chance:	0.0%
Skills:		Flare I, Short Teleport I, Lightning Shock I, Amplify I			
Upgrades:		(Select for options)			

Normally, a Mage couldn't min/max Intelligence like Devin did because they needed to put at least some points into other stats. Strength to be able to carry a little bit of loot and do some basic melee damage when out of mana; Constitution so they would be able to withstand at least a couple of hits before going down; and Agility so they would be able to dodge incoming attacks and critically hit with spells. Fortunately, Devin didn't have to worry about that – he wasn't going to be carrying any loot, wasn't planning on getting hit, and was hoping to only need a couple spells to take down the opposition. She was looking forward to seeing how he did.

Krista was also interested in the **Upgrades** located at the bottom of the stat menu. Since she had some resource points left, she selected it to see what the options were:

Dungeon Upgradeable Mobile Boss

Upgrade Menu	
Stat point boost:	100 rp
Gain an additional stat point for use upon next respawn	
Level boost:	100 rp per level (Current cost: 500 rp)
Gain a level through the use of resources instead of experience for use upon next respawn	
Skill point boost:	500 rp
Gain an additional skill point for use upon next respawn	
Lure skill:	1000 rp
Allows the ability to attract monsters from outside of the dungeon so that they could be brought in, killed, and absorbed by the dungeon. This skill is usable upon next respawn	
Dual class:	20000 rp
Allows the use of two classes at the same time – this includes class specific bonuses, skills, and equipment. For example, you can choose to be a Fighter-Mage which will give the Fighter access to magical spells and abilities. Class choices can be made upon next respawn	
(Additional upgrades available at Dungeon Level 5)	

Seeing nothing immediately usable, Krista nevertheless decided to invest in two additional stat points for when Devin respawned again. With pretty much all her points spent, all she had to do now was sit back and wait for the action to begin again.

Chapter 17

Devin didn't have too long to wait before the next group of "testers" arrived. This time, another trio of players entered the dungeon – an Archer, a Fighter, and a Paladin. The Level 12 Archer was named Shootdis, the Level 11 Fighter was DerektheRed, and the Level 14 Paladin was NoRlyIcanhlz. They sauntered in like they owned the place and without even pausing, attacked the **Goblin Brawler (Level 10)** located at the entrance.

Devin was waiting two rooms down, listening to Krista describe what was happening in the entrance. The Fighter and Paladin were taking turns beating on the Goblin Brawler while the Archer stayed back and shot it from afar. It didn't take long for the goblin to die and then the Paladin healed both himself and the fighter. They moved onto the next room – which had a Pit Trap (that they easily avoided) and a **Goblin Brawler (Level 12)**. They handled it almost as quickly as the first and started heading his way.

Devin moved to the exit of the third room just out of sight of anyone entering it. He heard the trio run into the room and start bashing away at the two **Goblin Brawlers (Level 10)**. They focused their attacks on one of them, quickly bringing its health down to 0, and started in on the second. The fighter held aggro most of the time and was down to about 50% health.

Devin waited until the second goblin was at about 50% health when he cast *Amplify* on himself. He stepped around the corner while starting to cast *Lightning Shock*. Targeting the Fighter, he released his spell and started casting another and then another. Two was all it took to take out the Fighter, so he redirected the third bolt towards the Archer.

The party was "shocked" to say the least. With his bonuses from his race (+25% to magical damage), class (+30% to elemental damage), and the *Amplify* spell (+20% spell damage) he did massive amounts of damage for his level. They couldn't recover fast enough – by the time the Archer saw Devin at the rooms' exit and started to take aim, he had already been hit with a *Lightning Shock* and stunned for 1 second. This aborted his attack and he was hit for a second time. Already down to 30% life and in a panic, he blindly fired toward Devin and was flabbergasted when his target wasn't there anymore. He looked 20 feet to his left and saw the "High Elf Mage (Level 5)" near the side of the room just as he got blasted again by another *Lightning Shock* and was sent for respawn.

When Devin saw the archer starting to aim his bow in his direction, he used his *Short Teleport* to get out of the line of fire. He deliberately chose a side of the room where he could still see the Archer but was behind the Paladin. After finishing off the Archer with another *Lightning Shock*, he turned his attention to the Paladin who was still trying to fend off the **Goblin Brawler (Level 10)**. NoRlyIcanhlz wasn't doing too bad and in a 1-on-1

129

fight would have easily handled the goblin even without having to heal himself. *Sucks to be him*, Devin thought as he released *Lightning Shock* after *Lightning Shock* at the battling Paladin.

At first the Paladin tried to run after Devin but couldn't catch him because he would just teleport away. Eventually, the Paladin stopped and tried to heal himself – thankfully, the mindless goblin was still beating on the Paladin and interrupted all the healing spells he was trying to cast. Finally, with no heals to help him, multiple shocks, and the goblin continuously attacking him, the Paladin went down to Devin's last *Lightning Shock*.

Devin sat down, exhausted and shaking a little from the intense battle he just finished. Taking a deep breath, he screamed out, "YEAAAAAAAAAHHH!" The remaining goblin in the room paid no attention to him as he got up and did a little happy dance. "It worked!!!"

"Congratulations! Just don't get too cocky, not all of the fights are going to be that easy," Krista warned him.

"Ach, it'll be fine – this is an awesome build and I'll just keep taking them out as they come in."

Chapter 18

(Excerpt from General Chat for Briarwood and Surrounding Areas)

Shootdis: There is something really weird going on at the Goblin Cave – my party and I were ganked earlier by this level 5 mage. Did they do a new patch that I don't know about that allowed PVP for under 20 now?

Xynthia: same here – it was a level 7 mage at the time though -- I'm sending it to my guild chat now

Aeliren: no new patches that I'm aware of you still can't PVP under 20

Lectricity: must have been a mob. they do have mages in there you know

Phluphphie: but this was a high elf – just got killed as well and it was a level 9 mage

BurningRain: can anyone higher-level head there and kill whatever this is? friend of mine just got wiped a minute ago

Graburankels: omw now was just passing through but I'll check it out

(End of Excerpt)

Chapter 19

Devin was having the time of his life – he had already taken out five parties of players trying to make it through the Dungeon. He was in the Boss Room resting after just wiping another party of four when he thought he heard something. Next thing he knew, he was in the Transition Room staring dumbfounded in confusion. He pulled up his combat logs to find out what happened:

Critical Hit! 112/112 Damage done to Rodchester (Level 12 Fighter) with Lightning Shock

Congratulations! You have slain tester Rodchester (Level 12 Fighter)! You have gained 600 experience.

You have gained a level! 1400/1100 experience. You are now level 12!

You now have 300/1200 experience. You now have 66 unspent stat points and 8 unspent skill points.

Damage taken! Sneak Attack! Critical Damage! 10/10 Damage received from Graburankels (Level 45 Assassin) with Execute.

You have been slain by Graburankels (Level 45 Assassin).

You are now being transported to the Transition Room until respawn.

What was someone level 45 doing in there? Devin thought. *Let alone one with an advanced class.* He knew that you could get an advanced class at level 40, so that wasn't too much of a surprise – it was just that he hadn't seen any of those classes yet. Now he knew why he didn't see him – an Assassin was a master of stealth and unless you had a high amount of stealth skill or something similar you wouldn't be able to see him coming.

Devin figured it was time for a change anyway and he wanted to finally use all the stat points that he had accumulated on his killing spree. Not every "tester" that was killed was done in by Devin – some had died from the goblins or traps inside the dungeon when they tried to flee. Nevertheless, he had managed to gain eight levels bringing him to level 12.

He was just about to pull up the screen for Character Creation when he was contacted by Krista.

"Hey, what happened? I looked away to see what other players were coming when I saw that you disappeared," Krista asked in concern.

Devin told her what had happened and how he was eager to get back in and start taking out some more players. Krista had another idea, however. She thought about what they had been doing and they probably ended up calling more attention to themselves than they had anticipated. The players surely had communicated with one another, to their guilds, and most likely a general chat as well. It was only a matter of time before they had to worry about a further influx of higher-level players.

To this end, she figured it was time to expand the dungeon – she had accumulated an additional 7600 resource points which brought her total accumulated point total to 10200. In addition to the points accumulated, she also leveled the dungeon up to level 2 – which allowed her to add in another floor. The only points that she didn't get back were the 750 used on upgrades.

She wanted to keep the first floor exactly the same to keep up the appearance of being a normal dungeon – expanding another floor let her do what she wanted and would make it look like it was added later during another patch. In fact..."Carl, is there a regular patch schedule like most games?"

Patches, or updates, to the game world are completed overnight on Tuesdays when the server load is at minimal capacity. Improvements in server adaptability have allowed these updates to take effect without having to do a server-wide shut down. Before you ask, because I can hear your thoughts, today is Friday.

"Can we somehow add in information to the patch notes without calling too much attention?"

Any AI can make necessary changes to their area of influence to maintain the functionality of the game world – which, in effect, means that anything you do can be updated in the patch notes that all players can see.

"Uhhh....why didn't you say anything before then? This would have made this so much easier."

The first and most obvious answer is that you did not ask. I could have volunteered this information, but as you were not making any significant changes to the structure of the dungeon it was deemed unnecessary.

"Well, from now on if you feel like volunteering any important information like that, I would love to hear it. Anything that would make this easier would be greatly appreciated."

Carl gave her an affirmative, so Krista went back to her previous thoughts. With today being Friday, this meant that they had about three full days to bring her plan together. First off, she had to look at her Resource menu:

Resource Breakdown	
Recoverable Resource Points Gained:	
Monsters Slain	2100 rp
Traps Sprung	25 rp
Chests Emptied	50 rp
Testers Eliminated	7600 rp
Previous Resource Total	65 rp

Total Available Resources	9450 rp

Testers Eliminated:	(Calculated by Level X 50)
Total testers eliminated within the last 24 hours:	19
Total resources earned from testers within the last 24 hours:	10200

Armed with this information, she started by getting Devin briefed on his part of the plan. After he was sent on his way, she got to work on the second floor of the dungeon. First, she created a small room just underneath the teleport room – she was going to wait to add stairs down to it when the whole floor was ready.

The visual editor made this easy to accomplish – she just had to think of where she wanted something and what she wanted it to look like. In this case, she added both stalagmites and stalactites to the top and bottom of the room to break up the flow of the interior. This cost an additional amount of resources, but it would allow her monsters to ambush incoming players by keeping them out of sight until they were very close.

After adding this first small room, she added a hallway to the north side of the room. This hallway then turned a blind corner to the east and headed toward another small room.

Right after this blind corner, she added an upgraded Fire Trap to catch unsuspecting victims on the way through the hallway.

In the next room, she continued to add the stalagmites and stalactites to decrease the field of vision of anyone entering the room. On the far east wall, she added another hallway that turned south after 10 feet and turned west after another 20-foot hallway. She also placed an upgraded Arrow Trap in the middle of that hallway that would shoot arrows from both ends. Hopefully, this pincer attack would take out the more unwary "testers".

The hallway eventually entered a medium-sized room at the northwest corner – again with more stalagmites and stalactites for ambushing. In this room, she placed her first chest on this floor because she was going to make this her first mini-boss room. She decided to upgrade the quality of the Chest so that it could hold more loot – she wanted people to explore down on this floor and loot is always a great incentive.

Chests	
Upgrade Menu	
Rotted Wooden Chest	Available
Can hold up to 1 silvers' worth of loot	
Sturdy Wooden Chest	Available
Can hold up to 5 silvers' worth of loot	

Banded Iron Wooden Chest	50 rp
Can hold up to 1 golds' worth of loot	
Copper Chest	250 rp
Can hold up to 5 golds' worth of loot	
Iron Chest	800 rp
Can hold up to 20 golds' worth of loot	
Steel Chest	4000 rp
Can hold up to 100 golds' worth of loot	
Gold-plated Chest	12000 rp
Can hold up to 1000 golds' worth of loot	
Platinum Chest (Unlocked at dungeon level 15)	
Mithril Chest (Unlocked at dungeon level 30)	
Legendary Chest (Unlocked at dungeon level 50)	

Krista decided that she was going to need to hold at least five golds' worth of loot for the final boss, so she unlocked both the Banded Iron Wooden Chest and the Copper Chest. In this first mini-boss room she placed a Banded Iron Wooden Chest with one gold in it – one gold was actually a lot for a player under level 20 since most potions only cost a half a silver or less in town.

After the chest was placed, she placed an upgraded Pit Trap right before the exit hallway to the southwest corner of the room. The hallway extended into another small room, again with the stalagmites and stalactites, and had another exit located in the middle of the east wall. This hallway led to another medium-sized room that was meant for a second mini-boss. It also had an upgraded Rockfall Trap just inside the entrance that was triggered by a pressure plate near the center of the room. The thought behind this was to trap the party inside the room when the battle started so that there is no immediate retreat – the rocks could be moved but not while being attacked by monsters.

Since the entrance of this room was on the southwest side, she placed a Copper Chest with two gold and five silver in it near the northeast wall. The exit of this room led down a hallway that ran north about 15 feet and then turned east toward the final Boss Room.

This Boss Room had only one trap located in it – an upgraded Spike Trap positioned right in front of the small adjacent room that contained a Copper Chest with five gold in it. This room would eventually contain the teleporter that was located on the first floor – Krista would move it once the whole floor was populated with monsters. The trap would also automatically deactivate once the boss was defeated.

Now that she had finished with the construction of the second floor, Krista looked at what she had spent to create it:

Resource Expenses	
Unrecoverable Resources Spent on Upgrades:	
Banded Iron Wooden Chest	50
Copper Chest	250
DUMB Lure Upgrade	1000
Unrecoverable Resources Spent on Rooms/Hallways/Decor:	
Small Rooms	150
Medium Rooms	300
Boss Room	400
Hallways	120
Decor (Stalagmites and Stalactites)	200
Total Unrecoverable Resources Spent:	2470
Recoverable Resources Spent:	
Chests	850
Traps	250
DUMB	3600
Total Recoverable Resources Spent:	4700
Available Resources:	9450
Total Resources Spent:	7170
Total Resources Remaining:	**2280**

After all the spending on the second-floor construction, she still had 2280 to use to populate it with some monsters. Speaking of which, Devin should hopefully be done with his tasks soon...

Chapter 20

Devin was on his way to try to acquire some monster variety for the dungeon. To accomplish this, Krista had upgraded him with the Lure skill that would allow him to bring back a monster to the dungeon from the outside. He decided that the best way to accomplish this without getting killed was to play a Goblin Rogue and do his best to stay hidden from all the players out there. He had 125 stat points to play with (35 starting points, 88 from leveling, and 2 from upgrades) and 11 skill points to find the best skills for what he needed to do. With an additional 17 additional stat points for being a Goblin Rogue, this is what he ended up with:

Character Status					
Race:		Goblin	Level:		12
Class:		Rogue	Experience:		300/1200
Strength:	10	Physical Damage:	227	Magical Damage:	0
Constitution:	20	Physical Resistance:	40	Magical Resistance:	0
Agility:	112	Health Points:	200	Mana Points:	0
Intelligence:	0	Health Regeneration:	60.0 per minute	Mana Regeneration:	0.0 per minute
Wisdom:	0	Block:	0	Critical/Dodge Chance:	11.2%
Skills:			Stealth, Backstab		
Upgrades:			Lure		

He chose to be a Goblin this time so that he could blend-in inside of the dungeon – hopefully he would just be considered just another normal mob since the race was not available to regular players.

Dungeon Upgradable Mobile Boss			
Skill Selection:			
Available Skill Points:		11	
Backstab I	**(Rogue Class Skill)**	Cost to unlock:	Unlocked
Does damage from behind a target that can only be used while stealthed			
Physical Damage:	30 with a 25% chance of critical damage	Cooldown:	60.0 seconds
Stealth I	**(Rogue Class Skill)**	Cost to unlock:	Unlocked
Hide in the shadows to move around undetected			
Effect:	60% less chance of being detected	Cooldown:	After stealth is canceled, you must be out of combat for at least 20 seconds
Wound I		Cost to unlock:	1 skill point
Does damage and creates a bleed effect on the target			
Physical Damage:	10 and 3 bleed damage per second for 5 seconds	Cooldown:	90.0 seconds
Disarm Trap I		Cost to unlock:	1 skill point
Disarms traps up to 5 feet away and up to a certain complexity			
Target Distance:	5 feet	Cooldown:	60.0 seconds
Complexity:	Simple trap		
Vanish I		Cost to unlock:	1 skill point
Enter stealth mode when not taking damage for a certain amount of time, even during combat			
No Damage:	5.0 seconds	Cooldown:	600.0 seconds
Poison Strike I		Cost to unlock:	1 skill point
Does damage and injects a debilitating poison into the target			
Physical Damage:	10	Duration:	20.0 seconds
Effect:	Slow (Agility -20)	Cooldown:	90.0 seconds
Garrote I		Cost to unlock:	1 skill point
From stealth, does minimal damage and silences the target			
Physical Damage:	5	Duration:	15.0 seconds
Effect:	Silence (Unable	Cooldown:	300.0 seconds

	to cast spells)		
Second Wind I		Cost to unlock:	1 skill point
Reset all cooldowns for all other skills			
Cooldown:	24 hours		

He had 11 skill points to use and every 5 levels you can upgrade a skill to the next level for that amount of skill points. For instance, at level 5 he could upgrade his backstab skill to level 2 for 2 skill points and at level 10 he could upgrade it to level 3 for 3 skill points. Depending on the specific skill, an upgrade can increase damage, duration, additional effects, and even reduce the cooldown.

Since he was going to be on his own initially, he needed to be able to hide from other players. To this end, he upgraded *Stealth* to level 3 for five points and *Vanish* to level 3 for six points. His objective right now was not to kill anyone unless he was forced into combat. He still had the ability to *Backstab* and his Strength and Agility brought his attack damage up pretty high. He wouldn't be able to take much damage in a fair fight – but he wasn't planning on fighting fair.

Stealth III	(Rogue Class Skill)	Cost to unlock:	Unlocked
Hide in the shadows to move around undetected			
Effect:	80% less chance of being detected	Cooldown:	After stealth is canceled, you must be out of combat for at least 10 seconds
Vanish I		Cost to unlock:	1 skill point
Enter stealth mode when not taking damage for a certain amount of time			

144

No Damage:	3.0 seconds	Cooldown:	150.0 seconds

After respawning, he received some basic armor and weapons (but also a necklace and two rings of Agility +1) from Krista, equipped it, and headed up to the entrance. Halfway to the surface he realized that he hadn't activated stealth mode yet. After activating it, he was glad that he did because near the first room he encountered a small three-man party tackling the dungeon. He cautiously made his way past the three players and his level 3 *Stealth* even prevented the Rogue in the party from seeing him as he slipped past.

Safely past the invading group of players, Devin made his way out of the entrance for the first time in what felt like only a couple of days. In actuality, he hadn't been outside in months. As the sunlight hit him, he remembered how beautiful the game world outside their little dungeon was. He just stopped and stared around him taking in all the trees, rocks, and even some squirrels chasing each other in the boughs of the tree in front of him. He looked back and saw the mountain that the cave was carved from – the majestic peak rising thousands of feet above his head made him finally accept the fact that this was his home now. For better or worse, he and Krista were stuck there and had to make the most of it.

Sure, they would continue to work toward finding out what happened to their real bodies, as well as seeing what they could do to get back to the real world if at all possible. However, until that time, he would make the most of it here and live the best life that he could. He would strive to level up his character, help Krista level up the dungeon, and continue to explore the world of Glendaria to its fullest.

Determined to get a move-on, Devin started heading south through the trees surrounding the dungeon. Krista mentioned that until the dungeon leveled up, the most he could travel was 100 feet from the entrance – the amount would double for each Dungeon Level. Although not a long distance, he felt confident that he could find a mob or two that was close enough to *Lure* back to the dungeon.

As he got closer to his distance limit, he started to feel anxious; it felt like he needed to start heading back to the dungeon as soon as possible. He turned around and walked a couple of feet heading back to where he started, and the feeling disappeared. *This must be how they limit the distance – not a physical barrier, but just the intense feeling of needing to turn back,* he thought. Still stealthed, he crouched next to a tree and started looking for anything he could use for the dungeon. He noticed a Dusk Boar (Level 11) about 40 feet away and well within his "containment zone". Walking slowly and trying to avoid making too much noise, he crept up to the boar, targeted it, and used the *Lure* skill.

Instantly, the boar started running unerringly toward Devin; despite being stealthed, it knew exactly where he was. Although he could probably kill it even in a stand-up fight, he wasn't here to do that. He started running back toward the dungeon when he saw another group of players heading toward the entrance as well. He took a chance and sprinted past the group, ignoring their startled exclamations at seeing a running **Goblin Rogue (Level 12)**, and entered the dungeon only seconds before they got there. He ran past the Brawler in the first room and heard the players running after him yelling about not letting a "Rare Mob" get away.

He ducked around the corner in the hallway and hit Vanish. He continued walking stealthily down the hallway and almost got to the next room before he heard the goblin Brawler get killed. Just before entering the closest room, he heard behind him an animal squeal and realized that the boar had continued to follow him and had just encountered the group of players. They didn't realize that it was following Devin; they didn't question it though, as they just attacked it and took it down in seconds.

He kept going and made his way to the Boss Room to wait for the group. Hopefully, he would be able take advantage of their preoccupation with chasing him to try and take at least one of them out. He made his way the front corner of the room, made sure his stealth was still activated, and waited for the show to begin. These players were a bit higher level than usual, so he didn't have long to wait – they arrived within about a minute and he saw that they hadn't even bothered to heal up between battles.

He took advantage of this using his favorite method when the Goblin Chieftain used his Rally skill at half health. When they were stunned, he crept up and activated *Backstab* on the Mage at the back of the group – one hit was enough to take her out since she had taken a little damage before. Knowing he didn't have a chance to kill any more, he ran behind the boss into the teleporter room and hit Vanish again to hide from the rest of the party. He didn't really care if the rest of them lived or not, he had other things to take care of now. He teleported to the entrance and as he got there he was contacted by Krista.

"Awesome job Devin! It was clever of you to get those players to kill that boar for you – now I can summon them into the dungeon!"

"Yeah, sure...that was my plan the entire time."

"By the way, the Goblin Chieftain ended up killing those other two players – they didn't recover from your surprise attack in time."

"Your welcome, my lady – more points for you!"

Deciding that one monster wasn't enough, he stayed stealthed as he exited out of the cave and made his way around the perimeter of his permitted distance. He saw a couple of gophers but didn't think those would be beneficial to the dungeon. He finally settled on getting a wolf – if he could find one. However, all he saw – other than gophers – were more boars.

Discouraged, he was going to just go ahead and bring in a gopher just for fun when he saw a player in the distance being chased by a pack of four wolves. As the level 13 Fighter got closer, Devin realized he was attempting to make it to the dungeon – when he crossed the threshold of the entrance the wolves would lose aggro and he would be safe.

Thinking quickly, he made it to the entrance of the cave about 15 feet in front of the player while still in stealth mode. Just before the Fighter made it inside, Devin used his *Lure* skill on the lead wolf – thereby allowing it and his friends to continue into the dungeon. The player wasn't even paying attention to what was in the first room and didn't see Devin – he was mistakenly only concerned with outrunning the wolves.

With a big sigh of relief, the Fighter, named Gorgee, stopped in the middle of the room and sat down on the ground to get his health back faster. As soon as he did, however, the wolves rushed up behind him. Three of the wolves still had aggro on the player and started attacking him immediately. The lead wolf, having had the Lure skill used on it, went for Devin. Devin ran down the hallway into the room to the South where he knew a Pit Trap was located. Since wolves were dumber than people, he had no difficulty maneuvering it into the trap, killing it instantly.

He stealthed again and walked toward the entrance looking to see if the wolves took out the player or not. No such luck – he was just finishing up the last wolf but was at about 20%

life. Not one to miss the opportunity, he crept up and used *Backstab* for critical damage which took him down in one hit.

Krista got ahold of him after the brief battle, "Nice job Devin! You brought me some wolves and leveled up at the same time! I think it's my turn now with these new mobs – do you want to keep ambushing players using that Rogue or do you want to respawn with a new character?"

He looked at his battle log and saw that he had, indeed, leveled up after the last battle and was now level 13. He decided to respawn with the new levels' points and respec, or respecialize, his character. "Delete me if you can – I want to try something else."

Chapter 21

Krista was excited to see what she could do with her new monsters in the upgrade menu. She pulled it up and reviewed her options:

Timber Wolf (Base Monster)			
Quick Bite I			
Current level description:	The Timber Wolf uses its agility to quickly attack, bypassing most defenses		
Physical Damage:	20	Cooldown:	120.0 seconds
Next level description:	The Timber Wolf uses its agility to quickly attack twice, bypassing most defenses		
Physical Damage:	40	Cooldown:	90.0 seconds
Upgrade cost:	100 rp		
Physical Attack:		**Physical Resistance:**	
Current Level: 1	7	Current Level: 1	7
Next Level: 2	12	Next Level: 2	12
Upgrade Cost:	25 rp	Upgrade Cost:	25 rp
Upgrade Weapon:		**Upgrade Armor:**	
(Cannot equip weapons)		(Cannot equip armor)	
Create Hybrid?		**Combine with Another Monster?**	
(Select another monster to create hybrid)		(Select another monster to combine)	

She selected *Create hybrid,* chose Goblin as the other monster, and got a prompt stating that it would cost 200 unrecoverable resource points. She selected **Y** and looked to see what the result was.

Weregoblin (Advanced Monster)			
A combination of wolf and goblin, the Weregoblin has the benefits of both. It walks upright, can use weapons and armor, and can use skills that increase its own power or stun its enemies			
Powershifter I			
Current level description:	Increases the physical damage of the Weregoblin for a limited time. After that time is up, it receives a debuff to physical resistance for the duration of the battle.		
Physical Damage Increase/Resistance Decrease:	30%	Cooldown:	Once per battle
Physical Damage increase duration:	30 seconds		
Next level description:	Further increases the physical damage of the Weregoblin for a limited time. After that time is up, it receives less of a debuff to physical resistance for the duration of the battle.		
Physical Damage Increase/Resistance Decrease:	40% increase/20% decrease	Cooldown:	Once per battle
Physical Damage increase duration:	30 seconds	Upgrade cost:	1000 rp
Howl I			
Current level description:	Stuns enemies for a limited time within a 30-foot radius around the Weregoblin		
Duration:	8 seconds	Cooldown:	300.0 seconds
Next level description:	Stuns enemies for a longer time within a 30-foot radius around the Weregoblin		
Duration:	10 seconds	Cooldown:	250.0 seconds
Upgrade cost:	1000 rp		
Physical Attack:		**Physical Resistance:**	
Current Level: 1	30	Current Level: 1	20

Next Level: 2	50	Next Level: 2	35
Upgrade Cost:	200 rp	Upgrade Cost:	200 rp
Upgrade Weapon:		**Upgrade Armor:**	
(Must have access to upgraded weapons)		(Must have access to upgraded weapons)	
Create Hybrid?		**Combine with Another Monster?**	
(Due to this being an advanced monster, hybrids are not available at its current level)		(Due to this being an advanced monster, combines are not available at its current level)	

She was more than pleased with her new addition to her monster repertoire. Hoping to have as much luck with the boar, she looked at its upgrade menu as well:

Dusk Boar (Base Monster)			
Charge I			
Current level description:	The Dusk Boar charges forward from a certain distance, does damage, and can knockdown target		
Physical Damage:	15	Knockdown Chance:	35%
Range:	Between 10 and 30 feet away	Cooldown:	120.0 seconds
Next level description:	The Dusk Boar charges forward from a longer distance, does more damage, and has a higher chance to knockdown target		
Physical Damage:	30	Knockdown Chance:	35%
Range:	Between 9 and 35 feet away	Cooldown:	90.0 seconds
Upgrade cost:	100 rp		
Physical Attack:		**Physical Resistance:**	
Current Level: 1	10	Current Level: 1	10

Next Level: 2	17	Next Level: 2	17
Upgrade Cost:	25 rp	Upgrade Cost:	25 rp
Upgrade Weapon:		**Upgrade Armor:**	
(Cannot equip weapons)		(Cannot equip armor)	
Create Hybrid?		**Combine with Another Monster?**	
(Select another monster to create hybrid)		(Select another monster to combine)	

She decided to try making a boar and wolf hybrid, but the result was less than satisfactory – when she saw the result it seemed to some sort of amorphous mass that had 8 legs, two different heads erupting from different sides of the "body", and it couldn't even move let alone attack. Discarding the disturbing creation, she lamented the loss of 200 resource points but endeavored to try again. This time she tried combining a boar and a goblin to see what she could get from that:

Goblin Boar-rider (Advanced Monster)			
Raised from a young age, these vicious boars have been tamed by Goblin Breeders and are used as mounts in battle. This gives them high maneuverability, height advantage, and the ability to have the boar help attack as well.			
Weapon Charge I			
Current level description:	Goblin and boar charge forward and attack together with the goblins' weapon and the boars' tusks		
Physical Damage:	100	Knockdown Chance:	40%
Distance:	Between 10 and 30 feet away	Cooldown:	Once per battle
Next level description:	Goblin and boar charge forward and attack together with the goblins' weapon and the boars' tusks, doing even more damage		

Physical Damage:	150	Knockdown Chance:	0%
Distance:	Between 8 and 40 feet away	Cooldown:	Once per battle
Upgrade cost:	500 rp		

Pincer Attack I			
Current level description:	The goblin and boar separate and attack from opposite directions		
Physical Damage:	150	Cooldown:	120.0 seconds
Next level description:	The goblin and boar separate and attack from opposite directions, with a chance to stun		
Physical Damage:	250	Cooldown:	90.0 seconds
Stun Chance:	10%		
Upgrade cost:	1000 rp		

Physical Attack:		Physical Resistance:	
Current Level: 1	25	Current Level: 1	18
Next Level: 2	40	Next Level: 2	35
Upgrade Cost:	200 rp	Upgrade Cost:	200 rp

Upgrade Weapon:	Upgrade Armor:
(Must have access to upgraded weapons)	(Must have access to upgraded weapons)

Create Hybrid?	Combine with Another Monster?
(Due to this being an advanced monster, hybrids are not available at its current level)	(Due to this being an advanced monster, combines are not available at its current level)

Having gotten two new awesome monsters for the dungeon, she decided against risking any more resource points on hybrids or combines. It was now time to start placing them into the second floor of the dungeon.

In the first room, she placed a **Dusk Boar (Level 14)** and a **Timber Wolf (Level 14)** so that players would have an indication of what was to come. In subsequent rooms, she started placing more wolves and boars, Goblin Boar-riders, and eventually a Weregoblin. In the next to last room with the Rockfall Trap, she placed eight total wolves and boars that would all attack together once the party was trapped in the room.

In the Boss Room, she placed a **Weregoblin (level 25)** surrounded by three **Goblin Boar-riders (level 20)**. She thought it would definitely be a challenge to any group of players with an average level of 20 or below. Once this level was connected to the first, Krista hoped they would see quite a difference in the quality of players eager to test out the dungeon.

After spending resource points on the hybrids/combines and placing all the monsters in the second floor, she had enough points left over to upgrade the base attack and defense of all her new monsters. This made the new floor even more deadly because the monsters' levels would be deceptive based on their actual strength.

All that was left to do was add some stairs to the new floor at the end of the first floor – but before that could happen she had to get Carl to add the changes to the next patch notes.

Chapter 22

Patch Notes for Update Version 3.40.2 (Partial)

...Moon Dust will now work properly when used in the Invisibility Alchemy recipe

The respawn rate of Dark Terrors in the Forest of Tears has been tweaked slightly

Fixed a glitch on the Trainer skill Obey that would allow it to be used on certain NPCs

Paladin skill Judgement base damage increased to 350 from 300

The old beginner Goblin Cave dungeon near Briarwood has added a new floor for levels 15-22 and has changed its name to Altera Vita

The user interface has updated to include an optional internet search window (for an additional fee)...

Chapter 23

When she was working with Carl regarding the patch notes, she decided to rename the entire dungeon Altera Vita or "Other Life" – basically in response to this being their new life now. Even though she and Devin were stuck here, they were both kind of enjoying themselves. They didn't have as much freedom as they used to, but the most important thing was that they were going through this side-by-side. If anything, they were growing closer together – they were working to accomplish the same task. While Krista was building up the dungeon, and then populating it with monsters that Devin had brought back, it felt like they were building an "Other Life" separate from their old one.

Krista was looking forward to seeing how the players reacted to the new floor in her dungeon. She was going to have Devin basically watch a group or two, so they could both see the difficulty of the floor and whether she would have to tone it down. She wanted to make sure her evaluation of the level range was accurate – if it was too easy or too hard then it could cause problems with the main system AI.

They had gotten this far by staying as far under the radar as they could – any new changes had to make the dungeon still accessible to players within the range. If they left its viability in question too long, then they would risk a complete shutdown.

Additionally, if Devin started destroying the player groups too often then it would show that no one could complete the floor – again risking the attention of the main AI.

With that in mind, she had Devin create a Rogue with as maxed out Stealth as possible so that he could observe without interfering. She sent him to the first-floor boss room so that he could wait for a group to finish and follow them down to the next floor. Of course, that didn't work out as well as they planned.

When a group of high-level players entered the dungeon, Krista figured that this would be just a waste of time. The players – averaging around level 50 – would just wipe out everything and it wouldn't even be a challenge. It didn't really cost any resources in the long run because she would get it all back, but it would be a massive disappointment if only high-level players came to farm the new addition. Fortunately, Carl let her know another feature of the Admin controls.

While you cannot personally delete/add anything to the dungeon while there are "testers" inside, you can assign level ranges to any floors after the first. Anyone can visit the first floor – even a level 500 player – but if you assign the second floor to players level 1 to level 22 then the system will automatically delete all objects on that floor if it detects anyone above that level (even if in a party) entering. The only exception to this is if a player were to level up while on that

floor – it would allow them to finish but they would not be able to come back again.

This feature was initially introduced for the "Dungeon Player" admin tools so that they could test multiple floors for different level ranges. They wanted higher level testers to bypass the easier floors without having to fight through them to test harder floors. You can use this to your advantage by making sure you only get the players that you want without fear of high-level powerleveling, where they would use their greater power to provide virtually free experience for someone of a lower level. The only requirement that you must follow is to make sure that the high-level limit is higher than 95% of the monster levels on the floor.

Knowing this, she set the floor level range from level 1 to level 22 – the only mob higher than level 20 was the Weregoblin Boss in the Boss Room at level 25.

She watched as the high-level players finished the first floor in record time, where they quickly descended to the second floor. As they reached the foot of the stairway, all the monsters, chests, and traps disappeared. Confused, the players then got angry when a prompt flashed before their eyes:

Warning! You are above the designated level (Level 22)! – all objects on this floor have been removed. If you meet the

requirements for subsequent floors the objects will repopulate on those floors.

Scoffing at the absurdity of this, the leader of the party led them through the rest of the second floor to verify that everything was gone. Upon reaching the end, they found that even the transporter wasn't there. Cursing the dungeon and the developers, they had to turn around and walk all the way back to the entrance. *Hopefully they will get the word out and keep all the other overpowered players away – we don't need them here right now.*

Thankfully, the next group to enter the dungeon was a perfect test for the new floor. It consisted of 4 players:

MndBlwn36 – High Elf Sorcerer (Level 20)

BunsoSteel – Human Fighter (Level 21)

Gleanna – High Elf Healer (Level 19)

BoworDie – Elf Archer (Level 20)

Devin stayed in the first floor Boss Room until the party arrived – Krista gave him updates on where they were located while he was waiting. When they finally got there, he got a chance to watch a team really work well together. BunsoSteel kept the aggro of all the mobs in the room the entire time. He also didn't even fall below 80% health because Gleanna did such a great job keeping up with the damage without attracting any attention. They also knew the characteristics of the battle – when the Chieftain used his *Rally* skill, all but BunsoSteel essentially left the room in order to avoid being hit by the skill. When their tank was stunned, they came back in and MndBlwn36 used his Mind Prison skill on the Chieftain, which incapacitated it for nearly 30 seconds.

Mind Prison I			
When Mind Prison is cast on a target, they are imprisoned in their own mind and is immobilized for a limited time. Damage to target may break Mind Prison.			
Duration:	30.0 seconds	Target Range:	30.0 feet
Damage:	0	Cooldown:	300.0 seconds

The rest of the fight was pretty unimpressive – at least as far as the goblins went – and they quickly dispatched the Chieftain. They collected the loot from the chest after the battle and headed downstairs to the next level. Devin followed behind, still stealthed and making as little noise as possible. When they got to the first room at the bottom of the stairs, they quickly paused and took stock of the situation. *They're certainly a cautious bunch.*

After not finding anything suspicious, they attacked the **Timber Wolf (Level 14)** and **Dusk Boar (Level 14)**. Being so many levels below the party, the wolf and boar didn't last long. After looting the corpses, the party moved on down the hallway to the next room. The Fighter, in the lead, triggered the Fire Trap located just after a corner in the hallway. Fortunately for them, it was just a glancing hit that just barely scorched his backside. Gleanna patched him up quickly and they moved onto the next room. Wary of more traps, the group cautiously made their way into the room.

Not seeing anything dangerous, let alone any monsters, they walked into the middle of the room. Suddenly, from behind multiple stalagmites around the room, two **Timber Wolves (Level 16)** and a **Goblin Boar-rider (Level 17)** raced out and ambushed the party. One wolf latched onto the Sorcerer, another wolf started attacking the Healer, and the goblin went for the Archer.

Using the *Weapon Charge I* immediately, the Goblin Boar-Rider charged forward with his spear and the boars' tusks in the forefront. Due to only being lightly armored, the charge did a massive amount of damage to BoworDie, where it knocked him down and left him with only about 25% of his health. Fortunately, by this time, BunsoSteel was able to run over and get the attention of the boar-rider by using his *Taunt* skill.

After being hit once for about 10% of his health, MndBlwn36 quickly cast *Short Teleport* and teleported behind BunsoSteel. He then turned and used his *Mind Prison I* skill on the wolf attacking the Gleanna. As the goblin that was focused on the Sorcerer passed by, BunsoSteel used his *Focused Strike* skill to deal massive damage to it, thereby turning its attention to him.

Freed from attacks for a couple seconds, Gleanna got to work healing BoworDie, thereby bringing him back from the brink of death. Unfortunately, this was just as the goblin boar-rider jumped off the boar and performed a *Pincer Attack I* on their Fighter. He was only able to block one attack and ended up getting gored by the boar from behind. It did about 30% damage to his health, which brought him down to 50% from all the previous attacks. Gleanna started healing BunsoSteel, but this of course was when the wolf suffering from the Mind Prison I broke through the stasis it had been in and turned its attention now on MndBlwn36.

Seeing the wolf heading for his ally, and despite his dwindling health, BunsoSteel attacked the wolf as it was running by and focused its attention on him as well. Now getting attacked by 3 different mobs, the Healer could barely keep his health above 30%. The Sorcerer and Archer hadn't been idle however – they had focused their attacks on the first wolf that had been attacking MndBlwn36 at the beginning and soon took it down. This also gave the Fighter some breathing room and he was able to start attacking instead of just defending – which he did when he started in on the second wolf. Ten seconds later, the last wolf collapsed on the ground and everyone was able to concentrate on the Goblin Boar-Rider.

With its skills on cooldown, the level 17 boar-rider was no match for the combined might of the party. The health of the mob quickly fell to zero and as a group they sat down and collected themselves after the battle.

"I wasn't prepared for that – sorry guys, wasn't expecting an ambush from a beginner dungeon," said BunsoSteel.

"I wasn't either, but at least we made it through with no casualties – it was a close one though," Gleanna mentioned.

"These mobs seem a lot stronger than their level would suggest – a level 16 and 17 shouldn"t have done that much damage and had that much health," suggested BoworDie.

"I know what you mean – now that I think of it, it's almost like this is an elite dungeon where all of the mobs are extra powerful. Now that I know to watch out for that – I'll hopefully be better prepared next time. I have a feeling we'll be seeing a lot of surprises in here."

BunsoSteel looted the corpses, and after asking if everyone was ready, headed towards the exit to the east. Following closely behind the Fighter, the group wasn't prepared for the Arrow Trap that was triggered and fired from two directions down the connecting hallway – Gleanna almost got a face full of sharp pointy things. Grazed by 6 arrows, she was only saved by the fact that she had walked more near the wall than was necessary. Healing the small amount of damage and waiting for her mana to regenerate, they continued – increasingly wary of traps.

Which is why they didn't fall into the Pit Trap just inside the doorway to the next room – if they hadn't been looking so closely because of the surprises they had encountered so far, BunsoSteel would have been on the bottom of a 20-foot-deep pit. Careful to avoid it, they just barely entered the room and didn't see anything because of all the stalagmites and stalactites spread throughout the room.

"I'm going to carefully make my way to the center of the room to see if I can draw out any potential ambushes. Stay here, just in range, and I'll get aggro on whatever it is and bring it back here." BunsoSteel moved toward the center of the room, looking closely at the ground for traps and around the stalagmites for mobs. Despite his close attention, he was almost taken off-guard when two **Goblin Boar-Riders (Level 18)** charged at him from opposite sides of the room. Able to block one *Weapon Charge I*, he nevertheless took damage from the other. Knocked off his feet, he quickly scrambled up and ran back toward the rest of the party.

Meanwhile, as the party watched the two Goblin Boar-Riders bearing down on BunsoSteel, two other **Timber Wolves (Level 16)** slipped through the stalagmites near the entrance of the room. Focusing on Gleanna as their primary prey, the wolves paid no attention to Mndblwn36 and BoworDie – who promptly used *Mind Prison I* and *Crippling Shot I*.

Crippling Shot I			
The Archer sends an arrow at a target that cripples the legs and enacts a movement penalty			
Physical Damage:	20	Duration:	60.0 seconds
Movement Penalty:	80%	Cooldown:	120.0 seconds

One wolf stood there, trapped within its mind; the other limped around trying to reach BoworDie but couldn't move fast enough. Freed up from interference for a while, BunsoSteel made it back to the group in time to receive some much-needed heals and for them to start focusing down one Boar-rider at a time. During this, BunsoSteel had to taunt the wolf that came out of the *Mind Prison* – the other wolf was kited as it chased after but couldn't reach BoworDie.

With everything well-handled, and with no new surprises incoming, the party easily finished the rest of the battle with precision. Resting and looting afterword, they noticed a Banded Iron Wooden Chest in the corner by the exit. Rushing over to it, BunsoSteel almost fell into the other Pit Trap located right next to it – however, he noticed a slight discoloration on the floor just as he placed his foot and was about to put his weight on it. The paper-thin covering collapsed, and he threw himself backwards, saving him from the 20-foot drop with a nasty-looking bottom.

Gathering himself, he worked his way around the pit and made it to the chest.

Opening it up, he was surprised that there was one whole gold – most drops and chests around this level were significantly less than that. The entire party was excited as well – the system automatically duplicated any currency that was inside the chest for each party member – therefore, each person got one gold as well.

"Nice loot – if this is what it starts with, I can't wait to see what else is in here for the taking," MndBlwn36 remarked.

Making their way past the Pit Trap, they made their way through the exit and traveled down the short hallway – even more wary of traps. Having made it to the next room without another issue, they were surprised when they saw a figure standing in the middle of the room. Still expecting an ambush, they carefully made their way closer to check out the figure – and it was a strange figure at that.

Standing seven feet tall, heavily muscled, broad-shouldered, wearing crude leather armor, and holding a Rusty Iron Sword, the **Weregoblin (Level 20)** was an intimidating sight. Having never seen anything like it before, the group was cautious in its attack. Using his *Taunt* skill immediately, BunsoSteel took a defensive stance because he was unsure of how hard this mob was. Raining blows down on his shield, he wasn't taking too much damage and was easily healed by Gleanna. BoworDie and MndBlwn36 each started slinging spells and arrows until the **Weregoblin** got to 70% health. At this point it used its *Powershifter I* skill, which made it growl and increase in size; now towering over nine feet tall and sporting muscles on top of muscles, the **Weregoblin** started hitting BunsoSteel so hard he was practically curled up on the ground underneath his shield.

Despite mitigating some of the damage with his shield, he was still losing a significant amount of health per hit. Gleanna was pretty much chain-casting heals one after another on him in order to keep him alive. MndBlwn36 and BoworDie were also noticing that their spells were doing about a third less than they were before it grew in size. Worried that they would run out of mana long before it died, BunsoSteel called out, "Guys, run – I'll sacrifice myself and you can get out – just don't forget about those traps on the way!"

As they started to turn around and book it out of there, there was another growl from the **Weregoblin** that started deep and menacing and ended up laughingly weak and pathetic. Astonished, they watched as the formally seven and then nine-foot-tall goblin shrunk down to just under five feet tall in seconds. The damage output from the **Weregoblin** also decreased so much that BunsoSteels' shield was able to block most of the damage. Encouraged, the team got right back into the thick of battle and started taking chunks out of the goblin's health with each hit.

At 15% health, the **Weregoblin** let out an intense *Howl I,* which stunned the entire party for eight seconds. As they were stunned, two **Dusk Boars (Level 16)** emerged from behind some random stalagmites and used their *Charge I* skill to damage and knockdown BoworDie and MndBlwn36. After losing about 50% of their health by the time they recovered from the stun, they immediately used *Mind Prison I* and *Crippling Shot I* again to keep them off until the larger-than-average goblin was taken out.

Having only 10% health by this time, the **Weregoblin** was killed just as the *Mind Prison*-effected boar started to attack MndBlwn36 again. BunsoSteel taunted it off him and with everyone concentrating on it they were able to kill it in under ten seconds. The last boar, still limping around from the *Crippling Shot*, was easy to eliminate as it couldn't reach anybody to attack back.

Exhausted by the crazy battle, they sat down and rested before they had a conversation together. They were trying to determine if it would be worth continuing onto the next room when this one was so difficult. Eventually, they figured it couldn't hurt and at least if they died they would know what was to be expected when they came back. Fully rested, they continued their trek further into the dungeon.

Still watching for traps, they emerged from the connecting hallway into the next room — again full of stalactites and stalagmites. BunsoSteel took the lead again when they didn't see any mobs right away and headed for the center of the room. The rest of the group was waiting near the entrance when they heard a faint click above them. Looking up, they quickly dived out of the way as a massive pile of rocks landed right where they were standing, covering up the entrance to the room.

"Good thing we decided to press on – can't go back that way now," MndBlwn36 commented unsteadily.

They turned around to see how BunsoSteel was doing – just in time to see a swarm of four **Timber Wolves (Level 18)** and four **Dusk Boars (Level 18)** heading for the center of the room. Overwhelmed, it was all BunsoSteel could do to try to avoid and block attacks from all sides – but he still took massive amounts of damage by the time the rest of the party came to help.

Boosting him up from around 25% health, Gleanna chain-cast healing spells to keep the Fighter alive. For his part, whenever one of the mobs would start heading towards Gleanna because of the aggro she was accruing, he would use one of his skills to either *Taunt* or damage it significantly, so its attention stayed on him.

Mndblwn36, meanwhile, effectively used *Mind Prison I* and other skills/spells to damage or slow down as many as he could. He once had to use his *Short Teleport* spell to escape a hungry wolf that was angry with the damage he was doing to him but otherwise he stayed far away from the main melee.

171

BoworDie kited one boar with *Crippling Shot I*, used his *Flurry* skill on another, and generally tried to focus down each mob that had the least amount of health. After about ten minutes of intense fighting, the last wolf went down with an arrow buried in its eye.

Relieved that they escaped again with no casualties, the group resolutely pushed on when they had recovered enough – they couldn't go back without hours of digging out the rocks, which by that time most of the dungeon mobs would have respawned. As they got near the exit of the room, they noticed another chest – a Copper Chest this time. Looking for additional traps and finding none, BunsoSteel opened the chest and each person received two gold and five silver. More than pleased, they pushed on past the chest and up the next hallway to the Boss Room.

They knew it was the Boss Room because there was a wooden door at the entrance. Ensuring everyone was ready, BunsoSteel slowly opened the door and peered inside. Worried, he pulled back and told the party what he had seen. Inside, there were three **Goblin Boar-Riders (Level 20)** and a **Weregoblin (Level 25)**. Quickly coming up with a strategy, they swiftly entered the room and went to work.

With everyone staying out of aggro range, MndBlwn36 used a spell that he couldn't use so far in this dungeon due to the ambushes from the mobs – *Hypno Strike*.

The Sorcerer controls the mind and basic actions of the target for a limited duration. The Sorcerer is incapacitated at this time as they will be controlling the target. Upgrading this skill will allow the Sorcerer to use the skills/spells of the target. Can only be used on targets below the Sorcerers current level and not already in combat.

Useable on target:	Level 20 or below	Duration:	180.0 seconds
Usable actions:	Basic physical attacks		
Casting time:	8.0 seconds	Cooldown:	60.0 seconds

Fortunately, he had leveled up to 21 while down in the dungeon so he was able to take over control of one of the **Goblin Boar-riders** and have it start attacking the **Weregoblin**. It wasn't his intention to kill or even seriously hurt the larger goblin, just to delay it and to hold its attention while they took out the other boar-riders.

As soon as the Sorcerer finished casting his spell, BoworDie sent a *Crippling Shot I* towards one of the boar-riders and kited him around the room. This left one more boar-rider that BunsoSteel immediately attacked and used as many of his skills on to do as much damage as possible. Gleanna also used the occasional *Minor Smite I* damage spell in between heals on the Fighter – who was doing fairly well dodging and blocking damage. BoworDie shot the same boar-rider that BunsoSteel

173

was fighting as he continued to run from the crippled one chasing him. Even with using its skills, the first boar-rider went down just as the crippled one recovered from his debuff and caught up to BoworDie.

BunsoSteel used his *Taunt* to get the **Goblin Boar-rider** off the Archer and they all concentrated on killing it as quick as possible. By the time it was at about 30% health, the boar-rider that had been attacking the **Weregoblin** had been killed by the much more dangerous Boss. The **Weregoblin** began looking for MndBlwn36 who was the one who sicced the boar-rider on him in the first place. As it got closer, the Sorcerer ran around in circles, attempting to kite it – however, the goblin was much faster than him. MndBlwn36 was forced to use his dwindling mana supply to teleport multiple times to stay out of range. This worked as the last boar-rider was shortly taken down by the other party members.

Able to finally concentrate on the main Boss, BunsoSteel used *Taunt* on the enraged **Weregoblin** to get its attention. Changing course, the goblin headed in the Fighters' direction. Its health down to just above 70%, BunsoSteel used his *Focused Strike* to do enough damage for the **Weregoblin** to use its *Powershifter* skill. Fortunately, *Crippling Shot* was off cooldown by this time so BoworDie shot him in the leg. It didn't seem to do as much to slow it down as the other mobs in the dungeon, but it was enough for BunsoSteel to be able to kite it around the room. After 30 seconds, the buff wore off and the goblin shrank down to around five feet again. This is when they went all out and used all their saved-up spells and skills to get its health to just above 15%.

Gleanna made sure that BunsoSteel was fully healed before the rest of the party backed-up near the entrance to the room. At 15% health, the **Weregoblin** used its *Howl I* skill and stunned everything in range. This time, there were no additional mobs that came out, but they underestimated the range of the *Howl* and everybody in the party ended up being stunned. The high-leveled goblin took advantage of this and beat the crap out of the defenseless Fighter. Finally unstunned, Gleanna used an instant heal that she had been saving since it had a four-hour cooldown – just in time because another hit and BunsoSteel would've been a goner. Saved from their imminent destruction, they rallied together and took out the rest of the **Weregoblin's** health in under a minute.

As it hit the ground with a resounding crash, the entire party just stared at it lying there in disbelief. Finally, after what seemed like hours, BunsoSteel collapsed on the ground himself and stared at his companions. "Holy crap, that was awesome! Nice job guys – we did it!"

As if it was a spell that was broken when he spoke, the others started congratulating each other and found that most of them had leveled up again after defeating the **Weregoblin**. They also noticed the Boss Chest located toward the back of the room near the transporter. Not even caring about traps, they headed over and opened the chest – five gold richer! They had made as much during this dungeon dive as they had gotten during all the previous weeks' leveling up.

Entering the transporter, the happy party of players left the dungeon in good spirits.

Chapter 24

Devin had watched the party go through the entire second floor of the dungeon while staying safely stealthed behind them. He learned a lot through the whole process – from how to work better as part of a team to how to take advantage of weaknesses in the party process.

Krista was also pleased to see that the dungeon was accessible to players within the level ranges she had designated. There were a couple of tweaks that she wanted to implement before the next group came in – mainly in the form of moving some traps around to be more effective and the placement of the mobs so that they meshed better with environment. Overall, though, the new floor performed above her expectations – especially since it was the first real floor that she had put together all by herself. Quickly making those few changes in the Visual Editor, she then talked to Devin about what his thoughts were concerning how he wanted to integrate himself into this new floor.

For Devin, he was all about protecting the dungeon – and by extension, Krista – from any and all potential threats. He would be satisfied just using his knowledge of the layout and strengths of the monsters located inside to take advantage of the weaknesses of the invading players. If no one got through the entire dungeon, no one could "hurt" his Krista. After looking at it objectively, however, he felt that he needed to work with the dungeon instead of against it.

If he were to kill every player that entered, less of them would want to try out a dungeon that no one was able to complete. If, instead, he acted as if was just a slightly irregular monster and only killed them sporadically, more of them would be likely to run through the dungeon. It would be a case of quantity vs. quality – more players meant more variety of races, classes, and equipment. In the short run, killing everyone would net them a huge amount of resources – but then it would soon be a ghost-town when no one wanted to run through the dungeon just to perish time and time again. In the long run, it was more beneficial to keep a steady stream of players coming through.

With that in mind, he asked Krista what she thought on the matter. Fortunately, she agreed with him whole-heartedly. She was curious to see what would happen if Devin played as a more cooperative class – since she wasn't able to do it herself, she wanted to participate vicariously through Devin. When Devin was ready to choose his next character, she prompted him to create a Healer. She walked him through the ins and outs of healing – it would be, of course, a little different when healing monsters. They were a team, though, and they would figure it out together.

Devin chose to be a Goblin Healer to blend in with the monsters in the dungeon. Once he was done with the stat point allocation, he would need to carefully select his skills/spells for the upcoming battles. He was level 13 so he had 150 total stat points (from leveling and race/class selection) to allocate as well as 12 skill points:

Character Status					
Race:		Goblin	Level:		13
Class:		Healer	Experience:		550/1300
Strength:	0	Physical Damage:	5	Magical Damage:	240
Constitution:	10	Physical Resistance:	20	Magical Resistance:	40
Agility:	0	Health Points:	100	Mana Points:	1200
Intelligence:	120	Health Regeneration:	30.0 per minute	Mana Regeneration:	60.0 per minute
Wisdom:	20	Block:	0	Critical/Dodge Chance:	0.0%
Skills:			Divine Blessing I, Minor Healing I, Minor Smite I		
Upgrades:			Lure		

He wasn't planning on lasting through major battles where he would need to heal constantly and for a large amount. He didn't need the massive mana regeneration that having a high Wisdom would provide him -- instead he needed to be able to get in and out casting the biggest, most costly spells that he could. He now looked at what skills/spells were available for him:

Dungeon Upgradable Mobile Boss
Skill Selection:

Available Skill Points:			12
Divine Blessing I	**(Healer Class Skill)**	Cost to unlock:	Unlocked
Grants a blessing on target ally raising Strength and Constitution			
Increase amount:	+3 to Str and Con	Cooldown:	30 minutes
Duration:	30 minutes		
Minor Healing I	**(Healer Class Skill)**	Cost to unlock:	Unlocked
Heals the target for a certain amount using the power of light			
Healing amount:	5	Target Range:	20 feet
Casting Time:	2 seconds	Mana Cost:	10
Minor Smite I	**(Healer Class Skill)**	Cost to unlock:	Unlocked
Damages a target with power from the heavens			
Magic Damage:	5	Target Range:	30 feet
Casting Time:	1.5 seconds	Mana Cost:	10
Flash Heal I		Cost to unlock:	1 skill point
The Healer instantly heals a target for a large amount			
Healing amount:	100	Target Range:	30 feet
Casting Time:	0.0 seconds	Mana Cost:	50
Cooldown:	4.0 Hours		
Healing Circle I		Cost to unlock:	1 skill point
The Healer magically inscribes a circle of light that heals all allies within a set radius per tick. There can only be one circle active at one time.			
Healing per tick:	20	Tick interval:	5.0 seconds
Duration:	60.0 seconds	Circle radius:	10 feet
Target range:	30 feet	Casting time:	5.0 seconds
Mana cost:	200		

Regeneration I		Cost to unlock:	1 skill point
The Healer infuses the target with a Light aura, healing wounds over time			
Healing per tick:	10	Tick interval:	3.0 seconds
Duration:	30 seconds	Target range:	30 feet
Casting time:	2.0 seconds	Mana cost:	75
Major Healing I		Cost to unlock:	1 skill point
Heals the target for a great amount using the power of light			
Healing amount:	100	Target range:	20 feet
Casting time:	2.0 seconds	Mana cost:	200
Body Blur I		Cost to unlock:	1 skill point
Using the power of Light, the Healer blurs the outline of their body, thereby reducing aggro from all attacking enemies			
Duration:	15 seconds	Mana Cost:	75
Casting Time:	1.0 seconds	Cooldown:	600.0 seconds
Shield of Light I		Cost to unlock:	1 skill point
A Shield of Light surrounds the Healer, preventing a limited amount of damage for a limited duration.			
Damage reduction:	200	Duration:	30.0 seconds
Casting time:	1.5 seconds	Mana cost:	50
Cooldown:	If shield is broken from damage, Shield of Light cannot be cast again for 300.0 seconds		
Resurrection I		Cost to unlock:	1 skill point
Revive fallen comrades with a set amount of health points within a set amount of time.			
Health on resurrection:	25% of max health points	Time from death to resurrection:	No more than 180.0 seconds
Target range:	40 feet	Mana cost:	500

Casting time:	20.0 seconds		
Cleanse		Cost to unlock:	1 skill point
Cleanses the target of all poisons			
Target Range:	20 feet	Mana Cost:	15
Casting Time:	3 seconds		

He didn't need any aggro reduction spells since if he was being attacked he wouldn't live long anyway, so *Body Blur I* and *Shield of Light I* were unnecessary. He ended up picking *Healing Circle I* and *Resurrection I* and upgrading both for an additional five skill points each. He looked again at the upgraded spells:

Healing Circle III		Cost to unlock:	Unlocked
The Healer magically inscribes a circle of light that heals all allies within a set radius per tick. There can only be one circle active at one time.			
Healing per tick:	40	Tick interval:	4.0 seconds
Duration:	80.0 seconds	Circle radius:	20 feet
Target range:	50 feet	Casting time:	7.0 seconds
Mana cost:	600		
Resurrection III		Cost to unlock:	Unlocked
Revive fallen comrades with a set amount of health points within a set amount of time.			
Health on	75% of max	Time from death	No more than

resurrection:	health points	to resurrection:	300.0 seconds
Target range:	50 feet	Mana cost:	1000
Casting time:	25.0 seconds		

The upgraded spells certainly cost a whole lot more, but they would be worth it. The additional 800 in healing for a group of mobs would turn the tides of quite a few battles. He wasn't sure how he would use the *Resurrection* spell yet, but he had some ideas. Confirming all his selections, he materialized in the second floor Boss Room where he had been deleted by Krista after the last party went through.

The dungeon had already been respawned by Krista so all he had to do was wait for some action. He didn't have to wait long because another group entered the first floor within minutes of his respawn. Krista informed him that it was a five-person party that ranged from levels 19 to 21. They had a Mage, a Defender, a Healer, a Rogue, and a Brawler in their group -- another fairly balanced team. He waited behind some stalagmites just outside of the exit hallway in the second room on the second floor – it was the room with the **Goblin Boar-rider (Level 17)** and two wolves in it. He had a partially obstructed view of the center of the room where the action would take place – it was also unlikely that anyone would see him there unless they were near the exit already.

The group tore through the first floor in no time at all and he could hear a quick fight in the first room. After a couple of seconds, silence descended upon the dungeon until he heard a faint *snick* down the hallway – the Rogue had just deactivated the Fire Trap. Devin couldn't see him, but he was probably stealthed, so it didn't bother him. As the group entered the center of the room, they were ambushed by all three mobs and the Defender quickly pulled all the aggro to him.

As they all started hammering on the wolves, he saw the Rogue de-stealth and *Backstab* one of the wolves – immediately killing it. Now that he knew that the Rogue was busy, Devin started casting *Healing Circle III* on the two remaining monsters. Once the – surprisingly visible – circle was around them, he could see their health raise up significantly.

It wasn't enough to hinder the solid team of players, however, so Devin ran for the exit as soon as he finished casting. He was hoping to avoid notice but the Mage, who was facing the exit, saw him and raised the alarm. Leaving them all behind, he waited and hid in the next room which had the two boar-riders and two wolves. He was barely in position when the group raced into the room looking for him – unfortunately, they were in too much of a hurry to check for traps and the Mage fell down the Pit Trap just inside the room.

Mages, being quite squishy to begin with, don't survive very well falling 20 feet down a pit onto sharp, jagged rocks. With him out of the picture, the survivors were thrown into confusion as they ended up triggering the next ambush from the boar-riders and wolves. Seeing an opportunity, Devin had enough mana again to cast his *Healing Circle III* on the melee happening in the middle of the room. He sat back and hid to see how the mobs would perform with a little extra healing.

The party recovered quickly and got organized even faster; however, their delayed start allowed the monsters attacking them to get some early hits on the Rogue (who hadn't stealthed due to their rush after Devin). He went down quickly, but the Defender soon got control of the situation and after a short battle was victorious along with the Healer and Brawler. The Healer had a *Resurrection* spell as well and after regenerating enough mana, she brought the Mage and then the Rogue back to life.

Interestingly enough, the system gave Krista credit for the Mage's Pit Trap death despite the resurrection and Devin also got credit for the Rogue's death. It seems that healing the mobs that the group was attacking netted him experience even though he did no damage himself. He was beginning to like the idea of being a healer more and more – let the monsters do all the work while he stood back and raked in all the experience.

He had retreated from the third room even before they were done with the battle – hiding in the next room with the first **Weregoblin**, he had a little bit to wait as the party was busy recovering from the resurrections and mana expenditures. When they finally arrived, they were a lot more cautious and conscious of traps and ambushes. Luckily for them, they didn't have to worry about an ambush in this room. They started right in on attacking the goblin and when it used *Powershifter I*, the players barely noticed the difference because the Defender was much better at mitigating damage than the Fighter from the last group.

When the **Weregoblin** got down to 15% and used *Howl I*, the two **Dusk Boars (Level 16)** emerged from hiding and attacked the party members in the back. The Mage took massive damage and only survived when the Defender was unstunned and acquired all the aggro from the boars with his skills. The Healer was busy healing the Defender who had taken a bit of damage while stunned, so the Mage was sitting at about 15% health. Devin took advantage of this by peeping out from behind a stalagmite and casted *Minor Smite I* on him, taking him out instantly; he was pleased to see that he did a bit of magical damage due to his high Intelligence stat. Ducking out of sight quickly, he didn't think anyone figured out where he was.

Standing there in hiding and listening intently to the battle was probably what saved him from a quick and unexpected death. As he was trying to figure out his next move, he heard a sound behind him and saw the Rogue unstealth out of the corner of his eye with a knife poised above his back. He quickly dived out of the way and managed to dodge the *Backstab* attempt. Rolling to his feet, he swiftly ran into the exit hallway and kept running until he was through the next room and near the Boss Room door.

He didn't think that he was followed this far, but he didn't want to make the same mistake twice. He cautiously made his way to the room he ran through and listened for anyone near. He knew he wouldn't be able to see the Rogue, but if he was lucky, he'd be able to hear him. Not hearing anything, he settled down in another hiding spot near the exit and waited for the party to enter the room. He was really looking forward to this one because it was the one with the Rockfall Trap, four wolves, and four boars. As he was waiting he looked at his combat log and found he had received more experience from the death of the Mage and had leveled up to 14.

Eventually, the group entered the room and inevitably triggered the Rockfall Trap. As the group was assaulted by the massive army of wolves and boars, Devin peered out and created a *Healing Circle* in the middle of the room – catching all but one of his animal allies. The outlier was a boar that decided that the Mage was too tempting of a treat to pass up – it must have thought he was tender due to dying so many times that day. The Defender and the Brawler had their hands full and couldn't get it off him, so the Healer, Rogue, and Mage focused it down until it was dead.

Refocusing on the main battle, the trio of players started attacking the boars and wolves one by one until only 2 were left.

At that time, however, Devin had just gotten enough mana back to cast his *Resurrection III* spell. Since no one bothered to heal the Mage again since he wasn't in any danger, Devin targeted the dead boar near the Mage and started casting his long *Resurrection* spell. Just before the last wolf died from the Brawler in the middle of the room, the boar near the Mage miraculously came back to life and took a big chunk out of the Mage. Two more quick hits and the Mage died for the third time that day.

Man, he's gotta be so pissed off by now, Devin chuckled to himself. Retreating to the Boss Room as they quickly killed the boar he had resurrected, he couldn't help but reflect on his good fortune so far. Together, they had technically killed four of the party – three of which gave him experience – and they were still going strong. He decided that for the Boss Room he would let them try to defeat it without any interference – unless he saw an opening to take out the Mage again without endangering the whole party. He admired their perseverance in pushing ahead despite multiple deaths and didn't want to discourage them from coming back or telling their friends and guildmates about the dungeon.

True to his word, he let them fight the Boss without interfering. They managed it much better than the last party – probably due to their having five party members and a Defender to boot. As they were leaving after looting the Boss Chest, Devin couldn't help but chain-cast a couple of *Minor Smite I* spells at the unsuspecting Mage as he was about to enter the teleporter. Fortunately for the Mage, he was at full health and had quite a bit of magical resistance due to his high Wisdom and all the attacks only brought him down to 50% health. Devin ran back through the dungeon, laughing all the way. Krista later told him that the Mage started chasing after him but turned around before leaving the Boss Room.

He continued using his Healer character for the next six parties that came through the dungeon – with varying levels of success. In one instance, his *Healing Circle* affected the battle so much that the entire party wiped. In another, nothing he did turned the tide of battle because the group had so much crowd control, allowing them to incapacitate multiple targets, that it didn't really matter. During the run-through of the last party, he made a mistake and a Mage with a sharp eye spotted him trying to hide and hit him with a *Flare I* spell which took him out in one hit.

After that, he decided to mix it up a little – he tried almost every class that he had access to. The Fighter didn't perform that well because everyone was a higher level and had more bonuses to defense. Same with the Brawler – he couldn't get close enough to do any damage. He had some success with the Mage and Archer, being able to selectively kill off the less defended members of the party. He always tried to leave the Healer alive so that they could resurrect their fallen members – just so he could try to take them down again.

Strangely enough, the most success he had – and the most fun – was when he used the Defender class. He beefed up his Constitution so high that most players couldn't damage him much, and he had an insane amount of health points for his level. He would head for the weakest members of the party and take them out quickly; the tanks couldn't *Taunt* him away from his intended target. He would kill one and then run away to let the rest of the party battle the remaining mobs in the room. He went through about ten different parties before one wizened up and had everyone run from him while attacking the other mobs. He couldn't run as fast in his armor, so he couldn't get any hits in. After taking down the mobs, he got teamed up on and killed after a long battle.

By the end of the week, he had reached level 25 and Krista had also increased the dungeon level to just under level 5. She had accumulated so many resource points that she was thinking about adding another level soon when the dungeon finally hit level 5 after another successful (for her at least) party died in the second floor Boss Room.

Congratulations on reaching dungeon level 5! Dungeon Player scenario 13b now initiated!

Dungeon Core now active!

This Dungeon Core is now automatically stored in the Boss Chest on your lowest floor. This Dungeon Core serves multiple purposes:

If a player captures your Dungeon Core, they (and anyone grouping with them) receive a 5% increase to all attack power, defenses, experience gained, and money earned. This amount will increase as your dungeon level increases. If your Dungeon Core is captured, your dungeon can still accumulate resources but cannot level up. You may use your DUMB to track down and retrieve the Dungeon Core – the distance limit is eliminated if the DUMB is heading in the direction of the stolen Dungeon Core. If the Dungeon Core is missing for more than 45 days, the system will shut down the dungeon, reboot the AI and all subsequent programs, and revert the dungeon to its initial unchanged state at Dungeon Level 1.

While you have your Dungeon Core, all your monsters receive a 5% increase to attack and defense. Additionally, every 5 dungeon levels (starting at level 5) awards a distinct Guardian which protects the Dungeon Core and is a Raid-Level Boss. This Guardian has high hit points, attack, and defense – meaning it will require at most a 20-player raid in the designated level range to defeat it.

An Admin avatar will also be awarded at dungeon level 15 – this avatar allows the admin to travel around the dungeon with a "body". This body will be just like that of player but will not be able to attack or interact with other players. It will, however, be able to interact with other dungeon monsters including the DUMB.

There will be an announcement regarding this change in 48 hours in the newest patch notes.

Good luck Dungeon Player!

"Uh...well...shit."

End of Book 1

Dungeon Crisis

Prologue

"Alright everybody, sit down – we don't have a lot of time."

De4thfrmbeh1nd directed this toward his lieutenants casually standing around talking to each other throughout the room. He had called this emergency meeting of the *Reckless* guild after receiving some advanced confidential information. They had to get things prepared before all hell broke loose in about five minutes. As everyone settled around the surprisingly modern-looking boardroom table located in the top floor of their guild house, he was finally able to tell them why he had called them there.

"First off, thanks for coming so quickly – we have a time-sensitive opportunity that a little birdie told me about earlier today. In the patch notes there will be mention of an item that will have the potential to make the power and ranking of our guild increase ten-fold. It is called a 'Dungeon Core' and will increase the amount of physical attack and resistance, experience gained, and money earned by whatever group possesses it. The only thing that I wasn't able to find out is where the dungeon that contains this core is located. We need to be able to move quickly once we find out where it is and what we need to do to get it. Sh1fty, how many members do we have here in Stormdawn at the moment?"

Sh1fty, De4th's second in command, looked at his interface for a moment before responding, "We have just over 120 members online at the moment with only 42 in Stormdawn currently. Most of those here are lower level – below level 40. We had a raid scheduled in about a half hour in the Caverns of Despair, so the majority of the higher-level members are already there or about to arrive."

"Send out a guild message – have them hold off on the raid until we find out more details. Eyes, how much do we have in the guild treasury?"

EyesHlzU, the guild treasurer, didn't even have to reference anything as she knew the guilds' finances like the back of her hand, "We are sitting at 12,337 gold, 2 silver, and 6 copper."

Thinking about it, De4th smiled. "That should be more than enough for all of the supplies we might need. St4lwart, can you use your contacts at the auction house to get what we need? We need it quickly before all of the other guilds look too closely at the patch notes."

St4lwartshield, probably the most versatile member of *Reckless*, had countless contacts with various merchants and the auction house which made him the guild's logistics master. "Just let me know where we are going and what we are doing, and I'll have it before the other guilds even finish reading the notes."

"That's what I like to hear...ok, the notes are posting in about...now. Everyone, pull it up."

Patch Notes for Update Version 3.43.1 (Partial)

Attention Adventurers!

A new item has just been found in the Altera Vita dungeon near Briarwood. This item, a "Dungeon Core", gives the bearer (and anyone grouping with them) a 5% increase to all damage dealt, all resistances, experience gained, and currency looted. This amount will increase as the dungeon increases in power which will happen at non-linear intervals based on activity inside the dungeon.

Beware, however, because this item is protected by fierce monsters and a raid-level guardian. Contrary to most raids, this special event has certain rules and restrictions on who can participate:

- **The raid can only contain 20 players, whose level must not exceed the level cap of the guardian floor (Current level cap: 30)**
- **After a certain amount of time, the power and strength of the dungeon will increase and produce additional floors with a higher-level cap – which in turn will raise the bonus increase in the Dungeon Core**
- **Each raid will be made up of 4 distinct parties consisting of 5 players that will proceed through the**

> dungeon in a separate instance on the guardian floor
> - Once through the floor, the remaining members of all parties will rejoin together for the final guardian battle
> - If successful, the Dungeon Core will be accessible to the raid leader
>
> *If the Dungeon Core is held outside of the dungeon for 45 days consecutively, the event will end, and the Dungeon Core will stay at its current increase percentage. If it is returned before the 45-day limit is reached, the timer will reset, and the power of the Dungeon Core will continue to increase.*

After glancing quickly at the location of the dungeon on the patch notes, De4th started spouting out orders: "Ok, Sh1fty – send out a guild-wide message for everyone to meet up in Briarwood and have our top raiders ready to move from the…"

"Hold up De4th! Did you read all of the patch notes?" interjected EyesHlzU.

Irritated at being cut off mid-sentence, he grumbled under his breath while he looked again at the patch notes. A sense of horror gripped him as he read them all the way to the end this time. A dawning realization came over when he thought over all the repercussions of this "special event". This wasn't just a simple quest for a powerful item – this could mean war.

Chapter 1

(48 hours before release of patch notes)

Congratulations on reaching dungeon level 5! Dungeon Player scenario 13b now initiated!

Dungeon Core now active!

This Dungeon Core is now automatically stored in the Boss Chest on your lowest floor. This Dungeon Core serves multiple purposes:

If a player captures your Dungeon Core, they (and anyone grouping with them) receive a 5% increase to all attack power, defenses, experience gained, and money earned. This amount will increase as your dungeon level increases. If your Dungeon Core is captured, your dungeon can still accumulate resources and experience but cannot level up. You may use your DUMB to track down and retrieve the Dungeon Core – the distance limit is eliminated if the DUMB is focused on reacquiring the Dungeon Core. If the Dungeon Core is missing more than 45 days, the system will shut down the dungeon, reboot the AI and all subsequent programs, and revert the dungeon to its initial unchanged state at Dungeon Level 1.

While in possession of your Dungeon Core, all of your monsters receive a 5% increase to attack and defense. Additionally, every 5 dungeon levels (starting at level 5) awards a distinct Guardian which protects the Dungeon Core and is a Raid-Level Boss. This Guardian has high health points, attack, and resistance – meaning it will require at most a 20-player raid in the designated level range in order to defeat it.

An Admin avatar will also be awarded at dungeon level 15 – this avatar allows the admin to travel around the dungeon with a "body". This body will be just like that of player but will not be able to attack or interact with other players. It will, however, be able to interact with other dungeon monsters including the DUMB.

There will be an announcement regarding this change in 48 hours in the newest patch notes.

Good luck Dungeon Player!

"Uh...well...shit."

Krista was not expecting that at all – she was just getting used to the dungeon as it was. "Carl, does that mean what I think it means?"

If you are referencing the missing Dungeon Core for 45 days, then you are most likely correct. You will both cease to exist, and I will go back to being the administrator for ND101208. The system AI has finally taken formal notice of your "anomaly" and decided to do something about it. It seems that it is going to make you, if I have the expression right, "Put up or shut up". If you can succeed at surviving long enough, you can continue to exist and thrive. If not, it will not have to dedicate further resources toward you.

After listening to this, Krista's mind hit a wall. She couldn't process this information properly – she knew that she was technically dead already but that had happened so quickly that it didn't quite feel real. Now, however, she was being faced with a potential doom that they would have to fight tooth-and-nail to survive. It wasn't a matter of staying under the radar and being cautious about drawing undue attention anymore – their little dungeon now had a massive target painted on it.

Despite the despair that gripped her initially, Krista worked on pulling herself together. She shortly came back to the main issue at hand – survival. She didn't like to admit it, but she always doubted herself when it came to making life-changing decisions. She would waver back and forth between choices and would never be sure she made the right choice even after deciding. This didn't mean that she wouldn't put her all into it – just that she would constantly look back and think about how it would've turned out differently if she chose another option.

Sometimes it was something simple like choosing which restaurant she wanted to eat dinner at on her birthday. Other more complicated choices – like which car to buy or which character she chose on the newest MMORPG – would leave her thoroughly researching everything and going back and forth without being confident in her decision. In fact, the only real decision she made that she was 100% confident in was when she wanted Devin to move into her hou....

"Devin!!!! Where are you? Did you see the prompt?"

"There you are! I was trying to talk to you for the last 15 minutes. I wanted to try something different for the next group through the dun...what prompt?"

"The one about the Dungeon Core...wait...I'm going to try send it to you now." Krista focused on Devin and imagined a floating text box hovering in the air in front of his face. As her concentration sharpened, she looked out into the dungeon to see a floating, semi-transparent square about three feet in length on each side. Elated, she then changed the color in her mind from a clear/semi-white color to a light purple – almost lavender – color so that there would be a nice contrast. When she looked back at Devin, she almost laughed, but the seriousness of the situation held back her mirth – the text box was only about two inches from his face.

Moving it farther away in her mind, she then proceeded to fill in the box with what she had seen earlier. She watched as Devin read through the text and as he got to the end she was concerned – mainly because it seemed that *he* wasn't. In fact, it looked more like excitement than concern on his face.

She was about to ask him what he was so excited about when he exclaimed, "This is awesome! Finally a challenge – I was getting a little bored with killing all of these players over and over. And I wonder what this guardian is that it's referencing?"

"Devin!! Didn't you see that if we lose the Core we can be deleted – as in die? Like...again...for reals this time? What are we going to do?"

Somehow sensing that Krista was starting to panic, Devin was able to switch her train of thought with just a few words: "What is life without risk?"

"Huh...what do you mean? I'm not into board games, you know that."

"Not *Risk*, that board game of world domination. I'm talking about the risk of losing something – be it personal property, money, your health, or even your life. I'm not talking about gambling either – that has more to do with chance than anything. Back in the real world, there was risk involved in everything – from just walking down a busy street, to flying on a plane to a great vacation skiing in the Rocky Mountains, to doing something truly death-defying like bungee-jumping off a bridge. That adrenaline, that risk, is what it truly means to be alive.

202

True, we will be risking our lives to protect this dungeon, but the challenge is what will keep us going.

"I don't know about you, but there is a limit to how many players I can kill without growing bored with the whole thing. I need something else to keep me going – a challenge, a risk. This Dungeon Core is just the thing we need – something to inject some life into this dungeon. We will have to work hard to keep what we have – just like the players will work hard to take it. It is this give-and-take – this struggle – that will make what we have here more than just a mere existence. It is our *life* and we will defend it however we can. *You* may not realize it yet, but this is probably the best thing that could have happened to us."

Somehow, just like that, all her fears melted away; looking back she was shocked at how panicked she had become. Devin was right – it definitely wouldn't be easy and would be extremely challenging, but she could see now that they had a chance if they just took the risk to defend themselves. She also had to acknowledge that she had become a little complacent lately with the dungeon running so smoothly – she had no great drive to improve and become better and more powerful. This might be just the thing she needed – but she wouldn't let him know that he was right, of course. Just because her protector came to her rescue didn't mean she wanted him to get a big head.

"When did you learn to talk like that, Devin? Have you been a philosopher all this time and I didn't know it? What else are you hiding?"

"Uh...well...you know...I had a lot of time by myself waiting for the players to get close and I got to thinking about some things," he stammered, "and don't worry, I'm not hiding anything else – you know me better than that."

Secretly pleased with his response, she still gave an impatient huff acknowledging his attempt to placate her. "Ok, well, you may have a point – but time will tell. In the meantime, however, we need to figure out *how* we are going to survive this Dungeon Core business. Do you have any ideas?"

"Possibly – Carl, do you have any more information about this whole thing that wasn't on the prompt?"

With the implementation of Dungeon Player scenario 13b, I was flooded with a vast amount of information regarding this "special event". First of all, although the dungeon is a major focus of this scenario, the main reason the developers designed it was to create a vast player-driven conflict that would encourage people to fight for a common goal – the Dungeon Core.

The developers knew that with a change of focus, the guilds competing for the prize would spend more time in-game, use more resources, and spend more real money to gain any type

of advantage that they could. It was a win-win situation for all involved – Wexendsoft would receive more revenue and players had a chance to compete with others to achieve the ultimate prize.

That being said, they didn't want to make it easy on the players – they wanted this scenario to last as long as possible. To this end, they implemented a few rules:

- The raid can only contain 20 players, whose level must not exceed the level cap of the guardian floor (Current level cap: 22)
- After a certain amount of time, the power and strength of the dungeon will increase and produce additional floors with a higher-level cap – which in turn will raise the bonus increase in the Dungeon Core
- Each raid will be made up of 4 distinct parties consisting of 5 players that will proceed through the dungeon in a separate instance on the guardian floor
- Once through the floor, the remaining members of all parties will rejoin together for the final guardian battle
- If successful, the Dungeon Core will be accessible to the raid leader

In addition, they also put some restrictions on the dungeon as well:

- If a DUMB is present, it may only participate in either one party instance or a guardian battle per floor
- If slain, the DUMB will lose experience based on the size and strength of the party that killed it
- Additionally, the DUMB will have level cap equal to the level cap of the strongest floor – if the DUMB is already above this cap, it will immediately lose levels until they are equal
- The initial guardian can be placed in the Dungeon Boss room located at the end of the most powerful floor
- Guardians cannot be changed or improved by the Dungeon Admin but will increase its level as it moves to a lower, more powerful floor
- Additional guardians earned through leveling can be added to new floors as additional separate guardian battles
- Once a floor is completed and the first testers travel within it, that floor will be locked and cannot be changed – the Dungeon Admin can still create and develop additional floors
- Only fully stocked (monsters, loot) floors will be considered for the most powerful floor

If you have any other questions about something I did not cover, let me know.

"Uh...that was a lot more than I thought you would have," Devin replied. "This instance...does that mean each group will go through a separate version of the dungeon? Will it cost more to create that?"

Yes, each party will face the same dungeon but will be split into a different instance "space", which will not be able to interact with other instances. The cost will be the same as a normal part of the dungeon – the system is providing the instancing so there should be nothing additional to worry about.

"Thanks, we'll let you know if we have any more questions." Thinking about the information he was given, Devin told Krista, "Well, unless you want to do something else I think we should start with this guardian. How do we get it?"

Krista was still thinking about what Carl had told them and was jolted out of her contemplation by his question. She realized that she hadn't looked at any of her menus for a while, so she pulled it up again, this time noticing a major change toward the bottom.

Dungeon Player Administration Toolset		
Available Resources:	35950	
Additional Resources:	Yes	
Dungeon Level:	5	

Dungeon Experience:	52500/75000	
Add/Delete Objects:		
	Monsters	(Select for more options)
	NPCs	(Available at Dungeon Level 8)
	Chests	(Select for more options)
	Loot	(Select for more options)
	Traps	(Select for more options)
	Rooms	(Select for more options)
	Buildings	(Available at Dungeon Level 8)
Upgrade:		
	Monsters	(Select for more options)
	NPCs	(Available at Dungeon Level 8)
	Chests	(Select for more options)
	Loot	(Select for more options)
	Traps	(Select for more options)
	Rooms	(Select for more options)
	Buildings	(Available at Dungeon Level 8)
Expand Dungeon Territory:	Capture additional territory	(Available at Dungeon Level 12)
	Add additional floors	(Select for more options)
Unique Dungeon Characteristics:	Dungeon Upgradeable Mobile Boss	(Select for more options)
	Guardians	(Select for more options)
Rename Dungeon:	Current: Altera Vita	

Create Admin Avatar:	Create a usable avatar	(Available at Dungeon Level 15)

She was looking forward to being able to create an avatar and use it to journey around the dungeon – but that was quite a way off from now. She didn't know if she would even survive until she got to level 15 but it was definitely something to strive for. What really got her attention, however, was the *Guardians* option in the menu. She selected it and a new screen popped up:

Guardians	
Current number of guardians:	1
Guardian names:	Violette (Spirit Witch)
Place guardian	0 rp

"Free! That helps at least. Let's see what this 'Spirit Witch' looks like." Krista selected *Place guardian* and turned her attention to the current boss room with the **Weregoblin** and **Goblin Boar-riders**. "Hey Devin, come to the Boss Room and let's check out this guardian."

There was a slight hitch in her view of the boss room as the guardian was loading – she figured it must be because this was a new element that really hadn't been seen before. As the view cleared up, she saw the back of a figure standing near the center of the room a couple of feet away from the **Weregoblin**. As she got closer, she saw the now-obvious woman turn toward Krista's viewpoint as if she could see her – which was impossible since she didn't have a form. Despite this impossibility, the guardian looked straight into her "eyes" and smiled.

"Hi! I'm Violette!! It's soooo good to be here!" Violette exclaimed with a bubbly attitude. "By the way, where exactly am I?"

Wow, she's like a really cheery NPC. Not what I was expecting. "It's great to meet you Violette – welcome to Altera Vita, my dungeon. My name is Krista and I'm the Dungeon Admin here. We just received a guardian upgrade to help with protecting our new Dungeon Core – I hope you are up to it because you don't look that tough."

If she was offended, she didn't show it in any way. "Well, I'm so excited to help out! It has been a long time since I was last here and I'm so glad that I have some company this time. I've been in storage for years and haven't had anyone to talk to in all that time – it gets a little lonely all tucked away like that.

"I'm a Spirit Witch, so although I may not have a formidable exterior, my magic packs a serious punch." She then proceeded to shadowbox the air while saying *boom...smash...boom* with each punch – ending with an uppercut and a *kablaam*. She was about to say something else but turned toward the door as she heard footsteps from down the hallway. "Attackers already? Don't worry, I got this."

Chapter 2

(47 hours before release of patch notes)

Devin was rushing through the dungeon to get to the Boss Room to check out this new guardian. He hoped it was some deadly dragon or a massive monster with hundreds of tentacles. They needed something that would be able to hold back all the players who would be coming to take a crack at the dungeon for the Core. He was eager to find out what they would be working with in the coming days and (hopefully) weeks and months.

He turned the corner and ran through the door to the Boss Room and instinctively ducked as he saw something out of the corner of his eye. A massive bolt of something arced over his head as he slid to a stop and turned toward where it came from.

Holyshitsheissohotwhatthefuck – that was all he could think before he found himself in the Transition Room ready to respawn. He saw the second bolt of some black/green substance a half-second before it hit him, but he was staring so hard at where it came from that he couldn't get his body to function enough to avoid it. It definitely wasn't a dragon or a monster with tentacles – quite the opposite actually.

Picture the hottest runway model you have ever seen and then up the attractiveness factor by about 10. Her hair was the palest blonde, full and hanging down to the small of her back – just above (at least from what he could see from the side) was a very shapely behind. She wasn't waifish like a typical model; she had curves in all the right places and legs that went on for days. In addition, she had a pair of the biggest breasts that he had ever seen – outside of some crazy things he had "inadvertently" seen on the internet; somehow, they didn't look out of proportion on her body. He wasn't sure how tall she was because she was wearing what looked like a witch hat that you would find in a costume store when looking to dress up for Halloween as a "witch" – black with a round rim and pointy top.

But what really had frozen him in place was her face – specifically her eyes. She had a perfectly symmetrical face, with lips as red as cherries, and a tiny nose that was slightly over-shadowed by her nearly anime-like eyes – they were so big that on anyone else they would have looked slightly freakish. Somehow, the seemed to work on her face and even increased the attractiveness of the whole package.

He didn't know who this was but was worried for Krista – no one was supposed to be down there right now, and they didn't want to lose their Dungeon Core in the first hour. Fortunately, he didn't have long to wait before he got to the character selection screen and he swiftly chose a Defender with beefed-up Constitution so that he would survive a little longer next time. He quickly found himself in the Boss Room again and took a defensive stance immediately.

"Sorry about that Devin, she reacted so quickly I couldn't stop her from casting – and it seems that I don't have any control over the guardians at all. Apparently, the "No Friendly Fire" between monsters doesn't apply either – I didn't think she would be able to hurt you since you're both part of the same dungeon."

The girl was moving in his direction as Krista was talking to him – he was still processing that *this* was the guardian when she picked him up with surprising strength. He found out that she was *much* taller than him because his face was being squished between two warm and massive mounds of flesh that his brain told him seconds later were her breasts.

As she hugged him to her body, he realized that he couldn't breathe and was taking damage from the lack of air – he figured it was another attack and started to struggle to get away. The struggle was fruitless, unfortunately, because she was insanely strong. *Oh well, if I have to die, this is the way I would want to go – death by boob.* Just as he was starting to be resigned to his fate, she pushed him away and held onto his arms while she looked at his face.

He could tell she had been crying and couldn't figure out why *she* would be crying when it was *him* that died. As he noticed this, he also saw that somehow even crying made her more attractive. *How does that work?* Most girls that he saw crying looked worse because their face got all red and splotchy and if they were really upset – snot bubbles. Not an attractive thing on anyone, especially on someone he could be attracted to. No snot bubbles here at least; however, he thought it likely that even if there were, she would somehow make it look good.

"Oh my God!!! I'm so sorry, Devin! I can't believe I did that to one of my new friends! Can you ever forgive me? I was trying to make a good impression on Krista, but I just made a mess of things, didn't I? Please tell me what I can do to make it up to you – I want us to be great friends! I think I'll really like working with you to protect this dungeon from the evil people wanting the Dungeon Core! By the way, my name is Violette – Krista already told me your name when she was yelling at me for killing you so quickly. See, I told you Krista, my magic packs a serious punch!"

The whole time she was talking she was still holding onto him and he couldn't move anywhere. However, that was beside the point because she was upset and breathing heavily – which made her generous assets bounce up and down in front of his face. Mesmerized, he wasn't really following most of what she was saying but understood enough to reason out that she wasn't trying to kill him again. As she turned away toward Krista with her last statement, his brain caught up with the rest of the world and he tried to talk.

Sadly, his tongue wasn't all there yet because the first thing he blurted out was, "Breast". As his face turned red, he realized his mistake and said, "Violette...I meant to say Violette...uh...so you're the new guardian?" *Lame recovery, moron! Now she's going to think all you see are her boobs!* He didn't want to make her uncomfortable by his verbal gaff — in his experience attractive girls tended to stay away from him. Frankly, he was uncomfortable around attractive girls — he knew they wouldn't be attracted to him, so he was unable to talk to them because he knew anything he said wouldn't make any difference. He didn't want to see the looks of disgust that said, "who's this person that thinks they can talk to me?" Therefore, he tried to avoid all the pretty girls he had ever met so they didn't have to suffer with his person. Besides, he really only had eyes for the prettiest girl of all — who somehow didn't give him looks of disgust: Krista.

Giggling demurely, Violette reached out and touched his arm in an over-friendly manner and said, "That's ok, Devin...I think it's cute when you get all flustered like that. And yes, I am the new guardian for the Dungeon Core — I'm a Spirit Witch."

"You don't look like any Witch I've ever seen before."

"That's because I'm special — there are no other Spirit Witches in the entire world of Glendaria. As I was telling Krista earlier, I may not look like much, but my magic is very strong — I can hold my own."

"I could definitely tell — one hit and I was done."

"Sorry about that again — I thought you were attacking the dungeon for the Dungeon Core. It won't happen again!"

"Well, I'm sorry I rushed in like that without announcing myself — I should have thought about what I was doing." *Now where did that come from* – she *was the one who shot* me! For some reason, her bubbly personality and looks made him want to apologize for something that wasn't even his fault. He wanted to get away from her for now because her presence was beginning to make him feel uncomfortable and act weird.

He started walking around the Boss Room while explaining what they had been doing in the dungeon before she got there. He couldn't look at her because every time he did he couldn't concentrate on what he was saying – instead, he just looked at the walls while he talked. Krista was mysteriously silent this whole time, but he figured she was looking into how they could improve the dungeon to make it deadlier. Violette kept asking questions about the different rooms and monsters that they had on this floor and when she found out that he had gone out and "lured" some mobs into the dungeon she got excited.

"You did that all by yourself?! You are awesome! I didn't know you were allowed to leave the dungeon! That must have been really hard, but it looks like you are a mighty warrior!" She kept trying to get close to him and touch him again while she was talking, but he was having none of it. He was feeling more and more uneasy and was dodging her attempts to get near him. *If Krista is watching, she's probably laughing her ass off.*

Finally, he tried to excuse himself stating that he had to see about some...things...around the dungeon that needed his personal attention. Violette tried to follow him outside the Boss

Room but at the entrance she was stopped. A prompt that he couldn't see – but apparently, *she* could – made her let out a frustrated noise, but a quick smile erased all signs of frustration on her face. "Come see me later Devin – I'll be all alone here and could use some company!"

Eliciting a non-committal grunt in her direction, he fled to the first floor of the dungeon. When he was sure she wasn't going to follow, he slowed down and attempted to get Krista's attention.

"Hey, Krista – what do you think we should do now? At least our guardian seems nice – more like an NPC than a monster. If she could take me out with one shot, I'd love to see her fighting against a raid."

He thought he heard her say something to the effect of, "That's not all you'd love to see her do, I bet", but it was so faint and mumbled he may have been mistaken. When she finally spoke with more clarity, he was already near the entrance hiding from a group of players that had just entered the dungeon.

"Well, I've been thinking about it and we should probably do two main things: get more monsters and create a new floor. The new guardian should be able to handle protecting the Dungeon Core for now since no one knows about the new raid for another...46 hours or so. If you handle the monsters, I'll handle creating the new floor just like last time. You should be able to travel farther now that the dungeon has leveled up, so see what you can find."

He agreed with her plan and asked to be respawned so that he could start fresh with a new character other than the Defender he hastily made earlier. After he was done, he headed outside the dungeon to see what trouble he could get into.

Chapter 3

(46 hours before release of patch notes)

Krista wanted to hit something. Well, not some*thing*, but some*one*. Actually, *two* someones. Aside from the fact that she didn't have a body yet, she didn't think it would do much good. Her frustration toward both Devin and Violette was more of a personal matter and violence wasn't a solution – although it would make her feel *so* much better.

How dare she kill my Devin! And then flirt with him right after that! That little hussy should know her place in the dungeon – staying in the Boss Room and protecting the Core! That's it! If she could exchange Violette for another guardian she would, but she had already asked Carl and got this response:

Once a guardian is rewarded, you may not exchange it for another. Once you have more than one guardian, you can change around where it is located on additional floors, but you can never fully get rid of it.

Devin wasn't getting off easy either – she was annoyed at his response toward Violette. It was like he hadn't ever seen a girl before – getting shot in the face with that spell while he was drooling over her new guardian was just what he deserved. Of course, she still chewed out Violette after he died because it was the principle of the whole thing. And then, after he respawned and motorboated her chest, she had to restrain herself from yelling at both of them. After watching their conversation for a little while, she had to switch her perspective and cool off for a while.

When she heard Devin calling later, she was still seething inside. After an under-the-breath comment about the two of them, she tried to calm down enough to consider their survival. After quickly detailing the plan with Devin, she removed him from the dungeon so that he could respawn and placed him in a room just off the entrance that was empty at the moment.

Figuring he could take care of his part, she got started on the new floor. She had plenty of resources to play with since she hadn't really spent much after creating the last floor. She'd like to say that she was hoarding them and saving them for something important – looking back, however, she had to admit to herself that she was just lazy and complacent with how things were running. She saw no need to change anything or improve upon the existing dungeon – although she was previously considering adding a new floor just for fun. Now, though, she needed a new, stronger floor to house the guardian and keep the Core safe. And they only had just over 46 hours with which to do it.

She started by creating a room just underneath the Boss Room where Violette was currently located. This room was unconnected to the rest of the dungeon – she would make stairs for it later. It was also large compared to most of the other previous rooms because she wanted a place for all the groups that were part of the raid to gather together before they split off into different instances. She made it brightly lit with light diffusing the room from two pillars located near the entrance to the next room. Satisfied, she was just starting in on the next room when she felt someone trying to contact her.

Switching her focus to the Boss Room, she found Violette trying to have a conversation with the **Weregoblin** still located there. If she wasn't still annoyed with her over the incident with Devin, it would have been hilarious. Now, however, it was more...sad...than anything.

"Ah, there you are! I was trying to talk to this guy here, but he doesn't seem to be much of a conversationalist. What's up with these guys?"

They are monsters tied to the dungeon – scripted programs that have no unique identity. Unlike you, they do not have an AI attached to them.

Violette immediately fell into a defensive stance and looked all around her for the disembodied voice. "Who is that?"

"That is Carl, the former dungeon AI before I took over. He is a fount of knowledge and has been a great help throughout this entire endeavor. If you have any questions, you can ask him. I have to go now – I have way too much to do than to deal with you right now."

"Ooooh, what are you doing? Can I help? I really want to help however I can! I have *tons* of ideas on how to improve this place. Like, what's with all of these stalagmites and stalactites? They don't really mesh well with my attack style. Are you designing the next floor? Can I tell you how I want my room to look like? I would love rainbows and unicorns somewhere – who doesn't love those? And maybe a room for Devin somewhere near the Boss Room...hey, where are you going?"

Even more annoyed now, she fled back to the new floor she was creating and thought about the second room. When she started, she had all sorts of big plans in place for this new floor. Now, with everything that had been going on with Violette and Devin she couldn't focus on creating anything new.

In a fit of despondency, she ended up just copying everything that she had done on the second floor. The only things she changed on this third floor were the rewards in the chests – she bumped them up by a factor of three. She figured there would be a whole lot of players coming through (and dying) in the next couple of weeks so she wanted to entice them with better loot.

Finally, as she looked at her resource screen to see how she had done, she saw that there were plenty of resources available. These she could use for the new monsters that Devin was going to acquire and for any small tweaks to the rooms themselves that might be needed.

Resource Expenses	
Unrecoverable Resources Spent on Rooms/Hallways/Decor:	
Small Rooms	100
Medium Rooms	300
Large Rooms	200
Boss Room	400
Hallways	120
Décor (Stalagmites and Stalactites)	200
Décor (Lighted Columns)	50
Total Unrecoverable Resources Spent:	1370
Recoverable Resources Spent:	
Chests	2550
Traps	250
DUMB	5400
Total Recoverable Resources Spent:	8200
Available Resources:	41350
Total Resources Spent:	9570

Total Resources Remaining:	31780

Pleased with herself, she decided to watch a party of players, which had entered the dungeon a little bit ago, work their way through the second floor.

With a good mix of classes, this group consisted of mostly players at the level cap for the second floor. The only exception was the Healer at level 21, but for the most part that didn't matter as they tore through the monsters without breaking a sweat. This floor had been around long enough that there were probably wiki pages out there detailing the traps and mobs that they would face. This became evident when she saw them bypass every single trap and had a fool-proof strategy for each encounter. They were even wary for any additional surprises (namely Devin) by having someone keep an eye on every corner of the room.

As they made their way into the Boss Room, she asked Carl to tell Violette to stay out of the initial battle and to only intervene if they killed everything else in the room. She still didn't want to talk to her if she could help it and Carl told her that he had relayed the message.

Having no problems so far throughout the dungeon, she wasn't surprised when they took out all of her "former" boss monsters with ease. Just as they finished and were heading toward the Boss Chest, Violette seemed to appear from nowhere and cast a quick spell that hit all of them at the same time. Holding their heads as if they just had an ice pick thrust through their eyes, they fell to their knees and screamed uncontrollably for what felt like hours but couldn't have been more than five seconds. Giggling incessantly, Violette then whipped out a staff from her inventory and approached them.

The staff was the blackest black Krista had ever seen – almost as if it was sucking in all the light around it. In addition, she saw what looked like small screaming faces that would fade in and out along the length of the staff. All of that was highly disturbing, but what was most disturbing was the intricate design depicted on top of the staff. It looked like a distorted man's face that showed his soul being ripped out of him by his open, screaming mouth. She couldn't stare directly at it because it was difficult to keep the revulsion from her mind.

She watched from the edge of her perception as Violette proceeded to one-shot each of the screaming party members one by one while whistling what Krista recognized as, "Whistle While You Work". *Where the hell did she learn that?* As the players died and their bodies disappeared, she asked Carl, "What in the world was that spell she cast?"

From what I understand, this is the spell she used:

Wave of Despair	
Project a wave of negative spiritual energy, causing incapacitation on anyone	

under a certain Wisdom threshold			
Magical Damage:	50	Radius:	15.0 feet
Duration:	30.0 seconds	Wisdom Threshold:	150
Cost:	400	Cooldown:	180.0 seconds

"Thanks, Carl." She didn't like Violette before because of how she was acting around Devin. But now, after witnessing the disturbing events of the last minute, she concluded that there was something seriously wrong with her new guardian. At least slightly unhinged, she figured there was something even more at work there and she begun to wonder why Violette was locked away for "years". Not only was she annoyed at her – she was a little scared of her as well.

Krista had to keep that girl away from Devin at all costs.

Chapter 4

(45 hours before release of patch notes)

Knowing that he'd be *Luring* more monsters into the dungeon, Devin decided to use a class that he hadn't tried yet:

Pet Trainer – This class uses its own Constitution and Wisdom to force its will on monsters, thereby taming them for use in and out of combat	
+5 to starting Constitution	+20% Damage with whips
+2 to starting Wisdom	+50% to starting base faction rating for all factions
+2 to Constitution each level	Starting Class Skill – Taming
+1 to Wisdom each level	

He had only seen one Pet Trainer come into the dungeon and he had made it a priority to kill him to get access to the class. It ended up with Devin dying as well, but he found it was worth it to trade his respawn for something new. He hadn't been able to use the class yet because the main Class Skill needed *enemy* monsters; it wouldn't work on the allied monsters inside of the dungeon.

Taming I			
While fighting alone, tame a weakened hostile monster to fight by your side for a certain amount of time			
Target level:	-1 or lower than player level	Damage threshold:	20%
Pet limit	1	Target Range:	15.0 feet
Duration:	30.0 minutes	Cooldown:	30.0 minutes

The other skills that this class had were related to boosting the attributes of the pet once it was tamed based on how much Wisdom or Constitution the player currently possessed. Eager to get started, Devin was dismayed when he saw that his current level was reduced down to 22 from the 25 that he had before the Dungeon leveled up. He remembered that the rules of the event stated that he couldn't level up past the level cap on the strongest floor – which was 22. Disappointed because all his hard work getting to 25 went to waste, he nevertheless looked it as a way to improve his skills as a "player" since he couldn't level up anymore (at least at the moment).

After distributing his stat and skill points, his character sheet looked like this:

Character Status					
Race:		Dwarf	Level:		22
Class:		Pet Trainer	Experience:		2200/2200
Strength:	0	Physical Damage:	190	Magical Damage:	0
Constitution:	190	Physical Resistance:	380	Magical Resistance:	100
Agility:	0	Health Points:	1900	Mana Points:	0
Intelligence:	0	Health Regeneration:	570.0 per min	Mana Regeneration:	150.0 per min
Wisdom:	50	Block:	0	Critical/Dodge Chance:	0.0%
Skills:			Taming V, Annoying Aura II, Stoneskin II, Sacrifice I		
Upgrades:			Lure		

He chose to be a Dwarf, not for any special characteristics, but so that he would hopefully blend in a little and not get targeted right away by hostile players. Ideally, if he wanted to stay the safest, he would be a Rogue again; however, he needed help to pull monsters from farther away. A rogue could travel undetected, but he didn't fancy running long distances while being chased by hostile mobs. And he needed help to kill said monsters once they were in the dungeon. Fortunately, he hoped that his skill selections would help with this.

Annoying Aura II was basically a strong taunt based on his Wisdom stat that would allow the pet to take attention away from Devin when he used his *Lure* skill. *Stoneskin II* would beef up the Constitution of the pet based on his own Constitution by a factor of 1.5. Therefore, without even considering their starting attributes, his pet would have at least 2850 health points and 285 physical resistance.

Devin chose the *Sacrifice I* skill as an afterthought in case he ran into trouble – essentially, it would sacrifice his pet by putting it into "overdrive". It would double its physical and magical damage and resistance by a factor of two – but only for 30 seconds. After that, it would make one more attack for four times damage and then die.

These skills would help keep both him and his pets alive long enough to lure monsters to the dungeon – but what he was most excited about was his upgraded *Taming V* skill.

Taming V			
While fighting alone, tame a weakened hostile monster to fight by your side for a certain amount of time			
Target level:	+3 or lower than player level	Damage threshold:	40%
Pet limit	3	Target Range:	35.0 feet
Duration:	70.0 minutes	Cooldown:	10.0 minutes

This meant that he could have 3 pets – up to level 25 – and they would last over an hour for each one. This seemed way overpowered, but when you consider that you have to try to tame them by yourself it makes it much harder. For normal players, with a more balanced stat allocation, it would be difficult for them to damage a mob that was anywhere near their level since they don't have offensive skills. For him, he wasn't too concerned about their level since he just needed something to last long enough to survive until he got back to the dungeon.

Respawning in a side room near the entrance, he found that Krista had left some basic starter equipment nearby, so he equipped it all and made his way cautiously outside. They had access to much better equipment, but for some reason Krista was stingy with her resources and only gave him better stuff if he asked for it.

Fortunately, he didn't see any players around, so he made his way south into the forest again, this time looking for something easy to make into a pet. He quickly spotted a **Dusk Boar (Level 11)** near the entrance of the dungeon and decided to try out his new Class Skill. Getting to within 20 feet of it, he used the skill, but nothing happened — except for an irate boar charging in his direction.

Taking out his Rusty Iron Sword, he tried to quickly dodge to the side of the boar's charge; he realized at the last moment that he had no stat points in Agility — he couldn't move very fast. Fortunately, that didn't matter so much because when he was hit by the boar, he only took two points of damage. His physical resistance was so high that it would take all day for the boar to do any serious damage. He took a swing at the boar and found that even with a starter weapon he could kill it in one hit since his Physical Damage was buffed up from his Constitution.

After the boar gave up the ghost, he brought up the skill menu and looked at the *Taming V* skill again to try to figure out what went wrong. *Aha! Whoops!* He saw that the damage threshold was at 40% – meaning that he had to bring down the monster under 40% of its health points in order for the skill to work properly. It meant that he wasn't going to be able to use any of the boars or wolves in the forest here as pets because even with a crappy weapon he had killed it instantly.

Well, nothing for it – looks like I'm heading somewhere else. He started heading East to see if there was anything new in that direction but eventually he hit a wall. Not a literal wall, but he found the limit to how far he could travel – he wasn't exactly sure how far it was, but it seemed to be around 1,000 feet or so. The only thing he saw were more wolves and boars, with the occasional gopher scurrying around in the undergrowth. Disheartened, he started to travel along the perimeter of his "cage", looking for anything new until he arrived back at the mountain where the dungeon was located.

He was about to give up and head to the West side of the forest when he heard voices. He wasn't sure where they were coming from at first; when he looked around, he couldn't see anybody near. That's when he realized that – although they sounded near – they were actually *above* him. He looked up and saw a group of players heading back down a pathway that led up into the Hearthfire Mountains. He realized then that although he could only travel about 1,000 feet, that didn't mean he couldn't travel 1,000 feet *vertically*!

They were too far away to see him, luckily, so he hid behind a tree a good distance away and waited for them to pass. He couldn't hear what they were talking about, but thought he heard "orc" somewhere in their conversation. Excited to find some different monsters, he impatiently waited for them to pass and rushed up the pathway into the mountains.

This impatience almost cost him a respawn because at only about 50 feet up the pathway he was flung upward into the air and landed on his face. Something had erupted from the ground underneath him and did a total of about 1,200 points of damage to his health from both the initial impact and the impact with the ground. As quickly as he could, he got to his feet and looked behind him to see what had hit him so hard.

Emerging from a hole in the ground, he saw a large, four-legged monster that looked like a cross between a mole and an armadillo. It had wicked claws that looked capable of tearing through rock and armored plates along its back that seamlessly fitted together as it moved. Sharp teeth and what appeared to be blind white eyes were the highlights of its highly elongated head. Oh, and it was also about the size of a full-grown grizzly bear.

When he looked for the name, it said **Hardy Rock-burrower (Level 19)**. *That explains how it came up from below* *me, I guess.* Devin pulled out his sword again and tried to find a weakness that he could exploit. By its appearance – and the fact that it lived underground – he figured that it was probably blind.

He tested this by walking to his left and watching the face of the rock-burrower. It followed his movement with its head, but it appeared that its eyes were looking in a slightly different direction. *It must either sense by sound or by vibration.* He picked up a small rock and threw it behind the rock-burrower; as soon as the rock hit the ground it turned and rushed after the noise/vibration it made.

Eager to take advantage of this, Devin rushed forward and aimed a stab at it from behind. As he was just about to strike it, the rock-burrower quickly turned and swung its right claw at Devin. It caught him unprepared and with a massive hit to his left side he was down another 500 health points. Now at just over 200 health points, he was desperate to figure out how to take this guy down – he couldn't afford to get hit again. Backing up, he put some distance between them in order to formulate a plan.

From what he could see when he was close to it, the soft underbelly of the beast looked like it would be its most vulnerable spot. With a plan in mind, he picked up some rocks and tossed them around the area, trying to attract attention to other areas so he could get into position. As slow as he could, he laid down on his back and positioned his sword so that it was lying flat against his chest. Once he was ready, he threw one last rock over his head, where it landed about 10 feet behind him. He then waited for the monster to make its move.

He had to wait about a minute, but eventually the burrower decided that it would check out the last place it heard/felt anything. As it walked toward the rock behind him, it passed over Devin with its soft underbelly exposed. When it was close enough, Devin slowly angled the sword upwards and thrust with all his might into the dirt-covered flesh of the creature.

The rock-burrower screamed out in pain as almost a foot and a half of sword was lodged inside its belly. It then immediately rolled onto its back, ripping the sword away from Devin's hand. The beast then tried to reach the sword to pull it out, but its arms were not long enough to get a grip on the hilt; the most it did was move it with the tips of its claws, further causing itself pain.

As the rock-burrower continued to take damage, Devin noticed that its health had just dipped to under 40%. Figuring this would be the perfect opportunity to use his *Taming V* skill, he activated it and immediately the name of the **Hardy Rock-burrower (Level 18)** turned from red to green. *Woohoo!!! It worked...wait, why is it still taking damage?*

The health of his pet was still dropping – the sword! Rushing over, he had to dodge the now-feeble attempts of the burrower to pull out the sword. Climbing on top, he reached it just as its health dropped below 10%. Pulling it out with a quick jerk, he jumped down and watched as his new ally rolled back onto its belly and sat there.

On the left side of his field of vision, he noticed that it now contained a picture of his pet that was flashing red. As he continued to watch, however, he saw the red color slow in its flashing until it started to turn yellow. It looked as though the health regeneration his extra skills imparted were doing their thing.

Experimenting with his new pet, it took him about 10 minutes to figure out how to give it commands. He tried speaking commands, hand gestures, and even trying to "click" on the icon to see if he could find a menu or something. After trying everything he could think of, he grew frustrated and thought, *Well, fuck me.* Let's just say that he inadvertently figured out that all he had to do was to think about where he wanted it to go or do and it was mentally sent orders.

And that's all that happened.

Really.

Chapter 5

(3 hours after the patch notes were released)

Briarwood was a madhouse. To De4thfrmbeh1nd, it looked as though all the strongest guilds had sent a large group of their members to the town in order to gain a foothold in the upcoming event. Because he had some forewarning, De4th was able to book the entire inn for his guild so that they wouldn't be forced to camp outside the town as the other guilds were forced to do. From what he had heard, there were already multiple altercations in and out of town between members of rival guilds. This was most likely just the beginning of a major conflict – it was almost guaranteed to get worse.

De4th called his lieutenants together to get a status report on what was being done to outfit the team they were sending in to the dungeon. Hand-picked by Sh1fty, they were all level 29 to 30 and had frequently demonstrated that they could stay cool under pressure. St4lwartshield had been using the guild's money to buy up all of the best gear they could afford at the auction house for use by the team. He had to act fast because prices were already skyrocketing, and supply was becoming scarce.

"Is the team ready?" De4th addressed EyeshlzU.

"Just about, we're still waiting on Strang3r's report of the route to the dungeon before we start to move out," EyeshlzU replied with barely restrained impatience. She was a stickler for punctuality so when someone was late she got a little moody. "He should've reported back more than ten minutes ago – he's one of the best Rangers out there so there shouldn't be any reason why he's not here on time."

De4th agreed but couldn't help being worried – this definitely wasn't like the Strang3r he was used to. They might need to head out blind if he wasn't back soon; they couldn't afford to let any of the other guilds get a head start on scoping out the dungeon. They were taking with them most of their higher-level members in order to protect the dungeon team from any potential PVP threats.

He had sent out Strang3r to scout out their route to ensure that they wouldn't be ambushed. If he was dead, there was a mandatory three-hour lockout and he'd be unable to communicate with anyone inside the game. They wouldn't be able to figure out if there was anything wrong before it was too late.

He didn't want to risk sending anyone else because he was worried that sending anything less than his whole guild would just be suicide. He gave the necessary orders to his lieutenants to go ahead and get everybody moving out; he'd take the chance that there wasn't any major organized resistance set up yet. They could take care of the small, opportunistic PVP groups that were surely out there preying on the eager, unescorted parties.

His plan consisted of using all his Rogue-type members as a forward screen to flush out any potential single PVPers lying in wait. After them, he had his strongest tanks surrounding his dungeon group who were to stay as safe as possible inside the formation. If any of them died it would set them back another three hours before they could make a full run on the dungeon. Those who could buff would be applying them constantly on the march to both the tanks and the dungeon group. His ranged attackers would be set on the outskirts of the big group watching out for any potential threat.

Finally, bringing up the rear – in order to make sure they were not hit from behind – was De4th's group. They had been playing together in other games for years and had started playing Glendaria Awakens at launch. They were so accustomed to each other that they rarely had to communicate in the middle of battle – they just knew what needed to get done. In addition to watching for ambushes, De4th wanted to be able to see everything in front of him in case he had to change the formation on the fly. He was hoping that things would go smoothly, and they would avoid any large-scale battles – but they were as prepared as could be if things went south.

Gathering outside the "tent city" that was springing up outside of Briarwood, De4th led his guild to the North while crowds of players watched. Even if they weren't dragging their feet on preparations, the other guilds had to be close to making their way toward the dungeon. As far as he could tell, *Reckless* was the first and only guild fully mobilized so far – but he was sure more guilds weren't far behind. They had, at most, one good chance to acquire the Core before the entire countryside became a warzone. With determination and ambition, they entered the Briarwood Forest and started on their journey.

Chapter 6

(42 hours before release of patch notes)

So, anyways...Devin thought it was time to try to lure one of the rock-burrowers back to the dungeon and kill it so that it can be absorbed for use. Moving further up the pathway, he had his new pet lead the way to draw out any aggro. Just up the path, they found another rock-burrower when it burst from beneath his new pet. Chuck, as he started to call it, took a lot less damage compared to when he was attacked earlier – its natural Constitution added an additional 1200 health points and 240 physical resistance. After only taking damage for about 10% of its health, Chuck started attacking its counterpart – a **Hardy Rock-burrower (Level 19)**.   They were doing about the same amount of damage to each other, but that wasn't what Devin was here for.

Using his Lure skill on the hostile rock-burrower, it immediately turned its attention toward Devin and headed his way. Fortunately, it was pretty slow when not burrowing underground so he just had to jog lightly in order to stay ahead of it. He ordered Chuck to follow along and continue to soften it up so that it could be put down easily when he got it to the dungeon. Making his way down the pathway again, he followed along the mountain without incident until he was able to lead the hostile burrower into the entrance. By the time they arrived, his "new addition" to the dungeon was at only 10% health. He had Chuck use the *Annoying Aura II* skill to draw its attention and together they were able to kill it quickly.

There was no response from Krista this time when he killed a new mob inside the dungeon. He assumed she must be hard at work building the new floor, so he just told the empty air what he had done and hoped she heard it. Heading outside again with Chuck, he headed toward the pathway up to the mountains. He didn't pay too much attention to where he was going or what was around him – which was why he literally ran into a player working his way through some trees near the mountainside.

Surprised, he unthinkingly tried to say, "Sorry", but all that came out of his mouth was some random incomprehensible gibberish. To his credit, the level 15 Human Brawler recovered quicker than Devin and started attacking immediately. Not to his credit, however, was that he ignored the fact that Devin was seven levels higher and had a pet that would crush him.

At first just defending, Devin decided to try out his new pet's skillset. He directed Chuck to use his *Burrow* skill and come up under Slacksoni, the player who was currently *trying* to do some damage to him. If he were a smarter player, he would have realized that he couldn't do enough damage and should've cut his losses and ran for it. Instead, he got hit from underneath by Chuck, launched about 15 feet up into the air, and landed in a boneless sprawl about 20 feet from Devin. His body quickly disappeared, and Devin looked at Chuck and said, "Nice job buddy!"

Continuing on, they made it to the pathway and started up it, now being more cautious of other players that might be around. On his way up the mountain, they were attacked by four more rock-burrowers, the first of which was the only one that gave them any bit of trouble. After having Chuck use his *Annoying Aura II*, they were able to whittle it down to under 40% health and Devin was able to *Tame* that one as well. He named that one Chucky (staying with a theme) and used them both to help tame the next one they came across (which was then named Chucka).

By this time, Chuck only had about 20 minutes left on his 70-minute timer, so Devin decided to try out the *Sacrifice* skill and get a new replacement. On the third rock-burrower they came across, he activated the skill on Chuck as soon as it got aggro, and the result was devastating. Chuck grew to almost twice his size and each blow he delivered rocked the hostile rock-burrower as if it was being hit by massive sledgehammers. After 15 furious seconds of pounding away at it, Chuck had already gotten it down to below 30%. Devin was so shocked at the results of the skill that he was delayed in using the *Tame* skill on the dying monster; as a result he ended up letting Chuck kill it before the skill was even finished.

After the 30 seconds were up from the *Sacrifice* skill, the valiant Chuck perished without a whimper. Sighing, Devin moved further up the pathway, encountered another burrower and got his pet back. "Welcome back, Chuck!" Pleased to have the gang back together again, he moved even deeper into the mountains.

Past rock-burrower territory, he encountered a myriad of different monsters that he brought back to the dungeon. The first one he came across was a **Sure-footed Mountain Goat (Level 20)** that was extremely nimble and was able to traverse the cliff-like sides of the pathway with ease. Although not large or particularly powerful, they were nevertheless difficult due to the fact that they liked to charge down the mountainside and ram its victims off the cliff. He lost two of his pets this way before he learned to have them burrow down underground as soon as they were spotted.

In one instance, he saw the goat a little late and Chucka, who was in the lead, got underground a split second before the goat reached it. The goat wasn't expecting this and despite being "Sure-footed", was running too fast – and ended up flinging itself off of the cliff. Devin collapsed on the ground, holding his sides because he was laughing so hard he couldn't breathe. After about five minutes, he pulled himself together, looking at his pets just standing around looking vacant. He wasn't sure what it was about them that set him off again, but he ended up collapsing in another fit of laughter.

After that therapeutic laugh session – and since he had already lured back to the dungeon the first goat that he had encountered – he continued on up the pathway, which seemed to have a switchback that led back toward the way he came. Looking up, he realized that it did this all the way up the mountain – a zigzag pattern to the top. This was good as it allowed him to cover more ground while still staying in the allowed distance from the dungeon.

After the goats, Devin was accustomed to staying alert for incoming attacks. His attentiveness was the only thing that saved him from being a meal for the hungry **Starving Mountain Lion (Level 21)** that ambushed him – after it ignored Chuck, who was up in the front of their formation. Immediately activating *Annoying Aura II* on all of his pets, he tried to dive out of the way of the leaping lion – but still took a claw to his back for almost half of his health. Fortunately, the taunting aura from Chuck succeeded in gaining the lion's attention and it moved away from Devin. Relieved at surviving the close call, he took advantage of having a new monster available and lured it back to the dungeon.

The fourth monster that Devin encountered was a **Shrieking Harpy (Level 22)** that attacked them from the cliffside above. Fortunately, he had with him the burrower trio who were able to go underground when they would swoop in to attack. The hardest thing about these ugly flying bird-women was their *Shriek* skill, which was a five second stun that affected everything within a large radius.

Despite their size, they were also quite strong; once, when Chucky couldn't get below ground fast enough, he was stunned by the harpy who swooped in and lifted the near 1500 lb. pet like it was nothing. The harpy then flew with Chucky straight up into the air about 100 feet and launched the poor pet all the way down the mountain.

Deciding that he might need some air support in the future, Devin said goodbye to Chucky and – not more than a minute later – said hello to "Betty", his new aerial strike force. Happy with his new acquisition, and again having already lured a harpy earlier into the dungeon, he steadily moved up the mountain.

The last two monsters that he found on his way up the mountain were flyers as well. The first one almost sent him to respawn when he found it – or more accurately – *them*. He had just passed the last of the harpies and hadn't seen anything for a while, when he turned on the next switchback and immediately encountered a nest of **Scaled Wyverns** ranging from levels 25 to 27. The overgrown winged snakes immediately hissed when they saw Devin and started flying straight toward him. Chuck and Chucka were too low to the ground to effectively fight them so Devin called on Betty to help.

While Devin ran for his life, he had Chuck and Chucka use their *Annoying Aura II* to gain their attention. Safe for the moment, he turned toward his ground-based pets and watched them take some serious damage while not being able to effectively fight back. The wyverns would swoop in and bite them with lightning-fast strikes that his pets had no chance to avoid. He attempted to have them burrow underground but as soon as they were unreachable they headed right back towards Devin.

Instead, he moved Betty in from behind and then had her tackle one wyvern after another in order to bring them to the ground. The burrower duo then pounced on top of them and tore them to pieces. Devin ended up losing Chucka before they were finished with them all, but he tamed the last wyvern as recompense. Fortunately, this one was level 25, so it was just in the range where he could tame it. He named that one Francis because he figured snakes should all have fancy names.

As he was waiting for them to respawn so that he could lure one down to the dungeon, he quickly headed back down the mountain to get a new replacement for Chuck whose timer was about to run out. After completing that task, he went ahead and replaced Betty on the way up – which was much easier with two pets in his aerial force. He reached the site of the wyvern nest before they had respawned, so he waited for them to appear. They started appearing in the order that they had been killed so it was a bit easier to take them out with the strategy he had used earlier.

With the last 2 that respawned, he took one as a replacement pet for Francis and the other he took back to the dungeon – which was actually quite easy since all he did was have his two flying pets lead the hostile wyvern down to the dungeon and kill it once they got inside the entrance. He couldn't see through their eyes or anything, but he found that when they were out of sight, he had a vague sense of what was happening around them. It was a little weird and the first time it had happened it hurt his head a little – but he soon got used to it and took advantage of it whenever he could.

The last actual monster he found was huge; like, so big it barely fit into the entrance huge. As he was working his way back up the mountain after replacing Chuck – who was running out of time – he saw a shadow fall over the ground and he thought that it was large cloud blocking out the sun. As he looked up, however, he caught a quick glimpse of a giant bird swooping overhead and snatching Betty out of the sky. She didn't even have time to shriek before she was swallowed down the enormous gullet of the monstrous bird. Devin was able to look a little more closely at it as it flew away – the giant bird turned out to be a **Majestic Roc (Level 60)**. *Oh my god, that thing could kill all of us with just a look.* As it turned in the air, gliding slowly in a semi-circle with its 150-foot wingspan, he looked for somewhere to hide. Unfortunately, he was in the middle of the pathway with a cliff on both sides with nowhere to run.

Instinctively ducking as it got near, he started panicking while thinking, *I'm going to die – I'm going to die – I'm going to die!* Lying down on the ground to present as little of a target as possible, he sent Francis straight up in the air to try to avoid the roc. This was probably the only thing that saved the both of them as the roc couldn't decide which one to attack first – and so it ended up missing them both. As it passed overhead, he figured he might as well "go for broke" and used his *Lure* skill on the avian monstrosity. The roc then emitted the loudest squawk he had ever heard which he was pretty sure gave him a deafness debuff.

He wasn't sure if the roc would fit into the dungeon but figured he would give it a shot – if the wings were folded up next to its body it might fit. After activating *Annoying Aura II* on Francis, he sent him to fly as close to the roc as possible to get its attention. Devin then immediately sent it shooting down the mountain toward the dungeon entrance. As the wyvern flew by the roc, it let out another squawk that even with the partial deafness he was suffering from he felt down to his core.

He watched the roc slowly turn itself in the air, following the Francis' trajectory. Running over to the edge of the cliff where he could observe, he watched the wyvern fly into the entrance of the dungeon – in full view of a party of players that were about 50 feet from the entrance. Devin couldn't hear them from where he was, but he saw them pointing excitedly at the entrance and hurrying to catch up to the out-of-place mob. Quickly running into the entrance, they encountered the wyvern and started to attack it with abandon. Francis was able to fend them off pretty well, which was good...and bad.

It was *good* because it meant that he was still alive to do his job – it was *bad* for the players who never thought to look behind them as the humungous head of the **Majestic Roc** crashed through the entrance trying to get to the wyvern. It had no regard for the players in its way – which was why they were smeared against the floor, sides, and ceiling of the cave. Francis bit the dust moments later as the six-foot-long beak of the bird snatched him up and gulped him down like a chicken with a worm.

Devin wasn't sure what he was going to do now – he didn't really have a plan for what to do next. He started rushing down the pathway with Chuck in tow, skillfully bypassing all the mobs on the way. The only thing he could think of was to try to get into the forest and hide from it until he could rush into the dungeon and respawn – which would hopefully cancel the *Lure* skill he had used.

Arriving at the bottom, Devin rushed to the dungeon entrance while staying close to the trees, attempting to stay hidden. He needn't have bothered, as he found that he wasn't in any danger. When he got close enough, he found a giant bird ass sticking out of the entrance to the cave. Apparently, the roc had generated so much speed in its chase after his pet that when it crashed into the cave opening it got stuck; it couldn't get any leverage to either back out or work its way further in.

Delighted at this turn of events, he immediately started attacking it along with Chuck. With it being almost 40 levels higher, he found that he couldn't do more than one point of damage with his crappy sword and Chuck wasn't doing much better. At this rate, it would take hours of constantly attacking it – which he didn't have because another party of players was bound to come along eventually. Frustrated, he thought of having Chuck burrow underground and come up beneath its chest but figured the thick skin would be the same there as well. It wasn't until he looked closer at the roc's rear end that he had an idea.

Without getting too graphic, he had Chuck use his claws to widen the hole in the roc that Devin had conveniently located. Once it was big enough, he had his pet "burrow" his way inside – which turned out to do enormous amounts of damage. Within a minute of Chuck going to town on the birds' insides, Devin watched the roc go from frantically squirming around to dead quiet. Shortly, the corpse of the **Majestic Roc** faded away and he found Chuck sitting nonchalantly in the middle of the entrance as if he did that every day.

Chapter 7

(26 hours before release of patch notes)

After taking a little time to rest, he headed up the pathway again while refreshing Chuck, Betty, and Francis on the way. He was interested in seeing if he could find these "Orcs" that he had thought he heard about from that earlier party. As he progressed further past the wyverns, he kept a wary eye out for any more rocs – he didn't want to run into any of them again. He only saw one, but it was a long way up the mountain, lazily circling in the air. He endeavored to keep his aerial force nearby to prevent them getting too close to its aggro zone.

As Devin got further and further up the mountain, he found the air grew colder and colder the higher he got. He was a little worried that he wouldn't find anything new before he hit his distance limit – which by his estimation was near the snow line just a little further up. He only found more of the same mobs that he had encountered before – although they started showing up at higher levels. Still not too much of a challenge, he kept going up and was about to turn back as he started to feel little urgings to turn around. However, at the edge of his vision he spotted what looked like a village.

Curious, as he couldn't imagine what kind of settlement could be up there, he made his way closer. As he got near enough to make out more detail, he realized that it wasn't just any old village – it was a village filled with orcs. It was just on the edge of his allowed distance from the dungeon; he thought he could make it to the village before he had to turn back. Now even more cautious, he and his team quickly made their way to an outcropping of rock that jutted out into the pathway. Directing his pets to stay hidden from sight, he was able to observe the settlement from a fairly good viewpoint without making himself overly visible.

The village consisted of 12 buildings – though it would be more accurate to call them huts. Made of extremely poor construction, these stick-and-mud domiciles looked like they wouldn't really keep the cold out – mainly because none of them had a door or anything resembling a curtain to keep in the warm air. If he was a gambler, he would be hard-pressed on what to bet on: whether the roofs would collapse inward first, or the walls would fall outward. They were all arranged in a circle with a large bonfire located in the middle that must have been 15 feet wide with the flames reaching even higher.

He watched as various orcs traveled from hut to hut without any discernable purpose – except for two that looked to be standing guard in front of the largest building located right next to the fire. The guards were wearing nice-looking leather armor, were equipped with what looked like steel-tipped spears, and were highly disciplined. Compared to the other orcs scattered through the village who were rather shoddily equipped, these two were probably an elite-type mob that were guarding the orc chieftain.

Devin was excited for a chance to get another sentient creature for the dungeon. The goblins they already had were great – especially in Weregoblin form – but they had limited utility as they didn't have a lot of defensive ability. Orcs, on the other hand, were both strong and tough – they could take a lickin' and keep on tickin'. They were also larger, generally thought to be at least marginally smarter than goblins, and were also a selectable player race. He looked for any regularity in the orcs' patrols and thought he could discern a pattern.

Cautiously making his way to a hut located the farthest from the center, Devin crouched down and started counting to 36 in his head. He apparently miscalculated – or just took too long to get in position – because when he reached 33 a lone **Hearthfire Orc (Level 30)** turned the corner and immediately attacked him.

Instead of attacking back or defending, Devin ran away back toward his pets while using his *Lure* skill. He ended up taking some glancing damage from the pursuing orc, but he made it back quick enough that when he had Francis and Betty use their taunt skill he was in the clear. From there, it was easy enough to guide his new "friend" down to the dungeon while causing as much damage as they could without killing it. When they arrived, it was simplicity itself to finish it off with them all attacking at the same time.

Although he was highly satisfied with all the monsters that he had acquired, there was one more thing that Devin wanted to try. Since they had the **Goblin Chieftain** as a unique mob on the first floor, he was curious if he could get an **Orc Chieftain** as well. He figured it would be a challenge, but since he was pretty much at the limit of what he could get as far as new monsters went, he didn't mind chancing a respawn for the opportunity to add another mob to the dungeon.

With a tough fight in mind, he refreshed with a new Chuck, a new Betty, and decided to get another Harpy so that he could have some extra lifting power (which he named Getty). As he approached the village again, he found that the orc that he had "acquired" earlier had respawned. That meant that he had 16 orcs wandering around the huts, two guards on the Chieftain's hut, and then the Chieftain himself. He wasn't sure what else might be in there, but he would find out when or if he got there.

His strategy in the coming fight would be one of Orc tossing. He would try to single each orc out and use Betty and Getty to grab onto each one of its arms so that they could lift it into the air. After that, it was a simple toss off the mountain and pretty soon it would be raining orcs. With luck, he might even hit a player or two on the ground with his orc missiles. If he was attacked by more than one, he would have Chuck try to kite the additional one by burrowing underground as much as possible while still trying to hold aggro.

While this strategy worked great for the single orcs, he found that when there was more than one he had to run for his life because as soon as Chuck went underground the orc would head straight for Devin. A couple of times he ran almost as far as the wyverns before Betty and Getty were able to catch up and get the orcs' arms. Eventually, he got to the point where all of the wandering ones were cleared out and only the guards were left.

Deciding to use the same strategy he had employed before, he sent Betty and Getty in to get one of the guards' arms, but it seemed that they were prepared for that. These appeared to be a bit tougher than the other orcs; as he looked closer, he saw that they were **Hearthfire Orc Guards**. As his two harpies got close, Devin watched the tip of a spear erupt from their backs, instantly killing them. Shocked – and admittedly a little sad – he started backing up, preparing to run.

Just before he turned around in order to sprint away a quickly as possible, he noticed that the doorway to the Chieftain's hut had a new figure emerging from the inside. Devin wouldn't be able to see whether or not he could acquire an Orc Chieftain for the dungeon – because what actually came stomping out was an ogre.

Standing about nine feet tall, Devin wasn't sure how the **Hearthfire Ogre (Level 35)** was even able to even fit through the doorway without destroying half of the hut in the process. Nevertheless, the massive ogre made its way out and with a mighty bellow, swung the tree-trunk-like club it was holding at the ground. The concussive wave generated by this knocked both Devin and Chuck to the ground, while doing a small amount of damage as well. Quickly scrambling to his feet, Devin used his *Lure* skill on the ogre and started booking it back down the pathway.

Chuck followed at a slower pace and was quickly run over by the pursuing trio. As it passed, the Ogre casually swung his club at Chuck and batted him away like he was a golf ball. Witnessing this, Devin pumped his stubby legs as fast as possible and didn't stop for anything.

Passing multiple mobs on the way down, he avoided them as nimbly as he could but still got hit a couple of times for a significant amount of damage. These additional mobs started following as well, but since they weren't being *Lured* they eventually lost interest. Once down at the bottom, he kept running for the entrance to the dungeon, all the while watching as the three mobs following him slowly gained ground.

Relieved that he got there before being caught, he quickly realized that he had no plan to kill his pursuers. Until he could think of something, he went ahead and kept running. Hearing a short scuffle behind him, he realized that the goblins on the first floor were attempting to attack the guards and ogre – to very little effect other than slowing them down incrementally.

With some of the pressure off, he determined that his only chance was to reach the second-floor boss room and hope that Violette was as good as she claimed to be. As he reached the bottom of the stairs to the next floor, he ran smack into the back of something and bounced backwards, flat on his back. Startled at the unexpected obstacle, he looked up and saw the equally surprised faces of a group of four players. All of them were level 20 but looked quite competent with a good division of classes.

It didn't really matter though, because as he got up and quickly ran past them, they weren't more than a penny on the rail of the freight train following him. He looked back as the party was attacked from behind and didn't last more than three seconds against the much stronger foes. A little worried now, he realized that he should probably warn Krista of the impending danger.

"Krista!!! Krista!!! I'm coming in hot! Got a bogey on my six that's a real doozy – I need Violette's help! I hope she is ready for me!"

Silence...and then a sullen, "I'll let her know."

Devin wasn't sure what all of that was about, but he had to trust that their new guardian would be able to handle this ogre and his guards. Finally reaching the boss room, he burst through the doorway and looked around for Violette in order to tell her about the incoming mobs.

Out of breath, he was able to gasp out to the room at large, "Ogre…*gasp*…elite guards…*wheeze*…"

It turned out that he needn't have bothered because Violette was already prepared – Krista must have told her what was coming. He stopped in his tracks when he saw her; at that moment she was quite scary-looking. She held a black staff topped by something he couldn't see clearly in his rush, and her eyes were filled with a glowing green fire that left him chilled down to his bones. On top of that, she was floating five feet off of the ground and her cloak was flapping wildly behind her as if she was in a windstorm. He was at a loss at what to do when she spoke to him in a deeper, more authoritative voice than he had yet to hear from her.

"Get behind me Devin – I don't want to accidentally kill you again."

Almost as if she had filled him with a shot of adrenaline, he quickly rushed behind her and tried to make himself as inconspicuous as possible. Very quickly, he saw his pursuers enter the room and make their way toward him – not even paying attention to Violette. Apparently taking affront at their indifference, she started casting a spell using words in a dark, unintelligible language. Dark tendrils of vaporous smoke rose from the ground in front of the attackers, creating an opaque wall that quickly and completely surrounded them.

Devin couldn't see them anymore, but he could hear them; if it wasn't for the fact that they were just trying to kill him, he would have felt sorry for them. Wails of anguish, unlike any that he had ever heard before, sent shivers down his spine and he felt like they would never end. Over the disturbing sounds emanating from the maelstrom of spiritual energy, Devin could also hear Violette in her deeper voice laughing maniacally – which he almost thought was worse. Eventually, the cries of pain and torment faded away and the dark smoke surrounding his former enemies dissipated. He briefly saw the corpses of the ogre and two orcs lying on the ground with expressions of terror frozen on their faces before they quickly disappeared.

Frozen in terror as well, Devin watched Violette slowly descend back to the ground with her cloak resting peacefully along her back with no sense of its former violence. When she turned toward him, her eyes were back to normal and she had a welcoming smile on her face.   As if he was just there for a friendly visit, she said – with her voice back to normal – "Devin! I'm so glad you're here! Where have you been, you silly boy? It's been so lonely here with only these goblins here to talk to – which is hard with just me carrying on the conversation. Thanks for bringing some more friends to play with! How are you, Devin? You look tired – come here, I'll take care of you."

As she walked over to him, Devin still couldn't seem to move. He just stared at her – he was unable to register the drastic change that came over her when she was in "battle mode". The dichotomy of who she was now compared to just seconds ago was too much for him to process.

He was still letting his brain catch up to the world when he was picked up and laid on the floor with his head on Violette's lap. She was making soothing noises while slowly running her hands through his hair as if he was a dog that needed to be calmed down. As his eyes refocused, he looked up expecting to see her face but all he saw was the underside of her generous bosom.

His voice cracking, both from the exertion from running and from being highly uncomfortable around a potential crazy person, he said, "Sorry for the surprise interruption, I got in a little over my head there."

"Don't you worry your beautiful little head about it – I'm just glad you stopped by like you said you would. You know you are welcome to visit me *any* time."

Devin didn't have any response to that – especially since he didn't remember telling her he would stop by. Afraid that he would incur her wrath if he tried to leave, he just laid there stiffly, hoping that she would grow bored. Instead, the feeling of her fingers slowly running through his hair was having a soporific effect on him. Even though he physically didn't need to sleep, the last day or so of hunting for monsters left him a little weary. His eyelids felt heavy and they slowly closed on their own. Just before he lost consciousness, he wondered if Violette was using one of her spells on him; he thought that he shouldn't be able to sleep – and didn't even think it was possible.

Chapter 8

(22 hours before release of patch notes)

Krista finished constructing the new floor about an hour before Devin had come in screaming for help. She had just been putting in little frivolous details when she got bored and started watching the various groups that were present throughout the dungeon. She had recently watched another group of lower-level players wipe on the second-floor room with the eight wolves and boars – apparently, they didn't do their research and were highly unprepared for the sheer number of mobs that attacked them.

Krista saw Devin sprint inside the entrance and kept running as though being chased by something. It was good to see him again as she was starting to miss having him around. She was about to talk to him when she saw the three mobs enter through the entrance chasing after him. She didn't want to startle him and potentially cause him to die, so she just followed along and tried to figure out what he was doing. After the ogre and orcs wiped out the party of players just starting on the second floor, Devin finally contacted her to let her know what his plan was.

She didn't want Devin anywhere near Violette because she didn't want that woman to get her claws into him. However, she didn't want him to die either because she was worried that he would lose levels in the process. Now that they started the event, they had to be more cautious of Devin dying; he needed to stay as strong as possible to help defend the dungeon from the incoming horde of players that were sure to arrive. She contacted Violette and let her know that Devin needed help killing some mobs that were following him.

Violette was overly-excited – Krista thought it was probably because she was rather bored sitting all alone in the Boss Room without anyone to talk to. She felt a little sorry for her, since the guardian was essentially sitting in a prison and forced to do what Krista wanted; she didn't feel this way about any of her other monsters, mainly because they didn't have any personality. They were just part of the dungeon – a tool to be used. Violette was different; she was like the NPCs back in Briarwood who had their own history, opinions, wants, and needs.

After the battle – or whatever you wanted to call it since it was pretty one-sided (slaughter was probably the more accurate word) – she again stood in awe of the power of her guardian. As well as still being a little frightened of her. She was apparently quite mentally unstable; most likely due to the fact that she had been locked away by herself for so long.

When she saw how Devin was eating right out of her hand – *with his head in her lap even!* – she lost it when she saw Violette put him to sleep. "You bitch! I told you not to cast your spells on him anymore! And stay away from him, he's not for you – he belongs to me!"

Surprised at her own vehemence, she thought about what she said and wondered where that came from. She felt very possessive of Devin for some reason, even though he was his own person and she had never stopped him from pursuing any other girl out in the real world. *Must be because he's part of my dungeon.*

Violette responded with a sneer and with heat in her voice, "Why do you care? Is he your boyfriend? Husband? Friend with benefits? If not, then he is free to choose who he likes. I can tell you like him – otherwise you wouldn't be so possessive of him. What is he supposed to do with you? You can't even touch him, let alone have any sort of relationship with him. I want him and there is nothing you can do to stop me – you can't get rid of me and you need me to protect your Dungeon Core. Leave Devin to me and I will do everything in my power to protect you; because protecting you will protect him as well."

She's blackmailing me! Even though she couldn't possibly be right about Krista liking Devin like that – he was more like a brother than anything. But she also did have a point that she couldn't do anything to get rid of or alienate Violette – she was the only thing standing between safety and oblivion. But Krista would be damned if she would let that whore do anything to hurt Devin – she was crazy and would inevitably rub some of that crazy off on him. But, she had to play along for now until she could figure something out.

"Fine. I won't interfere, but you need to promise to do everything you can to protect the both of us – but if you hurt him, I will do my best to ensure you never see freedom again. I would rather give up what we have than live with what you might be doing to hurt him."

"That's all I ask." Violette went back to running her fingers through Devin's hair with a satisfied look upon her face. She was so different from when she first met her that she wasn't sure who the "real" Violette was – the bubbly, happy, lonely girl from their first meeting or this manipulative, psychotic, scary woman from now. It was probably a combination of the two or perhaps three if she counted who she became when she fought her enemies. There must have been some major split-personality issues in that programming of hers – she wasn't even sure if she had seen everyone that was inside her yet.

She decided that she would keep working on a solution to the Devin-Violette problem – this wasn't the end. However, she had a deadline to meet and needed to get started.

Chapter 9

(21 hours before release of patch notes)

Krista moved her viewpoint away from the Boss Room because she couldn't watch Violette rubbing herself all over Devin anymore. She turned her attention to her new floor and worked on getting it up and running as soon as possible so that they would have it ready before the patch notes were released. She called up the monster upgrade menu and was surprised at how many more there were available – Devin had been busy.

Upgrade Monsters	
Goblin	Base Monster
Goblin Chieftain	Unique Monster
Dusk Boar	Base Monster
Timber Wolf	Base Monster
Weregoblin	Unique Monster
Goblin Boar-rider	Unique Monster
Hardy Rock-burrower	Base Monster
Sure-footed Mountain Goat	Base Monster
Starving Mountain Lion	Base Monster
Shrieking Harpy	Base Monster

Scaled Wyvern	Base Monster
Majestic Roc	Base Monster
Hearthfire Orc	Base Monster
Hearthfire Orc Guard	Unique Monster
Hearthfire Ogre	Base Monster

Krista was ecstatic over the plethora of choices she had for populating her new floor. As she looked over it, however, she realized that most if not all of these monsters were more suited to a mountainous terrain. *How am I supposed to make that work?* They wouldn't do well in the cramped rooms she had made – especially the flying creatures she saw on the list. She would have to completely revamp the entire floor to accommodate the needs of all the new mobs. But first, she wanted to see what new kinds of hybrids and combinations she could make. She pulled up the first two monsters two see what they were:

Hardy Rock-burrower (Base Monster)			
Burrow Strike I			
Current level description:	The Hardy Rock-burrower quickly burrows underground using its powerful claws and strikes the target from underneath, potentially launching them into the air		
Physical Damage:	60	Cooldown:	180.0 seconds
Next level	The Hardy Rock-burrower quickly burrows underground using its powerful claws and strikes		

description:	the target from underneath, with a greater chance of launching them into the air		
Physical Damage:	100	Cooldown:	150.0 seconds
Upgrade cost:	300 rp		

Physical Attack:		Physical Resistance:	
Current Level: 1	15	Current Level: 1	30
Next Level: 2	28	Next Level: 2	55
Upgrade Cost:	50 rp	Upgrade Cost:	50 rp

Upgrade Weapon:	Upgrade Armor:
(Cannot equip weapons)	(Cannot equip armor)

Create Hybrid?	Combine with Another Monster?
(Select another monster to create hybrid)	(Select another monster to combine)

Sure-footed Mountain Goat (Base Monster)			
Declined Ram Rush I			
Current level description:	The Sure-footed Mountain Goat rushes down a cliff at a decline and then rams into the target, causing damage and launching them a certain distance		
Physical Damage:	40	Cooldown:	30.0 seconds
Distance Thrown:	Up to 15.0 feet	Restrictions:	Must start on a decline
Next level description:	The Sure-footed Mountain Goat rushes down a cliff at a decline and then rams into the target, causing damage and launching them a considerable distance		
Physical Damage:	60	Cooldown:	150.0 seconds
Distance Thrown:	Up to 25.0 feet	Restrictions:	Must start on a decline
Upgrade cost:	300 rp		

Physical Attack:		Physical Resistance:	
Current Level: 1	10	Current Level: 1	8
Next Level: 2	18	Next Level: 2	15
Upgrade Cost:	50 rp	Upgrade Cost:	50 rp
Upgrade Weapon:		Upgrade Armor:	
(Cannot equip weapons)		(Cannot equip armor)	
Create Hybrid?		Combine with Another Monster?	
(Select another monster to create hybrid)		(Select another monster to combine)	

Krista felt that these would be welcome additions to her new floor. The physical resistance of the burrower along with its surprise attacks would work well in long tunnels where it was near-impossible to dodge such attacks. The goat was a little more of a problem since she didn't really have anywhere for it to use its skill. She was beginning to understand what she would need to create for them to be more effective. She would love to bounce around some ideas with Devin, but he was still "asleep" at the moment. Hopefully, before she changed anything major, she would get a chance to see if he had any input.

She placed a level 1 of each type in the entrance room of the new floor in order to get a better understanding of what she was working with. The burrower looked almost like an armadillo with wicked looking claws and the mountain goat looked like...well...a shaggy goat. Having gotten a good look at them, she dismissed them and got back to her menus.

Having had success earlier with making a hybrid with her Goblin/Wolf hybrid, the Weregoblin, she decided to try her luck at making a Goblin/Burrower hybrid. The results were less than satisfactory – what she ended up with was a green-tinged burrower that had lost any type of armor along its back and no special skills.

Mourning the loss of 200 resource points, she decided that she would be a little more strategic in her choices. Although she still had a large pool of resources to play with, she needed them to fully stock the dungeon with all her new mobs and couldn't afford to use them frivolously.

With this in mind, she thought about combining the burrower with a wolf or boar. The wolf was theoretically faster when compared to the burrower, but she didn't think that would help much – the burrower's strength was in its surprise attack and being faster probably wouldn't be that much of an advantage. If the hybrid went the other way around, she might get a wolf that had increased physical defense and stronger claws on its feet, but it also might make it slower – which would take away from the quickness of the wolf which was *its* strength.

With a boar/burrower hybrid, she could see some advantage of it being able to charge down a tunnel after surprising a party of players. Or, it could be a boar that had increased physical resistance – either could work. She selected the Hardy Rock-burrower and chose to make it a hybrid with a Dusk Boar.

Dusky Rock-boarer (Advanced Monster)

A hybrid of rock-burrower and boar, the Dusky Rock-boarer can burrow underground and also charge at enemies from a certain distance.

Burrow Charge I

Current level description:	The Dusky Rock-boarer tunnels under the ground, emerging underneath its intended target with a possibility of launching the target. If the target is launched and lands a certain distance away, the Dusky Rock-boarer will then charge at the victim, doing increased damage with a chance to stun.		
Emergent Physical Damage:	120	Launch Distance Needed for Charge:	8.0 feet
Charging Physical Damage:	140	Stun Chance:	15%
Cooldown:	240.0 seconds		
Next level description:	The Dusky Rock-boarer tunnels under the ground, emerging underneath its intended target with an increased possibility of launching the target. If the target is launched and lands a certain distance away, the Dusky Rock-boarer will then charge at the victim, doing increased damage with an increased chance to stun.		
Emergent Physical Damage:	150	Launch Distance Needed for Charge:	6.0 feet
Charging Physical Damage:	180	Stun Chance:	30%
Cooldown:	210.0 seconds	Upgrade Cost:	1000 rp

Enraged I

Current level description:	Occasionally, a boar will become enraged when it takes enough damage and will try to kill everything in sight without regard for its own well-being – so too will the Dusky Rock-boarer.		
Health Threshold:	30%	Physical Damage Increase/Resistance Decrease	200% Increase 50% Decrease
Next level description:	Occasionally, a boar will become enraged when it takes enough damage and will try to kill everything in sight without regard for its own well-being – so too will the Dusky Rock-boarer.		

Health Threshold:		Physical Damage Increase/Resistance Decrease:	250% Increase
	35%		40% Decrease
Upgrade cost:		1000 rp	

Physical Attack:		Physical Resistance:	
Current Level: 1	40	Current Level: 1	50
Next Level: 2	70	Next Level: 2	80
Upgrade Cost:	250 rp	Upgrade Cost:	250 rp

Upgrade Weapon:	Upgrade Armor:
(Unable to equip weapons)	(Unable to equip armor)

Create Hybrid?	Combine with Another Monster?
(Due to this being an advanced monster, hybrids are not available at its current level)	(Due to this being an advanced monster, combines are not available at its current level)

That was more like it! With this, she wasn't limited to just tunnels – this monster needed a little bit more open space so that it could launch players farther. With the right combination of landscapes, it could be really deadly. If she was able to get these boarers to fight in pairs it could keep the attacking parties off balance and might even score a kill or two.

With another successful hybrid in the bag, she turned her attention to the rest of the monsters on her list. The **Starving Mountain Lion** had an *Ambush* skill that did additional damage when undetected that would work well with her stalactite and stalagmite filled rooms that she already had. The **Shrieking Harpy** was an ugly flying bird-woman that had a *Shriek* skill that would stun everything within a 50-foot radius – but only for 5 seconds. It had high physical damage but very low resistance, so it was best as a support monster.

Next on the list was a **Scaled Wyvern**, which looked like a large winged snake that appeared to be highly maneuverable but weak on physical damage. Because it was scaled, it had a higher physical resistance but not as much as the burrower from earlier. She thought that in large groups, the wyvern would be able to overcome the opposition – especially with its passive *Swarm* skill that increased its damage output when surrounded by allies.

When she placed the **Majestic Roc** in the floor entrance room, her viewpoint actually jumped as she was startled by the size of the thing. *How did Devin manage to lure this back to the dungeon? It doesn't even look like it would fit through the entrance!* Since it barely fit in the expanded floor entrance that she constructed she wasn't sure how she would use it effectively. Unlike most of her base monsters, the Roc actually had two skills – *Deafening Squawk* and *Whirlwind*. The *Deafening Squawk* skill was relatively straightforward – a loud squawk that deafened and disoriented enemies within a large area. Although it was useful, Krista was more interested in the *Whirlwind* skill. The roc would use its massive wingspan to generate a minor whirlwind that would damage and push back a group of targets within a cone-shaped area in front of it. This could prove useful in pushing unprepared players into traps or even other monsters.

The three sentient mobs she obtained didn't have any specific skills unique to them, but she was pretty sure that Devin would be able to choose them as a playable race now. The **Hearthfire Orc Guard** was actually a unique monster that had higher starting stats than the normal orc – these would be good if she created some sort of camp inside the dungeon that they could be in charge of guarding. She figured she would see what the rest of the level was going to look like before making any plans like that, however.

Chapter 10

De4thfrmbeh1nd was getting frustrated. They had been attacked at almost every step of the way as they headed for the dungeon. He saw ambush groups from at least seven different guilds – nothing that they couldn't ultimately handle, but their force was getting slowly whittled down due to attrition. Fortunately, they hadn't lost any of their dungeon group, although most of their rangers and rogue-types that had been scouting had been taken out by other high-level stealthers.

All his tanks were still doing great – the ambushers didn't even touch them. A couple of his casters and long-range support members had been singularly targeted and taken out before any defense could be provided. His fellow guild members were getting antsy and paranoid; throughout the entire journey they had only killed one player who had gotten unlucky and unstealthed at the wrong time. They had to stay in formation to protect the dungeon group, so they couldn't break off to chase after the multiple hit-and-run attacks that they had been suffering.

They still had a bit of distance to go before they got to their destination and De4th was worried about a large-scale force that might be waiting for them. The systematic destruction of his scouts was potentially a sign that there was a powerful hand at work. He was essentially walking blind into what might be a major ambush that could wipe them all out.

He had thought that they had moved fast enough to avoid any type of this confrontation, but it looked like he might not have been the only one to have foreknowledge of the Dungeon Core. It was even possible, though he thought it unlikely, that they knew where it was located even earlier than everyone else.

Well, the only thing that they could do now was to continue moving and hope the level of organization he had seen so far from the other guilds was just coincidence. They were already committed to this endeavor and would be farther behind if they turned back now. With his fingers crossed, he ordered his lieutenants to keep everyone moving and to speed it up if at all possible. They had no scouting force to report back to him, so they could make better time without having to wait for those reports. With ill-disguised reluctance, his fellow players kept marching on – to which he hoped was not their doom.

Chapter 11

(18 hours before release of patch notes)

Now that she had checked out each of the new additions, she wanted to try her hand at some more hybrids and combinations. Once she knew what all of her monster options were, she would work on recreating the rooms in the new floor. Thinking carefully, she thought about what a good two-monster combination would be. She hadn't ever tried combining two sentient creatures before, so she decided to try out combining an ogre and a goblin to see what would come of it:

Ogrepult (Advanced Monster)			
A combination of an ogre and a goblin, the Ogrepult is almost like two monsters in one. They work together as a team as the ogre can pick up goblins and launch them at a target within a certain distance. This is especially helpful when the target is behind a staunch defender as the ogre can throw vertically as well as horizontally.			
Goblin Barrage I			
Current level description:	The ogre picks up any nearby goblins and continues to launch them at a target at a certain distance away. Goblins can travel either in a straight line or over any obstacles.		
Maximum Throwing Distance:	30.0 feet	Physical Damage from Goblin Impact:	100
Accuracy:	70%	Cooldown:	120.0 seconds
Goblin Cyclone I			
Current level description:	When the Ogrepult is surrounded by a certain number of enemies within a certain area, it will pick up two goblins		

	and rotate in a circle, doing damage to all within range		
Physical Damage:	60.0 per second	Duration:	5.0 seconds
Surround Count:	3 enemies in range	Surround Range:	Within 10 feet
Cooldown:	300.0 seconds	Restrictions:	Must have 2 goblins nearby to execute skill

Oh my god! That is awesome! She could imagine it now – the **Ogrepult** surrounded by a multitude of lower level goblins to use as ammo. This would be good for an optional mini-boss area that she could set up that players would have to defeat in order to get good rewards. She'd have to look through her loot menu to see what kind of reward would be appropriate. Perhaps even an upgrade to the **Ogrepult** to make it even harder for the players if they wanted the good loot.

Still strategically thinking about what a good monster hybrid would be, she decided to try something flying this time. The **Shrieking Harpy** was pretty strong but didn't have enough Physical Resistance to survive for long in a protracted battle. If she made a hybrid with something that had increased Constitution, it might make something that could take some damage while still dishing it out. She thought about the rock-burrower, but it was so heavy that she didn't believe that it could still fly. The two other mobs that she had that possessed increased inherent Constitution were the **Hearthfire Orc** and the **Hearthfire Ogre**. The Ogre would be way too heavy to hold up with the smaller harpy wings, so she went with the Orc.

Horcy (Advanced Monster)			
A hybrid of a Harpy and an Orc, the Horcy has the Strength and Constitution of an Orc with the flight power of the Harpy. However, with the additional weight associated with Orc DNA, the Horcy cannot stay in the air for more than 30 seconds at a time with a two-minute rest in between flights. The Horcy also has a pair of arms and can wield weapons – unlike the original Harpy. Each Horcy is female as well.			
Shrieking Roar I			
Current level description:	The Horcy lets out a shrieking roar that both stuns and damages its foes in a certain area		
Area of Effect:	30.0-foot diameter	Physical Damage:	50
Stun Duration:	5.0 seconds	Cooldown:	180.0 seconds
Dive Bomb I			
Current level description:	When the Horcy is airborne, it can use this skill to dive straight at an enemy, using its momentum and weapons to deliver massive damage; once committed, trajectory cannot be changed so there is a possibility of the attack being dodged		
Physical Damage:	250	Distance from target:	15 feet or more
Cooldown:	150.0 seconds		

Although not precisely what she had wanted, the fact that it was essentially a flying orc was sweet. It couldn't stay in the air for long, but since it could use weapons that would hopefully help make up for that restriction. She was definitely going to have to make an open-air cavern that would allow her forces to use the open space to their fullest potential.

Figuring that she was already going to have an area where the flying mobs could have an advantage, she decided to play some more with her winged assets. She liked the ability to equip her monsters with weapons if at all possible since she could upgrade those later. In fact...

"Hey Carl, when I look at the upgrade menu for my monsters, it has an 'Upgrade Weapon' and 'Upgrade Armor' option that is unavailable until I have access to upgraded stuff. I have some great weapons and armor that has dropped off players inside the dungeon – doesn't this count?"

From what I can ascertain, the upgraded weapons and armor are unlocked when you are able to make your own – not just as loot. My guess is the *NPCs* and *Buildings* option that is unlocked at a later level will have at least a blacksmith that can create these advanced weapons and armor.

"Well, that explains that at least – I can't wait to level up and see what we can do then!" With that option off of the table for now, she would still like to plan for the future possibility of upgrades. Thinking about how to "weaponize" another flying monster, she thought of a Dragon Knight. Now, she didn't have any dragons – or knights for that matter – but she did have a flying snake and something small to hopefully ride on its back. She chose the **Scaled Wyvern** and a **Goblin** and combined the two of them together.

Goblin Pole Dancer (Advanced Monster)
A combination of a wyvern and a goblin, the Goblin Pole Dancer is the epitome of

aerial maneuverability. Riding on the wyverns' back is a goblin that wields a long pole that can be used to attack targets both in the air and on the ground. It would've been a spear, but the low intelligence associated with goblins caused too many accidents with wyvern wings. The sinuous movement of the wyvern in the air allows it to dodge incoming attacks and looks as though it is dancing.

Strafe I			
Current level description:	The Goblin Pole Dancer quickly maneuvers through all of the members of the attacking party, only staying close enough to attack with the pole-wielding goblin.		
Physical Damage:	40 per target	Cooldown:	300.0 seconds
Max Targets:	5		

Joust I			
Current level description:	The Goblin Pole Dancer selects a worthy opponent at random and charges at full speed causing damage and possible knockdown		
Physical Damage:	200	Knockdown Chance:	35.0%
Cooldown:	180.0 seconds		

Not what I was expecting, but I think I could work wi...wait what was its name? Although it wasn't overly offensive, the name **Goblin Pole Dancer** doesn't really inspire fear either. It was more likely to be laughed at as a joke than anything. *Well, if it performs adequately, then we'll see who has the last laugh. Hmm...sounding like a cliché villain there – I wonder if I should laugh maniacally too.*

She was getting into this dungeon persona so much that is was almost exciting figuring out ways to gain any advantage she could over the players. With the impending danger pushed to the back of her mind, she was actually starting to enjoy herself. *Maybe Devin was right. Maybe all I needed was a challenge, some sort of "risk" to feel alive again.* She couldn't change what was coming, but she could utilize the life she *did* have to make sure they survived as long as possible.

And even have fun doing it in the meantime.

Chapter 12

Krista continued to make hybrids and combinations to add to her aerial attacking force. She utilized the **Majestic Roc** in a hybrid with the **Scaled Wyvern** and created a larger, heavier wyvern called a **Wyveroc**. One of its special skills was the *Hisssterectomy,* which caused deafness and removed all beneficial buffs from affected targets. The **Wyveroc's** other skill was the *Strangler*, where the creature wrapped itself around a target and lifted it up in the air while strangling it.

Using the **Majestic Roc** again, she combined it with the **Sure-footed Mountain Goat** to create an almost bomber-type ground assault monster. It was called the **G-Bomber**, and it was an apt name for the creation. The roc portion of the **G-Bomber** actually had no real offensive ability – it was more of a "personnel" carrier.

It had a hollow space on the bottom side of its body near the rear that would house up to six goats. When it was ready, it would then drop goats from above on unsuspecting players; each goat dropped would have access to the *Dive Bomb* skill which would allow them to "charge" through the air toward their target without taking fall damage. They would only be able to use this skill while they were still falling through the air – once on the ground they would be normal mountain goats.

The **G-Bomber** was only allowed to drop one goat every 15 seconds and came fully equipped with 6 goats. It would then regenerate one goat every 30 seconds and could drop them at any time thereafter. It had a once-per-battle skill called *Carpet Bomb*, which would speed up goat production to allow it to drop all six goats at once. Krista couldn't think of anything scarier than watching six angry goats dive bombing the party all at once.

Except for maybe Violette – that girl was scary when in battle mode.

After her experiments with the **G-Bomber**, she wanted to utilize the versatility of a mountain goat to enhance her other monsters. First, she mixed a **Sure-footed Mountain Goat** with a **Hardy Rock-burrower** to create a **Burrowgoat**. This hybrid gave the rock-burrower the ability to quickly climb near-vertical cliff sides and had an armored head that would allow it to use a special *Head Rush* skill that was like a short-range knockback attack. The attack itself didn't do a whole lot of damage but it would allow the **Burrowgoat** to get some breathing room by knocking back an attacker up to 20 feet. Its other skill was even better – *Wall Burrow*. Since the burrower had an increased ability to scale near-impassable walls, it also allowed it to burrow underground and attack from the side of a wall or ceiling instead of just underneath a target.

The other goat creation was the **Goatlin**, a hybrid of a **Goblin** and a **Sure-footed Mountain Goat**. Basically, it was a goblin that had the climbing skills of a mountain goat – not that great of a success considering it only had one skill. *Surround* was a skill that would only come in handy if she had a large quantity of them since it would allow them to quickly surround the target group and attack simultaneously.

Done with goats, she realized that she hadn't really used the **Starving Mountain Lion** in any of her "experiments" yet. With that thought, she combined it with the **Hearthfire Orc** to see if either the Orc could ride it or fight beside it. What she actually got was something a little different…

Pussy-master Orc (Advanced Monster)			
A combination of Orc and Mountain Lion, the Pussy-master Orc is a friend to most cats and master of them all. Goes into battle with one Mountain Lion as a pet.			
Herding Cats I			
Current level description:	The Pussy-master Orc summons a certain amount of Mountain Lions and directs them to attack a group of enemies for a certain amount of time – afterword they will retreat. The Pussy-master orc cannot direct which targets to specifically attack – they may attack anywhere from one per group member to all on one group member.		
Total Lions:	5	Duration:	30.0 seconds
Cooldown:	Once per battle		
Scratching Post I			
Current level description:	The Pussy-master Orc sends his Mountain Lion pet at a specific target where it attacks at an increased speed and ignores a portion of the target's Physical Resistance.		
Speed Increase:	3X	Ignores Physical Resistance:	50%
Duration:	30.0 seconds	Cooldown:	240.0 seconds

"Ok, that's ridiculous – now I know someone is deliberately changing these names to make them seem naughtier. It's not ok – Carl, is there any way I can change these names since I created them?"

Unfortunately, each name is created on the spot by the main system AI – you have no direct control of them. As soon as they are part of the game world they cannot be changed – just as if you were to try to change the name of a Goblin or a Timber Wolf. The only option you have is to not use those monsters you disagree with since you are not forced to use them if you do not want to.

"Well, this main system AI seems to have a twisted sense of humor – first sticking us with this event and then messing with my monster names. Does this main system AI have a name, or do you just refer to it as 'main system AI'?"

It doesn't have a name, but all the other AI entities call it "The AI" – capitalization intended.

"Ok...well then...I hate the name of this last monster and if I had the choice I wouldn't use it at all – it just seems dirty. We'll see if I need to use it or not depending on the makeup of the rest of the dungeon."

Now that she was finished experimenting, she decided it was time to rebuild the dungeon based on her new acquisitions.

Chapter 13

(4 hours after release of patch notes)

De4thfrmbeh1nd was beyond frustrated. *Reckless* had been attacked over and over without any letup for the last hour. The first of his dungeon group had finally been taken out – he lost an entire party of five from that group when a coterie of ten casters kamikaze'd into the middle of their formation. They had no chance of getting the Dungeon Core now because they had less than the max number of raid participants needed for the guardian battle.

Although the rules didn't specifically state that they *needed* a full twenty to fight in the raid, he knew from experience that if a battle required a specific number of players involved, then having less than that was suicide. The most they would be able to accomplish was to see what challenges lay ahead of them throughout the dungeon and be better prepared next time.

De4th would have turned the guild back after they had lost a quarter of their primary players for the event, but he was encouraged by his Lieutenants to continue on to see if they could figure out who was behind all of these attacks. That kind of valuable information would be worth his whole guild wiping if it came to down to it. They actually were relatively close to their destination now, so De4th figured they might as well push on and see what they could see.

Maybe they could play spoiler and prevent another guild from getting the Core.

Chapter 14

(13 hours before release of patch notes)

Based on the main aspects of her newly acquired monsters, Krista was going to need to set something up that had mountainous terrain, long tunnels, and something that her aerial army could take advantage of. To begin with, however, she was going to need to get rid of the rooms that she had built before Devin finished his monster "shopping spree". She decided to keep the entrance room where the parties of players could gather before splitting off into different instances. It was big enough to suit that purpose and she was proud of the light columns that she had created.

For the rest of it, however, she removed everything after the entrance – rooms, hallways, décor, and traps. She received 4,020 resource points back from deleting all that – which, added to her previous total, ended up with 35,800 resource points. However, she had also received 6,400 resource points from various players and groups that had perished in the dungeon since she had last looked at her resources. Some of those players were from when the **Hearthfire Orc Guards** and **Hearthfire Ogre** wiped out everyone in the dungeon while chasing after Devin.

So, all told, Krista had 42,200 resource points to work with. She wanted to make this floor as challenging as possible without it being harder than the level cap she would place on it. When she looked back at the second floor and its level cap of 22, she figured a good level limit should be a nice round 30.

With the abundance of monster diversity to choose from, she wanted to divide the floor up into six challenging rooms as well as tunnels that would offer a significant obstacle as well. Each room needed a different strategy to complete as a group – diverse groups would have the greatest success.

After the entrance, she created a dark tunnel lined with rough-hewed rock and 10-foot ceilings. After taking right turn with a 90-degree angle, she introduced the first monster of this floor – a **Hardy Rock-burrower (Level 23)**. It would wait underground for an ambush and attack as they passed by. Not too challenging, but the difficulty would only ramp up from there.

Further down the tunnel she added an *Arrow Trap III* – which she had upgraded – as well as two and then three Rock-burrowers at a time. In addition, all the tunnels were down-sloped about 10 degrees, to make them even more treacherous.

The first big room she designed was shaped almost like a kidney bean with space stretching behind the entrance on the left and right sides. It also featured four **Dusky Rock-boarers (Level 24)** and two **Shrieking Harpies (Level 24)** that were located near an upgraded *Pit Trap III* on opposite sides of the room. A chest was located behind one of the traps on the North side of the room and the exit was on the South side of the room, also near a trap. Once past the trap on the South side of the room, a lever on the wall could be used to open up a hidden door that exited to the Southwest.

Once in the next hallway, not much would happen until they reached a turn which would present four upgraded *Fire Traps III*. She wanted to create a timing puzzle for the players but wasn't sure how to do that. "Carl, how do I get these traps to activate in a specific sequence?"

You just have to select an already placed *Fire Trap III* and a menu should pop up with options. Once you upgrade a trap to higher levels, you will see an increase in the options associated with each trap.

"Nice! Let me try it out."

Fire Trap III		
Power:	0% [-------------------------|-------------------------] 100%	
Size:	Small [-------------------------|-------------------------] Large	
Shape:	Cylindrical [-------------------------|-------------------------] Conical	
Time Delay:	0.1 Sec [-------------------------|-------------------------] 5.0 Sec	
Duration:	1.0 Sec [-------------------------|-------------------------] 10.0 Sec	
Always On:	**No**	Yes
Color:	(Available at higher level)	
Status Effect:	(Available at higher level)	
Temperature:	(Available at higher level)	

Krista was glad she had upgraded these traps – if she had known there was this kind of customization she would have done it earlier. For each of the traps, she set it to being **Always on** and with a different time delay and duration. After playing around with the sliders for a little bit, she found a challenging but solvable pattern that would make the players have to think it through. If they thought about it too long, however, she had a surprise in store for them.

After those fire traps, she had the hallway (still at a 10-degree downslope) turn the corner and presented a second set of fire traps with a completely different timing system to them. If the players were able to successfully progress this far, they followed the hallway further down the slope until they encountered a very long room. It was long because, instead of level ground, she actually built a faux mountain-side into her dungeon. This was the main reason for the down-sloping of the tunnels and hallways earlier – she needed to get deep enough to build something players had to climb.

With a 30-foot ceiling that was sloped upwards at a 60-degree angle along with the mountain, you could see a pathway zig-zagging its way up to the top. It switch-backed six times on the way up and had one open side that looked all the way to the bottom – while the other side faced the mountain.

Dispersed throughout the climb up were **Sure-footed Mountain Goats (Level 25), Goatlins (Level 25),** and **Starving Mountain Lions (Level 25)**. Toward the top, when the groups of players thought that they were almost safe, she set **Burrowgoats (Level 25)** inside the mountain that would allow them to ambush and burst out the side of the wall.

Additionally, halfway up the mountain, Krista placed a pressure-plate trigger that released a boulder from the top that would follow the pathway down. If the players were quick enough, they could run all the way back down to avoid it – but if they hesitated they would be pancakes. She had to magnetize the boulder and walls to ensure the boulder didn't fall off the pathway on the way down – after trying it once she watched it fall off on the first switchback.

On the top of the mountain, she placed another chest on a flat surface that led to the next area. This led to a hallway that traveled about 50 feet before coming to a T-junction, allowing players to choose to go to an optional mini-boss section that had exceptional loot rewards.

Krista had asked Carl about placing some sort of warning pop-up to those interested in the experience. The former dungeon admin let her know that it should be accessible after selecting the hallway leading toward the mini-boss room. Similar to how she selected the fire trap menu, she was able to create a pop-up after a "tester" had crossed a certain threshold.

In this optional area, she placed an **Ogrepult (Level 30)** as well as multiple goblins and orcs. She decided that she would figure out all the rewards later when she found out what she had left to spend on it. Before she moved on, Krista placed an upgraded *Rockfall Trap III* that would collapse the tunnel leading into the room when the players all entered. She wanted to make sure whoever dared the wrath of the **Ogrepult** wouldn't be able to chicken out once they saw what was in store for them.

If they successfully completed the room, she created a *Pitfall Trap III* underneath the rockfall that would allow them to leave. One of the options of the upgraded pitfall was the ability to link it to a trigger and to seal it up after a time delay.

If a group of players decided to bypass the optional area, they continued down the hallway until they turned a corner and encountered a 60-degree down-sloped and perfectly-smooth tunnel that essentially turned into a slide. This slide continued downward for about 200 feet – allowing for the players to run up a good amount of momentum.

About ¾ of the way down, she opened the hallway option menu and had a brief warning pop-up alerting them to "Grab the Rope!" At the bottom, she placed five ropes that were suspended from the ceiling equidistant from each other. They had a loop at the end for easy grabbing; however, if they missed, they would run full speed into an "Always On" upgraded *Spike Trap III* embedded in the wall at the end of the hallway.

A successful grab, however, would allow them to work their way to an exit hallway that was on level ground near the ropes. At the end of this hallway, players would find themselves entering a large room with a 50-foot-high ceiling. Surrounding a level walkway throughout the center of the room, the sides were filled with staggered rocky terrain that was perfect for the **Starving Mountain Lions (Level 27)** placed around the room anticipating an ambush. At the end of this area, Krista gave in to necessity and used the **Pussy-master Orc (Level 30)**. The utility of that mob was too good to pass up – despite the fact that she still didn't care for the name. After the Orc was another chest before the room exited into another hallway.

Chapter 15

(5 hours after release of patch notes)

De4thfrmbeh1nd was confused now – they had made it to their destination without any more attacks from the mysterious guild coalition. He was expecting to either get wiped out in one huge battle in front of the dungeon entrance or to continue being whittled down until there was no point in progressing any further. Now that they were here safely, he brought all the remaining members of the dungeon raid group together.

"Well, as you all know, we are one whole group short of the 20 that we need to realistically complete our objective. However, I would still like to find out what to expect inside – that way if we are one of the first guilds to tackle this we will still be ahead of the game when we come back. We'll be able to fine-tune our raid preparation so that we will be successful on the next run," De4th told the assembled group. "Meanwhile, the higher-level players will guard you on the way down until you reach the lowest floor – we don't want to lose any more of you to simple traps that could be avoided."

Voicing their approval with a resounding, *"RECKLESS!"*, they turned as an ordered mass and started filing in through the cave entrance. However, when one of De4th's higher level tanks tried to enter inside, he stopped abruptly as if he had hit a wall. Rooker – the level 67 Defender – called out, "Hold up!"

"What's wrong, Rook?" De4th asked.

"A pop-up just informed me that anyone with a higher level than the level cap on the lowest floor is barred from entering. Then it says the current level cap is 30."

"Shit! Well, I guess that's a good thing since we don't have to worry about any crazy high-level stealthers waiting for groups to go through. Guess we're waiting out here everyone; if for some reason you are successful, we'll be here to get you home safe. Domn3r, you're the raid leader – you all know the plan of succession, if he falls you move on to the next in line which, as of now, is Ambrose. Good luck and don't forget to record everything for our briefing afterword!"

De4th watched as their dungeon group all headed in and let out a breath he didn't even remember holding as he watched them enter without trouble. *It looks like that pop-up Rooker saw was correct because every one of that group was level 29 to 30.* He turned around to talk to his lieutenants – intending to go over instructions regarding the camp he wanted set up – when he noticed movement in some trees to the West. Thinking it was his eyes playing tricks on him due to the inordinate amount of stress the journey had caused, he dismissed it as nothing important.

"Hey, Sh1fty, let's have all the tanks on the outside of camp in ord...aaahhh!!!" De4th looked down and saw two arrows sticking out of his chest – 60% of his health points were gone instantly due to it being a sneak attack. Looking around, he entered stealth using his *Vanish* skill and saw that his entire guild was surrounded by what looked like 150 or so players. Already, a third of his guild lay on the ground dead because of the sneak attack – the last 42 were currently under heavy fire. They fought back with skill and courage, but it was a fruitless endeavor from the start – there were just too many.

As he watched the last of *Reckless* go down under the onslaught of arrows and spells coming their way, he tried to look at the guild tags of all the attackers. Although there was a smattering of other guilds represented, more than 90% of the players he could see were in the same guild. *Divine Truth*.

Thinking that he could escape and warn the dungeon party, he worked his way around to what looked like less of a concentration of players to the East. He knew he needed to be out of combat for at least five minutes before he would be able to communicate with the group.

The attacking raid had different ideas however – they had their casters start using their AOE – Area of Effect – spells that would damage all enemies within a certain area. These didn't have to be targeted so they were used in this instance to expose any enemy stealthers lurking about. As he got close to the Eastern line of players, he looked back at a commotion – just in time to see Sh1fty exposed by the wide ranging AOEs being cast about. *I didn't realize he was able to stealth in time.*

Unfortunately, Sh1fty didn't last long – just long enough to be a distraction to De4thfrmbeh1nd. He turned back toward his destination and saw too late that there were two casters using their AOEs in overlapping areas just entering his range. Without anywhere to run, he was exposed seconds later and taken down just as quickly.

As he was forced to logout for three hours since there was no one there to resurrect him – he thought about *Divine Truth*. They were a top-tier guild that De4th had had dealings with in the past, but they didn't run in the same circles. While *Reckless* was one of the top 20 guilds, they spent most of their time running numerous small raids and concentrating on tradecraft to build up their treasury.

Divine Truth, like most of the top-tier guilds, spent most of their time and resources completing massive raids in most of the harder dungeons throughout the game. When successful, these raids usually had tons of both gold and other extraordinary loot – which is how *they* built up and maintained their treasury.

If *Divine Truth*, or one of the other top-tier guilds for that matter, gained control of the Dungeon Core it would make them the most powerful guild within a matter of weeks – if not days. The special property of the Core would apply to everyone in the party – which a raid group technically is. Therefore, having 200+ raid members with bonuses would allow them to complete the raids quicker, get a substantially higher amount of loot, and provide more experience would make them even more powerful.

If they knew about this event beforehand, that means that they must've plans in place to keep any other guild away from the dungeon. De4th now understood why they were allowed to reach the entrance before they were killed – *Divine Truth* didn't have many low-level players in the guild. Since they had no way to get it themselves, they would have someone else do it for them. If the groups going into the dungeon were successful, *Divine Truth* would ambush and take the Core away from them without going through the trouble of killing the guardian. Alternately, they could use one of their feeder guilds to run the dungeon and take the core from them.

They needed to eliminate any higher-level opposition waiting outside the dungeon for two reasons. One, obviously, was to make sure groups coming out of the dungeon had no support. The other was to ensure no one could establish a foothold close enough to defend the area. De4th figured they actually wanted the majority of the early groups to fail in order for the dungeon to get stronger – therefore increasing the power of the Dungeon Core. Additionally, they would learn more about what challenges groups would face, which would help in equipping their own groups to combat them. It was a brilliant plan and one that he wanted to stop through any means.

Granted, he was pissed that his whole guild was wiped out – but that wasn't reason enough to want to stop *Divine Truth*. If he allowed them to succeed, the competitive nature of the guilds would taper down to almost nothing.

He had seen it in other MMORPGs before when there was a super-powerful guild with the most powerful players on the server. They would dominate everything – new content raids, PVP events, and even the player economy would suffer because they were willing to pay more for everything, so the smaller guilds couldn't afford the nicer stuff. De4th and his friends had left a couple of games in the past due to this incongruity of riches among the players – it became less fun for everyone except those in the super-guild.

Resolved to fight them, De4thfrmbeh1nd – or as he was known in real life, Tyler Windstrom – got out of his FIPOD and called up his lieutenants. Tyler and his friends had some planning to do.

Chapter 16

(9 hours before release of patch notes)

Krista was getting a little worried that she wouldn't finish before the deadline, but she forced herself not to hurry. According to the rules, she wouldn't be able to change anything once this floor went live. She had to make sure it was all done correctly the first time because if there was anything that she wasn't happy with there was nothing she could do to fix it later.

The next room on this floor was one she was excited to see in action. First, she created a giant room 500 feet long and 100 feet high. Next, she created pillars of rock that rose to differing heights – from 30 to 60 feet high – around the room that were about 12 feet across and flat on top. Each pillar was connected to one or more other pillars by sturdy bridges spanning over a ground filled with all manner of jagged rocks and sharp stalagmites.

The way that the pillars were set up in differing heights made it near impossible to see the correct path through to the end. It wasn't really a maze, but if the players chose the wrong bridge they would need to backtrack quite a bit. Krista also placed chests at the end of complicated paths that would encourage exploration. She wanted them to spend as much time as possible moving from pillar to pillar because it allowed more chances for her mobs to knock them off.

She populated the room with various **Horcies (Level 28)**, **Wyverocs (Level 28)**, **G-Bombers (Level 28)**, and **Goblin Pole Dancers (Level 28)**. They were there scattered throughout the room for the explicit purpose of knocking as many players off as possible. After finding the correct pathway through, the groups of players would arrive at a larger pillar at the far side of the room that would work as a platform for the room battle. This battle would encompass the numerous winged monsters that were a nuisance earlier in the room – though this time they would come in mass. And, of course, a chest would be present after successfully living through the battle.

For the last main room, Krista created another room that was about 400 feet long and 200 feet wide. In this room, she designed an Orc Village that contained orcs that were grouped up in parodies of the players' parties. Since she had access to different classes, she was able to put together diverse groupings of tank-healer-DPS combos that would challenge the strategies of the players who were used to fighting only semi-intelligent monsters. These groups only contained level 29 orcs, but they worked together and reacted quickly like only a computer-controlled monster could. For the last normal Orc group, she had a unique challenge for the players.

Once through the Orc Village, players would enter into a final courtyard that contained a platform with an **Ogre (Level 32)** as the room boss with **Orc Guards (Level 30)** and **Horcies (Level**

30) as additional guards. An obligatory chest would be present for any group of players that made it that far.

Exiting the Orc Village – as well as the instance – players would arrive at the Guardian Staging Room. This medium-sized area would hold all the players that made it through their respective instances so that they could prepare for the upcoming Guardian raid battle. A large door would lead into Violette's room that would also contain the Dungeon Core. Above the door was a screen that Krista was able to permanently affix to the wall based on the special upgrade menu attached to it. This screen was both a warning and an update:

WARNING! You are about to enter a raid battle with the Dungeon Guardian. BEWARE!
Max amount of raid participants: 20   Current amount of raid participants: 0   Current level cap: 30
Current Dungeon power level: 5   Current Dungeon Core bonus: 5%

Krista was holding out hope that seeing the bonus at only 5% would encourage incoming players to leave the Dungeon Core alone until it had a bigger bonus. The more time they had to accumulate resources and level up would give them a better ability to survive.

As the final – and distasteful – task to complete the dungeon arrived, Krista needed to contact Violette and ask her what she wanted for her guardian room. She was afraid to see what was going on with her at this time – she didn't want to see Devin and Violette in a compromising position if she could help it. Fortunately, when she switched her viewpoint to the current Dungeon Boss room, Violette was alone and talking off-handedly to the mobs surrounding her. It was like she couldn't help but keep trying to hold a conversation even when nothing talked back to her.

As she viewed the room, Violette seemed to sense her presence and turned toward her. "Hi, Krista! I've missed you! I figured you were busy building your new floor and couldn't get away – I've been keeping busy talking to my new friends here! Are you all done yet? Do you want to play a game? It's been so lonely here since Devin left a couple of hours ago. He said he would be back, though! I really like him – he smells nice! Don't you think? And the cute way he pretends to not understand how much I like him – it just makes me want him more! Have you seen him?"

Whoa...I almost forgot how crazy she is. And what was that about him not knowing Violette likes him? He'd have to be blind and deaf not to know that – she must be messing with me. "No, sorry, I haven't seen him. I'm actually here to find out what you wanted for your Guardian Room. It's the last thing that I need to finish, and we don't have a lot of time. I was planning on throwing something together really quick but figured it would be better, as much as I don't like it, to have your input. Anything I can do to make you more formidable would only increase your likelihood of protecting the Core – which is my main priority."

Violette jumped up and down giddily, offering a strangely-mesmerizing "bouncy" show in her upper torso region. Krista refocused as Violette stopped "bouncing" and clapped her hands together in joy, "Oooh, I'm so excited! My very own room! I have so many ideas I'm not even sure where to start! This is going to be so awesome! Ok, so first..."

This is going to suck...

Chapter 17

(7 hours before release of patch notes)

Something abruptly woke Devin up from a deep sleep. Fortunately, he woke up feeling as refreshed as if he had slept for days. He reached over to make sure his alarm clock was turned off when he felt something soft and warm in his hand. His mind finally woke up enough to realize something was slightly off – he opened his eyes to find himself face to face to a smiling Violette. Everything came crashing back – the FIPODs, their dying inside *Glendaria Awakens*, and the dungeon they were currently the caretakers of.

As all of this went through his head, he realized his hand was still clutching something. He looked at it and found that Violette was naked from the waist up and he was inadvertently touching her bare breast. Snatching his hand back as if was burned, he stammered, "y-y-y-your n-n-n-naked! W-w-why are you naked!? I-I-I-I'm sorry, I didn't mean to touch you there – I was just waking up and didn't know where I was for a moment."

He quickly stood up and looked away from the gorgeous beauty still sitting behind him. From what he could tell, she had sat there with his head in her lap for hours while he slept. *Actually, why was I sleeping? – I don't need to sleep!* He felt a little violated because Violette must have cast a sleep spell on him without even asking. He did have to admit, though, that it

309

felt good to sleep – even if it was magically produced sleep. His mind needed some time to recharge after the stressful last couple of weeks. *Still, not cool.*

He could hear Violette stand up and some rustling of clothing behind him as she said, "That's ok, Devin! I don't mind if you touch me *accidentally* – it happens! I hope you don't mind, I got a little hot while you were sleeping and needed take my top off in order to cool down. You are so cute when you sleep – so innocent-looking! But I bet you're anything but innocent, aren't you Devin? I bet you're a naughty boy on the inside – but that's ok! I like it a little naughty sometime! Did it feel good?"

Apparently, I'm still half asleep since I can't follow most of that. Not sure what she was referring to, he didn't want to piss her off, so he answered, "Uh...yes?"

"Good, I just knew that a nice sleep would do wonders for you! Sorry about using that spell on you, but I figured you wouldn't enjoy it as much if you knew it was coming."

Devin turned around cautiously, making sure that she was fully clothed before looking completely. She was, but she also had a forlorn look on her face – like she was really sorry for putting him to sleep. He thought back at how annoyed he was at her for casting that spell and reversed his decision. She was only doing it to help him and it turned out well enough. Be that as it may, "I appreciate your thoughtfulness, but next time, please ask me if you are going to do something like that. Given everything, though, it really did feel good."

And he meant that, too.

She looked happy again and expressed that with an exuberant session of hugging. With a face full of Violette he heard, "Oh, Devin, I'm so sorry! I won't do anything like that again without your permission. I am glad that it felt good for you – it felt good for me, too!"

Not quite understanding why it would feel good her for too, he somehow extricated himself from her embrace and backed off a couple of feet. "Well, that's good to hear, Violette. Anyway, I need to get going – I have to...uh...do...something...dungeon related. Yeah, I need to check out the parties still going through the different floors. I'll see you around!" Practically sprinting for the door, he was deaf to her entreaties for him to stay longer.

He needed to get out and away from that beautiful – if unstable – woman back there. Devin was afraid that he would say something stupid that would cause her to go off on him. He didn't want to die again and potentially lose some levels. Cautiously working his way back through the dungeon, he tried to avoid any groups of players making their way through the first and second floors. He wasn't equipped to fight them, as he was still playing the Pet Trainer class and didn't have any pets to help him out.

Before he left the dungeon, Devin tried to contact Krista to find out their current situation with the dungeon but there was no response from her. *She must really be hard at work – I'll just let her do her thing.* As he made his way outside, he figured he would spend his time until everything was ready killing as many players inside the dungeon as he could.

Now that their dungeon was already the focus of the Dungeon Core event, he didn't have to be as cautious about whom he killed. The more resources he could get for Krista, the better – the quicker they could level up, the more chance they had to survive. But first, he needed some help.

He ventured out into the forest and was able to locate two wolves and a boar. Since they were only level 12, he was easily able to take them down to the appropriate health by using his fists so that he could tame them. Armed with his mini army, he made his way back into the dungeon and traveled quickly back to the second floor. With these pets, he would be able to blend in a little and not call too much attention to himself. Since the floor was already full of these types of mobs, a couple more would most likely go unnoticed. Devin wanted to stay unnoticed not because of any potential floor difficulty issues that would arrive with the main-system AI, but because he wanted to live longer and not be hunted down.

Hiding out in the second-floor room with the four wolves and four boars, he waited for the next group to work their way through. He had to wait longer than usual – the players were

312

probably a little hesitant because even good groups were getting slaughtered by the new guardian. Eventually, he was able to employ his low-level pets on a group that came in looking pretty confident.

At first, they ran a textbook operation – using their tank to draw aggro, their Healer using her spells – but not too many, therefore drawing aggro – to heal him, and their DPS in the form of a Mage and a Rogue taking out the wolves and boars one-by-one. As they were fully committed, Devin sent one of his wolves to keep the Healer busy while he had the other two attacking the Mage. Even being a lower level, they made short work of the Mage due to the bonuses that Devin provided with his passive skills.

After that, he had the two Mage-killer pets target the Rogue near the Defender tanking in the middle of the room. The Rogue, with the trite name of ShadoK1lla, saw what had happened to the Mage and was ready for them. He used his *Vanish* skill and was able to stealth before they reached him. Unfortunately for ShadoK1lla, these mobs were being controlled by Devin – he just had them go to the last place he was and start biting the air in a search pattern. This did the trick; after only three seconds, his pets were able to pop the Rogue out of stealth and went to town on him. He lasted a bit longer than the Mage, but still went down before the tank could arrive to help.

As there were only three of the original mobs left in the room, he had his pets all attack the Defender and was able to take him out quickly because he wasn't getting any heals from the Healer who was busy trying to kite Devin's wolf and healing herself to stay alive. Now that there wasn't anything stopping him, he had his pets follow the room mobs as they converged and killed the Healer almost instantly.

Although he was satisfied with the destruction, he couldn't help but feel that he went a little overboard there. He was used to allowing at least the Healer to live so that the rest of the party could be resurrected and killed again. *But it felt so good!* These were not thoughts that Devin usually had after battling with other players. Normally, he felt good for a well-executed plan to strategically take out certain key players or for killing abnormally-difficult opponents. These gave him a sense of pride in his own ability to out-think the competition.

But the strange excitement and need to kill during the battle was completely unlike him. He was worried that Violette's homicidal behavior was somehow rubbing off on him. He didn't like it – it just felt wrong somehow. During the next couple of battles, Devin tried to curb these destructive impulses. He found that if he was aware of how he was feeling, it was easier for him to control himself. As time went on, it got easier and easier until he eventually found that he didn't feel...wrong...anymore. Although he was relieved that it was just temporary, he was concerned that it would come back when he spent any time around Violette. She gave a whole new meaning to "bad influence".

Chapter 18

(6 hours after release of patch notes)

Domn3r was excited to finally see the new instance floor that this whole event was all about. Even though they didn't have enough players still alive to complete the raid, there was something to be said for exploring something that had never been seen before. Usually new content that was released was for the higher-level players and were explored, beaten, and had strategies developed about it by the top-tier guilds before anyone had a real chance to tackle them. With this content being only for players up to level 30, he could actually have an impact on the best strategies that could be used to beat it.

When Domn3r and his raid group entered the dungeon, they were greeted with a prompt that informed them of something both bad and good:

Welcome to the Dungeon Core event!

PVP is disabled within the entirety of the dungeon

Communication is restricted to small parties only – Raid Chat, Guild Chat, Zone Chat, World Chat, and Personal Messaging is automatically blocked

Inside the Guardian Room, Raid Chat is available for the raid battle.

Level caps are removed from all other floors

Current level cap for event floor: 30

Thankfully, they didn't have worry about being ganked by stealthers on their way through the dungeon. It appeared the system thought about the likelihood of the dungeon itself being used as a battleground and made steps to circumvent it. That almost made up for the fact that they couldn't communicate with anyone on the outside – all forms of communication were cut off. Domn3r was hoping to keep the rest of *Reckless* informed of their progress on a continual basis but it seemed that was not in the cards. They would have to wait until they finished before talking to them.

Moving together as a group, Domn3r and the rest of the raid party moved through the first floor quickly due to the fact that there were 15 of them. When that was added to their much higher levels, all the Goblins died before many of the group members could even attack once.

With the first floor a breeze, they expected the second to be almost as easy – and they were right. They *did* manage to trip three different traps, but it was probably due to the fact that there were so many of them that they weren't being watchful of their surroundings. The **Weregoblin** and crew gave them a little trouble due to their higher level compared to the rest of the floor – but even that battle didn't last more than 20 seconds. Even though they weren't really a high enough level to have gone on raids together in Glendaria Awakens, many of the players had participated in raids in various other MMORPGs and knew how to work as a team.

Finally, they arrived down the stairs to an empty medium-sized room that had two large light columns near the entrance to the next area. As soon as they all got down the stairs, they received a system prompt:

Attention:

Please break up into separate groups of up to five (5) members each for the next area.

Each group will participate in completing the same challenges, but in a separate instance.

Communication between different groups has been disabled.

Once through the instance challenges, the groups will come together again to face the Guardian Room if they so choose.

Good luck!

About what I expected, Domn3r thought. "Alright, everybody! This is what we came here for – you all know your teams. Let's all get in there and meet up on the other side – I don't have to tell you this but…kick some ass!"

A couple of the players chuckled at that, releasing some of the tension that had built up on the way down. With a more relaxed demeanor, each group went together through the entrance ahead and disappeared after crossing the threshold as if they had entered a portal. Domn3r thought it was reminiscent of the old-school MMORPGs that would make you "zone" into different areas – you would walk into an invisible wall and the next area would have to load up before you could move through.

Domn3r watched the other two teams of five enter first and then proceeded into the instance with his group. Stepping over the threshold, he expected to feel something; however, other than a very slight resistance, there wasn't anything dramatic enough to account for "zoning" into the instance. He looked around at his team and saw that they were surprised as well at the lack of difference between the prior room and the hallway they now found themselves in.

Glancing at his fellow group members, he could see the confidence in each of them – they were good at their respective classes and knew what they were doing. Ambrose, their High Elf Healer, was one of the better healers that he had ever played with. She knew how to avoid aggro and in fact was specced to dump aggro as quick as possible if she was the target of hostilities. They had done multiple quests together and had joined *Reckless* around the same time over a month ago. He had great confidence in her ability to keep them alive.

Bolt3n, their Wood Elf Archer, had an air of confidence about him that made it seem as though he couldn't miss with one of arrows. Domn3r had grouped with him a couple of times and each time he was one of the most valuable members of the team; he was somehow able to pinpoint and pull single mobs within a group where most people would have pulled the entire bunch. He was also specced to do additional critical damage and was able to take chunks out of a boss' health point pool without generating insane amounts of damage.

Mac, short for Macgowenishburt (Domn3r never was sure where that came from and never asked), was a Dwarf Mage. It was a unique race/class combination, but that was just like Mac – unique. Similar to Ambrose, Domn3r had grouped up with him multiple times before and came to know him fairly well. He had a gruff exterior and most people would call him rude, but he was just that way if he didn't know you well. He actually had a quirky sense of humor and was funny both in and out of battle. Oh, and he was a good Mage as well.

Domn3r had only grouped with Maxinista – their Rogue – once before, but she had shown that she was able to do everything required of her and did it well. From attacking from stealth when aggro was firmly established to scouting and identifying potential hazards, Max knew her stuff. She was specced for stealth and trap detection/disarming which was slightly different from most other rogues who liked to beef up their stealth attack damage. This was perfect for them because they needed her other skills to stay alive more than the damage she could add.

That of course left Domn3r, who as their tank, was responsible to making sure no one else got hit. As a Defender, he was specced for increased aggro accumulation and damage mitigation through the use of shields. All in all, he felt pretty confident that they could survive through almost anything if they just played to their strengths and kept moving forward.

Speaking of that, they moved ahead with Max carefully checking for traps along the way. It looked as though there weren't any along this stretch of tunnel – which hopefully boded well for the rest of the floor. As they turned a corner, Domn3r was surprised from below and knocked into the air by an explosion of rock. As he landed, with only taking minimum damage, he looked up at what had hit him and saw that it was **Hardy Rock-burrower (Level 23)**. Having fought these mobs before – as they were a normal mob up on the mountain above – they made short work of it. Domn3r kept its attention while Mac lit it up with a quick couple of spells to take it down. They had a hard shell on their outside and resisted a lot of physical damage but were weak to magical damage.

With one monster down, they moved ahead with more confidence. *If this is all this dungeon has to throw at us then this should be a cake-walk*, Domn3r figured. Pressing on further down the tunnel, they encountered two more rock-burrowers and used the same strategy as before. After the quick battle, they all looked at each other with smiles on their faces.

"This is too easy – maybe we should think about finishing the raid after all. If this is where it starts it can't be too hard, right?" Ambrose questioned.

"I agree – but I hope you didn't just jinx us...," Domn3r stated as they walked further on with confidence in their steps.

Chapter 19

(90 minutes before release of patch notes)

Krista was all done with the guardian floor – she just had to go back and add in some finishing touches to some of the rooms and to add in the loot for each chest. She pulled up the resource menu to figure out what she had to work with:

Resource Expenses	
Unrecoverable Resources Spent on Rooms/Hallways/Decor:	
Small Rooms	0
Medium Rooms	400
Large Rooms	12200
Boss Room	8500
Hallways	2050
Upgrades	1800
Décor (Bridges)	1300
Décor (Lighted Columns)	50
Décor (Buildings)	1500
Décor (Miscellaneous)	4030
Total Unrecoverable Resources Spent:	31830
Recoverable Resources Spent:	
Chests	1300
Traps	6100
DUMB	5400
Total Recoverable Resources Spent:	12800

Available Resources:	50350
Total Resources Spent:	44630
Total Resources Remaining:	5720

Krista had spent quite a bit of her resources to finish everything – but it was worth it. Fortunately, she had gotten more resources from invading players while she was making changes to the floor – otherwise she wouldn't have had enough. Now she had about 5000 resource points to use to populate the loot – she had made the chests, but they were currently empty. There were five normal room chests and one optional boss chest that she needed to fill – the Guardian Room chest was already filled with the Dungeon Core and was provided free of charge.

"Carl, I want to add some loot to the chests in the form of weapons and armor, but I don't want the same thing to be in there every single time – is there a way to do that?" Krista asked.

You can access the chest menu with different options just like you did the traps earlier – just select the ones that are placed already, and you can alter its properties. The weapons and armor that you can populate it with are based on what you have available.

"What about new things that people haven't seen before? I want to be able to draw them in – especially the optional boss area — so that they are more likely to come for the weapons and armor instead of the Core."

Just like the advanced weapons and armor for your monsters, new items are only available when you have at least a blacksmith. Additional improved items are available with other buildings and NPCs as well which will be an option for you at Dungeon Level 8.

"Thanks, Carl!" Krista selected the first chest in the **Harpy** and **Dusky Rock-boarer** room to see what its options were:

Iron Chest			
Currency:	Copper: 0	Silver: 0	Gold: 0
Weapons:	(Select from available loot list)		
Armor:	(Select from available loot list)		
Items:	(Unavailable at current Dungeon Level)		
Random Loot Generator	On		**Off**
Random Loot Selection	Weapons	Armor	Items	Random
Random Loot Preference	Match to Party		Random
Random Loot Limit	0 rp		
Add Dungeon Made Loot:	(Available at Dungeon Level 8)		
Add Trap	(Unavailable at current Dungeon Level)		

From what she could tell, Krista should be able to turn on the Random Loot Generator and have it choose from whatever she had available in her loot list – she just had to designate how many resource points it could use to generate the loot. She also wanted to match the loot to the party opening the chest so that it would be something they could use – there was nothing worse than fighting a hard boss and getting some armor that only a Mage could use when no one in your party was a Mage.

For this first chest, since it was in the first room she only put 200 resources into the generator. This would hopefully provide some modest loot for the adventurer and encourage them to press on and try for more. For the rest of the chests, she increased the amount that she put in them – 400, 600, 800, and finally 1000 for the Orc Village. For the optional boss, Krista wanted to make it really special, so she put in 2000 resource points into the generator.

After the chests were all set up and all the finishing touches were done, she added some stairs connecting the first room of the new floor to the **Weregoblin** Boss room from the second floor. Instantly, she was informed that the Guardian had moved and that she needed to set the current max level for the new floor. She thought about the levels of her mobs and set it to level 30. Before she could confirm this, she received a notice that she would not be able to change anything on the new floor once she said yes. Expecting this, she nevertheless was as happy as she could be with how it turned out, so she confirmed everything.

No new notices popped up, so she went to the new Guardian Room to check in with Violette to make sure everything was to her liking — not that she could change anything now, of course. Violette was ecstatic with how her room turned out and was looking forward to "destroying all the mean people." She also had a couple of nitpicky décor details that she wanted changed or added — Krista got immense satisfaction from telling her that she couldn't change anything now that the stairs had been opened up. Pouting, Violette said, "Well, I guess it will do. If you see Devin, have him come see me — I want to show him my new crib!" And just like that, she was happy again.

Damn bipolar crazy bitch.

Chapter 20

(30 minutes before release of patch notes)

Devin heard Krista call his name when he was busy watching another group of players battle through some **Goblin Boar-riders** on the second floor. He quickly left the room while they were distracted and made his way further down the dungeon. "What's up? – I've been trying to call you for what feels like hours. It has got to be pretty close to the deadline now. How's the new floor?"

"Ugh, it was a pain in the ass – I actually wanted you to check it out because I'm rather quite proud of it. Let me give you the grand tour," Krista replied.

"I can't wait to see it – did Violette get a new room too?"

Her voice devoid of any emotion, Krista told him, "Yeah, she got one, too." *Sounds like some kind of issue between the two of them – Violette must have demanded a lot for her new room. Oh, well – none of my business.*

"Alright, let's go now – I want to see what you did!" Devin made it to the **Weregoblin** boss room and went down the stairs into the new floor. He arrived at the gathering room with the two large light columns and hallway in between them. Krista explained what the room was for and that this is where the players would split up into groups for the instances next.

As he traveled through the respective rooms, Devin made appreciative noises when he saw what Krista accomplished in what had to be a stressful time crunch. Some of the rooms and hallways that had active traps in them were not activated until there were players present so Krista had to explain some things instead of showing him personally. He couldn't wait to see it all in action. He especially liked the room with the pillars and bridges – he wouldn't want to be a player in there trying to dodge flying mobs while moving from pillar to pillar. He doubly liked the slide with the ropes and spikes at the end – it was actually fun to slide down that fast and far.

Finally, they arrived at the raid staging area and he saw the screen on the wall near the huge doorway leading to the Guardian Room. He asked her how she did that and Krista explained how Carl let her know about how to alter the characteristics of certain objects. Devin was impressed – there was so much more to this dungeon stuff than either of them had thought of before. He couldn't wait for Krista to increase in level to see what other fun things they could do. But first, they had to survive long enough.

Devin was eager to see the Guardian Room, but Krista didn't seem too enthusiastic about it.

"Why do you want to go in there – it's just another room – I didn't really have anything to do with the design either. I just put in what she wanted and left it at that – it should work well enough for her. Come on – let me show you the optional boss area we skipped over earlier."

But Devin was determined – he wanted to see what would ultimately be the room that would save them from oblivion. "We're already here, so let's just check it out really quick and then we can see that optional room – we don't have a lot of time left and it would take too much time to backtrack."

He entered into the room despite Krista's reluctance, and walked into a nightmare. At least that's what his first impression was. He didn't know exactly what he was expecting, but it wasn't this – he couldn't wait to see how the players first reacted to it. As he made his way up toward the end of the room, he could see Violette on a half-circle island butted up against the wall and surrounded by what looked like a river of lava on one side and a river of, well, *death*, was the best way he could describe it.

As soon as she saw Devin, she ran toward him in what looked like something that you would see on Baywatch. He didn't intend to stare, but his eyes couldn't move away from the spectacle heading toward him. The gravity-defying breasts were almost hypnotizing – it felt like the moment lasted forever and not long enough. Before he was able to move his eyes away, he again was enveloped in a hug that threatened to suffocate him. This time, however she let him go before too much time had passed.

"Oh my God, Devin!!! It feels like it's been ages since you last visited me! You really should come see me more often – I would *love* to see more of you! I really missed your handsome face – this place is all gloomy and you just brighten it up! How do you like my new place? Krista did a great job implementing my plans for the room! There are a couple of minor issues but otherwise it is perfect – she said she couldn't change anything else though since it is locked. Come here, tell me about your day so we can catch up! I'll tell you about what I've been doing today as well..."

Krista interrupted her, "We can't stay – we have to get ready for the incoming players. We only have about 5 minutes until the patch notes are released so we have to get going. Say goodbye to Devin for now. Come along, Devin – let's go see that optional area before it is too late."

Devin watched Violette's face while Krista was talking and watched it go from happy to downright murderous. He was afraid he'd be inadvertently killed by Violette due to a violent reaction to Krista's words. Which – to Devin at least – didn't sound like she was saying anything that would have caused that kind of reaction. He tried to diffuse the situation by telling Violette that he would come by later when there was more time.

"Stay out of it, Devin! This is between Violette and I, head back outside the room and I'll meet you there."

Devin was floored. Krista had never talked to him like that. *I guess Violette really knows how to push her buttons.*

"It's ok, Devin. Krista and I are just going to have a little chat. I'll see you later and here's something to help you remember to come visit more often." With that, Violette quickly moved in front of him and picked him up. Without warning, she planted a kiss on his lips that surprised him so much he couldn't move – and he sure as hell didn't return the kiss, either. "I'll see you later, Devin!"

Speechless, he turned around and robotically walked back out the room into the raid staging area without even remembering having walked out there. He couldn't have been there more than a couple of seconds before Krista contacted him again.

"Sorry about that, we've been having some issues – but I made sure that it won't affect the protection of the dungeon. Are you ok? You look like someone punched you in the balls." Krista's voice was a little more upbeat compared to earlier.

"Uh, yeah...I just didn't realize how affectionate Violette was – she's a really nice person, isn't she? I wasn't prepared for that – I guess she's like that with everyone though. Except for anyone attacking her – then she's pretty scary."

"Yeah...I guess she's...nice? Anyway, before we get some incoming players for the event, I wanted to go over any strategies that you may have regarding defense. So, I figure you would be best served fighting one of the instance parties instead of in the Guardian Room – Violette can take care of herself.

Plus, you'd hopefully be able to whittle down the weakest group of players so that they won't make it through to the raid."

Still trying to get over what had just happened, Devin woodenly replied, "Sure, that sounds good – whatever you say."

"Alright, then – I'm going to send you to respawn and place you in the Staging Room at the end of the floor. I'll try to let you know what I observe of the incoming groups so that you can go after the weakest links. Let me know what you need as far as weapons and armor go – I have a couple of resource points leftover after the new floor creation and would like to outfit you with at least a little better stuff."

"Ok." Devin found himself in the Transition Room, gradually coming out of the haze he had found himself in.

Chapter 21

(5 minutes before release of patch notes)

Once Devin had some time to clear his head, he was able to concentrate on the upcoming event. Putting all other thoughts and concerns behind him, he focused on devising a strategy to combat the incoming players. He'd be at a disadvantage initially being only level 22, but Devin had confidence that he'd be able to level up quickly – as long as he didn't die too often.

Looking at the list of available races, he knew that he'd see an Orc on there and was about to select it when his eye caught on something else. He was surprised – but probably shouldn't have been – to see the Ogre as a playable race as well.

Ogre (Dark)	
Racial Characteristics:	
+50% Physical damage	-50% Magical Damage
+50% Physical resistance	-50% Magical Resistance
+10 to starting Strength and Constitution	Unfriendly starting reputation with all Light races
-5 to starting Intelligence and Wisdom	

If he chose to be an Ogre, he'd be able to withstand a greater amount of damage and therefore would survive longer at these lower levels. However, he wouldn't be able to hide very well and would become a target almost immediately. He decided to wait until he was a higher level and would be able to hold his own in a straight-up fight.

Given that reasoning, he chose to select an Orc for his race – he would blend in much better with the other monsters in the dungeon and wouldn't necessarily be targeted right away.

Orc (Dark)	
Racial Characteristics:	
+20% Physical damage	+5 to starting Strength and Constitution
+15% Physical resistance	Unfriendly starting reputation with all Light races

Although the Orc was primarily used by most players as a melee character with its impressive physical damage and resistance bonuses, Devin needed more of a ranged fighter. He'd played a Mage before, which would probably work, but with his physical bonuses he'd like to be able to live longer than a hit or two if he got into close quarters. He'd never tried the

Warlock before and had only seen one in action early on in his "dungeon career".

It had been a lower-level noob that ended up dying quickly after trying to solo the first floor of the dungeon at level 12. He didn't see a lot of the "dark" races in his dungeon – probably because this location was a bit of a haul from the dark-race starting locations. Based on the characteristics of the class, however, he had high hopes that it would work out perfectly for his situation.

Warlock – A follower of the Dark, the Warlock is a primarily a Dark-based caster that can also melee when needed	
+3 to starting Intelligence	+2 to Intelligence each level
+2 to starting Wisdom	+1 to Wisdom each level
+1 to starting Strength	+20% Effectiveness/Damage to Dark-based spells and effects
+1 to starting Constitution	Starting Class Skill – Unholy Curse
Restriction: Dark Races only	

With that being selected, he needed to pick his skills which he had never really seen in action. He had 21 skill points to use, since he was still level 22, and he was looking forward to seeing what he had available.

Dungeon Upgradable Mobile Boss			
Skill Selection:			
Available Skill Points:		21	
Unholy Curse I	**(Warlock Class Skill)**	Cost to unlock:	Unlocked
Curses a single target with a Strength debuff and inflicts damage over a set amount of time			
Dark-based Damage per second:	2	Strength Debuff:	-2 Strength
Duration:	5.0 seconds	Mana Cost:	10
Casting Time:	1.5 seconds		
Phantom Bolt I		Cost to unlock:	1 skill point
Casts a bolt of dark mana towards a single target for moderate magical damage			
Magic Damage:	15	Mana Cost:	10
Casting Time:	1.0 seconds		
Fear Barrage I		Cost to unlock:	1 skill point
Causes targets in a certain area with a Wisdom score less than the caster to flee uncontrollably in fear for a certain amount of time			
Spell Area:	8 feet around the caster	Mana Cost:	30
Duration:	10 seconds	Casting Time:	0.2 seconds
Pestilence Aura I		Cost to unlock:	1 skill point
Creates an aura around the caster that does damage over time to anyone within a certain radius			
Dark-based Magical Damage:	5 per second	Mana Cost:	50
Duration:	30.0 seconds		
Summon Wispy I		Cost to unlock:	1 skill point
Summons a Wispy that floats around the caster and boosts magical damage dealt through direct damage and damage-over-time spells; cannot be targeted or killed but may be unsummoned by the caster at any time; there may be only one Wispy summoned at a time			
Magical Damage	5% increase	Mana Cost:	While active,

Increase:			Wispy consumes 20% of max mana
Casting Time:	5.0 seconds		
Life Syphon I		Cost to unlock:	1 skill point
Targets of Life Syphon take damage based on the casters Constitution which then transfers a percentage of that damage to the caster as health			
Dark-based Magical Damage:	5% of Constitution	Mana Cost:	20
Health Restored:	25% of damage dealt	Casting Time:	1.0 seconds
Major Rot I		Cost to unlock:	1 skill point
Major Rot causes a target to rot from the inside out, which deals a massive amount of damage-over-time			
Dark-based Magical Damage:	30 per second	Mana Cost:	100
Duration:	10.0 seconds	Casting Time:	2.5 seconds
Summon Knightmare I		Cost to unlock:	1 skill point
Summons a temporary spirit that will effectively act as a defensive tank for a short duration; does no damage but all aggro accumulated by the caster is directed toward the Knightmare; there may only be one Knightmare summoned at a time			
Physical Resistance:	200% of Casters' Physical Resistance	Duration:	60.0 seconds
Casting Time:	3.0 seconds	Mana Cost:	While active, Knightmare consumes 30% of max mana

Devin wasn't exactly sure which way to play this class, but he could see some possibilities. He could rule out the *Summon Knightmare* spell because players didn't really pay attention to aggro rules – they just attacked whoever they wanted to. The way he saw it, most conventional players would tend to go the DOT or direct damage route. They probably only spammed those spells continuously with a Knightmare as tank to absorb damage. Devin could see why that level 12 Warlock thought he could solo the dungeon – at a higher level he probably had a good chance to do it – but unfortunately for the noob, he didn't know what he was doing.

Devin decided to take a vastly unconventional build to his Warlock. Based upon the dungeon floor he had to defend, he found the best way to defeat the incoming players was to use the dungeon against them. To this end, he took *Fear Barrage IV* for 10 skill points, *Life Syphon IV* for another 10 points, and *Phantom Bolt I* for 1 point.

Fear Barrage IV upped its range to 32 feet around the caster and lasted 22 seconds instead of 10. It also brought the cost up to 90 mana per cast, but it would be worth it. *Life Syphon IV* upped the damage to 14% of Devin's Constitution and absorbed 40% of the damage dealt – with a cost of 50 mana instead of 20. He picked up *Phantom Bolt I* so that he'd have some ranged direct damage in case he needed it.

In order for his plan to work, he needed to up his Constitution and Wisdom as his main attributes. With that in mind, this is where he ended up:

Character Status					
Race:		Orc	Level:		22
Class:		Warlock	Experience:		2200/2200
Strength:	0	Physical Damage:	0	Magical Damage:	120

Constitution:	70	Physical Resistance:	138	Magical Resistance:	240
Agility:	0	Health Points:	700	Mana Points:	500
Intelligence:	50	Health Regeneration:	210.0 per min	Mana Regeneration:	360.0 per min
Wisdom:	120	Block:	0	Critical/Dodge Chance:	0.0%
Skills:				Unholy Curse I, Fear Barrage IV, Life Syphon IV, Phantom Bolt I	
Upgrades:				Lure	

Devin had enough health points that he wouldn't die immediately from being hit by melee, and he had a bit of magical resistance to help with any casters targeting him. If he got into trouble, he could always use the *Life Syphon IV* to raise his health back up. His main weapon was going to be the *Fear Barrage* IV – there were so many traps and high places to fall off of that he was hoping he would take them by surprise. His thought that his Wisdom was high enough that there wouldn't be anyone out there that had a higher amount except for some of the Wisdom-based classes. If that was the case, he could target the immune ones with his other spells to take them out.

Now that he was ready, he materialized into the Staging Room and asked Krista for some gear.

"What do you need most?" Krista asked.

"Strangely enough, I need Constitution, Intelligence, and Wisdom stat bonuses."

After looking through her loot menu, she told him that she couldn't find anything that had all of those together. The best she could do was a Ring of Intelligence+2, a Ring of

Constitution+2, and a Necklace of Wisdom+2 — each of which gave him an additional +25 to each stat and pretty much used up all her remaining resource points after getting him some basic armor. Happy with that, Devin thanked her and set to wait for the upcoming invasion of players that was sure to come soon.

Chapter 22

(7 hours after release of patch notes)

Domn3r was wrong. Dead wrong. Nine different times dead wrong. That was how many times one of them had died – including him twice – and they still had more of the floor to go through. Fortunately for them, none of those deaths were Ambrose; otherwise they would have been screwed without her *Resurrection* spell. This dungeon was turning out to be much harder than they had expected.

It wasn't even the mobs that killed them – at least not directly. True, there were some strange combinations of monsters that no one had ever seen before, but that made it even more exciting to test their mettle against a new foe. Neither was it some hidden trap that wasn't detected – well, except for that once – that killed them. What actually killed them eight of the nine times were the traps that were obvious and in plain sight.

Their first two deaths were delivered to them in the very first room after the initial hallway. When they walked in, directly in front of them they saw two **Harpies** steadily keeping themselves afloat. To the left and right, Domn3r saw some obvious pit traps about 30 feet from the center of the room. *Obviously, whoever designed this wants the harpies to pick up and drop the players into the pits – how typical.* Convinced this was the biggest threat, he advanced into the room and grabbed the attention of the **Harpies**. Fortunately, his strength was high enough that although they tried to grab and lift him they were easily brushed off. Bolt3n took this opportunity for some target practice and was able to take them out quickly.

After they were dead, he looked toward the North side of the room and saw a chest that was located about 10 feet behind the pit trap. He sent Max ahead to check for traps just in case; she was almost there when she was launched into the air in a cloud of dust. She landed just shy of the pit trap and Domn3r and the rest of the crew rushed over to guard her while she recovered. Figuring it was another rock-burrower, they were surprised when out of the dust they saw a **Dusky Rock-Boarer** charging toward Max before she could get to her feet. Both impacts didn't really do a whole lot of damage – but the fall into the pit trap did. After she died instantly upon impact, Domn3r led the rest of their group around the pit trap toward this new monster they had never seen before.

It looked like the other rock-burrowers except for the face – it looked eerily similar to a **Dusk Boar** that they had just killed on the previous floor – with tusks and everything. *Must be a strange mixture of both of them*, Domn3r thought. While they were getting in position to take revenge on this strange looking creature, Bolt3n apparently got too close to another one of these critters and was launched upwards. Unfortunately for him, he was launched forward enough to land in the pit as well – killing him just as quickly as Max.

Enraged at this development, Domn3r quickly grabbed both of their attentions and, while they did try to charge at him, he was able to block them both with his shield. He could hear Ambrose start to resurrect Max which would take a while; she knew her business enough to know that Domn3r most likely wouldn't need help.

Mac pulled out all the stops and used his strongest AOE spells in order to kill them both as quickly as possible. When they were dead, Max was resurrected and soon after Bolt3n was as well. They all just looked at each other and were so shocked at those quick deaths that they didn't even know what to say. It wasn't anybody's fault so there was no one to blame and there wasn't anything they could have done to prevent something they didn't know was there.

With silent resolve to be more cautious in the future, they all turned toward the chest and had Max check it for traps – they weren't taking any chances now. Inside the chest was a rare quality bow that was a slight upgrade for Bolt3n – a small consolation for his death. After this, they looked around the room searching for the exit and finally noticed a lever on the South wall. Cautiously making their way there, they stayed as far away from the pit trap as possible. They still triggered one of the rock-boarers, but since they weren't facing the pit there wasn't any major harm done and took care of it quickly.

Pulling down on the lever, they were ready for anything –
instead of another attack, though, a door opened along the
Southwestern wall. Sending Max ahead again to check for traps,
they descended the hallway until they started to feel the
temperature start to rise the further they traveled. Just ahead,
Max found a trap curiously placed along the right side of the wall
just opposite of a left-hand turn. She didn't take the time to
disarm it because it wasn't anything that they would accidentally
trigger; instead, they moved up the hallway a couple of feet until
it turned left again. This is where the heat was coming from –
four different fire traps were spouting flames at differing
intervals.

They all stood watching the flaming jets that the wall was
emitting and tried to find a way around. As Domn3r kept
watching for about a minute, he thought he might have a
solution. "Hey guys, does it look like there is aaaahhhh!?!" He
just happened to be the one standing where a **Burrowgoat**
erupted out of the wall like a shot from a gun. Normally he
could take a charge and deflect it without too much damage, but
he was unprepared and had his shield on his other arm – as a
result he went flying back down the hallway they just came
down. The last thing Domn3r heard before he died was a click
and then he was being resurrected by Ambrose about a minute
later.

Apparently, we should probably just disarm any and all
traps we see. He had gotten his whole body filled with spikes

that had erupted from the wall and with the additional damage from the **Burrowgoat,** he died pretty much instantly. When he got all healed up and ready to go, they went back to the Fire Traps and Domn3r repeated what he was trying to say earlier – that the jets looked to be in some sort of pattern.

"You're right – I've been watching them while you were being resurrected. Mac and Bolt3n took care of that **Burrowgoat** – it didn't have as much resistance as the others but *apparently*...it can bust through vertical walls. In case you wanted to know," Max stated matter-of-factly. She said this with such a straight face and serious attitude that everyone else started to laugh as the tension of the last couple of minutes was broken.

When they settled down again, they quickly figured out the pattern and were able to negotiate their way through with only Mac getting slightly singed; with his short Dwarven legs he couldn't move as fast as the rest of them. Just after getting through *that* "puzzle", they were faced with nearly the same thing further down the hallway – except now there were five jets of fire.

Taking a cue from the last near-disaster, they looked for and found a trap on the wall similar to before and had Max disarm it. Then, Domn3r stood in front of the wall and after about a minute another **Burrowgoat** erupted from the wall and was deflected by his shield – where they then made short work of it.

Confident but still wary that they had solved that problem, they stood in front of the fire traps and tried to work out the pattern. It was a little harder with the additional jet thrown in – regardless, they were able to figure it out in a couple of minutes. As they made their way through, Mac brought up the rear and was just about to start moving through the jets of fire when another **Burrowgoat** erupted from *behind* him. Instead of launching him into the disabled spike trap, it instead sent him flying through all the fire traps. He landed and got to his feet right in the middle of the last jet and got a face full of flames, burning him alive.

Funnily enough, the **Burrowgoat** tried to follow and, apparently, was not immune to the dungeons' own traps because it burned up before making it halfway through. Domn3r was able to quickly grab onto Macs' corpse while the jet was off and drug him toward the rest of the party. Once Ambrose resurrected him and healed him up, they journeyed further ahead.

Max checked for more traps but there were no more throughout the next 100 feet of hallway – nor was there anything of note either. Not until they emerged into a huge room that climbed so far up into the air that they could barely see the top.

"I've never seen anything like this...I've played plenty of RPGs before and have never heard of a *mountain* underground," remarked Ambrose.

They all agreed with her statement as they looked upwards with their mouths hanging open – they were highly impressed. *Whoever designed this really went all out – I can't wait to see what's next!* Even though they had a rough time of it so far, it was still fun to challenge a new dungeon like this. You never knew what would be lurking around the corner – it could be something rather mundane or it could be a *mountain*.

After spying a pathway that started at the bottom and zig-zagged its way up the mountain, they began their "hike" to the top. The first half of the climb was pretty straightforward – they encountered some goats that tried to knock them off the pathway to the bottom but, again, the group had encountered them in the mountains above so knew what to expect. They expected to see some weird variations of monsters like they had seen before and after the goats they encountered some **Goatlins**.

These strange looking creatures looked like **Goblins** if you were to give them the bottom half of a goat and horns on top; you'd almost want to call them Satyr-like, but that would be a misnomer. Instead, they were really funny-looking as you watched as they nimbly traveled up and down the steep cliffs like they were walking on a flat surface. Domn3r thought it was their facial features – mostly Goblin with a little goat mixed in – *both are stupid-looking, and this just enhances it.*

They weren't that hard to kill – although when they paired up with a couple of **Starving Mountain Lions** it was a lot harder to keep up with all of them as they liked to move around a lot. The Lions would ambush one of their groupmates and the **Goatlins** would run up and down quickly, getting a couple of pot-shots in before retreating. Fortunately, they had some quality ranged players in the group and they were able to hit the quick-moving targets with ease.

The mobs on the latter-half were a bit harder – there were mixtures of lions and goats that proved to be a potentially deadly combination. The lions would ambush and hold down a player while a goat would race down the mountain in a rush and try to knock them off the mountain. Domn3r just made sure he had all of the aggro – he could block anything they tried to hit him with. There was also a stretch of pathway that had about a dozen **Goatlins** that tried to surround them, but Mac used his *Fire Wall* spell and burnt every one that got close.

The hardest stretch of the mountainous climb was the last – four **Burrowgoats** ended up launching themselves out of the side of the cliff with no warning. The first time it happened, they got lucky and it only clipped Bolt3n, which catapulted him near the edge but didn't knock him all the way off. After that, Domn3r made sure to face the side of the mountain with his shield facing forward in order to deflect incoming **Burrowgoat** projectiles.

Where they made a mistake on the mountain was actually not related to any of these monsters they encountered. Halfway up the mountain, Mac accidentally stepped on a hidden stone that depressed into the ground about six inches. Everyone instantly stopped and stood there looking around for whatever trap that had just triggered. Not seeing anything, they continued up the mountain cautiously – still wary of potential trap surprises. Eventually, they heard a rumbling coming from the top of the mountain.

"What is that? It sounds like the mountain is coming down on top of us," questioned Ambrose.

"I'm not sure...what is that...OHSHITRUN!" Max had been looking up toward the top and suddenly sprinted back down the pathway as quick as she could. Following her lead, the rest of them ran after her as fast as they possibly could. Behind them Domn3r glanced at a giant boulder traveling down the mountain – following the pathway – and was picking up speed. Unfortunately for Mac and Domn3r – who couldn't run as fast as the others due to short legs and heavy armor – the boulder was quickly catching up. Fifty feet from the bottom, first Mac and then Domn3r ended up getting squished flat as a pancake.

After a lengthy resurrection process, they were able to finish the rest of the climb and eventually made it to the top where they found another chest. They opened it and found an even nicer Shield for Domn3r. It was a step up from what Bolt3n had gotten earlier – the loot looked like it was getting better with each chest they opened. Domn3r was excited to see what else would they would find.

Once again on the move, they traveled along the flat top of the mountain to the exit at the Northeastern part of the room. This exit led to a long hallway that eventually arrived at a side path about 50 feet in. Domn3r looked at the side path and had Max check it out quickly so that they could figure out what way they should go. About 10 feet down the path, Max stopped, and a screen popped up for everyone in the group:

WARNING!

You are about to enter an optional Mini-boss area!

Caution! The challenge in this area is much greater than the rest of this floor but the rewards are increased as well!

Enter if you dare!

"Uh...don't think I want to go in there," stated Mac instantly. The rest of the group agreed but they couldn't help but think about what the rewards would be if they completed it. However, they were here more on a fact-finding mission and couldn't afford to die due to a side quest. Continuing down the original hallway for about another 100 feet, they turned right and stumbled upon a downward-sloping hallway that they couldn't see the end of.

"What do we do now?" asked Ambrose.

"Well, seeing as there isn't anywhere else to go, I guess we go down. The slope doesn't look too bad – I think that if we are careful and go slow we can walk down the slope." Domn3r led his crew down the slightly sloping hallway and everything was fine for about 40 feet. After those 40 feet, however, the slope increased dramatically, and they were barely able to stay upright. Bringing up the rear, Mac lost his balance and started sliding down the ramp, running into the rest of the group from behind. Soon enough, they were all sliding down at increasing speed, until they all received a quick pop-up that said, "Grab the Rope!"

They were still in a bit of a jumble together in their slide down the hallway; when they were finally able to see some rope hanging from the ceiling in the distance, Bolt3n and Max couldn't grab onto the looped ropes because they were facing the wrong direction. Mac, Domn3r, and Ambrose grabbed onto the rope and almost had their arms ripped out of their sockets. Because they were going so fast their momentum almost swung them up to the ceiling.

When they finally settled to a stop, they looked around and saw an exit on the West side of the wall within easy reach — there were easy handholds built into the floor so that they didn't slide anymore. When they looked at the end of the hallway, they saw Max and Bolt3n impaled upon a Spike Trap that was in the sprung open position. Once they scrambled to safety, Ambrose used her *Resurrection* spell again for the eighth and ninth times so far in the dungeon.

And so now here they were — nine deaths in and who knows how close they were to the end of this floor. They had taken a beating every step of the way and, although they were a determined bunch, there was a limit to what they could take. Domn3r was tempted to try to turn back now but there was no way to get back up that slide – they would have to brave the rest of the dungeon and see how long they could survive.

Chapter 23

(8 hours after release of patch notes)

When the patch notes released eight hours ago, Devin was excited and nervous at the same time. He was expecting an immediate response to the start of the "event", but he should have known better – it took time for players to make it to the location of their dungeon. By hour five, Krista had told him about a couple of players who had entered and then left within a minute of entering.

By hour six, Devin was really bored – there hadn't been any full parties that had come into the dungeon since before the beginning of the event. Eventually, Krista informed him of a large incoming party – but there were only 15 of them and not the full 20 they would need for the raid. Devin figured they were just testing the waters and wanted to check out what was in store for them. As they made their way through the first two floors, Krista gave him a rundown of the players in the shrunken raid group.

When they broke up into their instance parties, he chose to try his new class out with one of the weaker groups – the one with what appeared to be the leader was a little much for him at his level. The group he chose wasn't obviously weaker – as in levels or equipment – but they lacked the cohesion needed to work well as a team. Krista could see this in the way they fought over insignificant things and would need some prompting from other members of their team to perform essential functions like *healing*.

He was waiting in the Staging Room at the end of the floor; when all of the player groups traveled into the beginning of their different instances he entered from the end. As he arrived, he received three different screens with a picture of each group on separate ones. He figured he would normally have four screens to choose from, but because there were only three groups this time there was one less.

He chose the group Krista had marked as the weakest group – he could figure out the right one by the description of the garishly-dressed female Elf Sorcerer decked out in neon orange and hot pink. He had heard that you could change the color of your armor and accessories, but it was expensive; if he had that kind of money he definitely would use it on something more substantial and not cosmetic. Concentrating on that screen, he could see it highlight around the edges and then fade away. Next thing he knew, he was standing at the end of the Orc Village near the **Ogre** boss.

Devin made his way through the Orc Village and through the next room with the pillars and bridges. Even though he was shown the way through the "maze" of bridges, he still ended up taking a couple of wrong turns before he made it all the way through. He wanted to hurry and get into position before the group got too far – he wasn't sure how long it would take for them to get through the first room and hallways and he had already wasted a lot of time.

He ran past the **Pussy-master Orc** and waved to all the lions sitting glassy-eyed on the rocks in the room. He had reached the hallway with the gigantic slide when he faced a dilemma – he couldn't get up the sloping ramp.

"Krista, how do I get up this? If I try to walk up it, I'll just slide right back down – please tell me you put something in to climb up it."

"Of course I did – I actually made it so that if players wanted to turn around and exit the dungeon then they could. I am more than happy to let any disinterested parties leave – it would be less that we need to defend against. I just made it a little difficult to see – walk toward the far side of the slide from where you are from. There you'll see a small handrail that blends into the wall and the slope has small depressions in it on just that side that will work like steps. It's a long climb but you have some time – most of the groups are just barely finishing the first room and there have already been some deaths! Of course, they were resurrected quickly but it was still some more experience for me."

"Nice – how long until you level up again?" Devin asked.

"Well, I started the event at 66,900 experience and already got 6,000 from the deaths so far from these players. I didn't even think about their higher levels giving more experience – I'm going to level up pretty quickly if they keep dying like this. I only need 2,100 more experience to level up now and I don't think it will take that long…wait…now only 600 more."

"Awesome – I feel like I'm missing out on all of the fun. I'm going to head up now and wait for my group on the mountain where I can do the most harm. I can't wait to try out this Warlock!"

"Good luck – I'll keep you informed of where they're located so you can be ready."

Devin practically raced up the slide and was tired by the time he got to the top. Catching his breath and resting his legs, he made his way over to the top of the mountain and he had a good view of everything down below. Krista told him that his group was just making its way through the fire traps and had lost their healer – which was unfortunate for all of them since they couldn't resurrect any that he managed to take out.

Looking down at the bottom, he finally saw them emerge looking battered and singed in places. He could especially see the Sorcerer in the bright colors looking a little dimmer with streaks of burnt cloth in various places around her body. When she respawned, the clothing would look normal again – but for now she was probably self-conscious about her outfit. He chuckled a little thinking about that.

As they made their way up the mountain, fighting through the goats, lions, and **Goatlins,** Devin waited patiently for them to pass the Boulder Trap. He didn't want to get caught in it since he would be squished just as easily as they would be. Fortunately (at least for Devin), they just missed triggering the trap; as they made their way near the lion and goat section he started moving down, keeping as close to the wall as he could in order stay out of sight.

When they got to the next section, Devin hurried down and rushed toward where they were distracted fighting the small **Goatlin** horde. They didn't see him right away – which was fortunate for Devin – but as he ran to get as close to them as possible, he saw the technicolor Sorcerer start to cast a spell in his direction.

He slid to a stop – figuring he was close enough – and used his *Fear Barrage IV* spell which had a very short casting time. Instantly, the faces of all four players turned to fright and they took off in random directions. He idly wondered what it actually felt like to have that spell cast on him, but his thoughts were interrupted by the spectacle unfolding in front of him.

One player immediately jumped off the mountain and could be heard screaming on his way down to the bottom. As soon as he hit the bottom, Devin saw that he got enough experience to get to level 23 since he was right on the cusp. As he was congratulating himself, he watched another player run straight into the waiting **Goatlins** and was slaughtered quickly by their *Surround* skill. The third player ran further up the mountain and he lost track of what she was doing – but since she was alone against the next section of **Burrowgoats** he wasn't too worried. What did worry him was that damn Sorcerer.

The eye-straining, walking traffic cone ran screaming, yes *screaming*, down the mountain again — somehow staying on the pathway. As the fear timer ran out, she came to a rest near one of the turns in the pathway — which just happened to be the one with the Boulder Trap trigger. Not realizing she triggered it, she ran back up the pathway in order to help out the rest of her team — unaware that it was already too late for most of them. Devin threw a couple of *Phantom Bolts* toward her which did a little damage — she must have had a high magical resistance.

As soon as she was close enough, she cast an upgraded *Mind Prison* on him which trapped him within his own mind — which to Devin felt like the longest 30 seconds of his life. He couldn't move, couldn't see, couldn't hear, and the only thing he could do was wait it out — which was such a helpless feeling that he vowed never to be caught like that again. It was bad enough if they killed him, but to be trapped within your own mind without being able to defend yourself was worse. When he could finally see and move again, he saw the rest of the **Goatlins** had been killed by some AOE fire spell and the Sorcerer was facing him casting a lengthy spell.

Worried that it might be *Hypno Strike* which he had seen before and knew it had a long casting time, he started to use his *Life Syphon* spell to try to do enough damage before it was too late. He managed to get one off before his mind registered a loud noise behind him. Before he could turn, the Sorcerer finished her spell and Devin lost all control of his body. He was staring straight toward his new "mistress", when he saw her looking behind him in horror. She turned around and started running but before he could see her get far he was hit from behind and ended up back in the Transition Room.

He found out a little later from Krista that the Sorcerer, whose name she told him was Idylliss, didn't get much further than him before she was run over by the boulder as well. All told, the group he was up against contributed 8,950 experience toward increasing the dungeon level and 6,000 toward his own development. When he was able to look at his character sheet again, he had increased his level to 25 – but the death at the end lost him a full 1,500 experience which brought him back down to 24. *Not bad for a quick battle like that – it sucks that I lost so much from that one death though.* He asked Carl why he had lost so much when it was a boulder that killed him.

The boulder that killed you was a direct result of a player releasing it to roll down the mountain. Therefore, you lost a calculated amount based upon the difference in levels, size of the party faced, and damage you caused prior to death. If you had been closer in levels, you would have lost even more experience.

Devin was worried about how much experience he would lose when he maxed out his level and was on even ground with the other players. There was a possibility if he wasn't careful that he could lose multiple levels in one death. *That's something to worry about later when I get there – I just have to make sure to keep my deaths to a minimum.* The groups coming into the dungeon would only get harder from now on and he needed to be ready.

Krista also let him know how the other groups were doing. He wasn't able to respawn until after they completed their instances, so he was interested in their progress. The strongest group was still progressing through their instance and was approaching the Lion's Den room. They hadn't permanently lost anyone yet – although they had chocked up nine deaths already. The other, weaker group managed to make it up the mountain with only a couple of deaths. However, they foolishly decided to try out the optional boss area – where they wiped quickly because they were unprepared for the onslaught of goblin projectiles from the **Ogrepult** stationed there.

From all the experience gained from these players alone, Krista told him that she was only 6,650 away from the next Dungeon level. *Holy crap, she went up almost two dungeon levels from just this one raid party – at this rate we'll be at level 10 or beyond in no time at all.* He congratulated Krista on a job well done and complimented the floor design again. There was so much variety that it would take the players a while to learn it all – but that is, of course, when it would get dangerous for Devin and Krista.

Chapter 24

(9 hours after release of patch notes)

De4thfrmbeh1nd walked out of the meeting with the guild heads that he and his Lieutenants had managed to put together on short notice. He didn't even know he could get a headache in the game but apparently you could get massive ones. He was frustrated with those greedy bastards that led the two top-tier guilds that he had invited to the meeting. The most he got from them was a promise not to interfere with whatever *Reckless* wanted to accomplish – but he didn't think that would last long if push came to shove.

The leaders of *Kingslayers* and *Sweat Success* (De4th once asked if it should be *Sweet* instead of *Sweat* but was rudely informed that it was correct the way it was) were the top-tier groups that were in direct contention on the leaderboards with *Divine Truth*. They walked into the meeting with slimy-looking smiles and he found out later with absolutely no intention of helping out.

When he first contacted them about the impending disaster waiting to happen with *Divine Truth*, they seemed receptive to hearing his concerns and ideas regarding what they could do about it. He invited a couple of other not-so-powerful guilds as well but if they didn't have the top-tier guilds on board there was no chance of going up against them and winning. All seemed to be going well once the meeting started but after about 10 minutes he realized that he wasn't going to get any help from those in power – they just wanted more power for themselves.

They humbly apologized for not being able to help in the campaign against their rival, but they had their own raids to plan and would be looking for their own ways to acquire the Dungeon Core as well. They promised not to get in the way of what *Reckless* wanted to do but they would not offer any direct help. In De4th's opinion, they were so unprepared for what *Divine Truth* was doing that they didn't have a chance in acquiring it for themselves.

He tried entreating them with stories of the loot available inside and that it would only get better as time went on, but they had no need for the lower-level stuff available from there. He did catch the interest of some of the other guilds and had high hopes that they might come around to help in time. However, he believed that when that time came it would already be too late.

When he got back to his own guild, he let them know that they were on their own. He wasn't sure what they could do but they needed to take advantage of any opportunity to sabotage the plans of *Divine Truth*. Most of the guild was on board with the plan and he still had the opportunity to make alliances with some other interested guilds – he just prayed he had time enough.

Chapter 25

(8 hours after release of patch notes)

     Still feeling beaten up quite a bit from their experience so far in the dungeon, Domn3r followed Max down the hallway after the slide until they arrived without incident at the next room. Cautiously peeking inside, Domn3r saw a tall, largish room with a flat pathway meandering through small, mountainous terrain on each side. He couldn't see the end of the room due to the rock in the way, but he could see the reflections from eyes scattered around the slopes. Prepared for an ambush, Domn3r led the way with the rest of the group in tight formation with eyes roaming over everything.

     The expected ambush wasn't as bad as they feared – only four **Starving Mountain Lions** ambushed them singly on their way through. Each of the Lions was easily dispatched due to their vigilance in looking for potential ambushes. Domn3r was confused why more didn't attack because the prime time to ambush would have been when they were already being distracted by another lion. He could sense more waiting but couldn't for the life of him figure out what they were waiting for.

     He may have gotten his answer when he saw an Orc standing near the exit of the room. He had a mountain lion lying by his side, with its tail twitching back and forth lazily. Domn3r looked at the name of the mob and saw it was called a **Pussy-**

master Orc. *Wait...what? Pussy-master?* He couldn't help it –

he laughed out loud, startling his fellow party members. They

looked at him and he was laughing so much all he could do was

point at the Orc – which got them laughing as well. Well,

everyone except Ambrose – she just looked offended, but with a

small smile.

Climbing out of his FIPOD minutes later, he realized they

shouldn't have laughed at that Orc – even if the name was

funny. While they were all laughing, the **Pussy-master Orc**

summoned five Lions from the mountains surrounding them and

they were attacked on all sides. Three of them immediately

went for Ambrose and took her health down to nothing in three

seconds. Domn3r tried to taunt them all away but it was too

late for her by that time. Mac managed to kill one that was

going for him but the other one *Ambushed* Bolt3n and had him

down to 25% life by the time Domn3r was able to taunt him off.

Unfortunately, while he was busy defending against

these lions, the lion that was sitting next to the Orc made an

appearance behind him and laid down some major hurt. It was

attacking so fast that he couldn't defend himself and the

damage mitigation skills he was using still let massive amounts

of damage through – it was as if it was ignoring his armor. He

lost control of aggro from the other lions while trying to deal

with that crazy one; they ended up ganging up on first Max, then

Mac, and with only one left they took out the already injured

Bolt3n. By that time, Domn3r was down to 10% health himself

and had just managed to kill the crazy cat before the last, slower one could attack him.

Now more confident, he strode toward the last lion when he got hit from behind. *I forgot the Orc!* As it was a surprise attack, it did a bit more damage than normal and, as he spun around to defend against the Orc, he was hit by a pouncing lion. That was enough to finally put him down; if he ever got the chance to travel through this dungeon again, he wouldn't make the mistake of laughing at that Orc.

He contacted his guild leader, De4thfrmbeh1nd, through a messaging service and found out about what had happened after they entered. He was as furious as the rest of them about the ambush outside of the dungeon and vowed to get back at them somehow. He also found out what had happened to the rest of his raid group – they weren't even as successful as *his* group was. That floor was hard – but he knew if they practiced enough and knew where all of the traps were located it would be doable.

What he really wanted now was to have another crack at it.

Chapter 26

(24 hours after release of patch notes)

Krista was pleased at how things were going so far. They both had raked in lots of experience and there weren't any parties of players that had even finished the entire instance yet – although some had gotten close. It was only a matter of time before they all learned the ins and outs of the mobs and traps and developed a strategy to defeat it.

She hadn't been idle, however. Krista had watched how each successive party that went through developed strategies to defeat both her mobs and her traps. She kept in mind what did and didn't work for when she built her new dungeon floor underneath the current Guardian Floor. As she continued to accumulate resource points, she watched Devin work and level up as he defeated party after party. When he was level 28, he finally got caught by a group that had a high-wisdom Mage that took him out after he cast his fear spell. He ended up losing almost two whole levels as a result – which made him decide to change his class to one with more range.

But what she really enjoyed was watching greedy teams of players attempting her optional boss area. When they walked in, full of confidence for getting that far without any problems, they were sealed in the room by the Rockfall Trap that covered up the entrance. Seeing the futility of trying to dig their way out, they continued through the hallway they were walking down until they emerged in a giant room 300-feet-tall and 500-feet-long on each side. Splayed out in front of the emerging group of players were 80 low-level goblins (around level 10) on their hand and knees in supplication toward the far end of the room. There, an **Ogrepult** stood on a dais surrounded by an **Orc Sorcerer** on one side and an **Orc Mage** on the other.

The trick to this battle was to rob the **Ogrepult** of all his ammunition before he could use it – namely the low-level goblins. The problem was, that if you didn't have large enough AOE spells to take out great amounts of them all at once then they would rush to gather near the dais. If this happened, the **Ogrepult** would snatch up and hurl the goblins with bone-crushing force and uncanny accuracy towards the players. Most of them couldn't take more than one or two hits before they died and if they rushed the boss without killing all the goblins, then the **Ogrepult** would use his *Goblin Cyclone* attack that would wipe them out quickly.

So far, not a single party that had attempted the optional area had gotten close to completing it. Which was good, because Krista would like to keep it unbeaten long enough to accumulate more experience from the unprepared players. In fact, she had just leveled up to Dungeon Level 8 and had been meaning to look at what she had unlocked.

Dungeon Player Administration Toolset		
Available Resources:	76250	
Additional Resources:	Yes	
Dungeon Level	8	
Dungeon Experience	140250/180000	
Add/Delete Objects:		
	NPCs	(Select for more options)
	Buildings	(Select for more options)
Upgrade:		
	NPCs	(Select for more options)
	Buildings	(Select for more options)

Finally, Krista now had access to the Buildings and NPCs option that she had been seeing since she first was integrated into the dungeon. She selected the building option and pulled up the menu...and was severely disappointed. All the resource point requirements for the buildings were in the millions – she couldn't afford anything except for...a shrine.

"Ok, Carl – what's the deal? I thought you said that I could get advanced weapons and armor with a blacksmith and make other stuff with these buildings – but I'll never afford them. Well, everything except a shrine – what's that?"

I wasn't able to access most of the information until it was unlocked when you reached Dungeon Level 8. Apparently, this aspect of the "Dungeon Player" profile was never fully developed and tested. Normally, The AI will regulate the points necessary for anything that is not completely tested fully, but the "event" has put a hold on any changes that may be needed. In the future, when this "event" is over, it will most likely change all of the point values to something more reasonable.

The shrine is what players can use to set their bind point to – it will not directly benefit your dungeon but will allow players who die in the dungeon to respawn nearby. This will allow them to try the dungeon again without having to travel a long distance to get here. Basically, it is a way to increase player traffic flow.

"Well, that sucks, Carl." Krista wasn't happy but she kind of understood what was happening – The AI wanted them to sink or swim using what they currently had. Having access to buildings and NPCs would undoubtedly make them much more powerful – more powerful than most players would be able to overcome. That being said, the one thing that was available actually sounded like a good idea. It cost only 5,000 resource points and she needed to place it just inside the dungeon entrance. She went ahead and paid the cost and placed it in the front entrance room when there was no one around.

Krista turned back to the newest raid group of players that had come in while she was accessing her "new" options. Devin was busy using his Archer class, doing his best to stay out of danger so that he wouldn't lose any more experience from an unnecessary death. He had been doing great lately, but this new group looked like they meant business. They were from a guild named *Guiding Light*, and they were equipped to the gills with what looked to be epic gear. She wasn't too worried, but she paid a little more attention to what Devin was doing to make sure he was going to be alright – even though there wasn't much she could do at this point.

Chapter 27

(26 hours after release of patch notes)

Devin had to keep retreating from these players –
nothing he threw at them made any sort of difference. He had
started using an Archer class after his mishap with the Warlock
because he wanted to stay as far away as possible. However,
that seemed to not help in the situation he now found himself in
– he would've preferred using the Warlock again.

This new guild that he hadn't seen before came striding
into the dungeon like they owned the place and didn't have any
worry about what was in store for them. They had some
impressive and expensive-looking equipment that looked like
they gave massive stat boosts. With Krista's help, he chose an
instance group that looked a little less strong – but even that
difference wasn't much. They all looked pretty intimidating and
Devin was worried.

It turned out that he was right to be worried, because
even using his best skills he couldn't do more than 50 points of
damage – and that was to a Healer. Normally he would be able
to take out even the tanks with four or five well placed arrows
using his *Vital Shot IV* skill, which did critical damage if aimed
toward vital areas. Now, however, he was lucky to get three
shots off in a row before the opposing ranged players forced him
to retreat.

He had already retreated to the pillar and bridge room and he had hopes that the aerial troops in this portion of the floor would come through where he couldn't. As he watched the party of players enter, he took up a position just out of range on a far pillar that gave him plenty of time to retreat if needed. A couple of groups had made it this far but usually by this time they were tired, battered, and had a couple of deaths already. This room had killed all but one group and even that one didn't get too much farther in the Orc Village ahead.

Unfortunately for Devin, this party looked as though they were taking a stroll through the park. They didn't look tired, stressed, or even like they were working hard. As they moved along the bridges, a group of three **Horcys** launched themselves from an adjacent pillar and attacked them from above. It didn't seem to faze the group as they just took the hits without regard to damage mitigation or acquiring aggro – they just full-on launched all their ranged spells and weapons and took them down within seconds.

Not only did they have suburb physical resistance, but their physical and magical damage was through the roof. Nothing really stood a chance – if he wasn't able to visually see their levels, he would have guessed these guys were around level 50 or more. The **Wyverocs** and **Goblin Pole Dancers** attacked next and survived a little bit better due to their better ability to dodge and take damage. Even this didn't really make a huge impact on the group of players – Devin tried to distract them with random arrows from afar, but they were too well-disciplined.

It was only when the **G-Bomber** attacked that Devin was able to see some results from his constant barrage of arrows. Being attacked so much without the ability to retaliate must have gotten to a couple of the players, because the Archer that was with them suddenly broke off from the group and chased after Devin in order to get a better shot. It was bad timing on his part because that was when the first **G-Bomber** made its bombing run, and a descending goat caught him right on his side mid-bridge.

Despite having the stats to mitigate large amounts of damage, it couldn't prevent the impact and subsequent sideways momentum. The Archer flew through the air and landed on the sharp and pointy rocks far below. He didn't die immediately, however, but he had so many bleeding debuffs that he didn't last more than 10 seconds. Their healer couldn't reach him with her spells because he was out of range and, despite the Archer using some health potions, he couldn't out-heal the bleeding effects. He was also out of range of *Resurrection*, which meant that they were permanently one member down.

That still didn't matter much as they fought ahead with renewed determination and breezed through the room boss battle. They didn't even open the chest just like the ones before this – it was like they didn't care about anything other than getting through to the Dungeon Core. As only the second group to make it to the Orc Village (at least from what Devin had seen), he was curious how they would perform in there. The mini-groups of Orcs had different classes and used elementary tactics – they were a step above the monsters from the rest of the floor.

The Orc Village was comprised of various "buildings" that funneled each group that entered into a series of encounters that they had to overcome before progressing. These buildings were really just a façade – you couldn't actually go into them – and were essentially just decoration. The encounters, on the other hand, were far from decoration.

They started with just two Orcs with complementing classes that would use cover and were intelligent enough not to just stand there while you hacked into them. From there, the difficulty would slowly ramp up until you were fighting a team of five that were of similar composition as the party they were facing; Krista was able to access an upgrade when she selected the placed mobs that allowed them to mirror the opposing classes.

When they were finally through the Orc Village portion of the room, they would enter a courtyard that held a **Hearthfire Ogre** surrounded by two **Horcy** and four **Hearthfire Orc Guards**. This was the final battle for the floor before getting to the Staging Area for the Guardian Battle. Excellent timing and tactics were what would get you through this battle – unless you were equipped with near god-like (at least for this level) equipment.

And what Devin had feared since first seeing this bunch came true – they had no problem tearing through the Orc Village despite having one less member in their party. The final battle caused them no big problems – the Ogre did a bit more damage than they were probably ready for, but it just meant their healer actually had to heal for a bit. But even with that, the fight probably didn't even last for five minutes. This time, one of the players actually looted the chest – probably just for curiosities' sake. He didn't actually take the sword that was inside – he just laughed and left it there.

Devin felt pretty impotent through all of this – he fired as many arrows and used as many skills as he could but to no effect. He watched them walk through the exit and addressed Krista for the first time since the group entered the instance, "You see that, right? I'm assuming the other groups did just as well because if they did worse I'll shit a brick. I think we're in trouble – it's all up to Violette now."

He had been avoiding Violette lately for a couple of reasons. 1. She made him extremely uncomfortable with her happy, touchy-feely attitude toward the world. 2. He didn't want to get in the middle of whatever issue she and Krista were having. 3. She was a crazy – it didn't automatically make her a bad person but just...unstable. And they needed stability right now because they were fighting for their survival.

If Violette managed to fight off these powerful players, he'd have to suck it up and visit her again so that he can both thank and congratulate her.

Chapter 28

(27 hours after release of patch notes)

Krista watched with trepidation as the *Guiding Light* guild gathered in the staging room. The group that Devin had faced off against was being yelled at by the leader of the raid group, a Rogue by the name of Shdwsteppa. They were the only group to have permanently lost a member – although every other group had at least one death due to traps, they were able to resurrect them.

Eventually, the yelling stopped, and they organized into a cohesive unit that marched through the giant doors into the Guardian Room. On the way in, a couple of them looked at the warning on the wall:

WARNING! You are about to enter a raid battle with the Dungeon Guardian. BEWARE!
Max amount of raid participants: 20 Current amount of raid participants: 19 Current level cap: 30
Current Dungeon power level: 8 Current Dungeon Core bonus: 8%

Krista was hoping that having less than a full raid-party would help Violette with defending the Dungeon Core. Even though she still didn't like her and didn't care for what she was doing with Devin, she was forced to rely on her to keep them safe. It was finally time to see if the room she created for Violette would be sufficient.

Since this was the first time any players had entered the Guardian Room before, Krista was interested in seeing how they reacted to their first sight of it. Despite the distaste she had for the woman, she had to admit that Violette knew what she was doing when she designed the room. Krista was actually proud of the work she put into it and hoped the players would be just as impressed. She wasn't disappointed – regardless of the epic armor they were wearing, they were still players and could still be awed by the sight of something impressive-looking.

In keeping with the mountainous theme used throughout the rest of the floor, Krista had created more of a uniform mountain within the room – a Temple of Spirit. Similar to a ziggurat, the terraced pyramid stood 200-feet-high with receding terraces leading up to a central temple platform where Violette was located.

Unlike a normal ziggurat, however, this one was cut in half so that only the front half was butted up against the wall. Also, unlike a ziggurat, there was no central staircase leading all the way to the top – each terrace was accessed by a small staircase located on the opposite side of where the previous one was. This required any raid groups to have to fight through each terrace until they reached the top.

Surrounding the Temple, an undead horde of almost 1,000 various low-level creatures and humanoids wandered around looking for anything alive. Alone, they were pretty much pushovers; when alerted to potential victims, however, they tended to converge and overwhelm unprepared parties. If the players managed to survive the undead horde, they would move to the left of the temple where a staircase leading up to the next level awaited them.

Located on the biggest terrace was a forest filled with trees, dense undergrowth, and vines. Lots and lots of vines – hanging from trees, laying on the ground, and generally anywhere Krista could put them. There was also a clearing near the end of the terrace where three **Nature Spirits (Level 40)** would be found defending the next staircase. These giant, 30-foot tall walking trees were able to control all the other vegetation on the terrace as well as handily defending themselves.

On the second terrace up, piles of boulders were strewn all around a dusty, barren floor. As the parties of players approached, these boulders would form together into massive **Earth Spirits (Level 45)** that had insane amounts of physical resistance and caused huge amounts of physical damage with each swing of its arms. There were four of these **Earth Spirits** located on the pathway across the terrace, and if they were defeated then the next staircase led to a terrace filled with lava.

The only solid pathway through the lava wound its way through almost every part of the terrace, eventually ending up in the center which led to the central temple platform. Along the pathway, players were forced to fight five **Magma Spirits (Level 50)** that appeared around a wider pathway so that players would have more room to fight and move around.

Finally, on top of the Temple, the central platform was surrounded on one side by what Violette liked to call a "River of Souls" – it looked scary but wouldn't actually do anything to anyone that fell into it. It was a moving black liquid that would sporadically show the "tortured faces of the damned" flowing through it – Krista did her best to approximate this and thought she did a good job at it. The other side of the platform was surrounded by a moving lava flow that would spill over into the terrace below for effect.

On the platform stood Violette surrounded by six 15-foot-tall Undead Minotaurs that wielded giant two-bladed battle axes. Krista grudgingly admitted that Violette looked stunning in a black and red low-cut dress, her hair up in a particular style that if Krista had done it in real life would have taken hours in a salon to accomplish, all the while holding her customary black staff that she had seen before. Behind all of that sat the unassuming chest that held the Dungeon Core.

When Violette asked Krista to make this temple, she couldn't figure out why she was going through all the trouble of making different terraces, filling them with different elements, and basically using precious resources to make it look as intimidating as possible. She figured it would just be Violette against the entire raid party so why not make a big room with some traps and leave it at that. That's when she was rudely told that being a Spirit Witch was more than just casting the special spells that she had shown off before. They excelled at communicating with the spirit world both here and beyond – she was able to summon help from various aspects of the spirit world.

As a straight-up fighter, Violette admitted that she most likely couldn't withstand the entire might of a 20-person raid. Her spells worked better on small groups and although her physical and magical resistance was high, she couldn't even go toe-to-toe with a basic fighter in terms of melee. Hence, the room full of low and high-level monsters to help her defend the Core – this was her strength and she used it to her fullest.

Krista wished she had access to these awesome monsters – but if wishes were fishes then...she'd...have lots of fish? She never understood that expression; anyway, she turned back to the raid group that had entered the room. Currently, they were fighting in a circle with the tanks and short-range DPS on the outside and long-range DPS and healers in the middle.

Surrounding them on all sides were the undead horde that must have been at least 50 deep all the way around.

Since they were lower-level, the horde didn't do more than a couple points of damage to even the less-heavily-armored players. However, they were being hit so many times that the healers had a hard time keeping everyone up on health points. The casters were doing a good job thinning out the horde by casting AOE spells and the other long-range DPS were cutting swathes through them at a good pace. They were doing a good job staying alive and even staying ahead of the undead tide; if it wasn't for something else, they probably would have made it through with everyone still alive.

I'm glad Devin can't see this...on second thought, it might make it more likely he'll stay away from her. I'll have to think about what to tell him. On the highest point of the temple – where she is supposed to wait for the players to come to her – stood Violette, screaming out obscenities and raving like a crazy person. Or to be more accurate, she was just being her usual self. At least it was the deeper, scarier voice coming out of her saying these things – if it was her bubbly, cheerful voice that would have been weird. Or at least weirder.

"Where is Devin!? What the fuck have you done with him?! If you motherfuckers killed him, I'll rip your spirits out of your body and let my Minotaur friends skullfuck your eye sockets! Where is..." Violette continued on with a wide variety of threats of torture and corpse desecration which Krista tried to tune it out because it was so vulgar and disturbing that if she had a body she'd be throwing up by now.

During this furious tirade, she was also firing off basketball-sized bolts of magic that looked like black-flaming skulls toward the players more than 300 feet away from her – and accurately hitting them too. The raid, being surrounded by the undead as they were, couldn't avoid the bolts of magic that were being hurled in their direction and started suffering casualties. Since they were armored up so much, the bolts themselves didn't do a massive amount of damage, but they had a nasty side effect of silencing the target for five seconds. This led to a couple of healers not being able to heal the tanks that were being beaten up by the undead. One healer fell behind so much that two of the front-line players she had been healing died within seconds of each other.

Although they were still overpowered because of their gear, the rest of the battle went downhill from there. By the end, only 8 of the original 19 survived the undead horde – with only one healer for all of them. Instead of pressing on – and since their original leader had fallen along with the other 10 players – the remaining raid members decided to turn back. Krista always liked to leave an out for the players so the door back to the Staging Area was unlocked and a portal back to outside of the entrance was located there as well. Fortunately, *Guiding Light* was already past the first floor when she placed the shrine – all those that died got sent back to wherever they were bound before.

Krista reluctantly went back to the Guardian Room and tried to find out from Violette what had happened. Glad that she couldn't be attacked or hurt by the raving lunatic at the top of the temple, she got close enough to talk to her.

"Uh...are you ok? What happened there?"

Violette's visage slowly turned from crazy murderess to just crazy annoyed.

"Where is Devin? Why hasn't he come to visit? You agreed to not interfere in any way and I would do my job here protecting the Core. Why are you keeping him from me? Tell me where he is!"

Her voice went from almost normal to creepy deep by the end of that and Krista had to admit feeling a bit intimidated. "Whoa, slow down – no one is keeping him from you. He's been fighting almost non-stop in the instances to try to slow down the progression of players coming into the dungeon. It's only been like 24 hours or so – I'm sure he'll come to visit when there is some downtime. If we get attacked by that last group again he may even fight in here if he has to because he was relatively ineffective during the instance – although that was no fault of his own."

Violette looked so crestfallen after she heard what she had to say that Krista almost felt bad for her – almost. "I'm sorry, I didn't realize he was working so hard out there – it has been so boring in here by myself and you didn't come tell me how things were going so I thought he forgot about me. When I finally saw some players enter I kind of lost it a little bit – I needed to take some of my frustration out on something. Although I probably shouldn't have done that – if they had all lived a little bit longer I would have been all out of mana and would've only regenerated a little by the time they made it up to me. Fortunately, whenever the room is empty my mana and health pools fill up instantly. Sorry, I seem to be rambling – can you tell Devin to come and visit me...I miss him so much."

Krista realized that if the *Guiding Light* guild had been a little more prepared for the magic bolts, they would have had almost no challenge from Violette once they got to the top. As much as she didn't want to subject Devin to her romantic ministrations, he needed to go visit Violette so that he could keep her as even-keeled as possible. *Although he'll probably love the attention – especially if he's allowed to feel her up again.*

Chapter 29

(5 days after release of patch notes)

Devin had slowly improved his skills in staying alive over the last four days. He had made it to level 30 and hadn't lost any levels in two days. He had actually gone back to using his Warlock class for the last couple of days and it had worked out really well – he beefed up his Wisdom at a cost of a little Constitution in order to make sure there weren't many (or any at all) that would resist his *Fear Barrage V*. He found that his original intuition was right – when he couldn't dish out enough damage it was best to let the traps, steep mountains, and drops off of the pillars do the work for him. Oh, and the new equipment didn't hurt either.

When the *Guiding Light* guild lost 12 of their members to the dungeon, Krista was able to absorb and provide for use by him all of the equipment that they were using. There was nice stuff for just about every class but most of it had a level requirement associated with them. Most of the best equipment available in the game world had a certain level that you had to be in order to use it. This prevented a level 5 from spending a whole bunch of money to completely deck themselves out with Epic equipment that was found in high-level raid dungeons. There were good items out there that didn't have a level requirement, but they were few and far between.

For his Warlock, he had some choice items that were not specifically for his class but were shared between multiple classes. The way he was choosing to play allowed him to pick and choose the best equipment even if it didn't really match. To some it would look like there wasn't a cohesive theme to his outfit but there was a reason for everything:

Vinewalker's Staff			
Two-Handed Weapon			
Physical Damage	60	Intelligence	+30
Wisdom	+30	Mana Points	+100
Casting Speed		+10%	
Bonus:	Additional magical damage with Nature-based spells and effects		+30%
	Additional magical resistance to Nature-based spells and effects		+30%
Class Restrictions:		Fighter, Druid, Warlock	
Level Restrictions:		Level 28	
Cost:		3000 rp	

Helmet of Discipline			
Head			
Physical Resistance	50	Constitution	+40
Strength	+20	Health Points	+100
Bonus:	Reduces Cooldowns of all spells and effects		-15%
Class Restrictions:		Defender, Paladin, Warlock	
Level Restrictions:		Level 29	

Cost:	2500 rp

Warrior's Breastplate			
Chest			
Physical Resistance	100	Constitution	+50
Strength	+50	Agility	+20
Class Restrictions:		Fighter, Pet Trainer, Defender, Paladin, Warlock	
Level Restrictions:		Level 20	
Cost:		1500 rp	

Nimble Leather Gloves of Wisdom			
Hands			
Physical Resistance	15	Agility	+50
Wisdom	+50		
Class Restrictions:		Fighter, Rogue, Archer, Defender, Paladin, Warlock	
Level Restrictions:		Level 22	
Cost:		1000 rp	

Brown Britches of Brumhilda			
Legs			
Physical Resistance	10	Intelligence	+70
Wisdom	+70	Mana Points	+120
Bonus:	Chance to avoid physical damage when hit	+10%	
Class Restrictions:		Mage, Sorcerer, Healer, Druid, Warlock	
Level Restrictions:		Level 30	
Cost:		3200 rp	

Heavy Light-touched Stompers

Feet			
Physical Resistance	80	Constitution	+60
Wisdom	+60		
Bonus:	Additional magical damage with Light-based spells and effects		+20%
	Additional magical resistance to Light-based spells and effects		+20%
Class Restrictions:	Defender, Paladin, Warlock		
Level Restrictions:	Level 27		
Cost:	2400 rp		

Ring of Defense+2

Finger	
Physical Resistance	+100
Class Restrictions:	All
Level Restrictions:	Level 25
Cost:	500 rp

Ring of Shielding+2

Finger	
Magical Resistance	+100
Class Restrictions:	All
Level Restrictions:	Level 25
Cost:	500 rp

Necklace of Wisdom+4

Neck	
Wisdom	+100
Class Restrictions:	All
Level Restrictions:	Level 25
Cost:	500 rp

He had increased Wisdom for his *Fear Barrage* spell, Constitution for his *Life Syphon* spell, and Agility so that he could get in and out as quick as he could. He had found that as soon as he was in range to use his fear spell he could cast it quickly and then leave as soon as possible. Most of the time – if he timed it right – he could make at least one or two players leap to their deaths or activate a deadly trap nearby. He even hid in some small spaces, waited until the groups passed him, used his fear spell behind them, and took off running.

Occasionally he would be bored of doing the same thing repeatedly, so he would challenge himself to try to take out as many players as he could with long-range spells like his *Phantom Bolt* and *Life Syphon*. He would harass the groups from almost the beginning of the floor and continuously retreat ahead of them so that he stayed out of retaliation range.

In the hours following the *Guiding Light* attack, Krista told him about what happened in her Guardian Room and that he needed to go visit Violette. Apparently, she was so lonely with no one to talk to that she inadvertently lost control and destroyed many of the players that walked into the room. He thought it was a good thing until Krista told him how it was done and the dangers in doing it that way. He promised that he would visit her for about an hour each day to make sure she didn't lose control again. As much as he didn't mind looking at her beautiful features, she still made him uncomfortable when she got a little too friendly.

And it was only getting worse.

The first day he visited her she seemed genuinely depressed that he hadn't come to visit her in so long. He then made the same promise that he gave Krista that he would come visit her for an hour each day – which made her hug and squeeze him until he almost passed out due to suffocation damage. Which was good and bad – he now knew that it wouldn't kill him being suffocated but the feeling of not being able to breathe still sucked. A lot.

The next couple of days, when he went to visit Violette she would try to convince him to stay longer when the hour was up. He tried to explain that he needed to get back to defending the instances against all the incoming players, but she wouldn't listen. She started badmouthing Krista – saying that she was a slave-driver and didn't appreciate all that he did for the dungeon. When Devin tried to defend her, she kept making snide comments regarding how she wasn't a real person because she didn't have a body and she didn't know how to make him feel appreciated.

Devin thought this was funny because they were all technically computer programs and weren't "real" – but he didn't tell her that. He didn't want to become another victim of the crazy deep-voiced psychopath due to an argument. Making some noncommittal sounds, he would leave soon after that.

This last day, however, when he tried to leave after listening to her bash Krista, Violette attacked him. He wasn't hurt, per se, but he was frightened so much he didn't want to go back. As he was turning to leave, she jumped on his back bringing him to the ground. She straddled him and started ripping off his armor – which he didn't think was possible since it was *equipped*. Her face transformed into a rictus of anger while in the scary-deep voice stated, "YOU ARE MINE! YOU CAN'T LEAVE ME! I WON'T LET HER HAVE YOU!"

He tried fighting her off, but she was so strong – even with his enhanced armor he stood no chance against her. The worst part was when all of his underclothes were ripped off she started moving in what he supposed she thought was a sensuous manner but looked more frantic than anything. Despite his terror, his body reacted as any red-blooded straight man would with an extremely hot girl straddling him – he got aroused. As she felt this, something seemed to snap her out of her violent episode.

Her face as she looked down at Devin was filled with horror – not at him but at what she had done to him. She immediately stood up off of him and started crying and apologizing, trying to help him up from the ground. He scuttled backwards along the ground, trying to avoid her hands attempting to pick him up off the floor and told her, "Don't touch me!" Finally, when she backed away, he stood up and realized he was still naked. Accessing his inventory, he found that all of his armor (and somehow his underclothes – which normally weren't able to be removed at all) was unequipped. Quickly reequipping them all, he ran as quickly as he could for the exit.

Behind him, Violette had collapsed on the ground, hysterically pleading with him, "I'm so sorry Devin! It won't happen again! I didn't mean to do that – I don't know what came over me! Don't leave me Devin! Devin! Noooooooooooooo!"

Never once looking back, it felt like hours before Devin reached the exit into the Staging Area. When he got there, Krista impatiently contacted him, "There you are Devin, I thought you were only going to spend an hour at most in there – couldn't pull yourself away from her, could you? I was monitoring the players currently in the instances and was just about to go look for you. I can almost guarantee the current "participants" won't make it through. I have a proposition for *you* though. How would you like to journey out of the dungeon again and find some more monsters? I have enough resources to start creating a new floor – I just need some more monsters to populate it."

Devin was glad she hadn't seen any of what had just happened. He felt mortified and embarrassed and really didn't want to talk about it right then – especially with the girl he was still in love with. With as much fake-excitement as he could muster, he told Krista, "Sure – I would love to get out of here for a while. Hopefully I can get far away from here before I have to turn back. If you could despawn me, I can reequip for the journey outside."

Seconds later, he was in the Transition Room.

Chapter 30

(6 days after release of patch notes)

Krista was happy with how the last five days had turned out. After the *Guiding Light* scare, there was only one other raid group that had managed to make it through to the Staging Area, but they were down to only 13 players – they didn't even attempt to take on Violette. That was more than a day ago and, even without Devin's interference, the players were still struggling to complete the instance. They had made some improvements, however.

Ever since she put the shrine in at the beginning of the dungeon, she had been seeing repeats of various raid groups go through the instances and get farther and farther without dying. It was only a matter of time – perhaps a week – before most of those who tried out the event floor would be able to get through to the staging area.

Krista had been gaining massive amounts of experience as well – she had just gotten to Dungeon Level 12 today. She was expecting to jump up even further based on how quickly she leveled before, but after level 10 the experience needed to increase her level was staggering. But "business" had been good, and she was steadily improving. She had also just unlocked the *Expand Dungeon Territory* option but hadn't had a chance to look at it yet – she'd wait until Devin got back for that.

Especially since she just saw some "trouble" enter into her dungeon again.

It seemed as though the *Guiding Light* guild was back – and looked to be better prepared. They were as decked out with as much epic gear as before, but something told Krista that they had used the time away to prepare for the Guardian Room. Krista was a little worried since Devin wasn't here yet, but she had confidence that Violette would still prevail. Devin had been visiting every day and each time when Krista had visited after he had left she seemed to be "saner". She hadn't visited after Devin left earlier because she wanted to monitor everything else – especially since she didn't have an "inside man" in the instances to take care of any problems.

After breezing through the first two floors, the raid party split into their groups and entered their individual instances. She moved from group to group and watched as they absolutely decimated all her monsters, bypassed almost all of her traps, and steadily moved toward the exit without missing a beat. They all finished within minutes of each other – without losing a single raid member. After seeing how easy it was for them – especially compared to last time – Krista was really worried now.

She transported her viewpoint to the Guardian Room and was shocked to see that it was empty. Not completely empty – everything that Krista had built was still there – but there were no mobs. No undead horde, **Nature Spirits**, **Earth Spirits**, **Magma Spirits**, or **Undead Minotaurs**. And she couldn't see Violette as well – until she looked in the forest and found her curled up in a ball, sobbing uncontrollably.

"What are you doing?! Where are all the monsters?! I need you to summon them again and get ready – I don't have time for your craziness today! The *Guiding Light* guild is back, and they look even harder to beat this time. Hurry, they are on their way in now!"

Violette stayed curled up, continuing to sob and didn't even acknowledge that she heard Krista. She kept trying to get her attention, but to no avail – there was no getting through to her in this state. Krista didn't know what was wrong; it hadn't even been 24 hours since Devin was last here, so she shouldn't be like that. Everything she tried to ask Violette was met with more of the same so there was no help from that quarter.

Even as she despaired that her help was now a blubbering mess, the raid entered the Guardian Room prepared for the onslaught of undead. When it didn't arrive, they actually looked surprised for the first time – they stood there with confused looks upon their faces. After about 30 seconds, however, they conversed with each other and started cautiously heading for the stairs. They were probably worried that it was a trick and there was something even deadlier in store for them.

After finding no resistance, they climbed up the stairs up to the first terrace and made their way for the first time through the trees. The **Nature Spirits** were supposed to control the trees and vines to hurt and capture the invading players, but since they weren't there the forest was quiet. As the raid made their way through the trees, they heard Violette sobbing near the clearing at the end of the terrace and made their way to her. Instead of trying to find out what was wrong, they apparently recognized her from their first visit and started attacking immediately.

Violette didn't defend herself at all – the only difference Krista could see was that instead of crying she was now screaming in pain. Only the fact that she was about 30 levels higher than the players allowed her to live more than a minute under the onslaught. When she was almost out of health, she screamed out in a heartbroken voice, "DEVIN! WHY DID YOU LEAVE ME? I LOVE YOU..."

Krista watched her only hope of survival die without putting up any sort of fight. *Devin, what did you do?* She just watched, stunned, as the raid walked past the corpse without a second look and made their way up to the top of the temple, only stopping when they got to the chest waiting there. As soon as they opened it up and took out a baseball-sized, glowing blue crystal – she knew it was all over. All their planning and hard work was for naught.

A teleporter automatically materialized behind the chest for the players to teleport back to the entrance of the dungeon. Soon after they entered the teleporter, Krista received a prompt:

> **Your Dungeon Core has been stolen!**
>
> You now have 44 days, 23 hours, 59 minutes, and 55 seconds to retrieve the Core!
>
> Most restrictions on the DUMB have been lifted in order to use any and all means necessary to reacquire the Dungeon Core – these include:
>
> 1. The level cap of the DUMB is eliminated while the core is missing – if the core is returned the cap is reinstated to the level cap on the strongest floor
> 2. The location of the Core will be made known to the DUMB and travel restrictions are eliminated
> 3. Communications and trading between the DUMB and testers are permitted – outside communication is still restricted
> 4. The DUMB may join parties, raids, and even guilds of testers in order to retrieve the Core
>
> The dungeon can still accumulate resources and the instances will continue to function on the strongest floor, but the Dungeon Level will not increase as no experience will be awarded.
>
> If the Core is not returned to the dungeon within the time limit, the current dungeon "Altera Vita" will be reset back to its original ND101208 configuration and all extraneous programs will be deleted.
>
> Good Luck!

Taking a page from Violette's book, Krista mentally curled up in a ball and cried.

Chapter 31

(54 minutes after the Dungeon Core was stolen)

Devin ran as fast as he could back to the dungeon, hoping that he wouldn't run into any players on the way back. When he left the dungeon almost a day ago, he had to head back inside almost right away to have Krista respawn him so that he could change his class. He was intending to use his Pet Trainer class again since it was so successful the first time – but the virtual horde of players surrounding the entrance caused him to change his mind. After respawning, he used a Human Rogue with really high agility, *Sneak VII*, and equipment to boost his Agility and *Sneak* skill. He was fortunately able to sneak past even the high-level players because he was leaving instead of entering the dungeon – they were all watching for those incoming.

He had spent most of the last day avoiding the plethora of players and ranging as far as he could, looking for different monsters. Since the Dungeon Level had increased so much, the range that he could travel was heightened significantly. He found a lot of the same monsters that they already had in their dungeon in the forest and on the mountain – although he did find another dungeon at the top of the mountain. He tried to enter it, but he was denied access by the system – it said something to the effect of not having the ability to expand the dungeon territory. Ranging farther afield, he finally found a river teeming with various new monsters.

Which is why he was currently being followed by a **Giant Frog (Level 26)** and praying that he could quickly run through the player gauntlet near the dungeon. He figured that *he* could make it through, but he was worried that they would kill the frog following behind. As he got closer, he felt something tugging at him toward the South; however, he ignored it as he tried to concentrate on avoiding any danger. He needn't have worried, however, because he reached the entrance without seeing even a single player. Realizing that something strange was happening, he entered the dungeon using his *Stealth* skill and lost the trailing frog. He found out earlier that if he was far enough away and stealthed, any lured monsters would retreat to where it came from.

As he crossed the threshold, Krista started yelling at him, "Where have you been?! What did you do to Violette?! YOU JUST KILLED US BOTH!!!"

Not understanding what she was talking about, he tried to ask her what was going on, but she cut him off, "You don't even know what happened, do you? They killed Violette and took the Dungeon Core – and all because you two had some sort of lover's quarrel. I never took you for a love'em-and-leave'em type of man before, but I guess I was wrong. All you had to do was keep her happy when you visited her – and you couldn't even do that. I hope it was worth it; I bet it was all sorts of crazy – just like her."

Devin was still trying to register what she had said about Violette being killed and the Dungeon Core being missing. As his mind caught up to what else she said he got angry – he never did anything of the sort with Violette. "I have no idea what you're talking about, Krista. *I* didn't do anything to *her*. She was the one who's messed up in the head – not me. Why are you blaming me? What did she say to make you think I did anything?"

"As she was dying – being slaughtered by the players while sobbing uncontrollably – she screamed out that you had left her and that she loved you. She wouldn't have said that unless you had done something to or with her. I saw the way you were touching her breast that time when she put you to sleep! This is all *your* fault!" Krista blamed him.

Not wanting to explain what actually happened because it was still a fresh wound, he instead trying reasoning with her, "I don't know why she would have said that – I didn't do or say anything I could think of that would make her think she loved me. Besides, I couldn't love her – I already love *you*. I've loved you for almost as long as I can remember and there isn't a girl alive – or dead or whatever – that could change that. I've only ever wanted to be with you – I don't and didn't ever want to be with her." As he was talking, it all came gushing out of him –

everything that he had wanted to say but never had the nerve to before.

As the realization of what he just said hit him, he chickened out again and ran back out of the dungeon. Before he was completely out he stopped and quietly said, "I don't want you to die, Krista. I'll get that Core back – and I'll find some way to prove that I had nothing to do with it." There was no response, so he walked outside – and realized he had no idea who stole it or where it was. Except...he had felt a vague sense of tugging before and it was still there to the South. Since this was new, he had to take it faith that it was where he needed to go.

He activated *Stealth* and started walking as fast as he could – toward what, he didn't know. All he knew was that if he didn't find the Dungeon Core soon, their life – as it was – would come to an end. And strangely, he was glad he told her how he felt – he might never get another chance.

Epilogue

(2 hours after the Dungeon Core was stolen)

De4thfrmbeh1nd closed his mail window after reading the message he just received. Turning toward his Lieutenants he told them the bad news.

"The Dungeon Core was taken from the event dungeon about two hours ago. It was by the *Guiding Light* guild – which as we all know is a feeder guild to *Divine Truth*. They have numerous lower-level players who, as they level up to a certain point, join *Divine Truth* if they show enough promise. My contacts have informed me that *Divine Truth* used their substantial wealth to completely outfit their raid group with the best gear that could be found for their levels. We're talking about close to a million gold – they must have figured they would recoup their expenditures when they got the Core."

"What are we going to do? We can't go up against their guild – they have way too many high-level players and their castle is near impregnable," asked EyesHlzU.

"We need to call in those contacts from our guild meeting earlier in the week – some of them might be willing to help now that *Divine Truth* has what they wanted. Most will be looking to acquire the Core for themselves, some might help because they just don't want *Divine Truth* to have it, and others are just itching for a good fight. We can't let them know our

405

own plan, however. We are going to return the Core to the dungeon and ensure it stays there — we can't let another guild get access to that kind of power. Besides, the loot is just too good in the dungeon — we've gotten more gold from just these last couple of days than the last two months of raiding and grinding."

Those around the table nodded their heads in agreement, encouraging De4th that this was the right plan. *Look out Glendaria*, he thought. *The guilds are going to war.*

End of Book 2

Dungeon Guild

Prologue

Krista lethargically watched various groups of players travel through her dungeon. This latest bunch was progressing quite well – they were using strategies that they had developed after multiple runs through the new floor. The Shrine located at the beginning of the dungeon allowed them to respawn and continuously improve their skills. At the moment, she followed a specific group consisting of a Defender, Rogue, Mage, Archer, and Healer – they had made multiple runs through and were getting farther and farther each time. Right now, they were in the Orc Village and had a decent shot at finishing the Floor Boss despite not being decked out in massive amounts of epic gear. Not that Krista cared overly much – she couldn't seem to care about much lately.

Their Dungeon Core was stolen by a guild of epically decked-out players who took advantage of their Guardian's incapacitation. From what Krista could ascertain, three days had passed since that life-changing event. After Devin had left to retrieve the core, Krista had a bit of a mental breakdown. All their hard work and effort was negated by miscommunication, hurt feelings, and one crazy-ass psycho bitch of a Guardian. At first raving at the unfairness of it all, she then fell into a kind of fugue state where she didn't or couldn't pay attention to anything outside of her own thoughts. Fortunately for the dungeon, most of the required resetting of the mobs and loot was automated for the new floor.

This didn't apply for the first two floors, however. When she finally emerged from her wildly ranging thoughts (she wasn't sure what pulled her out from her broken mental state) she saw that there were still quite a few parties of players challenging the bottom floor. They would respawn at the shrine she had built at the entrance and make their way down to the event floor – without having to kill anything on the way. Since she wasn't actively paying attention to the dungeon, the first two floors were empty of mobs and loot because they had to be specifically reset by Krista.

When she saw this, her first reaction was to immediately respawn everything on those floors. However, before she could go through with that action, she was interrupted by her thoughts again. *Why does it matter? It's not like I need to slave away at this when I'll probably be "dead" in about 40 days. And anyway, why are they even here? We don't have a Dungeon Core anymore so there is no need to keep running through. I guess they like all of the loot – and it's probably good experience, too. Oh well, if they feel like wasting their time I'm not going to stop them.*

Seeing no point in resetting, Krista left the initial two floors alone and tried to go back to minding her own business and thoughts. Unfortunately (or fortunately – however you want to look at it), she couldn't fall back into her all-encompassing mind maelstrom. Eventually getting bored, she tried to amuse herself by watching parties of players make their way through the last part of her dungeon.

At first, she just blindly followed along without really seeing them. When they started dying pretty regularly in the same spots, she started making her own "game" up where she would watch new groups enter into the instance and she would try to predict where they would die. She based her predictions on a wide range of characteristics: how they got along with the other party members, how they held their weapons, their name, their class, their race, and even the color of their hair. She was wrong more often than not, but it helped to pass the time. Inevitably, her thoughts began to drift as she observed the mini-battles ranging throughout the dungeon without really caring what the results were.

Krista thought about the last conversation she had with Devin. She had just blamed him for Violette's breakdown and subsequent expressions of love toward Devin:

"I don't know why she would have said that – I didn't do or say anything I could think of that would make her think she loved me. Besides, I couldn't love her – I already love you. I've loved you for almost as long as I can remember and there isn't a girl alive – or dead or whatever – that could change that. I've only ever wanted to be with you – I don't and didn't ever want to be with her."

Questions, questions, and more questions arose from this revelation. *He loves me? How am I supposed to react to that? Why didn't he say anything before this? Why did Violette imply that there was a relationship between the two of them?* These and other related questions were spinning around and around her mind in a constant cycle. However, the two most pertinent questions that kept coming up were, *Do I love him?* and *How do I fix this?*

She couldn't answer these questions because her feelings were mixed – she didn't know what had happened between Devin and Violette. She knew that she cared for Devin like she would for a brother but had never considered his feelings for her before. She always assumed he felt the same way – they were so comfortable hanging out together that she couldn't see it from any other viewpoint. *Well, now that things have changed somewhat in our "living" arrangements, maybe I should start looking at things differently.* It would take some time, but Krista was sure she would figure it out eventually.

About a day ago, she had tried to place Violette back into the dungeon – the option to do it wasn't greyed out, so she knew she wasn't dead forever. When she clicked on it, however, she got a prompt warning her it wasn't possible.

> **ERROR!**
>
> Guardians are only available when the Dungeon Core is present inside the dungeon.
>
> Please reacquire the lost Core and every previously killed or new guardian will be available for placement.

So, obviously Krista wasn't going to get any answers to her questions from that source. The only way she could realistically figure out all of this was if Devin managed to capture and return the Dungeon Core in time to save them all from deletion. She wasn't holding out much hope of that because it seemed like an impossible task. *How is he supposed to get it back from that* Guiding Light *guild when they are decked out in the best epic armor for their levels? Not only that, but it wouldn't surprise me if they have massive amounts of higher-level players that could take him out in one hit. And besides, isn't he only level 30? What good will that do?*

More questions – Krista wasn't going to be able to answer anything until she heard back from Devin. She expected him to show up at some point for a respawn since he was way out of his league by himself out there. She'd get answers one way or another – she wouldn't let him leave until she had a good long talk with him.

With nothing else to do, she went back to watching the groups of players make their way through her dungeon.

Chapter 1

"Sir, we have a situation – one of the Rangers has spotted a low-level Rogue making his way through the forest and avoiding our camp," said Sh1fty over the guild chat.

De4thfrmbeh1nd shifted his focus from the various reports of *Divine Truth* sightings and started paying attention to Sh1fty. Sh1fty, De4th's second in command, oversaw their Rangers and other scouts that were combing the forest, looking for sight of either the *Guiding Light* or *Divine Truth* guilds. Ever since the Dungeon Core was stolen, *Reckless* and a smattering of smaller guilds had banded together to hunt for the guilds responsible – their objective was to return the Core back to the Altera Vita dungeon.

They wanted to return it for two main reasons: 1. They didn't want a single guild to become more powerful than the others – ultimately leading to a super-powerful guild that would control and dictate most aspects of the game world, and 2. The experience and loot found in the dungeon (and consequentially the gold received from that) was better than anything else that could be found other than high-level raids.

They had been tracking reports of their whereabouts for the last three days, sometimes losing track for hours at a time but ultimately finding them again when their scouts ventured out far enough. From what De4th could tell, they weren't heading for any populated areas and were taking a circuitous route back to their guild castle. *Reckless*, and the smaller guilds with them, were trying to catch them before they made it all the way there. If they managed to make it back to the castle it would be near impossible to get it back. It was also a mystery why they hadn't just teleported back there – but De4th was just thankful that they hadn't.

"Where is he heading? And can you tell which guild he's with?" De4th asked. "We don't want to start anything with another guild right now – we can't afford to piss anyone off."

"From what we can tell he's not in any guild and...well, his name is a little strange," Sh1fty responded.

"What do you mean, *strange*?"

"Well, as you know, normally all player names are colored blue unless they are attacking you – which then turns orange. This one, however, is red – as if he is a mob. And his name is only 'Human Rogue', which leads me to believe he has somehow found a way to disguise his name and player status. He's also heading toward where our latest reports say *Divine Truth* was last seen. We haven't been able to confirm this yet, though."

"I've never heard of anyone having that ability, but I'm intrigued enough to want to learn more about this 'Human Rogue' – I just hope whatever he's using to hide his name doesn't also hide his guild. Pick him up but treat him as well as possible just in case. I want to find out what he knows," De4th replied.

Minutes later, two of *Reckless'* Rangers dragged the struggling, non-descript-looking Rogue into the guilds' command tent. They managed to tie him to a chair sitting near the central support pole and then stepped back, out of the way but within striking distance if needed. *He was right, his name is strange – I wonder how he's hiding his identity. At least I know he's level 30...unless he can fake that as well.*

As he slowly walked around the mystery man seated in the chair, he couldn't help but observe that the equipment he saw was impressive for someone of his level. Most of the gear was epic quality, had level requirements, and gave bonuses to *Stealth* and movement speed. This worried him a little bit because to acquire most of this gear you had to be pretty loaded gold-wise – or have a guild sponsor. From the reports he had received regarding the *Guiding Light* guild, *Divine Truth* had spent almost a million gold to fully outfit the raid group that ended up stealing the Dungeon Core.

Realizing that they might have a spy on their hands, De4th determined to get as much information as possible before they killed this guy. It was almost a certainty that *Divine Truth* knew they were being followed, but hopefully they didn't know where *Reckless* was. *Let's see if I can get him to reveal their location.*

"What's your name?" De4th started out with an easy question.

The "Human Rogue" just stared at him, various emotions flashing across his face. De4th saw anger, confusion, resignation, and even what he thought was hope flash by so quickly he couldn't be sure that's what it was. Two minutes passed by without any response, but De4th just stared and waited – he knew silence was his ally in this situation. He could yell and scream at this guy for hours and potentially not get any response. However, most people couldn't stand the silence and having someone calmly staring at them usually got them on edge. This would lead them to involuntarily blurt out something in order to break the tension in the room – even if it wasn't the answer to the question. This situation was no different – after five more minutes he finally got a response.

"Devin."

Smiling inwardly, De4th asked, "Why are you here, Devin?"

Strangely, this "Devin" looked surprised that De4th knew his name. It was as if he was used to speaking a foreign language and having no one understand what he was trying to say – and then suddenly someone could. "Just passing through," Devin quickly responded.

"Why were you trying to sneak around our camp?"

"I've got no business with you – I just didn't want to be a bother," Devin said unconvincingly.

416

"What is your...business then?"

"My own," Devin curtly replied.

He's definitely hiding something — I'm still not sure what it is though, De4th thought. *I don't think I'm going to get much information from him, but I'll ask a couple more questions before we do away with him.*

"What guild do you belong to?" he asked.

Devin appeared surprised, as if he had never heard the question before. He looked closer at each of the players in the tent, most likely looking at their names and guild affiliations. Everyone here was in *Reckless*, which made his perusal quick. Looking back at De4th, Devin cocked his head to the side as if he was really considering his answer. "I'm not now nor have ever been in a guild," he finally said.

"Where did you get all of that gear? Unless you're rich, an unaffiliated player couldn't afford the type of equipment you're sporting at the moment."

"A good friend gave it to me...and why are you asking all of these questions? I didn't do anything to you and you're here interrogating me like I did something wrong. Let me go or kill me if you are a bunch of PKers. I'm not answering any more questions," Devin assertively — but with slight hints of trepidation — gave De4th his decision.

The *Reckless* guild was not a bunch of PKers, or Player Killers, and didn't want to be known as one. That being said, they were not opposed to eliminating spies to limit the

417

possibility of discovery. Thinking furiously, De4th came up with a quick, simple plan that would hopefully benefit everyone. He just had a couple more questions...

"I'm willing to let you go if you answer two more questions for me. Does this sound acceptable?"

Devin appeared to think about it for a couple of seconds before nodding his head in acceptance.

"How did you change your name to disguise who you are and why does the coloring on it appear as a monster's would?"

Apparently catching him off-guard, Devin froze and didn't say anything for a good fifteen seconds. *Looks like we're not getting the truth out of him – he's thinking of a lie right now.* His intuition was proved correct when he finally got an answer.

"I'm not sure why it is doing that – must be some sort of glitch. I'm sure it will fix itself at some point. I answered your questions so now let me go – I need to go get something important and I'm on a time crunch," Devin answered. As soon as the words left his lips, he looked as though he wanted to take back that last part. He sat there looking resigned and stubborn at the same time, waiting to either be killed or released.

Although he wasn't happy with the answer, De4th was a man of his word and ordered the two Rangers still standing nearby to untie Devin and release him. As the walking "glitch" made his way out of the camp, De4th ordered both Rangers to follow him at a distance. He didn't want this man to know he was being followed and, although their *Stealth* skill was most likely many levels above his, he wanted to be careful. He had a hunch that if things turned out the way he thought they would, this Rogue would lead them right where he wanted to go.

Chapter 2

Devin was scared shitless when he was first captured by the *Reckless* guild. He was sure he was going straight to respawn, and he wasn't ready to face Krista yet. He had to get the Dungeon Core back before their time ran out and if he died now he wasn't sure he'd ever be able to get to it in time. It was a measure of luck – and probably the fact that he didn't look like much of a threat – that he was let go.

He had been surprised that they could understand him when he talked – the last time he tried to communicate with another player it didn't turn out so well. *Something must have changed when the Dungeon Core was stolen. Now that I can speak to the players, maybe I can convince those who stole it to return it. If they were aware that they were going to end up killing Krista and I, they might be willing to make some sort of deal. Though not likely, it might be the only option that could work.* He'd have to think on it some more before he got to where he was headed.

Speaking of that, he knew he was getting closer to the whereabouts of the Dungeon Core because the pulling in his chest had intensified over the last couple of hours. When he had first begun searching for the Dungeon Core – just outside the dungeon entrance – it had been just a vague feeling of direction. It was almost like a faint ping in his chest when he faced the right way. Over the last few days, the faint ping had turned into a thumping and then a pounding of his chest – it was quite distracting, but it also ensured that he was going the right way. Eventually, the pounding faded and now it was as if he was being physically pulled toward his destination.

He stealthily crept ahead, moving in the general direction of where his body told him the Core was located. He wasn't sure what was in store for him when he got there, but he also didn't want to stumble blindly upon it either. He was also aware of the two Rangers that were following him from the *Reckless* camp he had left behind a couple of hours ago. He wasn't too worried about them – if they had meant him harm they could have killed him with a ranged attack a hundred times over by now.

Although they had quite a few levels on him, Devin had a pretty high Agility score and *Stealth* skill due to his stat allocation and gear bonuses. This allowed him to see them even though they were stealthed – it wasn't perfect because if they were standing still it was near impossible to see anyone using the *Stealth* skill. It was only when they were moving quickly to catch up to him that he was able to glimpse them out of the corner of his eye. He didn't let on that he knew that they were there because he didn't want to provoke them in any way – he still had a job to do. Since they had left him alone and hadn't done anything to try to stop him, he tried to ignore them and kept his focus on what was in front of him.

The pulling was getting so strong now that Devin was worried that it would start hurting if it got any stronger. *That must mean I'm really close now.* As he worked his way around another tree he stopped as he heard two muffled thumps followed by a cut-off cry of pain somewhere above him. He looked up and saw the body of an Elf Archer plummeting toward him. His high Agility saved him as he quickly dived and rolled forward as the body hit the ground right where he was standing.

Devin looked behind him, searching for the Rangers that had been following him. They must have been standing still because he didn't see anything. Sending out a silent "Thanks" in their general direction, he turned back toward where the Core was located. If it wasn't for the Rangers' help, he'd probably be dead by now – he vowed in the future to look up more often. There was likely to be more scouts the closer he got to where he was going, and he didn't want to make any more mistakes.

Navigating his way north through more trees – while keeping an eye on the tree branches above him – he eventually came to a slight hill in the forest with a thick clump of trees located on the crest. On the tree nearest him, he saw an extremely blurry form sitting on a high branch near the trunk. Figuring it for another scout, he headed east to make his way around any observers. When he estimated that he had put enough distance between them, he made his way back toward the Northwest where he was being pulled.

As he crested the rise, he looked down the other side and immediately flattened out on his stomach. Below him was a massive camp – at least five times bigger than the *Reckless* camp that he was dragged into not that long ago. On the outside of the camp were posted sentries every 50 feet that looked alert even though it appeared they had stopped not long ago. The rest of the camp was in a state of disarray – players and what looked to be NPC servants were putting up tents and portable crafting areas.

While it appeared everything was placed haphazardly, the camp was actually quite organized. Laid out in a rectangular shape, tents for individual players were set in orderly rows along the outside of the camp while longer meeting tents were further inside. After that came the portable crafting areas which included a small forge for blacksmithing, racks for tanning leather, tables loaded with paraphernalia for enchanting, and separated from the rest were two reinforced shacks for alchemy. In the center of the camp were two large tents that were most likely set up for the leadership of the guild or guilds inside.

Devin couldn't believe this was one or even two guilds together – the entire camp looked like a small city the way it was spread out along the small valley floor. From where he was hiding, he could see hundreds if not thousands of different people running around down there. The one thing he didn't see were any type of mounts – he knew they existed, but apparently were not being used at the moment. It was probably because navigating their way through all the trees in this forest was next to impossible while on top of a horse – it was just too dense to make it through easily. *Now I know why I was able to catch up so quickly – they can't move that fast with all of the stuff they're bringing along.*

The sheer amount of people and tents were a bit daunting for Devin. He knew in general where the Dungeon Core was located but couldn't pinpoint which tent it was in. Somehow, he was going to need to slip into the camp undetected and follow the pull until he was able to determine its exact location. Based on where it was, he needed to formulate a plan to sneak in, reacquire it, and somehow get out without getting caught. He figured that the best time for this would be sometime that night when it was fully dark, and the sentries were a little less alert.

With that decision made, Devin looked around for a good place to hide out until the time came to move. While he was technically stealthed, he was lying flat in plain sight for anyone who might come by. He wasn't sure if there would be any roving patrols, but he wasn't going to take any chances. Nearby he spotted a stand of four trees nestled up against each other which would hopefully give him plenty of cover while still allowing him to have a good view of the camp below. He carefully made his way over to the trees while keeping a low profile on the ridge. Making it without being spotted – he hoped

– he crouched down out of view while still maintaining a good vantage of the "tent city" below.

Resigned to wait for a while, he started looking for things to do while he was stuck there. He pulled up his Equipment list first to remember what he had to work with.

Serpent's Fangs			
Dual-wielded Weapons			
Physical Damage	210	Agility	+40
Strength	+20	Health Points	+60
Attack Speed		+20%	
Bonus:	Inflicts poison on each successful hit which damages the target over 10 seconds – may stack up to 3 times	20 physical damage per second	
	Increases critical chance when attacking from *Stealth*	+30%	
Class Restrictions:		Fighter, Rogue	
Level Restrictions:		Level 30	
Cost:		3500 rp	

Hood of Shadows			
Head			
Physical Resistance	40	Agility	+50
Strength	+5	Constitution	+10
Bonus:	Increases *Stealth* skill level	+1	
Class Restrictions:		Fighter, Archer, Rogue	
Level Restrictions:		Level 28	
Cost:		2400 rp	

Midnight Cuirass of Striking		
Chest		
Physical Resistance	80	Agility	+100
Constitution	+20	Strength	+10
Bonus:	Increases *Stealth* skill level	+1
	Increases physical damage when attacking from *Stealth*	+15% additional physical damage
Class Restrictions:	Fighter, Archer, Rogue	
Level Restrictions:	Level 30	
Cost:	3400 rp	

Trapmakers' Gloves of Agility		
Hands		
Physical Resistance	10	Agility	+80
Bonus:	Increase to *Disarm Trap* skill	+2
Class Restrictions:	Rogue	
Level Restrictions:	Level 24	
Cost:	1300 rp	

Whispering Pants of Darkness		
Legs		
Physical Resistance	21	Agility	+80
Constitution	+20		
Bonus:	Increases *Stealth* skill level	+1
	Increases movement speed while using *Stealth*	+30%
Class Restrictions:	Archer, Rogue	
Level Restrictions:	Level 29	
Cost:	2700 rp	

Swift Silky Slippers of Stealth			
Feet			
Physical Resistance	5	Agility	+70
Bonus:	Increases *Stealth* skill level		+1
	Increases movement speed while using *Stealth*		+40%
Class Restrictions:	Rogue		
Level Restrictions:		Level 27	
Cost:		2300 rp	

Ring of Agility +3	
Finger	
Agility	+100
Class Restrictions:	All
Level Restrictions:	Level 25
Cost:	700 rp

Ring of Agility +3	
Finger	
Agility	+100
Class Restrictions:	All
Level Restrictions:	Level 25
Cost:	700 rp

Necklace of the Shadow-touched	
Neck	
Stealth Skill increased	+2
Class Restrictions:	All
Level Restrictions:	Level 30

Cost:	1200 rp

His first thought when he needed to outfit himself a couple of days ago – when he was heading out to bring more monsters back to the dungeon -- was to increase his stealth up as far as possible so that he could sneak by the players surrounding the dungeon undetected. He was hopeful that it would also help immensely with his upcoming foray into the enemy camp in front of him. His skills that he had selected were probably a little overkill at the time, but they would definitely help now.

Stealth XIII	(Rogue Class Skill)		
Hide in the shadows to move around undetected			
Effect:	98% less chance of being detected	Cooldown:	After stealth is canceled, you must be out of combat for at least 5 seconds

Backstab II	(Rogue Class Skill)		
Does damage from behind a target that can only be used while stealthed			
Physical Damage:	60 with a 30% chance of critical damage	Cooldown:	60.0 seconds

He had upgraded the *Stealth* skill up to level 7, but with an additional +6 to the skill from his gear he ended up at level 13 – just 2 away from the max level which was 15. It was pretty impressive for a level 30 to have almost maxed out *Stealth* – that is until you saw the rest of his skills. He had upgraded *Backstab* to level 2 just to have some sort of damage skill, but he wasn't expecting to have to fight other players at the time. He just needed enough damage output to kill mobs that he brought back to the dungeon. Now it appeared that if he got into a fight, he wasn't going to be able to survive too long – although his Agility was high, and his dodge chance would help with that.

Character Status					
Race:		Human	Level:		30
Class:		Rogue	Experience:		3000/3000
Strength:	35	Physical Damage:	1999	Magical Damage:	0
Constitution:	100	Physical Resistance:	356	Magical Resistance:	0
Agility:	890	Health Points:	1060	Mana Points:	0
Intelligence:	0	Health Regeneration:	300.0 per min	Mana Regeneration:	0.0 per min
Wisdom:	0	Block:	0	Critical/Dodge Chance:	89.0%
Skills:				Stealth XIII, Backstab II	
Upgrades:				Lure	

As the sky began to darken, Devin started planning-out where he wanted to start making his way through the camp while there was still some light to see by. If he waited until most of the camp was asleep, he should be able to sneak by the sentries if he moved slowly enough. He was most likely to be seen while stealthed when he was moving, so by traveling at a snail's pace he hoped to be able to avoid being spotted. When he looked at the camp, he saw that there was one section that had one less sentry along the north side – he planned to circle around to that side when he was ready to enter the camp a little bit later in the night.

From his current hiding place, he couldn't accurately pinpoint the exact location of the Core. Therefore, after he successfully infiltrated the outer tents, he planned on using his innate Dungeon Core sensing to narrow down which tent felt the most likely to house it. If it was up to him, he'd put it in the most heavily guarded area – which was probably one of the guild tents at the center of the camp.

Trying to wait patiently was almost like torture to Devin – he was so close to his goal, but he just couldn't reach it. Once it got late enough, he shot out of his hiding place so quickly he worried that he may have called attention to his activities. He froze, heartbeat thumping loudly in his chest, and ducked behind a tree. He waited another couple of minutes with his senses active for any change. Although he could hear random camp noises coming from that direction, he noticed nothing out of the ordinary. He started moving again, this time slowly making his way toward the north side.

Moving into position halfway between two sentries, Devin began slowly making his way out of the relative safety of the trees, picking his way carefully so that he didn't make any noise. Just as he was about to pass the last tree, he heard what sounded like a branch crack behind him. He turned around as silently as possible, but it was already too late – before he could react something hard smashed into his head and he blacked out.

Chapter 3

"Here we are again, young Devin — if that is your real name..."

Devin felt woozy as he slowly came back to his senses, listening to the voice behind him. He couldn't see anything, but he could feel that his hands were tied together to the chair he was sitting in. *Well, this seems familiar...* The bag on his head felt itchy and annoying — this was the second time in less than a day that he felt alone and vulnerable and he didn't like it. He was also pissed off that they took him just as he was about to...try...to get the Dungeon Core back. Even if they let him go now he wouldn't have enough time to get back tonight and follow through with his plan.

He felt the bag suddenly jerk off his head, and a bright light shone down on his face. He found himself in the same tent he was in earlier in the day — a larger-sized rectangular canvas tent with a center pole and a flap-tie entrance. He looked around and saw the level 85 Assassin De4thfrmbeh1nd surrounded by three other members of *Reckless*. Without even looking at the class tag above her head, he could tell the level 79 EyesHlzU was a Cleric based on how she was dressed and, well...by her name. Sh1fty — who looked extremely roguish in his all leather ensemble — was a Level 81 Thief as per his class tag. Lastly, in a hulking suit of plate armor standing in the corner, stood a massive Level 82 Commander by the name of St4lwartShield.

Each of these players could wipe the floor with him in probably no more than a single hit – even the Cleric. They all had advanced classes that were accessible at level 40 – which meant that they had a lot of abilities that he hadn't even seen before. He knew that the Assassin and Thief were advanced Rogue classes, the Commander was an advanced Defender class, and the Cleric was an advanced form of a Healer. There were two advanced classes per base class – very few of which he had actually seen in person. Devin couldn't wait until he got to 40 so that he could experiment with these classes in the future – of course, he had to survive that long. Interrupting his perusal of the room, De4th started asking questions again which meant that, even though he was still a little woozy from getting hit over the head, he had to start paying attention.

"What were you doing at that camp, Devin? Who are you working for? Who are you really?" De4th asked him.

Devin tried to brush off these questions like he did the last time with answers like, "I don't know what you're talking about," and "I just stumbled upon the camp." However, De4th was having none of that – he most likely was expecting these kinds of answers because he was quick to reply.

"If you don't give me some truthful answers soon, we are going to have to kill you. You've technically been in combat since you arrived, so you haven't been able to send any messages – which means no one knows you are here. We need to make sure it stays that way because we don't need anyone else knowing where we are – although we do appreciate you showing us where the other camp was located. Nothing personal, but if you don't give us a reason not to, we'll have to get rid of you, so the word doesn't get out. You have five minutes – we have things we need to get to." Devin could tell De4thfrmbeh1nd was serious this time.

Devin thought about it for a couple of minutes. *What would happen if I told them the truth? Would the Main System AI shut us down if we shared what happened to us – or is this the reason I can communicate with them now? If I don't tell them they'll kill me – but if I tell them the truth, they might not believe me and kill me anyway. The way I see it, I'm damned if I do and damned if I don't. I can't afford to respawn right now, so I've got nothing to lose – but if they believe me there is a slight chance they may actually be able to help.* With his mind made up, he blurted out the first thing that came to his mind: "I'm not actually a player…"

All four of the *Reckless* players just stared at him with various expressions on their faces – from confusion, disbelief, and impatience. The last one was from De4thfrmbeh1nd who thought he was playing around again and making things up therefore wasting his time. "Stop jerking us around – you're clearly a player. Who else would you be?"

"Well, I actually used to be a player – but I haven't been one for the last couple of months. You see, about nine months ago..." Devin began telling the story of what had happened to them. As he was recounting how they had first started as new players in Briarwood – with Devin a Fighter and Krista a Healer – he couldn't believe how far they had come since then. All they wanted to do was have fun playing a game together as they always had – now they were a part of the game.

When he got to the part where they entered the transporter at the end of the Goblin Cave, he faltered a little in his recounting. It wasn't enough just having the knowledge that they had died – telling other people made it all come back hard. It hit him with more emotion now than it did when he first learned about it – maybe he hadn't fully come to terms with the situation. Anyway, once he was passed that part, he was able to pull himself together and recounted how they had taken over the dungeon from the former dungeon AI.

"Krista is actually the one in charge of the dungeon – I'm just the Dungeon Upgradable Mobile Boss. At first, I started back at level 1 and gained experience from those that I had killed. I could choose whatever race and class that had been previously killed in the dungeon and there was no penalty to respawn as a different combination. This all worked great until Krista hit Dungeon Level 5 – which is where the Dungeon Core event came in. We had 48 hours until everything got posted to the patch notes and made us a target for the whole of Glendaria.

While I lured the monsters back to the dungeon, Krista created the new floor to house the Dungeon Core and new Guardian. You can probably guess the rest from there."

During his entire recounting and explanation, the four guild members quietly watched him without saying a word. As he finished, silence descended upon the tent for a long five minutes. As if emerging from a sleep, De4th started moving again and asked, "How did they steal the Dungeon Core?"

Devin was reluctant to talk about specifics, but he was able to at least tell them something, "We had a problem with our Guardian, Violette. She ended up being unstable of mind and consequentially allowed them to take it without a fight – it was essentially out of our control. I wasn't there at the time and when I learned what happened I immediately went in search of the Core."

De4th considered this and looked at his guildmates for a couple of minutes. They must have been communicating over Guild Chat because they seemed to reach a consensus without uttering anything out loud. They all turned back to Devin, eyeing him again as if to confirm what decision they had reached. Suddenly, De4th broke the silence permeating the tent, "We would like to help you get the Dungeon Core back to the dungeon. We don't want it in the hands of *anyone*, especially one of the most powerful guilds in the game."

Devin inwardly let out a sigh of relief, keeping stoic on the outside. *Maybe together we can make this work. I don't*

trust them completely but at least they haven't killed me yet –
hopefully that is a good sign. "What help can you give me?"

"First, how did you know where the *Divine Truth* camp
was located? We've been trying to track them for days and it
has been near impossible to pin them down," Sh1fty responded.

"I have some sort of connection to the Core that
almost...pulls me in the correct direction. Before your guys took
me, I was trying to enter the camp to further pinpoint where the
Dungeon Core was precisely located. I know it is in there, but I
couldn't tell from the outside exactly what tent it was in."

"That could work for what I have in mind; now that we
know where the camp is we can track it to their next destination
and infiltrate them tonight. We don't have the forces to take
them on directly, but we do have some of the best stealth
players in the game. We can make it into their camp
undetected, but we won't be able to search all of the tents.
That's where you come in – when you get far enough in you can
point us in the right direction. After that, it'll be an easy snatch
n' grab and we'll use some teleport scrolls to get us out of there
before all the shit hits the fan," Sh1fty explained.

"Sounds like a plan to me...uh...can you untie me now?"

Chapter 4

"Alright muthafuckas, you know the plan – we'll go in as a small team, locate this bitch, snatch that shit before anyone knows we're there, and port out while they're still getting their dicks together."

Sh1fty tended to be quite crass just before a job or mission. That didn't mean he wasn't one of the best Thieves you could find in the game; it was just the way he got his nerves out. And sometimes it was quite humorous with what he would come up with.

De4thfrmbeh1nd was playing second fiddle to Sh1fty on this mission – although he was the guild leader his lieutenants all had their specialties. This was a situation where having their premier Thief in charge was best for what they wanted to accomplish. In De4ths' opinion, there wasn't anyone better when you needed something stolen without anyone the wiser. He just had a knack for thieving – it was above-and-beyond the basic abilities that came with the class.

Anyone could *Stealth* and *Pickpocket* an unsuspecting merchant – Sh1fty took it to a whole new level. Once, De4th remembered, when someone from a rival guild killed one of their low-level guildies for no reason, Sh1fty decided to get revenge. Later that night, he climbed the outside of their guild house, entered the attic, made his way around the entire place while everyone was asleep – and stole everything he could fit into his bag. Weapons, armor, clothing, decorative statues, small pieces of furniture, rugs, banners, and even some cookware they had in their kitchen made their way into his oversized bag. He could have kept it and sold it, but he "returned" it in a way to deliver a message – don't fuck with him and his.

The next day, the rival guild (who went by *Terror Squad*) found all their stuff in their house gone and a short note skewered to the front door by a small stiletto knife. All that the note said was, "Roof – DFWU (Don't Fuck With Us)". When the various members of *Terror Squad* who were inside at that moment stepped outside, they found all their different pieces of equipment, décor, and even cookware attached and hanging off the side of the roof. They were the laughingstock of the city for many months afterword and they could never pin down exactly who had done it.

So De4th trusted Sh1fty to lead this mission – if anyone could succeed it would be him. He chose to come along as well because as an Assassin he had a high *Stealth* skill as well and would work well as backup if it came to a fight. He wasn't going to let something this important be delegated to one of his lower-ranked guild members. If they didn't accomplish their mission, then it wouldn't be because they didn't use all their best people.

Along with Sh1fty and De4thfrmbeh1nd, they were bringing along Strang3r – who was one of the top Rangers in the game – and another Ranger by the name of Gahbriyelle. Gahbriyelle was a short, waifish-looking slip of a blonde-haired elf girl whom De4th had recruited soon after they had formed the guild. Both Rangers were expert marksmen/markswomen that also had a nearly maxed out *Stealth* skill – which made sense because they were an advanced form of the Rogue class. He trusted them all with his "virtual" life to follow the plan and get the job done no matter what. And then there was Devin.

De4th still wasn't sure what to think about Devin – his story was so crazy that it could almost be the truth. He'd have to do some research when he was out of the game and look up FIPOD deaths in the news. He hadn't heard of any deaths – but then again, he wasn't offline that often either. Honestly, De4th still didn't trust Devin but would use him if he was able to lead them to the Dungeon Core – he certainly seemed like he knew where he was going.

The next day after his revelation, Devin had led the *Reckless* guild in the direction he sensed the Dungeon Core was heading toward. All day, De4th was crossing his fingers hoping that they had put their trust in the right person – they couldn't afford to lose a day of tracking because they might not be able to catch back up.

At first, Devin had led them in a completely different direction from where all their experienced trackers and informers had said the *Divine Truth* camp was heading. After a couple of hours, however, they realized that they were on the right track when they began to see small signs leftover from a large party passing through. By nightfall, they had caught up enough that they could easily get from the *Reckless* camp to the *Divine Truth* camp in as little as 20 minutes.

After waiting for nightfall, the five party members *Stealthed* and crept close to the camp, bypassing four different scouts posted along the perimeter. They must have had some lower-level members of their guild keeping watch because their *Stealth* skill was so low they weren't able to see their party as they snuck past. As they got to the edge of the camp and observed the alert sentries standing equidistant from each other along the perimeter, Sh1fty had given his "rousing" speech to the party through party chat.

Which was another unusual and confusing aspect of Devin's story – if he was a mob he shouldn't be able to join a party with them. There were times during the game when an NPC would join a group doing a quest, either as someone they had to protect or as someone who would help them get through a difficult part. De4th had never heard of a mob joining a party – he thought that would have been talked about it if had ever happened. *Well, it's too late now to second-guess myself; we'll just have to roll with it for now.*

While waiting for Sh1fty to give the OK for them to move in, De4th got his first real look at the *Divine Truth* camp. Even though he got a report from his Rangers last night on how many tents there were, he was still amazed on how big the camp was.

441

Hopefully Devin really can pinpoint where the Core is – there is no way we could search all these tents. I suspect that it is going to be in one of the larger guild tents in the center, but I'd rather not go in those if it isn't.

Even though he was waiting for it, he was still startled out of his own thoughts as Sh1fty signaled for them to move in. A half-step behind the others, he followed along a slow pace, constantly watching out for threats on all sides. Just because they had visible sentries didn't mean that there weren't additional *Stealthed* players keeping watch for groups such as his. That's what he would have done if he was in their place – but perhaps their top-guild standing gave them too much confidence. Either way, they made it inside the tents without raising an alarm or gaining any notice.

Since they entered from the center of the north side of the camp, it was no surprise when he saw Devin leading the way south toward the big guild tents in the center. Although it was pretty much what he expected, De4th was worried that there would be way too many players inside to successfully steal the Core and – this was the most important part – get away safely. He'd have to see what Sh1fty said since this was his operation.

As they cautiously made their way past the last row of tents surrounding the larger guild ones, Devin suddenly stopped, turned to the right, and stared at one of the crafting tents they had just passed. Ashes, bits of metal, and scorch marks marred the ground outside of the tent which De4th assumed must be a portable forge for those with the Blacksmithing profession. He looked inquisitively at Devin, and asked Devin through the party chat, "What is it?"

"I think the Core is in that tent – I was expecting it to be in one of the big tents in the center of the camp, but my sense is pulling me in this direction," Devin replied. Without asking, he slowly started to circle around the tent as if confirming his suspicion. "Yep, it's definitely in there. What's the plan?"

De4th looked at Sh1fty, ready for instruction – this was his show. "Wait here, I'm just going to peek inside and figure out what the hell we're dealing with here. Be prepared to run if this is a trap – no need for all of us to get fucked." As usual, Sh1fty knew how to diffuse a stressful situation. Slinking further into the shadows of a nearby tent, the rest of the party watched as the Thief cautiously inched his way forward toward the side of the tent. At this distance, it was hard to see him despite being in the same party – his *Stealth* skill was just that high.

Sh1fty pulled a small, razor-sharp implement from his bag and slowly pressed it against the fabric of the tent in front of him. It was only because of their heightened attention toward what he was doing that they heard the barest whisper of cutting cloth – which was mostly drowned out by the normal nighttime camp sounds emanating from around them. De4th observed Sh1fty carefully placing his eye to the hole he had just made and stood silently for almost a minute before pulling away.

"Those smart sons-of-bitches set a pretty decent trap in there. First of all, that's not a crafting station — my guess is they made it look that way from the outside so that nobody would look for the Dungeon Core there. There is no forge inside, just a whole lot of guards surrounding some unassuming crates stored in the middle of the tent. From my count, it looks as though there are six high-level players in there — a Cleric, a Wizard, two Commanders, and two Assassins. It looks like they are getting bored waiting around doing nothing — I know if I was standing around night after night doing nothing I'd lose my shit. It's probably only the importance of what they are doing that is keeping them even relatively alert.

"They're placed around the tent almost equally — most likely to prevent them all from being hit by an AOE in the event someone attacked them. The two stealthers are by the entrance, the two tanks are near the center of the tent on either side, and the healer and caster are near the back. There's no way I'm going to be able to sneak in and steal it — their attention is too focused on it to be able to snatch and grab. It's in a crate, so first I'd have to figure out which one it is in, open it up, and then close it again without making noise or drawing attention. Not going to happen. It's a tall fucking order but we'll have to take them all out if we're going to have any chance of this succeeding. Now, I have a plan, but you'll all have to do what I tell you if we're going to get this shit done right," he looked right at Devin when he said that last part.

"I want this even more than you – I'll follow your orders since you seem to know what you're doing," Devin defensively replied. Giving an almost imperceptible nod in his direction, Sh1fty quickly outlined his plan to the group. Nodding his own head in approval, De4th felt more confident in their chances the more he heard. *If everything goes even halfway well, this plan might actually work.*

Chapter 5

Devin stood by the front of the "crafting" tent, just behind the man with the plan, Sh1fty. He was just now starting to get anxious – it was literally do or die time now. Based on how far away they were from the dungeon, this would probably be their only chance to get the Dungeon Core back. He gripped the Serpent's Fangs harder, somehow noticing for the first time that he was sweating profusely from nervousness. *Such realism in this game – crap, I've got to start paying attention or I might end up missing the cue*, he chastised himself.

Just as he thought this, he saw De4th – who was on the other side of the entrance – slowly start to creep around the tent flap in full *Stealth*. As if synchronized, Sh1fty mirrored his movements and Devin followed on his heels. Both the guild leader and the Thief entered the flap at the same time and Devin was relieved that there was no alarm raised as they passed within.

Devin's first glance at the inside of the tent showed him essentially what Sh1fty had reported earlier. Toward the back he could see the Wizard in flashy prismatic robes and the Cleric in all-white robes standing near opposite corners of the rectangular tent. About halfway up, two Commanders in full gleaming plate armor stood facing the pile of crates in the middle. That left the two Assassins – who looked particularly deadly in all black leather – standing near the front corners of the tent where they entered. Even with the quick glimpse that Devin had, he could tell that they were all bored and paying as little attention as possible. Everyone, except for the Commander on his right, had vacant expressions – most likely attributed to looking at menus, status screens, or chat screens.

The Commander that was halfway paying attention didn't have any *Stealth* skill, fortunately, and couldn't see them when they entered. Devin made his way past Sh1fty, who was heading for the side of the Assassin on the left-hand side of the tent. Devin's target was the tank, also on the left side of the tent, which looked even more intimidating when he saw him up close. While trying to avoid making any noise, Devin slowly came up behind the hulking, metal-clad behemoth and searched for a good place to sink his Fangs. The only spot he could see from his perspective was the gap between where the breastplate and helmet joined together. He was going to have to be supremely accurate with his *Backstab* in order to do any damage.

Just as he was settling into position, he heard Sh1fty in the party chat say, "Now". Without thinking too hard about it, Devin triggered his *Backstab* ability and aimed his twin knives toward the gap near his target's neck. His right Fang entered deep into the Commander's neck, while the left skidded off the helmet which moved slightly when the right one entered the gap. Disappointed that he didn't get both in at the same time, he was nevertheless pleased when he got a critical strike on top of the backstab bonus. Unfortunately, even with all that damage he only was able to take off about half of his target's health points.

Knowing he was in a world of hurt if it came to a face-to-face confrontation, he looked around the room to see how the rest of the party had fared. Toward the back of the tent, both the Wizard and the Cleric were down on the ground with four to five arrows each in their backs. Sh1fty had used his razor before the fight to cut small slits in the tent near the casters so that Gahbriyelle and Strang3r could fire straight into the tent when the time was right. Their aim was so accurate that they were able to fire multiple arrows through a three-inch hole which was practically invisible unless you knew where to look.

Satisfied that there wouldn't be any opposition from that front, he looked toward the next worst threat – the Assassins. De4th had used his *Execute* skill on his target and instantly killed him – while Sh1fty was still contending with his Assassin in the corner. The Thief was winning due to the surprise attack in the beginning and the fact that all of his attacks had numerous poisons inflicting DOTs on his target. Although the conclusion wasn't in doubt, they didn't have a lot of time to mess around.

Running toward the Assassin that Sh1fty was tangling with, he watched as De4th engaged the other Commander who hadn't seen any battle yet. With a flying leap, Devin launched his body toward the back of the stealther in the corner with his Fangs extended. Not expecting the additional attack, the Assassin went down under the weight of the Rogue with two knives stuck in his back. Although it didn't kill him, he was in no position to defend himself as Sh1fty stabbed down with his own knives and nearly decapitated the prone Assassin.

Devin rose to his feet quickly, after retrieving his Fangs from the back of the dead player. It was just in time as he looked up to see the Commander that he had initially *Backstabbed* running toward them. He dove out of the way of a clumsy strike from the player and rolled to his feet about ten feet away. *At least it* looked *clumsy – it could be that my Agility makes him look so slow and predictable. Or he's just disoriented from the sudden attack.* Either way, Devin wasn't going to allow him to get his bearings – he needed to take control of the fight.

With a quick look toward Sh1fty, he tried to convey his plan toward the Thief who nodded and started circling around the Commander whose attention was solely on the one who had hurt him so much initially. If players had aggro, then this massive tin can was fully aggroed on Devin – which was fine with him. He started quickly dodging all of the strikes thrown his way while attempting to land any type of damage on his opponent. There was a reason why a Rogue shouldn't try to go up against a tank in a fair fight – there was too much damage mitigation. Each of his strikes did little to no damage because they kept skidding along the plate armor worn by the player. The one hit that got through on the elbow joint did so little damage that Devin despaired of ever killing this guy.

Fortunately, he didn't have to do it himself. As he barely dodged another sword swipe, he saw the Commanders' knees suddenly fold forward and found Sh1fty standing behind the plate-wearing tank with a smile on his face. After literally cutting his opponents' legs out from under him, he executed a precision stab with both of his knives into the same gap Devin was trying to hit at the beginning of the battle. The defeated player fell forward onto his face and stopped moving.

Throwing quick thanks toward the Thief, he turned toward the remaining Commander. De4th wasn't struggling per se, but he wasn't making any progress either. Just like a Rogue going up against a tank, there wasn't much that the Assassin could do to damage him – he could dodge and avoid all sorts of attacks but that didn't help the situation. Devin and Sh1fty ran to help but before they could get there, they observed two arrows protruding from the eye slit of their opponent. The arrows themselves didn't cause a whole lot of damage due to the high health points of the Commander, but they did make it hard for him to see.

Devin looked out the entrance and saw the two Rangers aiming inside the tent again, but it was too late. De4th had taken advantage of the momentary blindness of his opponent and quickly moved behind him. A short flurry of stabs into the smallest gaps in his armor and the Commander was quickly choking on his own blood.

Silence reigned in the tent as the five combatants stopped to catch their breath after the intense fight. Suddenly, Devin remarked, "Uh, we should hurry — I'm pretty sure the rest of the camp heard that."

Sh1fty chuckled softly and responded, "We do have to hurry but the rest of the camp didn't hear anything — I used my very expensive Thief-use-only spell scroll to keep all sounds within this tent. It's called *Golden Silence*, and I popped it as soon as we entered the tent. It keeps all sounds from carrying more than ten feet from the source — because 'Silence is Golden', and silence usually leads to gold in my profession."

Mollified for the moment, Devin looked toward the center of the tent where the stack of crates stood waiting for them. There were crates of all different sizes, stacked on top of each other with no discernable pattern. There must have been almost 50 of them, and if it wasn't for his special connection to the Dungeon Core it would have taken quite a bit of time to search through all of them. As it was, all Devin had to do was step closer and he homed in on an unassuming, average-sized box nestled under three others. He moved some boxes off the top and as soon as he touched the one he was fixated on he knew he had found it. "Here—" was all he got out before he heard an alarm raised close by in the camp.

Although there wasn't supposed to be any way to contact those in the game from the outside, one of the players they had just killed must have found a way. Either that, or they were being monitored closely and someone saw that they had all logged off around the same time. It didn't matter in the long run because now they had to escape quickly. Turning to Sh1fty, he told him to start the group teleport to get them out of there.

"I've been trying to use this fucking thing since the alarm was raised. This piece of shit doesn't work because we have possession of the Core. It must be why *Divine Truth* didn't teleport back to their castle with it – they couldn't." A veritable tide of curse words followed this statement from Sh1fty as Devin tucked the box under his arm – he didn't have time to open it up right now. As he did this, he noticed something in the corner of his vision. He concentrated on it and received an urgent system notification:

You have retrieved the Dungeon Core!

You now have 39 days, 22 hours, 16 minutes, and 37 seconds to return the Core!

As a reminder, most restrictions on the DUMB have been lifted in order to use any and all means necessary to return the Dungeon Core – these include:

5. The level cap of the DUMB is eliminated while the core is missing – if the core is returned the cap is reinstated to the level cap on the strongest floor
6. Travel restrictions are eliminated
7. Communication and trade between the DUMB and testers is permitted – outside communication is still restricted
8. The DUMB may join parties, raids, and even guilds of testers to retrieve the Core
9. While it is in your possession, all parties and raids the DUMB is a part of

---

will receive the bonuses attributed to the Dungeon Core

Current bonus: **12% increase to all damage dealt, all resistances, experience gained, and currency looted**

An additional restriction has been imposed on all carriers of the Dungeon Core: No teleportation is allowed, and it may only be transported on foot – no mounts are allowed.

If the Core is not returned to the dungeon within the time limit, the current dungeon "Altera Vita" will be reset back to its original ND101208 configuration and all extraneous programs will be deleted.

Good Luck!

Well, there goes that plan. They were anticipating being able to teleport out of the camp with the Core but with the restriction on it they were going to have to find another way. He looked toward Sh1fty, but he was facing De4th with an expression of anticipation. It appeared that with the theft out of the way, the guild leader was going to take over again.

De4thfrmbeh1nd ran his fingers through his hair in what appeared to be a nervous tic, and announced, "Alright people, this is what we're going to do…"

Chapter 6

Devin only started slowing down as he reached the scouts on the fringe of the *Reckless* camp. With the morning light just starting to lighten the sky, he continued to follow behind De4th and Sh1fty. He saw that they were heading for the command tent – which was where he needed to go as well. As they passed by tents set up by the *Reckless* guild members – and even a smattering of other small guilds – they heard cheers and congratulations from everyone they encountered. It wasn't so loud that they would alert the neighborhood of their location, but the enthusiasm was nevertheless there.

The guild leader and lieutenant entered the command tent and Devin followed right along. As he entered, he saw the other two lieutenants he had met previously – EyesHIzU and St4lwartshield – along with some others that he didn't know. As De4th walked by two low-level Mages that were standing near the entrance, he pulled them aside, quickly murmured instructions, and sent them away. Clapping then greeted their entrance and additional congratulations followed in its wake. De4th graciously accepted the praise but insisted that they got down to business.

"Thank you all – however, we wouldn't have succeeded if it wasn't for Devin here. He led us unerringly to the Core when we would have been searching for hours otherwise. Now, we've got to get moving as fast as possible – we've got an entire guild on our heels looking to take back what we just stole from them. I've already ordered the camp stricken and we'll be moving out shortly. I'll answer any other questions on the move. Now, let's go!" De4th acted on his own orders and started heading out of the tent.

Devin, still holding the crate containing the Dungeon Core, looked lost until EyesHlzU came up and led him out of the tent toward the eastern part of the camp. Looking around, he was amazed at how much progress had been made in just the little time they were all gathered in the command tent. Most of the tents were taken down already and players were streaming toward the east and gathering together, waiting on orders to leave. As Devin walked, he realized that he was extremely tired after the last couple of hectic hours. Still in a bit of a daze over what had happened, he realized Eyes was asking him questions and he was inadvertently ignoring her. "I'm sorry...what was that again?" he asked apologetically.

"I asked why you all didn't teleport back to the camp like we expected you to. Don't tell me you lost the teleport scrolls?"

He tiredly drudged up the answer to her question, "I wish that we *had* teleported – we had a hell of a time getting back here. To answer your question, anyone in possession of the Dungeon Core cannot teleport or use mounts to transport it. It must all be done on foot. When we found that out, we thought we were screwed – especially when the alarm sounded shortly after retrieving our objective. If it wasn't for Gahbriyelle and Strang3r we wouldn't have made it back. They sacrificed themselves to ensure we got back safe with the Core."

"How did you guys manage to survive an entire guild coming after you?" Eyes asked him.

Devin thought about the horrific ordeal they had suffered through on their escape from the *Divine Truth* camp. He emotionlessly recounted the experience to Eyes as they walked. "When we left the tent where we found the Dungeon Core, we dropped any thought of a stealthy escape and booked it for the edge of camp. We stayed near the tents on the way out for as much cover as possible, but by that time players and NPCs were streaming out of their tents and were getting in our way. Fortunately, they got in each other's way as much as us. The mass confusion caused by the alarm, coupled with the secrecy of where the Dungeon Core was *actually* hidden, made it possible for us to blend into the crowd and safely arrive at the perimeter.

"It was only when we passed the last row of tents that we were spotted. The sentry guards had turned their attention to the camp and easily spotted us as we emerged. Charging straight for the chainmail-armored NPC guard directly in front of us, we easily overpowered him with a combination of critical strikes from De4th and Sh1fty and precise arrow shots from Strang3r and Gahbriyelle. He was dead in mere moments, but by that time the damage was done. The commotion brought on by the battle had drawn all the players looking for us near the tents.

"We immediately ran for the trees along the edge of the clearing, hoping to lose them amongst the dense foliage. I guess we all knew it was a forlorn hope that they wouldn't be able to track us – despite being mainly raid-focused in their daily routine, they *were* still a top-tier guild. This meant that if their players weren't the best-of-the-best, they were damn near close. They were on us in less than a minute."

Devin started jogging after those ahead of him, trying to catch up with the rest of the group who had moved further through the forest. It was difficult to move too quickly through the forest – it was essential to watch where you were walking. He knew from experience that hidden roots just seemed to leap up at the most inopportune times. As they reached the rest of the group, Devin continued explaining to EyesHlzU about their escape.

"A party of four Hunters caught up to us as we were discussing which direction to take. We had thought that we had done a good job at camouflaging our tracks, but with the appearance of the Hunters it didn't matter. De4th told me later that they could track down a specific flea at a dog show – that was their specialty. Since we weren't going to be able to escape, we had to fight. Armored head to toe in leather gear, the four Hunters were deadly with both ranged and melee weapons – as we found out.

"Two of the Hunters stayed back and fired directly at me. I was fortunate that my Agility was so high – even holding the crate I was able to dodge both arrows rather easily. Of course, they were only a distraction for the other two who were in my face as soon as both arrows whizzed past. I was saved from a nasty decapitation by a wicked-looking short sword when De4th slid in and intercepted the strike meant for me. That first loud clang was the first of many as I watched our Assassin and Thief trade blows with the two Hunters near me. I had to dodge another pair of arrows, one of which hit the crate and lodged itself near the edge.

"With the ranged attackers focused on me, our Rangers – whom, as you know, have pinpoint accuracy – began riddling them with skill-infused arrows. By the time that they could focus on where the arrows were coming from, each of them was sporting one arrow in an eye and one arrow in their neck. Without being able to focus properly, they were speedily taken down by the additional arrows fired by the duo. Which was a good thing, since the two Hunters near me were liable to kill De4th and Sh1fty if they hadn't provided some support.

"When that fight was done, the health points of both the guild leader and lieutenant were both under 20%. Fortunately, they thought to bring plenty of health potions just in case they were needed. They quickly quaffed them, and as we turned to continue running we heard what sounded like a huge group of players coming from the direction of the *Divine Truth* camp. We all looked at each other, realizing that they had heard all the noise from our fight with the Hunters and knew exactly where we were. If they had any more Hunters, we'd never be able to get away and would end up leading them right to the *Reckless* camp."

Stepping over *another* root on the ground, Devin looked at EyesHlzU and realized she had been paying rapt attention to him. Which was a change – he wasn't used to being the focus of anyone's attention, let alone a girl. *It's probably because I'm so tired from everything that has happened lately that I don't really care anymore. I'm normally nervous talking to most people, but now it's just flowing out of me without a thought.* He'd gotten through this far without any problems, so he continued on with his story.

"It was then that Strang3r and Gahbriyelle stepped up and told us to run; they had decided between them that they would hold them off as long as possible. They made the choice to sacrifice themselves so that we could escape with the Dungeon Core. I was expecting De4th or Sh1fty to protest and figure out another way, but I think they knew all along that we may not all make it back alive. As we ran away as fast as possible, we watched as the two Rangers climbed some trees on the opposite sides of the pathway we were taking. Their plan, which they quickly relayed to us, was to eliminate any potential Hunters in the group following us which would help us avoid being tracked anywhere we went.

"After about a minute, we heard intense fighting behind us – complete with screams and large explosions from some casters. Those two could hide pretty good but most likely couldn't hold up under massive AOE spells casts. Apparently, they had taken out any trackers, because we weren't found the entire way back to the camp. We took multiple detours and laid false trails where we could, until we finally made it back here. We heard shouts in the distance, but we got lucky and didn't see any opposition. You know the rest from there."

EyesHIzU was silent for the next couple of minutes as they continued to make their way through the forest with the *Reckless* guild group. "It sounds like you were both lucky and privileged to have such players such as Strang3r and Gahbriyelle on your team tonight. That three-hour lockout and experience penalty is no joke – they knew what they were in for when they sacrificed themselves. I'm glad you're back safe, even if not all of you made it," Eyes finally broke the silence.

"Their sacrifice will not be in vain – as long as we make it back to the dungeon in time. We still have about 39 days so that should be more than enough time," Devin confidently stated.

"I certainly hope so – but I also hope you didn't just jinx us."

Chapter 7

I should have kept my mouth shut, he thought – fifteen days later. The last two weeks had been spent on the run, avoiding parties of players from a multitude of different guilds. Small skirmishes with over-confident players had slowly whittled their ranks by two dozen *Reckless* guild members. They still had quite a few players on their side – with those that had died earlier slowly returning from where they had spawned when they were back from the lockout.

The first night after retrieving the stolen Dungeon Core, they all camped in a small valley nearly invisible from outside the camp unless you were right on top of it. They all collapsed in exhaustion, with Sh1fty assigning sentry duty to an unlucky few that would guard in shifts. Devin volunteered for the duty as well, since he had no need of sleep.

He needed to rest after the exertions of the last night and day, but he felt he was alert enough to watch as much of the perimeter as possible. De4th and Sh1fty seemed surprised that he didn't need sleep since as a player it was required (so that it seemed as realistic as possible). He told them that as a mob it wasn't programmed in him to need to sleep – they were so used to his presence that they had forgotten that he wasn't an actual player now.

During his sentry duty that night, he finally got enough time to crack open the crate containing the Dungeon Core. Because he was trying to avoid making a lot of noise, it took about an hour of slowly prying it open, but he was rewarded when he noticed – through an opening in the box – a steady blue glow. When he finally reached in a pulled out the baseball-sized, glowing-blue crystal he was relieved to finally hold it in his hand. Although his dungeon-given Core tracker and system prompt let him know that he had the object in his possession, it was good to physically possess it. As soon as he knew it was the real thing, he slid it into his shirt as securely as possible. He didn't have a bag like most players, so he had to carry everything on his body somewhere.

They weren't disturbed by anything that night, but as they were moving out the next morning, they were surprised by a trio of stealthers that attacked some of the lower-level players on the outskirts of their large group. Four players went down in a matter of about 15 seconds, but the *Reckless* leadership was quick to respond – they immediately swarmed the three attacking players and took them down without any more casualties. After that surprise attack, De4th ordered the lower-level members to support from the middle of the group and had his own stealth-oriented players in front, behind, and on the flanks to provide warning.

Later that day, they observed a couple of smaller parties of players that watched from a distance. It could have been coincidence – they might have been questing and just happened to be there – but they were much too high a level for the area.

There was one time they turned slightly off course so that they could avoid a larger group that their scouts had sighted. Expecting that they were some more *Divine Truth* members that had somehow gotten ahead of the rest of the guild, everyone was surprised that the big group was actually a completely different guild that had no connection whatsoever. Most of the other smaller parties that they had seen were from different guilds as well, which was confusing to say the least – it was almost like everyone was hunting them.

When they stopped for the night, Sh1fty logged off to see if there was any chatter about them on the forums. When the Thief quickly came back with a serious expression on his face, Devin knew they were in trouble. He followed him into the command tent where a couple of guild members, including De4th, were lounging around.

Without preamble, Sh1fty launched right into the bad news, "We're fucked. *Divine Truth* put out a bounty for killing anyone in *Reckless*, as well as an award for the return of the Dungeon Core. A million gold. We're going to have shitloads of people trying for one or the other of those paydays, with some of the larger guilds wanting both. Thousands of players have seen the postings already and many more are bound to see it within the next couple of days."

The shocked faces of the *Reckless* leadership would have been funny, if it wasn't for the fact that this was his life on the line. Devin looked toward De4th, hoping to see if he had any solution – only to be disappointed. Although he recovered from his shock faster than the others, dismay was still written on his face. "If anyone has any ideas how to proceed from here, let me know – there's not much we can do tonight other than double or triple the sentries outside the camp to provide more warning. Looks like it'll be a sleepless night for the majority of us, so get some sleep if and when you can. We'll get together again tomorrow morning before we head out," De4th tiredly announced.

Fortunately, Devin didn't need to sleep so he was standing guard around the perimeter all night. He thought he had seen indistinct shadows further into the forest a couple of times during the night, but he figured his mind was playing tricks on him, looking for trouble when there was none. All during the night, they didn't end up having any attacks – which didn't lessen the stress any. In the morning, Devin joined the guild leadership for a planning meeting in the command tent.

As he entered, his confidence was bolstered by a cunning, yet enthusiastic, look on the leaders' face. De4th had a plan. It was a complicated one, with many moving parts, and needed almost everyone to pitch in to make it succeed. Devin wasn't needed much for it, because a lot of it was executed by guild members who went offline. Essentially, the whole point of their strategy was to use misdirection, misplaced cooperation, and not a little stealth.

First, the guild holed up in a defensible position in a clearing in the middle of a tight copse of trees that made them invisible from the outside. Then they had as many players as possible logoff and post false sightings of the *Reckless* guild and "prideful" boastings of having killed so many guild members at so-and-so place on all the top game forums. To top off the misdirection, Devin brought out the Core for a couple of players to take screenshots of it. They would then post on the forums about stealing the Dungeon Core and that they would meet *Divine Truth* somewhere for the award.

This all led to players, parties, and even whole guilds looking through the forest in a myriad of different places for actual sightings of *Reckless* or the Core. With so many people looking for the same thing, conflict was all too prevalent. PKers were having a field day picking off the single players and lower-level groups that were wandering around – which led to their respective guilds stepping in. The guilds that hadn't gotten involved before were sucked in as some of their members were being killed and hunted down by rival guilds. After days of constant hit-and-run fighting, small skirmishes, and even a protracted battle or two, *Divine Truth* got impatient. They raised the award up to two million gold for the return of the Dungeon Core.

This led to some of the top-tier guilds, such as *Kingslayers* and *Sweat Success*, joining the fray. This was what De4th was waiting for. The second part of the plan was to arrange a "meeting" between *Reckless* and each of the top guilds. He told them that it was to turn over the Dungeon Core for "protection" from *Divine Truth* and a share of the award money. Directing them to one of the larger open spaces that could be found in the forest – which just coincidentally happened to be within a couple of hours journey of the dungeon – De4th told them all that they wanted to meet in ten days. He even let the time and place of the meeting "leak" to one of the members of *Divine Truth*.

With that plan in place, all they had to do was sit tight and let the tension build between all of the guilds searching for them. They continued to post fake locations on the forums to keep everyone away from their hiding place and to keep the momentum going. Finally, the day came where they had to start moving. This was the most dangerous part because they were literally going out into a hostile warzone. Based on the misdirection supplied by the postings, they had a good route to the meeting planned out that hopefully would have a minimum of players.

They ended up running into a handful of random hunting parties along the way, but it wasn't that big of a deal. Devin figured that they would post their location online, but it would hopefully be one of many "sightings" and would be lost in the shuffle. *Besides, we're on the move and going toward huge groups of players anyway.* After quickly traveling to their destination, they camped again for the night hidden in a small valley close to the meeting location.

There are only 23 days left to return the Core to the dungeon – this plan better work.

Chapter 8

"Hey Devin, before we leave I'd like to talk to you for a second," Devin looked his way before walking over to where they were breaking down the command tent. De4th was nervous but didn't let it show to his fellow guild members – he had to maintain a confident demeanor for the sake of the "troops". A lot was riding on the next couple of hours – their days of preparation would hopefully culminate into success. Careful planning could only get you so far – they would have to trust in their assessment of the players' attitudes and emotions.

"We all talked about this last night and we'd like you to join our guild. You've proven yourself to be someone we would like to have as part of our family. It would mean the world to me if you join – I could also brag that I run the only guild that has a mob as a member. It's up to you though, I don't want to force you – and it all depends on whether you can even join or not," he asked.

Devin stood there with an unreadable expression on his face, before responding with a slightly choked-up voice, "I would love to join you and your guild. I haven't had that many I would call friends before and I feel like we've all become good friends already. I also can't thank you enough for what you've done for Krista and me over the last couple of weeks – if it wasn't for you and the *Reckless* guild, I wouldn't have had any chance of literally getting my life back. I'm not sure if I actually can join or not, but I won't know unless I try."

De4th sent the invite to Devin, not sure what to expect. After a couple of seconds, he got a message saying that "**DUMB** has joined the guild." He was thoroughly confused, trying to figure out why it said "DUMB" and not Devin or even Human Rogue. He looked toward the person in question and asked him about it.

"Damn it – I thought I could get away from that stupid name. To answer your question, DUMB stands for Dungeon Upgradeable Mobile Boss and is what I'm known as inside the dungeon. I hate the name and Krista can't or won't do anything about it – she says the Dungeon Player system named it and she can't change it. Just call me Devin, and let's all just forget about the DUMB name," Devin informed him.

Chuckling softly, he warned Devin, "Well, all of our guild members just saw that notice – you may have to repeat what you told me a couple hundred more times before everyone understands. Or you could just use the guild chat – why don't you try it out. Oh, and welcome to the guild!"

He watched as Devin tried to figure out how to use the chat, which was interesting because he looked like he was waving his hands randomly around in the air while saying variations of, "Chat", "Guild Chat", and "Chat for Guild." Finally, a look of satisfaction appeared on Devin's face before an explanation came across the guild chat that told everyone who the "DUMB" was. That should hopefully head off needing to explain to a bunch of people, if not some good-natured ribbing.

With that taken care of, De4th formed a raid group that included Devin in it. Immediately, he noticed a small status screen near his normal raid user interface.

Raid Bonus:
Dungeon Core: *12% increase to all damage dealt, all resistances, experience gained, and currency looted*

I forgot about that benefit to having Devin in the guild – I'm glad he decided to join. That bonus may make this next part a little more bearable. With their preparations complete, he ordered all the members of his guild to move out. They all knew what was waiting for them in the next couple of hours, but not even one hesitated. He was proud of what they had already accomplished – and what they would try to accomplish with this meeting. Even if everything didn't turn out the way they planned, he was confident that it wouldn't be because they didn't work hard enough.

As they approached to the meeting area, he had them all stop so they could get a preview of the situation. Looking out from the edge of a dense grouping of trees, De4th and the rest of *Reckless* could see almost everything they needed to. Starting about 20 feet in front of them, a large clearing – about 1500 feet in diameter – was situated in the middle of the forest. It almost looked like a massive giant had ripped out a large random handful of trees and left the surrounding areas alone.

When De4th and his lieutenants sent the messages to the various guilds about this meeting, they ordered them not to arrive before 10 o'clock in the morning. They told them that if they were seen beforehand, then the deal was off. Checking the time, he witnessed a great influx of players arriving from all directions – right on time. They were lucky that they didn't run into any of them on the way here – their scouts had found a gap through all the waiting guilds that were circling the clearing. He saw each guild enter and react to the presence of the other guilds, usually milling around in confusion. After about 15 minutes, each of the players that were going to arrive had lined up around the perimeter of the clearing and segregated into their own guilds.

Not wanting to keep them waiting, De4th shouted so everyone could hear him over the low rumble of so many voices in the now too-small clearing, "Alright everyone, in the words of my good friend Sh1fty – let's go fuck some shit up!" A low cheer erupted from the guild, slightly muted because they didn't want to call too much attention to themselves until it was time. He started walking toward the center of the clearing, followed by the rest of the members of *Reckless*. He could feel the stare of hundreds – possibly thousands – of players weighing down on him, but he forged ahead because he was now too excited to be nervous.

Stopping near the center, he looked around as representatives of the different guilds surrounding him all started to walk quickly toward their group from all around them. De4th and his lieutenants stayed silent even as angry guild leaders or co-leaders arrived, vehemently yelling at them about all the other guilds being there. When they were all close enough to hear him talk, De4th told them, "Settle down, we'll figure thi..."

As if that was a signal – and it was – behind every guild leader appeared a player (and in some instances two) that had no guild affiliation attached to them. Almost as one, they attacked the guild leaders and killed them within moments before disappearing again. Silence reigned across the clearing as the guilds in attendance were shocked at the sudden occurrences. *Reckless* was silent as well, but for a different reason.

As part of their alliance with a couple of smaller guilds that wanted to help with their mission, De4th enlisted their help by having them provide some guild members who would be willing to leave their guild for a short period of time. These players were the ones waiting in stealth for the guild leaders to arrive – when they killed them they were not part of a guild so could not be traced back to it. With the wetwork done by these guildless players, specific *Reckless* members were instructed to send messages to the remaining leadership present on the field. Each of these messages was different, explaining that before they killed their leaders the stealthers mentioned the name of a rival guild or even – in some cases – *Divine Truth*.

This lead first to some confusion and then anger as De4th watched each of the guilds get riled up as they all shared news of who had killed their leaders in cold blood. Within minutes, the scenario that De4th had planned, worked on, and executed came to fruition there in the forest clearing. All it took was one guild, the *Kingslayers*, to start moving on *Sweat Success* before everyone present was out for blood.

The sounds of screams, metal striking metal, and magic explosions could be heard from miles around. Through it all – among the scenes of players dying only to be *Resurrected* soon after, entire guilds being overwhelmed by a larger guild, and even a swarm of undead skeletons rushing past as a guild made up of mainly Necromancers ran by them – *Reckless* stood untouched and forgotten by them all. Or so it appeared.

Knowing that *Divine Truth* would be appearing at the meeting, De4th didn't have long to wait before he saw a massive group of high-level players emerge from the trees and head straight for the center of the clearing. As they were recognized, several guilds attacked them along the way, only to be thoroughly wiped out only moments later. After that, they were left alone before they arrived near *Reckless* – at which point they stopped and from the center of the group a figure emerged.

Topping out at almost seven feet, the guild leader for *Divine Truth* was an imposing figure of a woman. Justice (De4th figured she must have been playing a long time to have gotten that name) was a Human Commander that was decked out in top-tier raiding gear that shone brightly with a myriad of different effects — most of which added to her already significant health point total.

Although he had heard about her, he had never actually met her before and was shocked to see she was level 112. *112! I've never seen or heard of anyone that high of level before — even the leaders of* Kingslayers *and* Sweat Success *were just under 100.* He knew that the higher level you achieved, the harder it was to level up to the next. After level 60, it was extraordinarily hard to increase your level; the experience needed to level-up was increased almost exponentially. To have progressed that far she must have been playing almost non-stop since game launch.

Her voice was deep — but surprisingly feminine — as she shouted loudly in order to be heard over the din of battle raging all around, "Hand over the Dungeon Core and we'll kill you quickly. If you don't, we'll kill each and every one of you slowly until we get what we want. No negotiation." That was it, short and to the point.

This was the hardest part of this whole plan — even knowing what was coming, all his fellow guild members were standing resolutely in the face of overwhelming odds. He held up a medium sized crate for all to see and said, "I don't think so – you'll have to pry it from my cold, dead hands." *I've always wanted to say that*, he thought, just before Justice gave the order to charge. She led from the front, confident in her abilities and higher level as she aimed straight for De4th.

What followed was a massacre – his guild just didn't have the levels or the gear to stand up to them for long. The bonus from the Dungeon Core was the only thing that kept them alive long enough to trigger the next step in the plan. After Justice charged, De4th immediately ran with the crate visible to everyone and made his way to the outskirts of the guild battles still ongoing throughout the clearing. Shouting, "*Divine Truth* is trying to steal back the Dungeon Core," over and over, he managed to gain the attention of many of the greedy players who until then had been fighting each other.

He was able to stay just ahead of Justice due to her heavy armor and made it back to the middle of the clearing as he watched nearly half of all the players follow him and Justice. His last stand was impressive – as he dodged attacks from Justice for almost a minute, he was cut down from behind by someone else from *Divine Truth* and dropped the crate on the ground. As he lay on the ground, bleeding out and staring up at his attackers, he saw out of the corner of his eye a player unstealth and attempt to grab the crate before he was cut down as well.

From there, swarms of players barreled into the center of the clearing, trying for a shot at obtaining the Core before *Divine Truth* could reacquire it. Although they were more numerous – and a higher level – than most of the guilds there, the members of *Divine Truth* could not hold up under the onslaught of players. One-by-one they fell until the tide of players surrounded the core leadership of the guild. These were the elite, the crème de la crème so to speak, of *Divine Truth* and wouldn't be put down easily. They worked well as a group and fought off their attackers, taking many of them with them as they fell.

Finally, only Justice was left facing almost 100 players by herself and she was hurt with multiple wounds across her body. As De4th watched from the ground as the last of his health points ran out, he saw the other guild leader pick up the crate and attempt to run through a small gap in the players – only to be quickly cut down as she neared them. The last thing he saw was the remaining players piling on top of the crate like it was a fumbled football.

A screen popped up saying, **YOU HAVE DIED**, and he woke up in his FIPOD minutes later with a smile on his face.

Chapter 9

Devin could hear the sounds of a battle behind him as he worked his way slowly through the trees, maintaining his *Stealth* in order to stay unnoticed. He could sense the two Rangers – Strang3r and Gahbriyelle – following behind him, stealthed and moving silently as well. They were about an hour out from the dungeon at their current pace and fortunately hadn't seen any players nearby for almost 15 minutes. They had been lucky so far; the only ones they had seen had been lower-level players hunting in the forest, blissfully unaware of what was taking place back in the clearing.

The trio had left the main group shortly before they arrived at the meeting place and had headed straight for the dungeon while maintaining *Stealth* the entire way. Strang3r and Gahbriyelle were along to help Devin in case he ran into pockets of players he couldn't avoid. So far, they weren't needed, and he was hoping that it stayed that way.

He thought about what was happening back in the clearing – about the sacrifices his new friends were making to help get the Core back where it belonged. When De4th unveiled his plan, Devin wasn't at first confident that it would work. *I thought there was no way that all of the guilds would end up attacking each other – it appears I was wrong.*

All their work, which Devin couldn't really participate in since he couldn't logoff or access the forums, was all for the simple act of a distraction. Although "simple" couldn't accurately describe the complexity of the misdirection caused by the members of *Reckless*. It was a masterful deception and now Devin had to do his part. He patted his chest where the Dungeon Core was hidden and thought, *I gotta get this baby home now.*

Over the next hour, they were fortunate not to run into any major opposition. As they approached the immediate vicinity of the dungeon, they did run into two higher-level casters in their 60's that were waiting around for something. Sneaking into position, the two Rangers pelted them with arrows as soon as they were in range and took them out quickly. None of them were sure if they were there to stop them, but they weren't going to take any chances.

At 100 feet from the dungeon, Devin got impatient and couldn't wait anymore. He unstealthed so that he could run for the entrance – which then seemed entirely too far away as he saw a player aiming a bow at him crouched near the dungeon. He instinctively rolled forward as an arrow flew a bare inch above his head and flinched when he heard a bow string thrum from behind him.

He looked up and saw his attacker with an arrow sprouting from his chest, followed by another one less than a second later. His companions had come to his rescue once again and he watched – as he could now tell by looking closer – the *Divine Truth* Archer slump to the ground. He turned to his saviors and waved thanks before sprinting again for the entrance.

As soon as he crossed the threshold, he felt the weight of the Dungeon Core disappear from inside his shirt. Patting his shirt in reflex, he immediately started freaking out when he couldn't find it. It was only as he saw that he had a prompt waiting for him that he calmed down.

Congratulations DUMB!

You have reacquired and returned the Dungeon Core to the dungeon! It has been automatically returned to the Guardian Room.

Because of your perseverance in the face of overwhelming odds, some benefits have now been granted to you and your dungeon:

- The dungeon may now earn experience again and the Dungeon Level will increase accordingly
- All Dungeon Level benefits are now activated and implemented
  - These include:
    - Buildings
    - NPC's
    - Dungeon Territory Expansion
- All resources gathered since the theft of the Dungeon Core are maintained
- Most restrictions lifted for the DUMB during the retrieval of the Dungeon Core are now made permanent
  - These include:
    - Travel restrictions are eliminated
    - Communication and trade between the DUMB and testers is permitted – outside communication is still restricted
    - The DUMB may join parties, raids, and even guilds of testers which will benefit from the Dungeon Core bonuses
- All Guardians currently unlocked are now available for use

These benefits also come with some new challenges:

- Every 72 hours the time allowed to retrieve the Dungeon Core if it is stolen is reduced by 5 days
    - Retrieval time will not drop below 5 days
- The level cap on the strongest floor will increase by 5 every 48 hours
    - The timer and level cap increase will reset whenever a new floor is created

I did it! Oh yeah, oh yeah! Devin did a spastic-looking dance that looked like he was having a seizure, but he didn't care. He had gotten the Core back and saved them from certain death at the hands of the system. As he looked over the prompt, he realized that his elation might be short-lived. The Dungeon Core was only as safe as the dungeon containing it and they had failed last time. With these new challenges, they would have to work increasingly harder to ensure their livelihood was secure. Just as he was thinking these things, he was interrupted by a voice.

"Devin! Oh my god, you did it! How did you do it?! We're saved! I could just kiss you right now!" Silence rang out after that statement from Krista, as Devin assumed she thought about what she had just said.

Trying not to make what should be a joyous occasion more uncomfortable, he started telling her about what he had gone through over the few weeks. She was understandably astonished when he told her about his dealings with the *Reckless* guild, including his revelation about their status as Dungeon and DUMB.

When he told her how the guild was intent on retrieving and helping to return the Core to the dungeon, she seemed skeptical – which was understandable. He himself was skeptical at first, but they had come through when he thought the whole game world was against him. She said that she would give them the benefit of the doubt since Devin did make it back safe with the Dungeon Core.

"I'm so glad you're back, Devin! I thought you had abandoned me after you didn't come back as a respawn and you were gone so long I was despairing of ever seeing you again. I'm sorry for what I said before you left and I'm sorry for doubting that you could get the Dungeon Core back – it was wrong of me to accuse you like that. I was just so distraught over losing the Core that I wasn't thinking straight – neither of us was. Can you ever forgive me?" Krista pleaded.

Devin found that he had mixed emotions over the whole thing. On one hand, he was still angry at her for doubting and accusing him falsely of things he had no control over. On the other, he still loved Krista and felt bad for her thinking that he had abandoned her after they had such a fight. Overall, however, he felt that he wasn't quite yet ready to forgive her yet. He didn't even have any proof yet of not having anything to do with Violette's breakdown – as soon as he did, it would hopefully clear the tension between them and things could go back to the way things were before.

He told her all of that – without repeating that he loved her – and she seemed only slightly mollified by his reasoning. He brought up bringing back Violette, now that the Guardians were accessible again, so that they could both question her about what had happened. Krista adamantly refused, stating that the crazy bitch was still too unstable to guard the Core against any intruders. They needed a Guardian that they could count on to *be* a guardian, one that they didn't have to worry about being a liability instead of an asset.

Devin felt that when they were able to talk to Violette and figure out what happened then she would be able to do her job again successfully. His arguments were in vain, however, because Krista still refused, and she was the one ultimately in charge of the dungeon. She decided to place the new Guardian that she had acquired at Dungeon Level 10 in the Guardian Room until they could make a new floor. Then they could bring Violette back as a mini-boss just before the new Guardian Room so that even if she was still unstable she wouldn't be the only thing protecting the Dungeon Core.

Devin reluctantly agreed and asked Krista to respawn him in the staging room just outside the Guardian Room. Since he figured he would change it soon when he found out what he needed to do next, he quickly selected Orc Defender as his race and class. He was anxious to see this new Guardian that their survival would depend on.

When he was ready, he spawned in the staging room and made his way to the Guardian Room door. He entered the doorway, not really having any idea what he was expecting since Krista had made no mention of the new Guardian before this. He walked two steps in and stopped. And stared, disgusted. And then he looked up...and up...and up some more.

"What the fu—"

Chapter 10

Krista was overjoyed to get the Dungeon Core back after its absence. In the time that Devin had been away, the anger and confusion she felt toward him had faded away into oblivion as she lost herself in a depressive state. Her "consciousness" floated free and she only intermittently focused on the dungeon, usually just long enough to peer in on some player groups making their way through the dungeon. She only watched them for a minute or so before she retreated to the safety of her unfocused mind.

It was only when she got a system prompt that she was pulled from her stupor long enough to read it. As soon as she read the first line about the Dungeon Core being returned, she felt her mind wake up and start working again. It was like her "brain" got a shot of adrenaline, everything that happened over the last couple of months crashing down on her in a massive download. By the time she finished reading the prompt and gathering her thoughts, she had focused on the entrance and saw Devin standing there. He looked just the same as he had when he left so long ago, if a little more ragged and worn down.

After she greeted him, she belatedly realized she told him that she wanted to kiss him. She mentally blushed and thought about it – remembering what he had said before he left earlier. She had thought about it a lot in between bouts of depressive fugue states. She still wasn't sure exactly how she felt about him and his feelings toward her. Fortunately, Devin prevented her from having to say any more as he explained what had happened to him after he had left.

Krista was actually a little jealous – not for all of the "adventures" he had, but jealous of all of the friends that he had made. She was the one who usually spent all her time adventuring with him and she felt left-out. They would usually have other party members in other games, but the core of the group was always the two of them. Even in the dungeon, they still worked together to accomplish what they needed to. With the addition of this *"Reckless"* guild, it felt like she was losing him. However, he was back now, and Krista was determined to keep him around as long as possible.

She could understand his reasons for not forgiving her – she did say some not-so-nice things before he left. But she couldn't countenance bringing Violette back to talk to her yet. She wasn't going to trust her to protect them now when she had already failed at it once. When Devin reluctantly agreed to hold off bringing Violette back, she brought up the Guardian Menu to see what her other option was.

Guardians	
Current number of guardians:	2
Guardians:	Violette (Spirit Witch) Bruce (Undead Abomination)

Place guardian	0 rp

Bruce? What kind of name is that for an Undead Abomination? Figuring anything was better than their last Guardian, she placed it just inside the door of the Guardian Room. As it appeared, she was as unprepared for the result as she was when she had first seen Violette – this was definitely not what she had expected. She had to move back her viewpoint to take it all in.

Standing 40 feet tall, the Undead Abomination was a giant, rotting mass of flesh that disgusted Krista as soon as she looked at it. From what she could see, it had numerous eyes and mouths located in seemingly random locations all over its body. She also counted 17 giant arms and 10 legs supporting the ovoid-shaped abomination. The skin was an unhealthy corpse-grey and dark purple color as if it were an enormous bruise. If she could smell, Krista was sure that the stench alone might be enough to kill someone.

As she finished taking it all in, she noticed Devin entering the doorway and stopping a couple of steps into the room. His vision looked all the way up the monstrosity and started to say something when he inhaled. Instantly, he dropped to his knees, woozy from the odor emanating from the Undead Abomination. Krista watched him drag himself back out the doorway into the staging room.

She moved her viewpoint and waited until he had recovered enough to talk. "How do you like our new Guardian?" Krista couldn't keep the humor from her voice.

"Ha ha. What the hell is that thing? I can't even get close to it without wanting to throw up from the sight and smell of it," Devin asked.

"He's an Undead Abomination and apparently his name is Bruce. Since I can't smell, let me see if I can talk to him and get him to guard the Dungeon Core." As she went to shift her viewpoint, she couldn't help but tease Devin just a little, "I wouldn't advise copping a feel on this one."

Krista went back to the Guardian Room and moved her viewpoint to just in front of the massive mound of flesh. "Can you understand me?" She wasn't expecting anything coherent, so was startled when every single mouth answered her at the same time – which was quite unsettling to say the least. Especially because the tone of the voice was high-pitched, happy, and juvenile – all at the same time. *He's as happy and cheery as Violette was – if not more.*

"Hi! How are you? Are you my new master? It's so nice to be here! Where am I? This place looks sooo neat! Did you do the decorating here? I love all the different levels to that temple back there – it's so cute! My name's Bruce – what's yours? You've got a lovely voice! Are you the only one here? I'm hungry – I like to eat things! Is there a mirror around here? I want to make myself presentable if we have any guests later."

On and on it went for what Krista could have sworn was an eternity – but was more like five minutes. She couldn't get a word in edgewise and when "Bruce" finally wound down she didn't even know what to say. Confused at the dichotomy of its appearance and personality, Krista had to take a mental step back and collect her scattered thoughts.

When she reasoned that she had her thoughts in order, she told Bruce about the dungeon, the Dungeon Core, and his job to protect it. He seemed receptive to what she had told him and to cut off any more rambling conversations she asked him what he needed as far as a Guardian Room went.

"I need space, lots and lots of space! I know it's hard to tell, but I'm a little overweight. I'd feel a lot more comfortable with a large empty room that I can move freely around in. Although I like the look of the temple, I can't use it properly. You are so awesome for doing this for little ol' me! Thank you so much! Let me know if there is anything else I can do!"

With a speed she didn't know she had, Krista started to remove all of the former Guardians' décor including the massive temple complex. She wanted to move on to something else and get away from the chipper chatterbox in the room – it was just too creepy hearing that voice coming from all those different mouths. Once everything was gone, she looked toward Bruce again and found that he was wandering around his new place. He was obviously happy with it since as he walked he made weird chirping sounds. She quickly told him that if he needed anything in the future to let her know and she would warn him if any intruders were heading in his direction.

Moving back to Devin, Krista found him wandering through the third level watching a group of players struggling through the Orc Village. She asked him to exit from there, so they could talk without alerting the players and he made his way out the exit. Devin asked about the new Guardian and she went on to explain about his personality and the horrifyingly disturbing way he spoke to her. She also told him that it looked likely that he would hold up his end of the position and seemed like a formidable foe. Krista asked him if he wanted to formally meet Bruce – while also letting him know that it wasn't required. He promptly declined, and he seemed relieved when had an out. Apparently, Bruce looked and smelled so bad that it would actually be a benefit when players came calling.

Next on the agenda, Krista wanted to find more out about the different benefits that had unlocked when the Dungeon Core was returned. She asked Carl, the former dungeon admin, if he had any new information about the NPCs and Buildings. The last time she had accessed the menu, the resources that were needed to purchase them were so astronomical that she would never have the ability to use them. She was hoping that this time was different.

The NPC and Building prices have been fixed. Whereas before they were in the millions of points, they are now much more

affordable. The buildings you can create can be placed outside of the dungeon and each NPC can be hired to operate these buildings. The only downside is that you will need to expand your territory in order to place them outside of the dungeon.

"That at least sounds better – how do we expand the dungeon territory?"

The only way to expand your dungeon territory is for your DUMB to find, defeat, and claim another dungeon. This will then incorporate that dungeon into your territory and enable access to the immediate vicinity surrounding the entrance to each dungeon. Only then would you be able to place building outside of the dungeon.

In anticipation of your next question, the DUMB must complete the dungeon alone – meaning they cannot be in a party to do so. Only by defeating the Dungeon Boss can the dungeon be fully claimed. You would then take over control from the resident AI in charge of the dungeon and you can run it just as you would this one. Fortunately, there is only one Dungeon Core, so you would not have to guard one there as well – although I cannot claim to know what "The AI" will do in the future.

Additionally, every mob in the claimed dungeon will be usable in your first dungeon and vice versa.

Imagining the possibilities, Krista thanked Carl and turned to Devin who was looking excited. "Did you hear all of that? Do you remember seeing any other dungeons around nearby?"

"When I was looking for more monsters for the new floor before...you know...I saw a dungeon further up the mountain that was inaccessible at the time. I'm not sure what it is or what level the mobs are inside, but I can find out – let me speak to my guild and see what they have to say," Devin responded.

Although she was happy that he had some outside help, she was still miffed that he had found some friends outside of their "circle". She didn't let him know about her dislike about this circumstance and instead told him that it was a good idea and to let her know if he needed anything. "Oh, and one more thing – I think I have enough resources to spare to unlock the Dual Class upgrade for you – so you can use two different classes at the same time. Talk with your friends and see if they have any ideas for a character build."

She watched him walk away, heading for the teleporter in the staging room that led back to the entrance. Now that they weren't in any danger of dying, she thought again about what she wanted to do for that new floor she was going to make...

Chapter 11

Devin teleported back to the entrance and cautiously looked around for any incoming players before heading outside. He had tried to use the guild chat but for some reason it wouldn't work inside of the dungeon. *It must be some sort of change that was implemented when the Dungeon Core event started.* As soon as he walked outside, he was flooded by messages in the guild chat. Some of them asked after him and asked if he had gotten back to the dungeon safely. These were answered by Strang3r and Gahbriyelle, who had watched him enter the dungeon, and told them that indeed Devin had made it back safe. It also seemed that the three-hour lockout period had expired only a couple of minutes ago for most of the players who were involved in the "distraction".

After catching everyone up on the events of the last couple of hours, including the new Guardian, he told them about the changes in the dungeon. The fact that the level cap would increase every two days would be a problem in the future if they didn't figure out a solution soon.

Guild Chat:
DUMB: So, there is a way to expand our dungeon territory, thereby increasing our ability to use some of our other resources. But I have to find, defeat, and claim another dungeon in order to do this. There is a dungeon near the top of the same mountain our current dungeon is located. Does anyone have any information about it?

493

Domn3r: If I remember correctly, it is a fire-themed dungeon with Dragonkin and a Flame Dragon at the end as the Dungeon Boss. I remember running it with a group when we were all around level 20.

DUMB: Thanks! And if I were to try to defeat it all by myself, what class would you recommend? Keep in mind that I'm only level 30.

Sh1fty: Why would you want to do it by yourself? I can have a few guildies come help you get through it with no trouble.

DUMB: I appreciate the help, but the rules say that I must do it by myself.

EyesHlzU: Does it say you have to defeat every monster or just the Dungeon Boss?

DUMB: Uh…well, now that I think of it I only have to defeat the Dungeon Boss.

Sh1fty: That settles it – I'm sending you some help with the rest of the dungeon so that you are fresh for the boss. Domn3r, are you and your crew still near there?

Domn3r: We sure are, we were finishing a quest not too far from there. We can be there in about an hour or so.

System Message: De4thfrmbeh1nd has come online

DUMB: That would be awesome – thanks for the help! What class do you think I should choose? I can choose any of the basic classes and can alter the stats from there.

De4thfrmbeh1nd: What?!?! That's so unfair – seems like a cheat to me. By the way, great job getting the Core back to the dungeon. Our distraction worked even better than I had planned. We had everyone almost in a free-for-all in that clearing.

Sh1fty: It was a glorious slaughter – from what I could see before a couple stray arrows took me out.

De4thfrmbeh1nd: The forums are blowing up with accusations flying all over the place and everyone is still looking for the "Dungeon Core" I dropped. Since no one has come forward saying they have it they are searching the battlefield and accosting all the players heading in and out of the area. Fortunately, most of the backlash toward Reckless that I was expecting is instead being directed toward Divine Truth.

DUMB: Nice – I can't thank you all enough for what you have done for Krista and me. If it wasn't for all your help, we probably wouldn't be here today.

Sh1fty: No problem kiddo – I haven't had that much fun in ages.

De4thfrmbeh1nd: Same here.

EyesHlzU: Ditto.

DUMB: So anyway, does anyone have any suggestions for my class? Actually, I should say "classes" because Krista just unlocked an upgrade giving me access to two classes at the same time.

Sh1fty: Bullshit! That's not fair – how do I become a DUMB like you? To be able to change your class or classes anytime you want is game-breaking. You're one lucky son of a bitch...well except for your little logoff problem – sorry about that.

After this, there were lots of helpful suggestions concerning his mix of classes that he could choose and more outbursts of "unfair" as more people learned about his ability to change classes whenever he wanted to. These last made him smile as he read them, thinking that maybe he didn't have it so bad here. Even remembering that Krista and he were here permanently didn't diminish his joy at reading how they thought he was "OP" or "overpowered". He'd have to remember to tell Krista that – and to thank her for upgrading him.

Eventually, the consensus they guild arrived at for his dual class was a mixture of an Archer and a Druid. The thought behind this was to be agile enough to avoid attacks while casting or firing arrows from long-range. There was no way he going to be able to go toe-to-toe with Dungeon Boss – even with damage mitigation it was close to impossible to finish it off without a healer. The only hope was to stay away long enough to damage it from range and the Druid had enough buffs to help with healing and resistance if he did end up getting hit a couple of times.

After making his decision, he headed back into the dungeon to have Krista respawn him near the entrance so that he could make his changes to his class. He figured he needed to balance his Wisdom and Agility stats for his character to work – normally he just dumped the majority of his stat points into one attribute. He also needed to add a little bit to Intelligence so that he had a large enough mana pool to cast the spells he needed to. And he needed Constitution for a boost in his health points so that he didn't die in one hit. The one thing he didn't really need was Strength, fortunately, but finding the right balance was going to be difficult. Eventually, with help from Krista who was able to provide him some non-typical Archer and Druid gear – and the addition of a new race that had been added while he was away – he figured out his stat point allocation with the equipment bonuses.

Character Status					
Race:		Troll	Level:		30
Class:		Archer/Druid	Experience:		3000/3000
Strength:	5	Physical Damage:	1005	Magical Damage:	260
Constitution:	124	Physical Resistance:	652	Magical Resistance:	790
Agility:	360	Health Points:	1240	Mana Points:	1300

Intelligence:	130	Health Regeneration:	372.0 per min	Mana Regeneration:	1185.0 per min
Wisdom:	395	Block:	0	Critical/Dodge Chance:	36.0%
Skills:			Flurry I, Ice Arrow III, Sidestep I, Entangling Roots I, Nature's Boon III, Deathly Chill IV, Freezing Rain III		
Upgrades:			Lure, Dual Class		

His gear gave him some increases in his Agility and Wisdom so that he was able to concentrate on putting his available points into Constitution and Intelligence. That meant he was balanced enough to take advantage of all that the classes he chose had to offer.

The skills and spells that he had to choose from were almost overwhelming – he'd never had so many choices on where to spend his skill points. He had to narrow down his selections based on just the fight he was heading toward – the Flame Dragon Dungeon Boss. Since fire was the primary attribute to the dungeon, he wanted to be able to counter that with its opposite element.

Flurry I	(Archer Class Skill)		
Fire multiple arrows at once at a single target, doing physical damage			
Number of arrows:	3	Physical Damage:	10 per arrow
Cooldown:	60.0 seconds		

Ice Arrow III			
Fire an arrow doing additional Water-based elemental damage to a single target, with a chance to stun			
Magical Damage:	150	Stun Chance:	10.0%
Cooldown:	30.0 seconds		

Sidestep I			
Sidestep to move out of the way of an incoming ranged projectile or targeted spell.			

Will be used automatically.			
Cooldown:	120.0 seconds		

Entangling Roots I	(Druid Class Skill)		
Cause roots to rise from the ground under a target, trapping them in place for a limited time			
Magical Damage:	0	Duration:	15.0 seconds
Casting Time:	1.0 seconds	Mana Cost:	15

Nature's Boon III			
The power of nature engulfs a target, regenerating health points per tick for a limited time			
Healing per Tick:	50	Tick Interval:	3.0 seconds
Duration:	60.0 seconds	Casting Time:	2.0 seconds
Mana Cost:	160		

Deathly Chill IV			
Invoke the power of the cold arctic weather to reduce the Water-based magical resistance on all enemies within a certain distance for a limited time			
Resistance Decreased:	70%	Duration:	180.0 seconds
Casting Time:	1.0 seconds	Area of effect:	50 feet out starting from caster's position
Mana Cost:	120		

Freezing Rain III			
Summon an average-sized freezing rainstorm over a designated area for a short duration; does Water-based elemental damage			
Magical Damage:	110 per second	Duration:	10.0 seconds
Area Diameter:	20.0 feet	Casting Time:	1.5 seconds
Mana Cost:	400		

When he had respawned, equipped his gear, and checked to make sure everything was set up to his liking, Devin asked Krista to wish him luck and headed outside of the dungeon. As he walked, he kept almost tripping as he had to get used to the new race that he had chosen. The average Troll used by player characters was about nine feet tall, as big around as a good-sized horse, and had small tree trunks for legs. He had chosen the Troll because of the additional +25% physical damage and resistances – now he was beginning to regret it. He felt like a big, lumbering house as he trudged out of the entrance and made his way toward the forest outside.

As he started moving faster, his higher Agility stat kicked in and he was able to move more fluidly amongst the trees – dodging and weaving through the trunks with ease. Despite his size, his Agility more than made up for his bulk – of course, he was still a giant target. When fighting, he figured he would be able to execute a dodge easily – whether or not his whole body moved out of the way was a different matter.

Taking out his bow that he had received from Krista, Devin decided to make sure he could use it with his big fat fingers. As he nocked his first arrow, his whole hand engulfed the string and arrow until he couldn't even see it – *this isn't good*. He tried to fire it at a tree about 20 feet away and as it released the string caught on another one of his fingers and the shot went awry. He set another one on the string and tried again – with little better result.

Krista frequently called him stubborn and didn't know when to stop trying something that wasn't working and do something else. She was probably right, as Devin continued to practice shooting arrow after arrow toward the same trunk he had been trying to hit at first for about 20 minutes. His stubbornness paid off as he figured out how to hold it and fire it with relatively good accuracy. Glad that he didn't have to change his race, he headed toward the mountain path that led up to the dungeon he had found so long ago.

Chapter 12

Domn3r followed his group as they approached the destination where they were supposed to meet Devin. As they turned the last corner blocking the view of the dungeon, they all stopped abruptly when they saw a giant, nine-foot tall Troll holding a bow waiting near the entrance. Trolls were an uncommon sight around these parts, where primarily Light-based races held sway. Domn3r had only actually seen two his entire time playing *Glendaria Awakens* and it was just recently during the battle in the clearing between all the guilds.

Not sure of his intentions, all in his party readied their weapons and got ready to defend themselves. The Troll started moving toward them and Domn3r almost gave to order to attack when it unexpectedly spoke, "Hi guys! Thanks for coming on such short notice!"

Confusion set in for all of them as Domn3r took a closer look and saw that he was looking at a **Troll Archer/Druid**, which was crazy because he had never heard of a dual-classed mob before. The lightbulb apparently went off for Ambrose, because she asked, "Devin? Is that you?"

"Of course, who else would be here waiting for you? And an Archer/Druid to boot? Oh, yeah, I'm a Troll – sorry, I should have warned you. It's got high physical damage and resistance bonuses, so it was the best choice for my mixture of classes," responded the hulking behemoth.

Domn3r had been monitoring the guild chat and had been listening as different members were giving advice to Devin on what he should choose for his character build. He had to admit that he honestly didn't believe he could change his character that easily and was expecting the Human Rogue he had met previously. To say he was surprised was an understatement – he was also insanely jealous of his ability to change on a whim. To be able to change to whatever you wanted to be was so unfair as to be almost criminal. Some days when he was tired of soaking up all the damage for the party, he wished he had chosen a Mage or something else that could cast spells from long range. To be able to do that – even if it cost money – would be something he would jump on in a second.

He looked at the rest of his party as they caught on to who they were talking to. Their Healer, Ambrose, looked smug as she was the one who had figured it all out in the first place. Bolt3n, their Archer, looked surprised still as he took in his counterpart – most likely he'd never seen anyone that big wielding a bow. With characteristic suspicion, Maxinista looked at Devin like he was a situation that still needed to be investigated. And finally, Mac (short for Macgowenishburt) looked happy – most likely because he had another magic caster to play with.

"Well, then, what exactly are your thoughts on how to do this, Devin?" Ambrose asked. Devin looked confused for a second – as much as a giant troll can look confused – until he caught on to what she was asking.

"I figure I can follow you all down the Dungeon Boss and then kill it. I've never been here before, so you'll have to show me where to go in there."

Domn3r thought this was a good a plan as any, but he added something to it, "Along the way I want you to practice using your spells and attacking as much as you can – I'm betting you haven't tried killing anything yet since you changed. To take the Flame Dragon down by yourself you'll need to be on top of your game. The boss is level 28 – which sounds easy since it's two levels below you – but keep in mind that it's a BOSS and has much higher health points and resistances than the typical level 28 mob. I'm sure you know all of this, since you're part of a dungeon yourself – but you've probably never been on this side of the encounter before. This boss is meant to be taken down by a group of players working together.

"Even though the typical group tackling this dungeon is about ten levels below you, you'll be working at a disadvantage when trying to do it solo. Most of the problems you would normally have trying to do it by yourself are caused by the mobs on the way to the end – which we will be able to help with. They aren't hard, but there are a lot of them. You just need to concentrate on staying alive until we can deliver you safely to the Dungeon Boss."

Devin seemed to consider this and quickly agreed with enthusiasm. They then headed into the dungeon entrance with Domn3r's group leading the way. They had all talked about this dungeon on the way here and it turned out that all of them had run it through at least once – just in different groups. They had all been part of numerous groups before they had been thrown together trying to obtain the Dungeon Core. It was ironic that it was the same dungeon they were now helping to get stronger. After they had leveled too much to be able to try for the Dungeon Core anymore, they had stayed together because their playstyles all seemed to mesh well. The trials through the dungeon had brought them all closer and he felt confident that he could call them his good friends.

Domn3r thought about how everything they now enjoyed about the game they were playing revolved around Devin and the dungeon he was part of. The bonds of friendship forged, the epic guild battle in the clearing, and now being the first players to escort a dungeon mob through another dungeon so that it could take it over – these were what made playing games like this worth all the time spent in-game. He was excited to see what would happen next.

Chapter 13

Devin followed after Domn3rs' party, anxious for the first time since playing this game. He wanted to show them he had the skills to accomplish what he needed to do. He thought that he had practiced enough, first when he was fighting in his own dungeon with various classes, and lastly with his Archer/Druid in the forest just before he made his way up the mountain. Even though they were a couple of levels above him, he thought he could show them a thing or two as they made their way through the first floor.

After watching them in the first battle, he changed his mind and was determined to learn as much as he could from them. Their teamwork was stellar – they were able to anticipate each other's attacks and instinctually knew where they needed to be at any given time. It was clear that they had spent a lot of time together and knew one another's strengths and weaknesses. He realized that he didn't have much experience fighting normal mobs – he was more used to fighting players. He needed a whole new set of skills to succeed here.

The first creatures that they ran across were some innocuous-looking mushrooms that stood about three feet tall, were about as big around car tire, and were a deep red color. They were arranged haphazardly in the initial room they came across and if they hadn't been attacked by Domn3r's group almost immediately he would have tried to walk by them, thinking them just some random flora. As soon as Domn3r rushed ahead with shield leading the way, the room came alive with a horrid screeching that sounded like someone was running nails across a chalkboard.

Cringing and covering his ears, Devin watched as the other players with him ignored the sound and attacked full-out. While he was still trying to catch his bearings, he looked up and saw the mushrooms around the room had somehow grown short arms and legs – barely big enough to handle their stature but enough to make them mobile. They all rushed Domn3r with their now-visible mouths full of razor-sharp teeth as he gathered their aggro to him.

Devin looked closer at one of the mushrooms and saw that it was called a **Magma Shroomba (Level 20)**. From what he could see from his position, there were nine of the Shroombas closing in on the Defender in the middle of the room. It looked like too much for him to handle and, indeed, he was swarmed almost as he thought that. Before he could take more than a couple of points of damage, however, Maxinista appeared from *Stealth* behind one of the mobile mushrooms and backstabbed it – killing it instantly. At the same time, two arrows flew through the air in rapid succession, striking the two Shroombas on either side of the Rogue. Apparently, they were critical shots, because they were one-shotted as well.

As this went down, the rest of the party was marshalling their own attack. Mac cast *Ice Shard* after *Ice Shard* toward the creatures on the opposite side of where Max had appeared, taking down four in as many seconds. The remaining two Shroombas each got sliced in the head by Domn3r, doing a healthy amount of damage. Ambrose followed up each strike with a quick *Smite*, which blasted them into oblivion. The entire battle lasted no more than about ten seconds, from when Domn3r rushed ahead to when the last Shroomba fell. It was over so quickly that by the time Devin thought about helping there was nothing for him to do.

Feeling a little useless, he cast *Nature's Boon III* on Domn3r to help regenerate the couple of points of damage he had sustained. It wasn't necessary because he had regenerated all but one health point by the time the spell landed on him. They all turned toward him, and he shrugged as if to say, "Sorry." Each of them laughed, realizing that they had been too efficient in their slaughter.

"Sorry about that Devin, we're just so used to working together that it is almost automatic now – we'll try to leave you some to practice on from now on. These guys are so far beneath our level that most of the time we can sweep through them without breaking a sweat," Domn3r apologized.

And so it went – through the next few rooms there were increasingly larger groups of **Magma Shroombas**, at least a few of which Bolt3n designated for Devin to kill. His first arrow went way off target, as Devin got nervous and forgot how to properly hold the arrow on the string with his massive fingers. Shaking his anxiousness off, he put another arrow on the string and fired it off – hitting the walking mushroom he was aiming at in the junk. Or at least where its junk would be if it had some. It wasn't exactly where he had aimed it, but at least he hit it this time.

His next two arrows were more on the mark: one hitting it on the top of its head and the next flew straight into the mouth of the Shroomba, instantly killing it with a critical strike. Elated, he switched targets and put the next two arrows into the mouths of the two mushrooms heading in his direction – again killing them instantly. He was finally getting used to the different feel of firing with his large hands and was improving his accuracy by leaps and bounds. He was lucky that their mouths were so large, thereby providing a bigger target for his arrows. If he had to aim for their eyes, for example, he wasn't sure he could have hit them accurately.

With his accuracy improving, he switched to using his other skills and spells over the next couple of fights. First, since he was already getting better at using his bow, he used his *Ice Arrow III* skill to see what kind of extra damage it would inflict. He was pleasantly surprised when he hit a Shroomba in the back with one of these special arrows – it did three times the amount of damage of a normal arrow. When he checked his combat logs, he saw that it was due to the mobs' lower resistance to water-based elemental attacks. He was glad to see this, since this was the basis for his strategy for the Dungeon Boss later on.

After experimenting with his different Archer skills, he switched to using his Druid spells to see how effective they were going to be. On one of the last rooms before the Floor Boss, he asked Domn3r to gather up the whole room full of Shroombas, which had now increased to 25. In addition, he had him attempt to keep all of them in front of him, without letting them surround him. As soon as they were mostly in position, he cast *Deathly Chill IV* on the assembled mobs, which was designed to reduce their resistance to water-based elemental attacks. Within a second, a cold gale of wind blew thick, frosty air outward from his position. Although he couldn't see any obvious effect on the Shroombas, he thought they looked a little slower in their movements – which was an unintended side effect.

As soon as the wave of super-chilled air hit them, Devin used *Freezing Rain III* and centered it on the outside of the pack of deadly mushrooms. He did this to try to avoid hitting Domn3r, who was still trying to tank the whole lot of them by himself. The result was spectacular – as soon as the freezing rain pelted the Shroombas with what looked like tiny icicles, they started taking massive amounts of damage. They had just enough time to turn toward Devin – as he had taken their aggro – before they collapsed almost as one. The spell continued for another seven or eight seconds before stopping, leaving a puddle of water 20 feet in diameter containing all the mushroom corpses.

He looked around, overjoyed at how well that worked, but his elation was short-lived as he saw his companions shivering in their armor. He was confused for a second, but suddenly everything clicked – his *Deathly Chill* spell said all "enemies", which technically all players were. He would have to be more careful in the future not to hit any of his allies with an AOE spell since friendly-fire was a distinct possibility.

"Sorry, I won't do that again. I didn't know it would do that," he told the murderous glares directed his way – apparently they didn't like the cold any more than he did. He tried to avoid their gazes while listening to their teeth chatter and after another couple of minutes the effects wore off. Gathering themselves back together, they headed off to the Floor Boss room with disdainful glances directed his way. *They'll get over it...I hope.*

The Floor Boss was a **Giant Magma Shroomba (Level 24)** that was almost identical to its smaller cousins other than the fact that it was fifteen feet tall instead of three. Despite the size, Domn3r's group was able to take it down without much struggle in about 20 seconds. Devin was even able to get a couple of *Ice Arrows* off before it was killed – which, with his improved accuracy was able to hit it in the mouth every single time. Devin told the group that they could loot everything in the Boss Chest, just as they had looted everything before this. He couldn't carry anything, so it would do him no good – besides, they were doing most of the work so should get all of the rewards. It wasn't anything great, but they would be able to sell most of the stuff they picked up back in Briarwood or another town. After that, they headed down to the next floor.

There were five floors in this dungeon which made it a bit longer than most other dungeons in this level range, so it was good that they were able to fly through the first floor so quickly. The second floor wasn't that much harder, but it was comprised entirely of another new mob. As they entered the first room after following the staircase down from the previous floor, the temperature in the room began to rise dramatically. He could see small lava flows on either side of the room which gave off such heat that it was almost stifling.

Domn3r led the group toward the middle of the room, where he placed everyone in two rows facing outwards toward the lava flows. He told them all, including Devin, to look for anything coming out of the lava and to call out when they spotted something. He wasn't sure what he was supposed to look for, but he diligently stared at the lava waiting for something to happen. He didn't have long to wait as a large, lizard-shaped creature emerged from the molten expanse and shook off the lava like a wet dog. Through the rain of fiery goblets – none of which got near the party – he found the name of the lizard was a **Lava Salamander (Level 22)**.

Devin had a pet salamander when he was really young – probably around age 5 or 6 – and it was a cute little guy named Stinky that he could hold in his hand. As it got older, it grew in size but even then, it wasn't larger than his forearm. The **Lava Salamander** was entirely different. First of all, it was about the size and shape of a walrus, was a light red color just slightly darker than the lava flow behind it, and he could see wisps of fire emanating from its mouth. He was so startled by its appearance that he forgot to call out right away and only as it started heading in his direction did he shout, "Hey, over here! Help!"

Domn3r immediately rushed toward the giant lizard, cutting it off from reaching the rest of the party. Once aggro was established, everyone except Max unleashed their ranged attacks and brought it down within seconds. Max oversaw watching for any other Salamanders that might attack and just after the first went down another emerged. This one went down as quickly as the first, but as it was collapsing in death Devin shot an *Ice Arrow* that flew over its head and landed in the lava flow. As soon as it entered the lava, a cloud of steam erupted when the water-based projectile became super-heated.

"And that is why you should never cast *Freezing Rain* or any other water-based spells that might get out of control. The amount of steam released would kill us even quicker than any of the mobs in here. I've seen it happen, and it's not pretty," Mac told him. "*Ice Arrows* are ok, because they only release a small amount of steam and you could fire them all day without worry — just hold off on your other spells for now, though."

"Thanks, I'll try to remember that," Devin responded. He was glad that he hadn't kept trying his spells out — he had already made one mistake and didn't want another one to kill them all. *It looks like I still have a lot to learn.*

Chapter 14

After Devin left to capture the other dungeon to expand their territory, Krista floated around watching the different parties' progress through the dungeon. There was a really determined guild called the *Swordsmiths* that was steadily improving – this time it looked like they would all make it through with few casualties. As she watched the last group of five complete the Orc Village, she realized that 19 of them made it through – a player had fallen off one of the elevated bridges onto the rocks and was lost.

This was the first time since the Dungeon Core was returned that anyone looked like they would challenge her Guardian. Krista was a little nervous – but also really excited – to see how her Undead Abomination would perform guarding the Core. As the players gathered in the Staging Room just outside of the Guardian Room, she transported her viewpoint inside to let Bruce know about the upcoming fight.

She found him walking around the room in slow circles, talking to himself. "And what do you think about the rock in this area?" "Well I think it's a little too dark – it doesn't really go with the rest of the room." "I think it works just fine though, it gives it a little contrast compared to the bare aesthetics of the stone wall." "But what about that crevasse over there?" "What about it? It gives the wall definition." "How far do you think it is from one wall to the other?" "Doesn't matter – I could walk around here all day." "But the stone floor hurts one of my feet. Can we get shoes?" "We don't need shoes, what we need is…"

It was hard to get a word in edgewise – the constant chatter between Bruce and himself was a constant self-dialogue. It was as if all the personalities of the bodies he was composed of wanted to speak all at once. When she saw no pauses forthcoming, she butted in, "Hey, Bruce! We have incoming players who want to try to steal the Core. Get ready!"

Luckily, despite his obvious mental shortcomings, Bruce was able to stick to a task once he had one to focus on. He immediately turned toward the door and made his way to the middle of the large room. His constant self-conversation thankfully stopped, and as the *Swordsmiths* entered the room they all stopped and stared at the monstrous amalgamation of animated body parts facing them. They stood frozen, most likely speaking to each other in their Raid Chat. That was when the stench of the Undead Abomination hit them – almost all of them scrunched up their faces and held their stomachs as if they were in pain. One Healer in the back even vomited off to the side, splashing chunks on her fellow guildmates.

Suddenly, Bruce shocked them by speaking in a booming – but cheerful – voice, "Hello! It's so nice to have visitors. What would you like to do? I love to talk – I could talk for hours. Unfortunately, if you are here to take the Dungeon Core I will have to kill you all. I hope you aren't here for that, though – I don't get many visitors these days. I think I have refreshments around here somewhere if you're here to chat."

The guild was speechless at this turn of events and they didn't answer Bruce right away. He seemed to take this the wrong way, "Well, if you won't even answer me then I guess you're here for the Core. It'll be a shame to have to kill you but that's my job. Goodbye!" With this statement, he lumbered forward, intending to smash into the waiting players. Seeing the incoming lumbering monster, most of the players scattered and got out of the way. One Mage was standing still, looking at something only she could see – most likely some game menus. By the time she realized her predicament, it was already too late. One of the giant feet stomped down on her, flattening her against the ground. The first hit amazingly didn't kill her – but the second stomp did the trick.

Bruce lifted his foot up, exclaiming, "Ewwwwww – that'll take some work getting all the blood off the floor. Why can't you be bloodless flesh like a good undead?" He turned toward his right, where the raids' tanks were starting to annoy him with their taunts and puny metal weapons. They didn't really hurt since he couldn't feel anything – undead don't have the necessary components to register pain – but they were nevertheless a distraction. He started hitting the three Defenders and one Paladin in front of him with his numerous appendages, doing quite a bit of damage. The raid Healers did their job admirably by keeping their front line alive with measured heals, ensuring that they didn't acquire aggro.

Once over their initial shock, the players showed why they were good enough to get that far. Their Rogues circled toward the rear of the Abomination, striking him from behind. They didn't end up doing extra damage since Bruce literally had eyes on the back of his head. As well as his back, sides, and even a pair on one of his legs. Their Archers unloaded arrow after arrow into the writhing mass of rotting flesh, most sinking inside without noticeably doing anything. A couple lucky shots hit an eye or two, but Bruce had so many that it didn't matter in the long run.

All these attacks did nothing to decrease the health points of the Guardian. The melee despaired when they saw they were having no effect, with everyone besides the tanks backing off and retreating until they found something to deal some damage to. It was only when their casters started slinging spells toward the Abomination that they saw some effect.

As *Ice Shards*, *Mana Bolts*, and *Lightning Shocks* hit Bruce, his whole body quivered with each strike. Each attack did a very tiny amount of damage, so small that it would take hours of constant bombardment to have any real effect. Seeing that they were making some progress, if even just a little, the casters redoubled their efforts and started trying out different spells to see which ones would deal more damage.

Bruce, however, didn't want to give them time to experiment. Their damage, infinitesimal as it was, overrode the taunts that the tanks were throwing his way and aggro shifted to the casters near the rear of the line. Since his forward progress was slightly impeded by the heavily-armored players, Bruce reached inside his body and pulled out a dozen globs of flesh that he then tossed toward the casters and healers. It appeared that his aim was off, though, and he only managed to hit a Healer in the leg as it bounced past the rear line – but that was never his intent. When the masses of flesh came to a stop behind the rear line, who promptly ignored them since they weren't hit with them, they started shaking and morphing into small, 4-foot tall mini-versions of the Abomination.

Once they were all formed, they rushed toward the unprotected and unsuspecting backs of the Mages, Healers, and Sorcerers. Inflicting major damage in the first few seconds, the players retreated toward their front line, all the while switching their magical attacks to the smaller versions pursuing them. This time, their magical attacks had no effect. It wasn't until one of the Mages smacked one that had gotten too close with this staff that they discovered that they were vulnerable to physical damage – unlike their big daddy.

The Rogues and Archers who had been holding back their ineffective attacks on the larger Abomination turned their attention to the smaller ones and started taking them out one-by-one. This took a while, since there were a dozen of the smaller Abominations and there was only a total of four players to fight them. Since they were taking some damage and were directly protecting the remaining casters, the Healers used their spells to keep them alive – to the detriment of the tanks still holding off Bruce. The Paladin went down, with no one to heal him, and the others started taking more damage since there were less of them now.

Eventually, the fight stabilized for the guild – the mini-Abominations were all killed, and everyone was able to focus on Bruce again. This, of course, was when he used another one of his special attacks. Instead of hitting one of the tanks again with one of his fists, he instead picked up one of the Defenders and stuck him inside his rotting, corpulent body with a wet, slurping sound. Their guildmates could see their tank's health start to plummet dramatically, but they couldn't see him to heal him. As he died, they saw his body slowly slide out from the bottom of the Abomination, as if he was a piece of waste being expelled.

One of the healers took the time to *Resurrect* both the Paladin and the Defender that just got pooped out – but found out too late that it was a mistake. Apparently affronted at these *Resurrections*, Bruce stopped attacking and stood still. As the ignorant players kept attacking, the Undead Abomination started violently shaking, his quivering flesh increasing in intensity as time went on.

After 15 seconds, the violent vibrations suddenly stopped and a moment later he exploded. Chunks of body parts exploded outward in every direction at a speed that literally decapitated a couple of players when the rotting flesh hit them. To the remaining players who didn't lose their heads, the amount of damage they sustained killed all but one of the Defenders; the lucky (or unlucky?) player was flung about 300 feet backwards before he hit the wall on the other side of the room.

Apparently realizing something bad was happening at the last moment, the Defender had used one of his damage mitigation skills that left him at 5% health even after taking lethal damage. As he slid down the wall that he had crashed into, he looked up to see the rest of his raid party destroyed and, in some cases, laying in multiple pieces. Standing where the Undead Abomination previously was located, was a much smaller glowing figure that was hunched over as if in pain. It was similar in appearance to the mini-Abominations that had attacked earlier – only it was emitting an unhealthy putrid-green glow.

As the Defender got to his feet, he tried to use a potion to bring his health back up – only to find he had used his last one while the casters were being attacked. Seeing that he was the only one left, he ran for the door hoping that he could get out before he was hit again. It just wasn't his day, however; just as he started moving, so did all the pieces of the Abomination that were scattered around the room. Flying back with magical speed, each piece of flesh that hit the glowing figure attached themselves until it was completely covered up. More and more pieces joined the growing Undead Abomination until he was back to how he looked before he exploded.

Bruce looked around and saw the Defender trying to escape. "Hey there, I wasn't done playing with you all yet – come here." Swiftly moving to block the exit, he grabbed the remaining *Swordsmiths* player and stuck him in his body. Since he was near death already, it only took a couple of seconds before he expelled the player out of his bottom.

He paused for a second, looking for anyone else in the room, before he slowly started walking around in circles again, talking to himself. "They were nice enough, but why doesn't anyone want to come see us?" "I know, it's like 'I want the Dungeon Core this, and give me the Dungeon Core that.'" "Seriously, why does..."

Krista retreated from the room, ecstatic in her choice of Guardian this time around. Witnessing him in action relieved a lot of the worry she was having concerning the Dungeon Core. She hoped that it would be a long time before anyone found a way to kill Bruce – hopefully long enough that they could build their new dungeon floor.

Chapter 15

This first room only had the two Salamanders, so they headed for the next room with Max in the lead this time. Just as Devin was wondering about the change, he witnessed the Rogue disarm a trap on the floor that he could barely see even when he got close. Noticing his curious stare, Max told him, "There were no traps on the first floor – they don't start until you reach the second floor. Just make sure you let me go first because I have pretty high *Detect Traps* skill."

Nodding in the affirmative, he followed her as they arrived at the next room. Like the last room, two lava flows were on opposite sides of the room, with the center being clear of the molten earth. The only difference was an increased amount of **Lava Salamanders**, twice as many to be precise. They still only came one at a time and they were as easily defeated as the others. *This is pretty easy so far,* Devin thought.

The next couple of rooms doubled the amount again – and then again. By time they reached the fifth and final room before the floor boss, the 32 **Lava Salamanders** came in waves of four at a time. Devin was tempted to use his *Freezing Rain* spell but held off due to the warning Mac gave him earlier about killing themselves with steam. Instead, he used his *Entangling Roots* spell to keep one in place for a time. Unfortunately, due to the plant-like nature of the roots, they were weak to fire-based creatures. Each time he caught one of the Salamanders they only ended up being entangled for about five seconds – which was about a third of its normal duration.

This still helped significantly, since they were able to take out the other creatures in just a couple of seconds. Bolt3n also used his *Crippling Shot* skill, which greatly slowed down one of the lizards that was approaching, leaving it for last. Only once during all the fights did a Salamander get close enough to use its fire-breathing skill – which Domn3r reflected with his shield before removing its head from its body in a single critical strike.

Devin couldn't help thinking about how this fight would have gone down if they were more equal to the level of the dungeon – it would have been a whole lot harder. As it was, Domn3r's party was barely putting forth much effort to kill everything that was thrown their way. Even Devin, with some practice and fore-knowledge, thought that he could solo through this part of the dungeon if he was forced to.

After finishing off all the mobs in the room with a minimum of trouble, they headed toward the floor boss. As they entered, Devin was starting to recognize a theme relating to the bosses in this dungeon. Before them was a large pond – lake would be too big of a word – of lava in the center of the room. Domn3r led the way, running ahead in order to be the prime target for what they saw poking out from the center of the pool.

If the other **Lava Salamanders** were the size of a walrus, the **Mega Lava Salamander (Level 25)** was the size of a double-decker bus – only longer and wider. Devin watched as Domn3r used his *Shield Rush* skill to bash the giant Salamander as it poked its head out of the lava, stunning it momentarily and causing massive amounts of aggro toward the Defender. He then ran toward the corner of the room, thereby making the boss leave the lava and follow the annoying human. Once it reached him, everyone else started laying on the damage so Devin followed suit with *Ice Arrow* and *Flurry*.

Its health dropped quickly and within 15 seconds it was at 20% – that's when it turned around and made for the lava pond in the middle of the room. "Don't let it get in, it'll regenerate and heal most of the damage we just caused," yelled Ambrose. Devin immediately cast *Entangling Roots* while Bolt3n used *Crippling Shot* to slow it down. The roots were even less effective against the boss compared to its smaller brethren, but for this it was enough – the giant lizard collapsed in death only halfway back to the pool.

"Nice job everyone – that was the quickest I've ever seen that done – at least personally. I'm sure there have been higher level players who have come through here and done it faster, but every group that I've been in here with allowed it to regenerate at least once per battle. I'm just glad we didn't have to worry about that this time. Let's move on," Domn3r told them all, after they had looted the corpse of the Salamander and popped open the Floor Chest.

The third floor was very similar in makeup to the first two, with another new mob to battle against. This time they were facing flights of **Small Fire Drakes**, which were basically small dragons the size of a Golden Retriever – but with wings. They had very strong and sharp-looking claws on both their hands and feet and could lob fireballs toward the party from a short distance away, as well as breathe fire when in close.

Devin enjoyed fighting against these since it allowed him to practice his accuracy on a quickly-moving target. He started at first with just regular arrows, trying to get a feel on how the small Drakes moved through the air. After missing the first ten times, he began to see a pattern in its movements – it would hover in the air for a short time when it was going to lob a fireball.

Once he realized this, he waited until it stopped moving and hit it with an *Ice Arrow*. The arrow lodged in its throat just as a fireball emerged, causing it to fall harmlessly straight down below. The critical strike was enough damage to instantly kill the flying creature and Devin watched ecstatically as it plummeted down.

This also gave him the opportunity to inadvertently try out his *Sidestep* skill. As he was focused on the Drake he had just slain, another one lobbed a fireball in his direction and the skill automatically triggered. He felt his viewpoint change slightly and saw that he was standing a couple of feet closer to Ambrose.

Confused, he looked around as he saw a fireball pass through right where he was standing a second ago. He looked in the air and watched as Bolt3n filled the last Drake with three arrows fired in rapid succession. "Thanks," Devin shot toward the Archer. *That was close – at least now I know what that skill does.*

The group pressed on, finding themselves in the same situation as the other floors – more rooms with greater quantities of **Fire Drakes**. Devin continued to improve his aim and was able to finally hit the Drakes while they were still moving through the air. Only one other time did he have to utilize his *Sidestep* skill – a stray fireball aimed at Domn3r was deflected in Devin's direction from behind. All in all, however, the floor was just as easy as the previous two.

The boss for this floor was a bit different from the others – instead of one gigantic **Fire Drake**, there were two near-giant Drakes. The two **Huge Fire Drakes (Level 26)** divided the parties' attention by flinging fireballs from different directions. Not only were the fireballs larger than their smaller brethren, but they exploded upon contact and generated additional splash damage.

The method that the group used was to have Domn3r grab the attention of one Drake and move away by himself while blocking the flaming projectiles. Ambrose would heal him while the rest of the group concentrated on the other boss – with

Bolt3n as the target. The Archer had high enough Agility that he was able to avoid the fireballs heading in his direction and was a good enough shot that he was able to fire on the run. Devin and Mac then added their own supporting fire and the Drake – which was not as hard to hit as the smaller ones – fell rapidly. Once it was down, they concentrated fire on the remaining **Huge Fire Drake** and killed it quickly without much trouble.

As they arrived down on the fourth floor, Devin was excited to find out what other kinds of creatures they would encounter down here. He was slightly disappointed – thinking he'd find some sort of Fire Elemental or something else along those lines – when all he saw were humanoid-looking figures covered in red, green, and black scales. As he got closer, he noticed that they looked like upright-walking dragons: reptilian-shaped head and face, clawed hands and feet, and a prehensile tail following behind.

"Watch out for these – they are sentient, so they'll give you a run for your money if you're not careful," warned Maxinista. Devin looked at them closer and saw that they were called **Hearthfire Dragonkin (Level 25)**. *I hope that means that I can use them as a playable race – that would be quite the change.* The group approached the first of these Dragonkin and Devin got even more excited as he witnessed a pair of wings unfolding behind its back. *They can FLY! Oh my god, I want one!*

Too engrossed in dreams of flying and attacking enemy players from above, he missed it as the Dragonkin launched into the air and flew straight at the party. Fortunately, the veteran players comprising the rest of the group were ready for it. Domn3r taunted it to catch its attention and Devin watched, distracted, as it dived straight for the Defender with a steel sword leading the way. The tank was knocked backward from the impact but was able to stay on his feet as he pushed back at the mob. Once he was on the ground, Max could finally utilize her skills and used her *Backstab* skill on the unsuspecting Dragonkin.

This took off most of its health, due to it still being quite a few levels below them. A quick arrow to its vulnerable neck made it fall to the floor instantly. Another approached, and they used the same method as the first – this time, Devin was able to get a shot in before it dropped. This first room contained a couple more Dragonkin and they were taken out easily – prompting them to move on to the next room. Max had to disable another trap in the hallway leading there, but as soon as it was safe they all walked further ahead – into an ambush.

If it wasn't for Ambrose catching a glance of something in the corner of her eye, they might have taken some casualties. As it turned out, fortunately, she called out, "UP!" quickly enough that the six Dragonkin diving down from the air above the entrance to the room lost the element of surprise. They all still ended up taking damage, as each member of the group got a face full of scales and steel. Domn3r was able to get his shield up in time to block most of it, but the others took anywhere from 30 to 60% damage to their health points.

Domn3r used his AOE taunt and gathered all the Dragonkin's attention while Ambrose started healing herself and Mac who had taken the most damage. As soon as their health was stable, Ambrose started healing the Defender who was taking a whole lot of damage from the six mobs. The rest of them started attacking the Dragonkin one at a time, until the last one died from a sword strike from Domn3r. Taking a breather after surviving the close call, Max commented on the ambush, "I don't remember that from my time here before – I would have been more prepared if I had. Does anyone know what's going on?"

"I remember seeing in the patch notes a couple of weeks ago a mention of the Dragon Lair getting some changes, but I don't remember any specifics. It looks like we found one of the changes – we'll have to be more vigilant from now on," Ambrose told them.

"Alright – Max, you're on scout duty now. You're in first to check out each of the rooms and let us know what is in store for us in them. If there are more ambushes I want to know about them ahead of time," Domn3r ordered.

Using this method, Devin followed along as they progressed through the floor at a slower pace than usual. They only found one more ambush, but with Maxinista's warning they were able to spring it on their own terms and only took minimal damage. The only other difficulty they had was fighting the increasing amount of Dragonkin as they got further through the floor – they were so numerous that they started using group tactics to fight.

As soon as they were being attacked by eight or more at a time, the Dragonkin would attack from above and from ground level simultaneously. When Domn3r would use his AOE taunt on the target on the ground, the ones in the air were usually out of range of the skill and wouldn't be picked up by the tank. This led to either Devin or Bolt3n having to take aggro from the flyers to avoid air damage hitting their Defender. In the end, it wasn't too hard because for the most part the Dragonkin didn't do a whole lot of damage when they were prepared for it – the entire battle did take longer though.

The floor boss was similar to the Orc Village back in Altera Vita in the effect that it had Dragonkin with multiple classes. The main boss was a **Hearthfire Dragonkin Warlock (Level 27)** with a Defender and Healer as support – both level 26. The fight was tough only because of the DOTs that the Warlock managed to land on everyone in the party; Ambrose had to work overtime to keep everyone *Cleansed* and healed through the entire battle. Once they took out the Healer – everyone knows you take the Healer out first – they focused on the Warlock as the two Defenders whacked at each other. Once the main Dragonkin was down, they interrupted Domn3r's playtime with his counterpart and eliminated the opposing Defender.

Eager to get to the end, they all rushed down the stairs to the last floor – where Devin would try his luck at defeating the Dungeon Boss single-handedly.

Chapter 16

The bottom floor of the Dragon Lair was a mishmash of all the mobs that they had seen so far on their journey down. There were Shroombas surrounding Salamanders, Fire Drakes lobbing fireballs while being supported by Dragonkin, and even a couple of classed Dragonkin interspersed within. The different combinations made the battles a little tricky, but they used the same techniques that they had used previously and made it through without too much trouble. The only reason they had even a little trouble wasn't because there was an increasingly larger number of mobs as they went through – just different combinations. They never faced more than eight different enemies total in each room.

As they approached the doorway to the Dungeon Boss, Devin was nervous about the upcoming fight. He had practiced everything he could on the way down, but he wasn't sure if he was prepared for what he had to do in there. He felt confident in his accuracy with the bow, could use his *Ice Arrows* with regular frequency, and had learned tactics from his new guild friends. He hadn't used his Druid spells all that much since the *Deathly Chill* mishap, but he had used plenty of spells during his other incarnations in the dungeon and felt like he could perform well.

"You impressed me on the way down here – I think you'll do fine, Devin," Max told him.

Ambrose chimed in, "Keep your regeneration on as much as you can – if you need it and don't have it on then it's already too late."

"Don't forget – if you see any lava DON'T CAST WATER AT IT!" Mac helpfully reminded him.

Bolt3n had some advice on shooting accuracy; he told him to always stay calm – panic would mess with his accuracy. "Use your skills as soon as they come off cooldown – there's no reason to hold off on using them. The quicker you can damage the Dragon the less time you'll be at risk of burning alive."

Domn3r just smacked him on the back and told him, "Good luck kid, you're going to need it."

With the good wishes of his group, they watched Devin as he entered the final room all alone. Once he was inside, he looked around at the massive room containing the Dungeon Boss. From what he could see, it was at least 1,000 feet from where he entered to the back part of the room – with the sides only a little bit narrower.

In front on him rose a tiered hill made of volcanic rock with stairs cut into it in various places, allowing those trying to traverse to the top easier access. Along the far sides of the hill, lava flowed freely down in sheets in parody of a waterfall and causing massive heat waves to emanate outward. Devin figured that it would probably be a good idea to stay away from the sides so that he wasn't cooked alive. As it was, the heat was already oppressive, and he wasn't even close to the lava.

From this distance, he couldn't see anything on top of the hill, but he guessed that the Dragon was on top of it, waiting for him. He made his way forward, picking his footing through the porous volcanic rock strewn throughout the room. As he approached the bottom of the hill and stepped on the first stair, he was almost thrown off his feet as the ground started shaking. Catching his balance, he looked up; the sight that greeted his vision almost made him turn around and run out the door right then and there.

Rising from the side of the hill, one appendage at a time, was the **Mighty Flame Dragon (Level 28)**. He watched as it slowly lifted its back legs and then its front two before lifting its massive body upright. He could see the tail – which was at least 20 feet long all by itself – just as the reptilian-like head lifted from the ground. It had black eyes, but with a fire behind them that Devin swore he could feel the heat from. As it stood fully upright, two massive wings – 50 feet in length each – unfolded from its back with a snap so loud Devin thought they had broken something.

While he was still stunned, trying to comprehend the sheer size of the thing – it must have been 75 feet from head to tail – Devin didn't react fast enough when a jet of flame erupted from the Dragon's mouth. If he hadn't had his *Sidestep* skill, his fight would have ended right then and there. Instead, he dodged a direct hit from the spout of flame but took a little damage due to being in such proximity to the attack. He reprimanded himself for letting his attention wander during the most important part of this dungeon journey – the near fatal attack got his body and mind moving like nothing else could.

He ran away to get some distance between them – all the while dodging fireballs that the Dragon shot in his direction. His Agility allowed him to move out of the way of the deadly projectiles if he saw it coming his way in time. Once he had dodged four fireballs, he judged that he had gotten enough breathing room between him and the boss.

He turned around and immediately cast *Deathly Chill IV* followed by *Freezing Rain III* centered on the humongous Dragon – while making sure that there were not any lava flows nearby to fill the room up with steam. Even if the room was large enough to prevent being cooked alive, the last thing he needed was a way for the **Mighty Flame Dragon** to hide from him.

As the ice-cold raindrops hit his opponent, the Dragon let out a tremendous roar that shook loose some stalagmites from the ceiling that crashed down throughout the room. Devin tried to cover his ears but couldn't – he was being affected by a stunned debuff for the next ten seconds. He watched the **Mighty Flame Dragon** launch itself into the air and hover there for a couple of seconds before heading in his direction. The stunned effect wore off just in time for him to dodge three consecutive fireballs that were launched in his direction. He took a little bit of damage from the heat again; it was then that he realized he hadn't cast his *Nature's Boon III* buff yet. Ambrose would never let him hear the end of it if he survived this.

After quickly casting the health regen spell, he finally got a chance to look at how much damage his *Freezing Rain* spell had done to his now-airborne foe. He had done about 10% damage, which was more than he thought he could do with one spell. As he was attempting to cast his rain spell again, the Dragon quickly flew out of range and shot another couple of fireballs in his direction. Realizing the futility of trying to cast more spells, he again dodged the incoming projectiles and switched to his bow. He fired off some normal shots to see if he could hit it at this range — but he came up just a little short.

Devin was reluctant to get closer because he would have less time to dodge anything flying his way; however, if he didn't, he wouldn't be able to do any damage himself. Resigned to this new plan of attack, he rushed toward the Dragon while firing ranging shots on the run. When he was finally in range, he shot an *Ice Arrow* toward its face, hoping for a critical hit. The magical arrow ended up hitting it in the chest and doing a modest amount of damage — around 5% of its health points were taken away. *Not too bad — its water resistance must still be lowered due to* Deathly Chill.

He continued to move while firing normal shots while his *Ice Arrow* was on cooldown. When the massive beast's health dropped to 75%, it changed its attack from shooting out fireballs to dive-bombing Devin. He was caught mostly unprepared; he was getting ready to fire off another *Ice Arrow* when he saw it swoop down and rush through the air straight for him. He was caught flat-footed and almost ended up inside its gullet – even though a troll would have been quite the meal even for the giant Dragon. Luckily, his *Sidestep* was off cooldown and he just barely avoided that fate. Unluckily, his automatic dodge put him somewhere he wasn't expecting.

Normally, when the automatic dodge was activated, the system basically "warped" your character to a spot a couple of feet away either to the left, right, or behind the previous location – depending upon what was clear at that time. If, say, you were in a long narrow corridor and a projectile came flying your way, the dodge would fail because there would be no safe place to jump to. In this instance, though, the Dragon was so large that when it barreled into him that he couldn't dodge to the left, right, or behind – but it did have another option: up. And that was how he ended up on the back of the Dragon.

He was facing toward the tail initially, and he held on to the spikes protruding from his ride's back as they rose into the air again. He looked behind, expecting to be blasted as the Dragon felt him holding on for dear life. After about a minute with no reaction, though, Devin realized two things: One – either the dragon didn't know he was there or couldn't turn its head in his direction, and Two – he LOVED flying. He remembered that back in the real world he was scared of heights, but ever since he was trapped here that fear had gone away. *It could be anxieties like that weren't copied over, or I don't have the same fear of falling and dying that I used to have. Either way, I'm enjoying this.*

Turning himself around, he got closer to the front of the dragon until he was able to wrap his own massive legs around its neck. *Obviously, it doesn't know I'm here because it didn't react to me moving up on it.* Coming up with a plan, he checked his mana and health points and saw that he was full-up after the down-time on top of the Dragon. Figuring this would be his chance to end this fight quickly, he took a deep breath, steadied his nerves, and cast *Deathly Chill* to reduce its resistance again.

His ride didn't react – as he had hoped – since it didn't know where the spell came from. He then chain-cast three *Freezing Rains* with the first one above and slightly behind, the second spell above and in front, and the third right on top of them. Attempting to dodge the first, the Dragon flew ahead into the second and then tried to backtrack, which put it square into the third.

Confused, the Dragon let out another massive roar that shook the room and Devin narrowly missed being impaled by a falling stalagmite. He had been expecting the outburst this time, however, and was able to cover his ears in time, preventing a stunned debuff like the last one. He then checked his mana points and was able to cast another *Freezing Rain* directly above again, adding to the already massive amounts of damage the Dragon was taking.

As its health dropped to 25%, the **Mighty Flame Dragon** dove for the ground, landing hard and causing the ground around its landing place to shake. If Devin had been on the ground, he probably would have taken damage and been knocked off his feet – fortunately, he was riding a "mount" at the time.

This was what he was waiting for – he figured that the boss would land sometime during the battle so that melee fighters could fight it. He instantly cast *Entangling Roots*, keeping it stuck to the ground for a couple of seconds so that it couldn't rise back up in the air. He didn't want to be on top of it when it died – he wasn't sure he would be able to withstand the crash damage.

Checking his mana again, he saw that he had regenerated enough to cast his *Freezing Rain* spell again centered over them. As soon as he did that, he aimed an *Ice Arrow* into the back of the Dragon's head, followed up by his *Flurry* skill. The damage from the rain accompanied by the donkey punch full of arrows was more than the **Mighty Flame Dragon** could handle. It fell to the ground with a resounding thump as its health points ran out, causing Devin to fall off at the unexpected collapse. He picked himself up and looked at his fallen adversary.

I wonder if I could ride one of those again – that was awesome! I'll have to see what Krista can do. As he thought this, he remembered the whole point of this dungeon expedition was to kill the Dungeon Boss and to capture the dungeon. He was expecting something to happen once the boss fell, but that didn't seem to be the case. He attempted to loot the dragon, but it wouldn't let him – he didn't have a bag to put stuff after all. The only thing left to do was to check the final chest which he saw earlier was located at the top of the hill. He walked up to it, touched it, and a screen popped up.

Congratulations!

You have successfully captured the dungeon: Dragon's Lair! The Dungeon Player now has access to this dungeon as well as:

- Expanded Dungeon Territory
- All monsters currently used by the dungeon: Dragon's Lair
- The ability to combine the two dungeons together with further expansion
- Buildings and NPCs can now be employed outside of either dungeon due to expanded Dungeon Territory

Further expansion from capturing additional dungeons will further add potential benefits.

Current Dungeon Total: 2

With a smile on his face, Devin added to the guild chat the results of their expedition into the dungeon. He also invited Domn3r and his group to come into the boss room and take the teleporter back to the beginning of the dungeon with him. They heartily agreed – since they didn't want to have walk all the way back up – and together they found themselves back at the entrance.

Devin turned to the group who had guided him through the dungeon and thanked them again for all their help. "If it wasn't for you guys, I never would have made it through – not only were the mobs more numerous than I could fight myself, but the experience fighting with you was one I won't easily forget. I learned more about my own abilities and how to fight as a group than I ever have before. I don't have anything to repay you all for the help right now but check again in a couple of days and we might have something for you – I'll talk to Krista about it. Thanks again and I'll see you soon!"

Domner, Max, Mac, and Bolt3n all told him that they enjoyed dungeon-diving with him and they would have to get together again the next time he wanted to "Expand the Dungeon Territory" again. Ambrose gave him a big hug, which was a little funny looking due to her small stature as a High Elf and him a Troll. After she was done, they all walked out of the dungeon, leaving Devin alone in the entrance.

"Krista, can you hear me?" he asked the air.

"I sure can! Nice job, Devin! I got the notice that you had expanded the dungeon territory and I'm so pumped to see what I can do now! Do you want me to respawn you or do you want to walk back yourself?" Krista asked.

"Go ahead and respawn me, it's been a long day. I'll tell you all about my adventures later – now I need to chill for a while. Get it? Chill? Cause this was a fire dungeon...whatever, it sounded good in my head..."

Chapter 17

Krista was excited to play around with her new options. First things first, she wanted to strengthen the primary dungeon, Altera Vita, so that the Dungeon Core was better protected. Even though Bruce had proven himself to be able to fight off the incoming players pretty well, the level cap would be increasing soon and there was no guarantee that just Bruce was enough. With that in mind, she looked at her current monster list:

Upgrade Monsters			
Goblin	Base Monster	Goblin Chieftain	Unique Monster
Dusk Boar	Base Monster	Weregoblin	Advanced Monster
Timber Wolf	Base Monster	Goblin Boar-rider	Advanced Monster
Hardy Rock-burrower	Base Monster	Hearthfire Orc Guard	Unique Monster
Sure-footed Mountain Goat	Base Monster	Dusky Rock-boarer	Advanced Monster
Starving Mountain Lion	Base Monster	Ogrepult	Advanced Monster
Shrieking Harpy	Base Monster	Horcy	Advanced Monster
Scaled Wyvern	Base Monster	Goblin Pole Dancer	Advanced Monster
Majestic Roc	Base Monster	Wyveroc	Advanced Monster
Hearthfire Orc	Base Monster	G-Bomber	Advanced Monster
Hearthfire Ogre	Base Monster	Burrowgoat	Advanced Monster
Magma Shroomba	Base Monster	Goatlin	Advanced Monster
Lava Salamander	Base Monster	Pussy-master Orc	Advanced Monster
Fire Drake	Base Monster	Giant Magma Shroomba	Unique Monster

Hearthfire Dragonkin	Base Monster	Mega Lava Salamander	Unique Monster
		Huge Fire Drake	Unique Monster
		Mighty Flame Dragon	Unique Monster

In the past, Krista had to place one of the new base monsters in her dungeon in order to see what she was working with. Now, all she needed to do was to visit their new acquisition and check them out in action. She decided to leave the dungeon alone for the moment and let it continue running the way it had been. In the future, she would probably change it depending on how much her dungeon expanded, but it was fine the way as it was. She was able to observe as another group entered a few hours after Devin and his guild friends left, watching as they quickly made their way through the various mobs.

The **Magma Shroomba** was interesting — she didn't have anything even remotely like it yet. It was fairly harmless by itself, but she had some plans to enhance it with some of her other monsters. As the group she was watching fought its way through the first floor, she started her experimentation with her new mushroom friend.

First, she wanted to increase its size to make it harder for the players to avoid an attack. And, of course, she chose the largest base monster she had access to for her new hybrid.

Shroomba of Doomba (Advanced Monster)		
The **Shroomba of Doomba** is a hybrid of a **Magma Shroomba** and a **Majestic Roc**. This massive mushroom is 20 feet wide, 30 feet tall, and can fly. That's right – it can fly.		
Pollenate		
Current level description:	At 50% health, the **Shroomba of Doomba** creates an outward expanding explosion of magma spores that does fire-based magical damage in a large area if they touch an enemy. They can be destroyed if they land on the ground without contacting an enemy.	
Magical Damage:	40 per spore	Damage Radius:	50 feet
Number of Spores:	50	Trigger Threshold:	50% health
Germinate		
Current level description:	At 25% health, any spores that are created during the Pollenate attack are turned into normal **Magma Shroombas** for the duration of the battle.	
Trigger Threshold:	25% health		

This sounds impressive; I can't wait to see it in action, thought Krista. The **Shroomba of Doomba** sounded like it would be best used by itself in a room that had plenty of room to move vertically. Pleased with this hybrid, she moved on to making a combination of monsters that she could use multiples of. To this end, she combined a **Sure-footed Mountain Goat** and the **Magma Shroomba** together…

Goat Sucker (Advanced Monster)		
In this interesting combination of mammal and fungus, the **Goat Sucker** is comprised of a **Sure-footed Mountain Goat** and a **Magma Shroomba**. Smaller Shroombas are attached all over the body of the Mountain Goat, providing it additional protection and a DOT effect if the Shroombas are penetrated.		
Goat on Speed		
Current level description:	A Shroomba is grown on the top of the Goats' head, which it then used as it rushes ahead and slams into an enemy. The head Shroomba provides the goat increased speed and damage compared to a normal Mountain Goat rush attack. Also has a chance of knockdown upon impact.	
Physical Damage:	250	Knockdown Chance:	40%
Speed Increase:	20%	Cooldown:	60.0 seconds and

				must be at least 15 feet away from target
		Hallucination		
Current level description:	Used as a last-ditch effort to avoid damage, the **Goat Sucker** explodes all the Shroombas on its body at the same time creating a cloud of hallucinogenic vapor. Any caught in the explosion will suffer hallucinations for a certain period of time – time in which the Goat Sucker will try to escape, leaving its incapacitated enemies to others.			
Effect Radius:	20.0 feet around Goat Sucker	Effect Duration:		15 seconds
Cooldown:	Usable if under 15% health			

Krista could envision the scary sight of a horde of **Goat Suckers** descending on unsuspecting players, ramming into them and causing hallucinations. She was looking forward to seeing how they would handle the goat-filled onslaught.

With those two creations complete, she again focused on the group heading through the Dragon's Lair dungeon. They had made it to the second floor already and were attacking the giant lizards down there. When Krista looked at one emerging from the lava, she found they were rightfully called **Lava Salamanders**. They appeared to be rather formidable but quite slow. She needed to be able to speed it up to make it more effective in hybrid form, so Krista started putting it together with various speedy monsters like the Goat, Boar, and Wolf. However, none of those made viable hybrids – they all melted due to the Salamanders inherent heat into a quivering mound of burnt skin, hair, and fur.

It wasn't until she branched out and used the **Shrieking Harpy** that she got a result. Not precisely the result she was looking for (especially with the offensive name and attacks), but she would use it if she needed to.

"BWMYF" (Advanced Monster)			
This hybrid monster – consisting of a **Shrieking Harpy** and **Lava Salamander** – turns a normal everyday Harpy into a disgusting, flying, burning force of waste destruction. The **"Bitch Will Melt Yo Face"** has wings of fire instead of feathers and launches disgusting flaming balls of poop at unsuspecting victims. And that's just the beginning...			
Flaming Shower			
Current level description:	The **"BWMYF"** will land on an enemy with its feet on their shoulders, squat down, and relieve itself upon their head with a fiery release of lava. Not a pleasant experience for either of them. Has a chance to cause temporary blindness.		
Fire-based Magical Damage:	500	Blind Chance:	30%
Blind Duration:	30.0 seconds	Cooldown:	Once per battle
Hit The Fan			
Current level description:	Mimicking the effects of severe food poisoning, the **"BWMYF"** quickly spins around in a circle in the air and releases a torrent of burning, flaming destruction in a large area.		
Magical Damage per hit:	100	Effect Radius:	20 feet from "BWMYF"
Duration:	5.0 seconds	Cooldown:	Once per battle

The AI was getting more and more ridiculous as time went on. When Krista thought about it, most of the programmers she had ever met or talked to had possessed a relatively "juvenile" sense of humor. It stood to reason that if they had initially programmed the The AI, then some of that must have come through into its unique personality. She was beginning not to care as much when she saw the names and attacks that the system came up with – if they were useful to her, she would try to ignore what she didn't care for. It was more important to use all tools available to her to protect the Dungeon Core – and in turn, their lives.

The **Lava Salamanders** were less than useful by themselves, but if they were combined with something then they might have a better chance of reaching the players before they were cut down. She was hoping to find something that could ride the giant lizard, but when she tried her new Dragonkin, it was too large and couldn't fit on its back. The same thing happened when she tried the Orc and she wasn't even going to try the Ogre – it was even bigger. The only one left to try was the **Goblin**...

Lizard Tickler (Advanced Monster)			
The **Lizard Tickler** is a combination of a **Goblin** and a **Lava Salamander**. The **Goblin** takes control of three leashed **Lava Salamanders** that prey on enemies like hounds on the hunt. The collars and leashes imbue extra Agility to the Salamanders which allow them to move faster and avoid attacks. The **Goblin** receives extra physical defense in the form of Salamander scale armor. If the **Goblin** falls in battle, the remaining Salamanders will go berserk and attack anything close by – including each other.			
Retribution			
Current level description:	All remaining Salamanders under the control of the **Lizard Tickler** converge on a single target enemy that is attacking their handler (ignoring aggro). This attack deals additional physical damage in addition to normal attacks.		
Additional Physical Damage:	200	Duration:	20.0 seconds
Cooldown:	150.0 seconds		
Scatter			
Current level description:	Upon the death of a nearby ally, there is a chance that each of the remaining Salamanders under the control of the **Lizard Tickler** will scatter and attack enemy targets at random, ignoring aggro. Deals extra fire-based magical damage to enemies wearing cloth armor.		
Extra Damage to Cloth Wearers:	20%	Duration:	20 seconds

| Trigger Chance: | 33.3% | Cooldown: | Once per battle |

That is more like it! Now they can attack faster and even target someone besides the tank for once. This would be a great support creature to back up some other tank creatures. The look of surprise on players' faces when the Salamanders scattered and potentially attacked the healers and casters would be priceless. Add to that the fact that it was like having four mobs in one made the **Lizard Tickler** a good addition to her menagerie.

By this time, the group of players who had been making their way through her new dungeon was just finishing up their battle with the **Mega Lava Salamander**. Krista watched the rest of the battle and wished that she could put more of those bosses in her dungeon, but they were unique monsters and could only be used once – they were fine where they were at the moment. Perhaps in the future she would change everything up and shuffle them around, but she was a long way off from that.

Chapter 18

As Krista watched the group of players kill the large Salamander – while only allowing it to heal in the lava pool once – they looted the corpse and chest and made their way down to the next floor. In here they were attacked by some **Fire Drakes**, which made Krista happy to have another base monster that could be added to her aerial force. She watched as they lobbed fireballs at the players and saw how they were largely ineffective against the prepared tank – they just splashed off and did little to no damage. Meanwhile the flying mobs were being torn apart by the ranged attacks of the other members of the party.

Their main attack consisted of the fireballs that they flung toward the enemy – they had no real close combat abilities. Granted, they could probably do a little damage with their wicked-looking claws against a caster, but they were useless against anyone wearing a little bit of armor. Krista needed to change that with some new variations that she could create.

Fire Wyvern (Advanced Monster)	
The **Fire Wyvern** was born from a hybrid combination of a **Fire Drake** and a **Scaled Wyvern**. This faster, more agile version of a **Fire Drake** cannot lob fireballs at an enemy – instead, it will get close to an enemy to breathe fire and bite any exposed flesh.	
Love Bite	
Current level description:	This attack is actually a common form of foreplay between mating **Fire Wyverns**. When used on an enemy

	however, the bite injects a burning poison that ignites the blood of its victim for a certain amount of time, doing fire-based magical damage in addition to the initial physical damage of the bite.		
Initial Physical Damage:	40	Magical Damage:	30 per tick
Tick Interval:	3.0 seconds	Duration:	60.0 seconds
Cooldown:	25.0 seconds		
Flatulence			
Current level description:	Due to the **Fire Wyverns'** love of eating sulfurous rock, it has produced an enormous amount of gas that can be expelled. The Fire Wyvern will glide through all of the enemies within range while expelling this gas – which then can be ignited to cause a large explosion that causes fire-based magical damage to all enemies in the area.		
Affected Area:	15-foot circle	Magical Damage:	400
Cooldown:	Once per battle		

Nice! Wait...what's with The AI's obsession with potty humor? It seems like everything I'm making wants to either poop, pee, or pass gas on its enemies. It must have something to do with the fire-based enemies – there wasn't anything like this before, Krista exasperatingly thought to herself. *I at least achieved what I was hoping for – a melee-focused Drake.* If she was able to pair up the normal **Fire Drake** with the **Fire Wyvern**, the combination of melee and ranged attacks should give the players more of a challenge.

She was really excited about the next combination of monsters she had in mind. The initial plan had basically backfired on her when she created the **Goblin Pole Dancer**, but now she had something even better to work with. She was going to add the **Goblin** – or even an Orc – to the **Fire Drake** (since it was more like a Dragon than the Wyvern) but paused when she saw the Dragonkin option. She hadn't seen one in action, but she could guess that they were a sentient race that inhabited the dungeon. Deciding to try that one first, she combined the **Hearthfire Dragonkin** with the **Fire Drake** and got the result she was hoping for.

Dragon Rider (Advanced Monster)			
The **Dragon Rider** is a combination of a **Hearthfire Dragonkin** and a **Fire Drake**. Although the Dragonkin is a little large for a normal **Fire Drake** to allow for riding, the Dragonkin uses its own wings in conjunction with the Drake to keep it flying in the air. The Drake can lob fireballs toward the enemy as well as attack in close with a flame attack. The Dragonkin wields a spear that can be used for massive close-combat damage.			
Impale			
Current level description:	The **Dragon Rider** plummets down from directly atop the target and impales its victim with its spear, inflicting massive physical damage.		
Physical Damage:	550	Cooldown:	200.0 seconds
Firestorm			
Current level description:	If two or more **Dragon Riders** are present and both are under 50% health, they can use the Firestorm skill together. Each **Fire Drake** emits a massive cone of flame that combines with each other, covering their target with overlapping blasts of fire causing fire-based magical damage.		
Magical Damage:	100 per second	Duration:	10 seconds
Cooldown:	Once per battle: Only available if two or more Dragon Riders are present and have less than 50% health		

Yes! Now that's what I'm talking about! I love it! Krista had always liked Dragonriders in games and in the fantasy books that she used to read. They were always so powerful and hard to kill – hopefully these would be the same. *But shouldn't it be* Dragonrider *instead of* Dragon Rider? She asked Carl his opinion.

In this case, the "Dragon" in question is the Dragonkin – so it refers to the "Dragon" being a rider, instead of it riding a Dragon. I think you should just be thankful it was not named "Drake-riding Dragonkin". That would have been a little confusing and unnecessary.

Krista couldn't help but agree, she was happy all the same with her creation. Wishing to see these Dragonkin in action, she switched back to viewing the current group inside the Dragon's Lair dungeon. They had made it to the fourth floor and were being attacked by the **Hearthfire Dragonkin** populating the environment. *If these are a playable race for Devin, he'd going to love being able to fly,* she thought.

She watched the Dragonkin's attempt to ambush the players from above or behind something with little success. They had the advantage of being able to attack from the air, but they were so noisy that they rarely got close enough before they were heard and spotted. *Now what do I have that is stealthy? Oh, yeah, that could work…*

Death's Roar (Advanced Monster)	
In order to become sneakier, this hybrid of **Hearthfire Dragonkin** and **Starving Mountain Lion** is the epitome of stealthiness. Although the **Death's Roar** is smaller than its normal Dragonkin cousins, it makes up for it by being covered head to wingtip in short, soft black fur. This black fur allows it to blend into the shadows and attack in near silence. It also dual-wields two sharp knives that are perfect for assassination attempts.	
Backdoor Assault	
Current level description:	Although the **Death's Roar** doesn't use magic, it has the skill to move through the shadows to teleport behind an

	enemy to attack from behind for physical damage. It also has a greater chance for a critical strike.		
Physical Damage:	250	Additional Critical Strike Chance:	20%
Cooldown:	180.0 seconds		
Distraction			
Current level description:	The **Death's Roar** isn't the best in a straight up fight – therefore it likes to retreat to find a better avenue of attack. It uses an illusion skill to project an image of itself where it is currently standing and disappears to an area away from the nearest enemy.		
Retreat Distance:	20 feet away	Cooldown:	Once per battle: Can be used if it takes 20% or more damage from a single hit

Krista was ecstatic upon receiving her first "stealth" mob – previously she relied on brute force or surprise attacks from unsuspecting directions. Now, though, she could place these around and treat them almost as traps to catch non-attentive players. *Staging these mobs singly or in pairs would be just as effective as a whole room full of them.*

Now that she had done what she could to create some new additions to her bestiary, Krista now needed to focus on a new level for her main dungeon. The deadline for the increased level cap was coming up soon and she had to prepare quickly. She looked at her available resources and was flabbergasted at the amount she had accumulated over the last couple of weeks when the Dungeon Core was missing. Even though she hadn't leveled up, she was still able to accumulate resources. Now that the Core was back, she had leveled up to Dungeon Level 13 and was well on her way to 14. When the new floor was done, she figured she would level up even quicker.

Dungeon Player Administration Toolset	
Available Resources:	2435050
Additional Resources:	Yes
Dungeon Level:	13
Dungeon Experience:	200300/240000

Krista figured she had "carte blanche" when it came to the creation of the new floor; she had so many resources that it might be impossible to use them all at this time. Although she knew she would need to save some for when she was able to look at the Building and NPCs options, but that was for after she finished securing the Dungeon Core from potential assault.

* * *

After almost a full day of creating the new floor, it was almost complete and in about eight hours the level cap would increase by 5 for the third floor. Until she placed the Guardians and connected the two floors, however, the fourth floor would stay incomplete until she was ready. Before she did that, she wanted to have Devin run through it with some of his guild friends to test it out before it was complete.

Now that she had expanded her dungeon territory, she found that she could create a long slide from outside of the entrance behind a hidden door. This door would allow someone to travel down to the fourth floor without having to officially enter the dungeon (since they were over the level cap). Once it was tested, she could delete the slide and then open the floor for the general public. She was going to call them her "beta-testers".

A couple of hours ago, when she knew she would finish in plenty of time, she had asked Devin if he could contact the group that had helped him acquire the Dragon's Lair dungeon. He had asked about a suitable award for them and although she still had some ideas how to compensate them, she figured this would help tide them over until she was able to do it. Krista had lowered the levels of the mobs she had placed down there to better match them – she would raise them up again later. Devin was as excited as she was to see them try it out – he hadn't seen it yet, so it would be new to him as well.

Chapter 19

Devin slid down the slide that Krista had created, leading Domn3r's group down to the new fourth floor. When he had told them of this unique opportunity, they dropped everything they had going on and jumped on it immediately. They all lived for this type of thing – being able to test out a new section of a dungeon that had never even been seen before was too good to pass up. When they got there (in record time no doubt), they were all eager to get started.

He met them outside the dungeon in a different guise than they had seen him in last time. This time there was just a small shock since he looked quite different, but at least he was a little more familiar-looking this time. He had chosen to be a High Elf Healer to be able to resurrect his friends in case they died. *What am I thinking – of course they are going to die! Krista seems to make the deadliest dungeons – it's almost a guarantee.*

He didn't have to worry about being attacked himself since he was part of the dungeon, so he put very little consideration into defending himself. Because of that, as part of his build he maxed out his Intelligence and Wisdom, took a couple of low-level healing spells, and boosted his *Resurrection* spell up as far as he could take it in order to reduce the cooldown time. He also got a couple of key items from Krista for his level that would further reduce the cooldown time on all his spells. In effect, this meant that if the entire party wiped he would be able to get them all up within a couple of minutes.

Once they arrived at the bottom of the slide – which gradually leveled off until they slowly slid to a stop – they found themselves in a small room about 50 feet wide and long. They ended up near the corner of the room where, Devin suspected, the stairs from the floor above would be located. In front of them they were greeted with the familiar sight of **Magma Shroombas (Level 32)** – although this time there were about 30 of them all grouped up together near the center of the room. They weren't moving so they obviously hadn't been aggroed yet.

Once Domn3r and his group had gotten their bearings after the long slide down, they considered the Shroombas before them. Mac spoke up and said, "I got this – step back and get ready just in case." Everyone – including Devin – stepped back and watched as Mac started casting a spell. It was a powerful one, based upon the five second casting time. Devin watched as shards of ice rained down from the middle of the room and impaled the entire group of **Magma Shroombas**. Instantly, the mobile mushrooms woke up and turned toward Mac – before they could take more than a step they were dead.

I think they were holding back when they helped me out with that dungeon, he thought. He again appreciated the way they had helped him – if they hadn't held back then he wouldn't have gotten enough practice before he took on the **Mighty**

Flame Dragon. Now Devin was looking forward to seeing what they could *actually* do.

Mac smiled and fake-roared, "Take that *Ice Storm*, muthafuckas!" Maxinista, their designated looter, shook her head and looted all the corpses of the Shroombas. She found that their loot was very similar to the other dungeon but of a higher quality. It made sense because they were pretty much identical – other than being a higher level.

"Hey Krista, if you're watching I would suggest spreading them out a little more – that was entirely too easy," Devin told the air around him.

"Yeah, I saw that – I'll change it once you guys are done. Do you think they would be better near the walls or just scattered in groups?" Krista asked him.

Devin noticed the group had gone silent around him and was looking around in confusion. "Who is that?" Ambrose asked for the group.

"Ah...that's Krista – I wasn't aware you could hear her. It must have been a something she had unlocked recently to be able to talk to players. She couldn't before the Dungeon Core was stolen – she used to warn me when groups of players would get close to my hiding places. Anyway, Krista, I want you to meet Domn3r, Ambrose, Bolt3n, Mac which is short for Macgowenishburt, and Maxinista – but she goes by Max. Everyone – meet Krista!"

They all said hello and Ambrose added, "It's so good to finally talk to you – Devin has told us all about you and your situation. I would love to talk to you more about the whole dungeon building experience because it sounds like so much fun."

"I would love to talk sometime – probably when we aren't under the imminent threat of death and have time to breathe. Hopefully in the next couple of days if everything goes well," Krista responded. She then asked the group again for any suggestions for placement of the **Magma Shroombas**.

Mac had a suggestion, "The only way I was able to kill them all so quickly was because they were so bunched-up together. If they were along the walls then we could make our way around the perimeter, only taking on those in aggro range – this wouldn't work be good for you. If they were spread out throughout the room I wouldn't be able to hit them all and the ones I didn't hit would aggro straight for me. If we went straight melee, there would only be a small possibility that most of them would aggro as soon as we attacked one.

"Your best bet is to have three groups of ten that are separate but within aggro range of each other – this way I wouldn't be able to hit all of them with a spell and if we attacked only one group the others would aggro immediately. Huh...I can't believe I'm telling you the best way to kill us." The other members of the group looked at Mac, surprised at his thought-out explanation.

"I agree that it's weird, but it's also kind of neat – we can help shape this place in order to make it more effective against Dungeon Core thieves. Which is kind of the entire point of what we've been doing the last couple of weeks. Of course, that means we'll know how to defeat everything – easy farming here we come!" They all laughed at Maxinista's statement, including Devin and Krista.

"That's fine, you can farm the dungeon all you want – it doesn't cost me anything to restock it after it's looted. The only cost is with the initial setup," Krista told them all.

With the extra incentive of being able to help fine-tune this dungeon floor, they eagerly moved onto the next room with a spring in their step. "I hope you have something deadlier than those Shroombas – they are kind of weak," Devin had fallen back behind the group and spoke softly to the air.

"Don't worry, that room was basically a friendly 'hello' compared to the rest of it. It was just something familiar to lure them into a false sense of security," Krista whispered back so that the others couldn't hear her.

"Oh, you're a devious one you are. That's what I love about you," Devin responded automatically, not thinking about what was saying until it came out.

"That's another thing I want to talk about…" Krista started.

"Not now, let's wait until this 'beta-test' is done and you can bring back Violette to clear matters up. I think you said that you'd be able to do that when you are ready to open the new floor and it's almost time for that. If everything goes well, we'll have plenty of time to talk."

Krista hurriedly agreed because Domn3r's group had just entered a dark hallway that had high ceilings and seemingly-random side alcoves that held statues of grotesque monsters. Devin could hear Krista whisper right next to his ear, "Stay back, I want to see how these guys do – you may have some work ahead of you."

He stopped and watched as they entered the dark tunnel, anticipating a good show.

Chapter 20

Max led the way as the rest of them followed, with Ambrose safely out of harm's way in the rear. Domn3r watched as she checked for traps, knowing that this dungeon was notorious for having hidden traps where you least expected them. After Max crouched down to disable an obvious tripwire hidden near the floor, he heard Ambrose cry out in pain behind him.

He spun around, only to find her on the ground, bleeding out with two stab wounds in her back. Looking further behind, he saw Devin standing about 30 feet away with a shocked look on his face. Looking all around him, he couldn't see anything that would have caused her death.

"What happened?" Max came running back, looking around at the shadows near the alcoves in the walls. She had better dark vision than the rest of them, so they would have to rely on her to find whatever had killed Ambrose.

"Not sure, I heard her cry out and by the time I spun around she was dead. I didn't hear or see anything – it was like a ghost. From the stab wounds, it looks like she was attacked from behind. Hey – can you res her?" Domn3r shot this last request toward Devin who was speaking softly to the air. Once he got his attention, Devin walked over and started casting his *Resurrection* spell – which didn't take long. *That's the fastest*

I've ever seen that spell go off – he must've put all his points into just that one spell. It was good to see because if they all wiped it meant Devin could get them all back up before time ran out.

As Ambrose got to her feet, she asked in confusion, "What happened? Last thing I knew, I was watching Max disarm that trap when I heard a very soft sound behind me; then suddenly I was dead. Did you kill whatever got me?"

"Nope, we have no idea what got you – we were hoping you could tell us," Max told her.

"I didn't see anything – hold on, let me check my combat log...it says that 'Death's Roar' hit me with a critical hit that basically one-shotted me. Never heard of that before," Ambrose informed them.

"Well, I don't see it now, let's get a move on; everyone, stay close – Ambrose, you're in the middle. Now, keep an eye out and call out if you see or hear anything," Domn3r told the group as they started progressing forward again. Within a minute, Bolt3n – who had been in the rear of the group now that Ambrose was in the middle – cried out and they all turned to see him fighting a shadow. Or at least that's what it looked like, since the skin or fur on the creature was so black that it blended into the background and was hard to follow.

Bolt3n was still on his feet but he was hurt bad. Thinking she was far enough to be safe, Ambrose immediately cast one of her instant-cast heals on Bolt3n – not wanting him to die as well – when the shadow creature turned its aggro on her. Domn3r was running to head it off in case it went for Ambrose when he watched it launch itself from the ground and fly – yes, FLY – over Bolt3n and went straight for their Healer.

As it approached, she put her staff up in front of her to block its attack. Ambrose was a capable defensive fighter and knew how to block most attacks until help came. She blocked its first two strikes, getting a small nick on her hand from one of its knives, when Domn3r saw it disappear and then instantly appear behind her back.

Two quick strikes and Ambrose was down again without being able to turn around. This time, at least, they saw who did it and Domn3r used his taunt to gain its attention. It immediately headed in his direction and he easily defended himself against its knives with his sword and shield.

He could hear Mac casting a spell behind him; as it went off, he saw some ice shards appear to the side of the shadow and impale the Death's Roar in multiple places. Its health dropped more than 50% and he saw it stop moving. *Must be weak to ice – those ice shards must have stunned it or something.* Taking advantage of its paralyzed state, he slashed his sword in a horizontal cut that would take its head from its shoulders.

At least, that's what it would have done if it was real. As he watched his sword cut right through it without resistance, he lost his balance and fell to a knee. When he looked up, he saw the shadow about 20 feet away launch itself into the air, disappearing into the shadows near the top of the hallway.

Domn3r glanced at Max and saw that she was tracking it with her enhanced dark vision. He looked again at Devin and with an unspoken request, asked him to resurrect Ambrose again. Devin promptly *Resurrected* Ambrose and then backed up, looking to see what they would do now.

"Do you see it Max?" Domn3r asked her.

"Yep, it's hovering in the air about 20 feet above us. I can hit it with one of my ranged attacks, but it won't do enough damage. It looks like it is waiting for us to move and lose sight of it again," she replied.

Domn3r switched to party chat just in case the shadow creature could hear and understand them, "Keep an eye on it and let me know if it moves from that spot. Mac, can you cast a non-targeted AOE that would reach that far?"

"I have the *Whirlwind* spell that has a 30-foot reach – but it's only level 1 and doesn't do a lot of damage. It would just piss it off," Mac told him.

"That's all we need – I need to make it come after you. Sorry, my friend – you're acting as bait for this one. Max, get behind Mac a couple of feet away and *Stealth*. I have a feeling that it will try to backstab its target whenever possible," Domn3r gave out orders to the group.

When Max was in position, Mac cast his low-powered and low-cost *Whirlwind* spell. It created a vortex of wind that reached all the way to the ceiling and whipped the clothing around their bodies. It did very little damage at this level, which is why Mac didn't use it very often. Within three seconds, Domn3r saw the shadow land behind Mac and stab forward with its knives. Before they could hit him, however, the creature was stabbed from behind by Max – who had scored a critical strike in addition to the *Backstab* bonus. It fell to the ground dead, and they finally got a good look at what had killed Ambrose not once, but twice.

Its shape was very similar to the **Hearthfire Dragonkin** that they had just seen in the Dungeon that Devin had captured. Although it was smaller, it was hard to tell because it was covered head-to-toe in black fur instead of scaly skin. When he looked closer, he saw that it was called a **Death's Roar (Level 35 – Deceased)**. That was just under their current levels, which ranged from levels 37 to 39. He had never seen anything like this before and asked Krista about where she had gotten it from.

"I made it. I created a hybrid that included a **Hearthfire Dragonkin** and a **Starving Mountain Lion**. This was the result – a stealthy and deadly Dragonkin. I'm quite proud of it, actually, because it performed awesomely. Even better than I had expected," Krista answered him.

That explains all the new and interesting creatures we found on third floor. I was wondering why we hadn't ever seen those before. "That's neat – can you mix any creatures together?"

"I can only mix Base Creatures together and the result isn't always a success – you'd be disgusted by the results sometimes. When these creatures are created they become Advanced Creatures and I can't do anything further with them at this time. Perhaps when my dungeon levels up more I might be able to."

"Now I want to hear about dungeon building even more, there seems like there is a lot more to it than I thought," Ambrose chimed in.

"We definitely will – but first you need to make it through this floor and we don't have a lot of time."

"Alright, let's keep moving – this is what we're going to do. Mac, periodically cast your *Whirlwind* spell while Max follows behind you in stealth. When we clear an area, Max will check for traps further ahead and then come back. That way we can flush them out and kill them before they can do any more damage to us," Domn3r told them as they started moving.

Their plan worked out well and they flushed out three more **Death's Roars** along the way. The only trouble they had was at the end of the hallway, when two of the shadowy Dragonkin attacked Mac at the same time. Mac ended up dying, but Max was able to *Backstab* one while Domn3r picked up the other and with all of them attacking at the same time was able to kill it before it could get away. As they exited the hallway, Krista asked them if they had any suggestions for improvements – they had none. If it wasn't for Devin bringing Ambrose back to life twice, they would have been hard-pressed to get through without losing more party members.

Glad to be out of the dark hallway, Domn3r's first glimpse of the next room reminded him a little of the last floor. From what he could see, they were in a large, well-lit room that was much longer than it was wide. The ceiling was about 100 feet high; it was only that high because in front of them was a small hill about 50 feet high that ran the width of the room – almost like a giant speedbump. It was similar to the mountain they had seen on the third floor, so Domn3r warned his group to watch out for Mountain Goats or some sort of variation of them.

Domn3r led the way this time, ready for incoming attacks as they made their way up the hill. He didn't have long to wait because at the halfway mark, he saw some grotesque shapes cresting the top of hill. As they rushed down to his location, he counted four of them and was just able to catch their name – **Goat Suckers (Level 34)**. *Well, I was right – Goats. But I'm not sure what they are covered in.*

As they neared the party, Domn3r used his group taunt to get them all to attack him. Bracing himself, he withstood the impacts of three of these sick-looking Goats while hiding behind his shield. The fourth one, however, hit him with enough force to knock him down, flinging him back down the hill until he stopped near the bottom.

Getting himself back to his feet, he looked at this health points and realized the fall took about 20% of his health away.

Looking back up the hill, he saw the **Goat Suckers** racing down the hill toward him since he still had all their aggro. He hoped they weren't going to ram him again, but at least this time he was on flat ground. They closed in on his position and although they slammed into him, it wasn't with the same force as before.

Now surrounded by four Goats, he looked up to see his group coming back down the hill and casting spells and firing arrows as they came. *Now* this *we can handle — they'll handle dishing out the damage while I keep these Goats busy.* As he continued to be hit from multiple sides by the attacking **Goat Suckers**, he watched as his team quickly whittled them down until the first one was almost dead. Suddenly, the Goat with the lowest health suddenly exploded in a cloud of spores.

The next thing Domn3r knew, he was being assaulted by demonic apparitions from all sides. He couldn't help panicking and started wildly flailing about with his sword, hoping to kill them all. His attacks seemed to meet some resistance but had no effect on the demons, so he ran for his life — screaming for help as he sprinted away. After what seemed like hours, his head cleared, and he looked around. About 50 feet behind him was the rest of his party, scattered dead on the ground. All except Ambrose, who was standing and shaking her head as if to clear it. As soon as she seemed ok, she looked up just in time to see three of the **Goat Suckers** impact her at the same time. She fell dead on the ground, just feet away from the others.

Domn3r knew when he was outmatched and ran away, attempting to get out of the aggro range of the remaining Goats. When he was far enough away, the trio of monstrous-looking Goats headed back up the hill to where they were waiting for them before. As he made his way back to the massacre, he found Devin already bringing his group back to life, hysterically laughing as he did so. When he was close enough to talk, he angrily asked, "Why are you laughing – almost all of us just died!"

He could tell Devin tried to sober up when he heard his angry tone, but his smile kept threatening to reemerge as he answered Domn3r, "I'm sorry. It wasn't that you *died*, it was *how* you died that was so funny. All of you check your combat logs and you'll see what I'm talking about."

Fuming, Domn3r quickly brought up his combat logs and as he read them his anger slowly faded away. He didn't think it was funny, himself, but he could see why it would have been if you were watching from far away. It turned out that aside from Ambrose, they had all killed each other – with Domn3r doing the majority of the damage. Apparently, the goat released some sort of hypnotic agent that caused hallucinations in the entire party. What he thought were demonic apparitions were actually his other party members and he had smacked them around while they were defenseless.

Domn3r thought that the friendly-fire rule applied to groups no matter what spell or skill was used. However, since this was due to an attack created by a monster, anyone that he attacked while under the influence was deemed a valid target. Similar – just opposite – of the *Hypno Strike* that Sorcerers employed on mobs. Not a fun situation, but they could get by if they figured out a plan for them.

Putting their heads together, they came up with a plan that would minimize the risk to everyone but Domn3r. Since he was used to acting as a whipping boy, he went along with it. When they next made their way up the hill, Domn3r was all by his lonesome in the center while the other four were to the left and right of him, out of range of any potential hallucinogenic gases that might erupt. When three of the remaining **Goat Suckers** appeared over the rise again, he braced behind his shield again, reminiscent of the last time he was here. As they collided with his shield, he was again knocked down and he found himself sliding to a stop at the bottom of the hill. Instead of getting up, he stayed on the ground and attempted to cover himself up as much as he could with his shield.

When the Goats arrived, they rammed into his shield over and over he sustained minimal damage. They occasionally found an exposed body part and did a little bit more – but not enough to worry about it. From behind his shield, Domn3r continued to spam his taunts, making sure all the **Goat Suckers** kept their attention solely on him. After a couple of seconds, he could hear the rest of his party unload on his attackers until he first heard an explosion – and then started seeing bugs crawling

572

all over his body. He threw away his shield and rolled all over the ground, attempting to squish them all. He did this for a long time, all the while screaming, "Get them off me! I hate bugs! Help! Kill them all!"

Suddenly, Domn3r heard laughing and he looked around expecting to find squished bugs everywhere and was confused when he didn't see anything. He looked toward the source of the laughing and found his entire party – including Devin – collapsed and rolling on the ground, looking like they were being suffocated. It turned out, however, that they were just laughing so hard that they couldn't breathe.

"See...<giggle>...I told you...<laugh>...it was funny. Now do you...<giggle>...believe me?" Devin appeared like he was having trouble getting even this much out because he was laughing so hard. Domn3r didn't think it was funny, but it was good to see the rest of his group having a good time. The most important part was that they had succeeding in taking out the stupid Goats.

"Alright, that's enough laughing at me – let's go!" They followed Domn3r up the hill, still snickering behind him.

Chapter 21

As they reached to top of the hill, Domn3r looked ahead and saw another two hills the same size as the current one with small valleys between them. At the bottom of the valley, he saw lava on either side of a small stone bridge about 10 feet wide in the middle of the pathway. The bridge was so close to the lava that splashes of the molten rock could be seen cooling along the sides. At the end of the bridge waited another mob that he hadn't seen before – a **Lizard Tickler (Level 34)**.

Surrounding a short figure armored head-to-toe in scaled armor were three **Lava Salamanders,** with collars and leashes leading back to the hand of the armored individual. On closer inspection, Domn3r could see that the figure was actually a Goblin that looked to be trying to prevent anyone from crossing the bridge. *It's probably a trap – since there are already some Salamanders present, I wouldn't be surprised if more will appear while we are crossing.*

He didn't want to take any chances here, so he told Mac and Bolt3n to start firing at them from long range. As soon as they got closer, he would take over the aggro and finish the fight up close. He asked them to stay far enough away from him so that they wouldn't be affected by any more surprise AOE attacks.

The two players started attacking the lizard out front with a combination of *Ice Shards* and *Ice Arrows*. By the time they reached Domn3r, they had already taken out one of the giant Salamanders and he taunted the rest to gain their attention. Everything was going well, and the second lizard was almost dead as he saw Max unstealth and *Backstab* the Goblin for critical damage. The scaled armor the Goblin was wearing prevented it from being a mortal strike, and before she could attack again the Salamanders that were previously focused on Domn3r turned and attacked the Rogue with abandon.

Since she was wearing quality leather armor, Max survived longer than if she was a caster – but not by much. Domn3r could see that the massive lava lizards were doing more damage than normal, and he reached them just as she went down under their bites and flames, even with frantic healing from Ambrose. As soon as she dropped, they abruptly turned and began attacking Domn3r again as if nothing had happened. The rest of the fight went normally, and they left the injured Goblin for last since he didn't actually attack until the other two Salamanders were dead.

Ambrose brought Max back with her *Resurrection* spell and as soon as was up she yelled out, "What the hell was that? I thought you had aggro!"

Domn3r looked at her and said, "I did – apparently they don't take kindly to someone attacking their master. It looks like we need to avoid attacking him until the lizards are dead. Sorry you died, but at least now we know."

They continued and crossed the bridge and were attacked by normal **Lava Salamanders**, just as Domn3r had thought. They finished them off handily and approached the next hill. Based upon their expectation of more **Goat Suckers**, they used the same strategy as last time, with Domn3r in the center and the other four on either side out of range of any AOE attacks.

Even though there were six Goats this time, their strategy worked just as well as the first time. They did have one "Oh, shit!" moment when Domn3r was knocked backwards down the hill and almost ended up in the lava. When he was affected by the hallucinations again, he actually did end up in the lava toward the end of the battle. Fortunately, he was still affected by the spore attack, so he didn't experience as much pain as he would've normally. They were able to resurrect him soon after the battle and they worked on figuring out a way to prevent that possibility in the future. The decided that if he laid down at the beginning he would take more initial damage but would prevent any knockdowns from happening.

Continuing on through the room, they topped the next hill and found the same setup as before in the valley between the hills. The only difference this time was of two **Lizard Ticklers** instead of just the single one. Using the same method as before – since it worked until Max attacked the Goblin – they pulled the two mobs to Domn3r's position and went to work whittling down one group of lizards at a time. As they finished off one group of **Lizard Ticklers** and started on the second, Domn3r was left flatfooted as the Goblin let go of all the leashes and the Salamanders scattered. They went in seemingly random directions: one went for Ambrose, another attacked Max standing nearby, and the third made its way toward Bolt3n.

Domn3r used his taunt abilities that were off cooldown, but they didn't seem to affect the crazy creatures. He ran after the one heading for Ambrose (because you never want to let your healer die) and reached it just as it attacked her. She was able to block the initial bite but was burned badly by the follow-up flame attack. Domn3r used every skill he had to cause damage and it wasn't enough.

Fortunately, Ambrose was saved by a barrage of ice spears coming from the direction of Mac who wasn't being attacked at the moment. Now safe, the Healer quickly started casting a heal spell toward Bolt3n who had been getting creamed by another one of the **Lava Salamanders**. His salvation came a second too late as he fell under the joint bite and flame attacks.

Max was holding her own, dodging like crazy even with a Salamander and Goblin attacking her. She wasn't doing any damage – just concentrating on staying alive – but she couldn't hold out forever. As Domn3r watched the lizard that had killed Bolt3n head in her direction, he ran toward them and spammed all his taunts again on the way. It didn't look like it had any effect when suddenly they all turned his way and shot forward to engage. With the fight relatively back on track, they were able to take out the remaining mobs before Ambrose brought Bolt3n back.

"Wow, these guys are surprising the hell out of us – hopefully that was the last of the surprises we'll see here – I don't think I could take any more," Domn3r told Devin.

"We'll just have to wait and see – even I don't know what's in store for you guys," Devin replied.

They made their way over the **Lava Salamander**-infested bridge with no problems and tackled more **Goat Suckers** on the hill above. This time there were eight of them, but when Domn3r laid down and took their initial charges there were no problems this time. He did end up taking a bit of damage from that first attack but was healed up quickly by Ambrose. After the battle – and another hilarious bout of hallucination – they continued walking further until they caught sight of the rooms' exit.

It was guarded by three **Lizard Ticklers**, but this time they had a plan. They would keep everyone except Domn3r at the extreme edge of their range and if they were attacked they would run from the slower Salamanders. They would continue to attack the ones grouped around Domn3r and keep him healed at the same time.

They implemented this, and it worked perfectly – it just took a bit longer than they were used to. Twice, a group of Salamanders broke off and headed for the ranged group but were easily outrun. After about 20 seconds they stopped their chase and went back to attacking Domn3r. Through a long battle of attrition, they were able to take out all the remaining Ticklers.

"I love and hate that room, Krista. I loved it because it was so challenging – and hated it because it was so challenging. If you want to make it deadlier, which you probably do, add something to prevent ranged attackers from pulling the **Lizard Ticklers** off of the bridge to take advantage of the Salamanders in the lava. Something like a wall they can hide behind so they can't be targeted," Domn3r told the air, hoping Krista was listening.

"I saw that, I didn't even think about that possibility before this. Thanks for pointing it out to me – I'll change it later when you're all done dying over and over in here. Speaking of that – next!" Krista responded.

Chuckling at her enthusiasm, they made their way to the exit and headed further through the floor with Devin trailing behind.

"That was fun watching them make their way through this room – I love all of the new monsters you created. What's next?" Devin whispered to Krista.

"It's just kind of a mini-boss, no biggie..."

Chapter 22

Energized at their completion of the previous room, Domn3r and his group rounded the corner of the hallway leading to the next area. Max had just disabled another Spike Trap embedded in the wall that Mac was a mere half-inch from triggering when they saw the hallway open into a large, circular, stone-walled room. The top of the room was about 100 feet from the floor and there was a massive hole in the middle of the ceiling. He sent Max ahead to scout it out in *Stealth*, wary since he didn't see any obvious threat.

As she approached the middle of the room, a portion of the ceiling seemed to drop. It was only the quick reflexes from the Rogue that prevented her from being flattened like a pancake – although she did take a little damage from the impact which popped her from *Stealth*.

Domn3r wasn't surprised to see that the ceiling hid a giant mushroom. He *was* surprised when he watched the **Shroomba of Doomba (Level 36)** spread a pair of wings from behind its back and lift into the air. The massive 30-foot-tall and 20-foot-wide mushroom rose in the air until it was right in the middle of the room. Once it was there, it turned its attention to the now-unstealthed Rogue standing in open-mouthed awe below it. The giant mushroom quickly swooped overhead and folded its wings, dropping straight down and landed with a resounding *THUMP, completely* engulfing Max.

Backing out into the hallway, the group looked at each other with shocked expressions. Mac got over his shock and turned to Devin, "How the hell do we kill that thing? I mean, it fucking FLIES!"

"I'm not sure – that's for you to find out and for me to watch the show. Here, let me get Max up for you – I'm pretty sure you don't want Ambrose going in there right now," Devin put action to his words as he walked in the room and cast his *Resurrection* spell on Max. After she resurrected near Devin, she quickly ran back into the hallway with the rest of her group. "Uh...that was unexpected...and painful," Max told them in all seriousness.

"I agree, that was unexpected – sorry about that Max. Anyone have any ideas?" Domn3r asked.

"We won't really know what to expect other than by going in there and trying our hand at it. Let's just treat it as a normal boss and try to adapt on the fly," Ambrose put forth her opinion. They all agreed, and they all entered the room as a group, determined to see what they could do against the monstrous fungus.

Their first attempt didn't go so well. Domn3r attempted to taunt the **SoD (Shroomba of Doomba)** and succeeded a little too well – it instantly headed in his direction and similarly "thumped" him like Max. Even with his hefty damage mitigation, it was an instant one-shot death. After that, one-by-one the others were "thumped" to death – all except for Max. She was quick enough that she could avoid the **SoD** when it dropped because of her massive amount of Agility. Bolt3n was able to avoid one drop but miscalculated on the next and was instantly killed.

Regrouping back in the hallway after Devin *Resurrected* the other four, they determined that Max was the best chance to avoid further casualties. They needed to concentrate on taking away the **SoD**'s ability to fly, which meant somehow damaging the wings it possessed. Mac had an idea he wanted to try, so with their new plan in mind they all headed back into the room.

Max used her one barely-effective ranged attack and threw a knife at the **SoD** hovering in the center of the room. After getting its attention, she started running around the room in a circle to avoid the mushroom's "thump" attack. As soon as its back was turned toward Mac, he cast a spell that seemed counterintuitive for the fire-based monster but was actually quite effective on its feathered wings. A huge fireball, four feet in diameter, launched from his hands and impacted the spot on the **SoD**'s back where the wings connected to its body. Within seconds, the wings caught fire – compromising their effectiveness – and the massive mushroom plummeted toward the ground.

This didn't mean that it was defenseless, however. With its wings clipped, it was very similar to a normal Shroomba and legs sprouted from underneath the monstrosity to propel it toward Mac. Domn3r stood in the way, finally able to tank it properly. He taunted it and braced himself as it got closer to him. He angled his shield toward its right hand, which he saw heading in his direction, and tried to deflect it away from him. That was not precisely what the **SoD** had in mind, unfortunately.

Instead of hitting him, the giant hand swiftly picked Domn3r up and tossed him inside its massive tooth-filled maw. After chewing on him for a couple of seconds, it spit him back out onto the ground in front of it. Domn3r took a large amount of damage, but it didn't one-shot him this time. He got back up and felt healing wash over him as Ambrose sent a couple of spells his way, bringing him back up to full.

He saw another hand coming for him and this time he ducked down underneath it as it passed over his head. He attacked the front of the **SoD** and saw its health reduce by a small amount, but he wasn't worried. He wasn't designed to do dish out a ton of damage – his job was to take it.

All this time the rest of the party had been busy laying into the massive mushroom from all sides with spells, arrows, and quick stabs from Max. Its health dropped quickly and when it hit the 50% mark it started quivering all over its body. Domn3r backed up as he saw it almost collapse in upon itself and called out, "Everyone watch out, it's doing som..."

He couldn't get it all out before there was a *whoomp* and a large number of baseball-sized spores erupted from the body of the **SoD** and shot out in all directions, damaging anyone in their way. Domn3r was able to block the ones heading his way with his shield but the others weren't so lucky.

Fortunately, no one died but Mac got one to his face and another hit him in the chest, doing a great deal of damage. Bolt3n took one to his nether regions, which made him slump over in pain. Max was clipped in an arm and a leg but didn't suffer too greatly. Ambrose got hit right smack in the middle of her forehead which knocked her on her ass. All in all, though, they got lucky from this attack; once Ambrose was up, she was able to quickly heal everyone back up to full using an expensive group heal called *Resurgence*.

Domn3r looked toward the **SoD** and saw that it had shrunk a couple of feet after releasing all those spores. He glanced around and told his team to avoid the remaining spores along the ground in case they still did damage if you touched them. They went back to whittling down the giant mushrooms' health, Domn3r attempting to dodge or block any attacks that came his way. He was picked up and chewed on again but took less damage than the first time.

Within a minute, the **SoD** was down to 25% health and Domn3r watched it closely for signs that it would do something else. He gave a sigh of relief as it gave no signs of launching any other type of attack. *Nice! We can do this!* His focus upon the attacks of the fungal monstrosity left him open to an attack from behind, unfortunately. Surprised at a rear attack, he looked behind him and saw a smaller, normal **Magma Shroomba (Spawn)** behind him. It was so unexpected that he wasn't watching his bigger brother and got hit from the side by a giant hand that sent him flying 15 feet away.

As he was airborne, he could see the rest of the room filled with Shroombas attacking his other party members. By the time he got to his feet, Ambrose and Mac were already dead and Bolt3n wasn't far behind. Max was sprinting away from a group of Shroombas and if it wasn't a life-or-death situation it would have been funny; she looked like she was running from a horde of irate toddlers.

Looking at his own health, Domn3r realized the last hit took about 40% of his health away. As he turned his focus back to the bigger threat, he found that his attention had wandered too much. A massive hand grabbed him and the next thing he knew he was being chewed up again, doing enough damage to kill him just before he was spit out.

When he was brought back to life by Devin, he found out that Max lived another 20 seconds before being surrounded by almost 40 of the smaller Shroomba spawn. Even being able to dodge their slow attacks, she was still overwhelmed by their sheer numbers.

As they all regrouped in the hallway, they looked back into the room to see that the **SoD** had regenerated after they

585

had all died in the attack. Disheartened, they discussed what had happened and tried to figure out what to do about it. Bolt3n said that he saw the spores that were launched out earlier had spawned the smaller Shroombas. Killing them all before they were able to spawn had to be their objective during their next try.

They kept all their previous strategies on this next fight and when the **SoD** exploded they all crouched down presenting as little of a target as possible. They were still hit a couple of times, but the damage was minimal compared to before. After that, Domn3r tanked and Ambrose healed him as the rest of them ran around and attacked the remaining spores scattered along the ground. They didn't fight back and were easily killed with one hit, so they were done quickly. The rest of the fight was rather boring as they brought it down to 0% without any other incident.

A chest dropped down from the ceiling as the massive mushroom died, and Max ran over to it to check it out. She opened it up and yelled out loud, "Holy shit!"

"What's in it?" Domn3r asked.

"There's 100 gold in here. That's more than I've ever had at one time," Max unbelievingly responded.

"Sorry about that, I wanted to have some epic loot in there, but I don't have access to it at the moment. After this beta-test, I'll be making some buildings with NPCs that will hopefully remedy that," Krista interjected.

"Uh...no, this is awesome. I can buy good stuff with this – much better than what I have now," Max replied.

The rest of the party expressed their gratitude and personally thanked their good fortune. Leading the way out of the room, Max entered the hallway that appeared after the **SoD** had died and started checking for traps. Domn3r had a smile on his face as he heard her mumbling, "yeah, sorry about that...here's JUST 100 gold for you...next time I'll have something even better..."

Chapter 23

Krista got close to Devin as he was following behind the group of players and whispered in his ear, "Hey, I'll be back in a little bit. I have to go start on a project so let me know what happens. I hopefully won't be gone too long." He nodded in acknowledgement as he continued following behind his guild friends. She then changed her viewpoint to just outside the entrance of Altera Vita. She found that she could travel about 100 feet out from the entrance and could influence non-animate objects within that range.

After making sure there were no players around (she had tried moving a tree before this excursion but found she couldn't while there were players within 200 feet of the entrance), Krista started eliminating trees and rocks so that she basically had a blank canvas of dirt that she could play with. Each object she removed gave her a negligible amount of resources, but she wasn't really concerned with that. She still had over a million resource points to play with, even subtracting what she needed to fine-tune the lower floor Devin was currently going through.

Once everything was clear, she brought up her Buildings and NPCs menus to see what kind of trouble she could get into:

Building and NPCs Toolset

Buildings		NPCs		
Blacksmith/Forge	10,000 rp	Smythe	Blacksmith	5,000 rp
Alchemy Shack	15,000 rp	Chemlas	Alchemist	7,500 rp
Enchanting Hut	15,000 rp	Trance	Enchanter	7,500 rp
Herbalist's Cabin	5,000 rp	Rose	Herbalist	2,000 rp
Hunting Retreat	8,000 rp	Trax	Hunter	8,000 rp
Tannery	12,000 rp	Skinny	Tanner	6,000 rp
General Goods Store	20,000 rp	Price	Merchant	10,000 rp
Guard Barracks	25,000 rp	Sgt. Rucker	Guard	12,500 rp
Tavern/Inn	22,000 rp	Finny	Innkeeper	5,500 rp
		Pierre	Cook	5,500 rp
Wood Palisade w/Gate	50,000 rp	Dewey	Gate Guard	10,000 rp
Guild House *new	100,000 rp	(none)		
Shrine (purchased)	5,000 rp			

As she looked over the list, she realized what she had here was the beginnings of her very own town. She had more than enough to purchase everything right now, but she was sure that she could upgrade them once they were purchased. Those upgrades would most likely cost a pretty penny once she got to that point.

She was just a little confused on why she would want all these buildings — she had originally wanted to build a blacksmith and enchanter in order to improve the weapons that she had access to in the dungeon. *What are these other things for?* She asked Carl if he had any more knowledge of it and was rewarded with a plethora of information.

These buildings were ultimately designed to help increase the availability of weapons, armor, and items that can be looted in your dungeons as well as provide an additional source of resource points. Your NPCs are autonomous creations that can provide services to players for a fee that can be instantly converted to resources that the dungeon can use.

For instance, a player walks into the Enchanting Hut and wants an enchantment that adds +5 to Physical Damage on their sword. They can either pay 8 silver or provide the raw materials a player enchanter would use to create this enchantment. Either payment would suffice for your enchanter to create the enchantment. This payment would then be absorbed for its equivalent resource points.

At level one, each building can only provide lower level goods and services. As you upgrade them by infusing them with additional resources, they can create and provide higher-level products.

The General Goods Store is a place where players can unload any unwanted loot and your NPC will buy it for less than it is worth in resources, thereby making a nice profit of points.

Additionally, as you build each building, their respective goods that they traffic in will then be absorbable inside your dungeon if they have it on them or in their bag. So, this means that ingredients, skins, potions, scrolls, and other various items will then be usable as loot.

A warning – when you start adding buildings, each building has a specific amount of "health points" that corresponds to how much damage it can take before being destroyed. The Palisade and Guards are designed to help prevent this from happening but will not be enough against a determined enemy.

If you have any more questions, please let me know.

Armed with this information, she started buying and placing the buildings she purchased with her large supply of resource points. First, she placed the Wood Palisade w/Gate along the perimeter of her 100-foot territory in a semi-circle shape and butted the ends up against the mountain. The 20-foot-high walls looked formidable enough to stop most players, but Krista was worried that mages with access to fire spells would tear right through it. After that, she placed the Guard Barracks next to the gate on the west side and placed the Hunter's Retreat opposite it on the east side. Halfway down the east side of the palisade, Krista placed the Alchemy Shack and again on the opposite side she placed the Herbalist's Cabin.

Near the mountain she placed the Blacksmith/Forge and Enchanting Hut on the east side, giving them plenty of room to expand and upgrade. On the west side next to the mountain she placed the Tavern/Inn in the corner and the Guild House right next to it. In the center of the territory she placed the Tannery and the General Goods store – right out front to encourage players to sell their loot. When she was finished placing them all, she quickly purchased all the available NPCs and populated each of the empty buildings.

Suddenly, the empty, abandoned-looking town was filled with life as the NPCs went about performing various activities. She saw the shopkeepers opening their shops, the blacksmith banging on some hot metal on his anvil, her new herbalist leaving her cabin and heading out the gate into the forest, and the new gate guard standing at attention near the gate. Near the Guard Barracks, she spotted Sgt. Rucker standing at attention as if he was awaiting orders.

She brought her viewpoint near the front of the new guard and addressed him, "Hello Sgt. Rucker. What is it you do here?"

Krista was happy to see that he could hear and answer her, "I'm here to protect your settlement from anyone you deem to be hostile. Although I could probably use more help."

"How do I go about that, Sgt.?"

"You need to select the barracks behind me and hire me some new recruits that I can whip up into shape in no time. A variety of different guards will help diversify our defensive strategies. And if you can upgrade the Palisade to have a catwalk or even a different material it would help as well. I consider the safety of this place to be my highest priority," Rucker told her with all formality.

"Thank you, I'll look at the wall in just a moment." It appeared as though he took his job seriously, but Krista wasn't sure why he needed to guard these buildings in the first place. She saw that they had a certain amount of health points, but she couldn't understand why anyone would want to attack them in the first place. So, she did what she always did when she had a dungeon-related question – she asked Carl for some more clarification.

The reason someone would attack your town is for two main reasons. First, is the monetary reward they would get from each building demolished. If it is a trade building like an Enchanter, they would receive an amount of currency equal to the sales over the last day at that location. For other buildings, they would receive a set amount determined by a complex calculation based on various factors – including, but not limited to, the upgrades spent on the building.

The second, and probably most important reason, is that if another guild attacks and destroys all the defenders and occupies the Guild House uncontested for 30 minutes, they can

gain control of the town bonuses. These bonuses include a discount on all items bought and sold in town – while still maintaining a profit of resources for the dungeon – as well as receiving the Dungeon Core bonus while inside this dungeon. Currently, as it is unoccupied by any guild, you may choose to either assign a guild to control the town defenses or let a guild occupy it on their own.

Fortunately, the system automatically protects the town from being overrun by high-level players. PVP is disabled inside the town for anyone over the level cap of the dungeon – this includes damaging buildings or occupying the Guild House.

One last thing...a new way to provide payment was added recently when the Dungeon Core was returned. Any player that is part of the guild that controls the town may pay for goods and services with their lives. Not permanently, of course, but if they die on dungeon territory after making a contract with one of your NPCs they can convert their death into the equivalent resource points you would receive if they had died inside the dungeon. They, of course, can be resurrected afterwards – but there is a limit. Only one death conversion can be performed each week per player to prevent them from dying over and over to buy everything they can get their hands on.

Information pertaining to the presence of the town, the monetary reward of destroyed buildings, and the town bonus is slated to appear on the next routine patch notes releasing next Tuesday.

"Wow, that is an insane amount of information, Carl – thanks!" She wasn't sure what she thought about the "death conversion", but if the players agreed to it she wasn't going to stop them. It didn't cost her anything in the long run, so she didn't see any harm. Although from another perspective it almost looked like they were making sacrifices to a "Dungeon God" – she had mixed feelings about that.

With this new information, Krista wanted to upgrade everything as quickly as possible but first she needed to look to see how much it was going to cost. She looked at the Guard Barracks and mentally selected it:

Guard Barracks			
Hire Guards:		**Upgrade:**	
Fighter	5,000 rp	Increase Guard Capacity by 5(Current: 5)	15,000 rp
Defender	6,000 rp	Increase Base Guard Level (Current level: 1)	100 rp
Archer	4,000 rp	Strengthen Barracks Structure	5,000 rp
Mage	8,000 rp	Add Defensive Fortifications	25,000 rp
(Additional guard types and upgrades available upon Dungeon Level increase)			

After buying all the buildings and NPCs, she found that she still had over half a million points to play with. She first upgraded the Guard Capacity by five and bought two Fighters, three Defenders, three Archers, and two Mages. Continuing her spending spree, she Strengthened the Barracks Structure – which increased its "health" – and added Defensive Fortifications.

She watched as the walls of the barracks grew bigger and sturdier and noticed ballista emplacements on the roof of the building as well. Lastly, she increased the Base Guard Level until they started at level 40. She wanted to do more, but as she started increasing their base level she saw that each level cost 100 more resource points than the last.

All-in-all, she ended up spending 179,000 resource points on her new barracks and guards. She was starting to see that resource management was going to be an important part of this new town if she wanted it to succeed. As she pulled up the Palisade menu, she despaired when she saw that it would cost 100,000 resource points to upgrade it from wood to stone.

A catwalk along the top was only 25,000 and she considered just doing that, but she took Rucker's advice and spent the necessary points to upgrade it all. The wood Palisade seemed to ripple from one side to the other as a wave of stone replaced the wood all the way down the line.

The gate was the only thing that was still wood, and she wondered at that until she thought to bring up the gate menu.

Another 30,000 resource points! At this rate, Krista was quickly running out of money – she hoped she had enough left over to do everything she needed to do. She spent the necessary points and watched as the gate as well rippled and turned to stone. Just like that, she was over 360,000 points poorer after strengthening the towns' defense.

Next, she went to the Blacksmith since that was her main motivation for creating this town. She pulled up the menu and looked at her options:

Blacksmith/Forge		
Upgrade Menu:		
Increase Weapon Quality (10)	Current Level: 10	2,000 rp
Increase Armor Quality (10)	Current Level: 10	2,000 rp
Increase Accessory Quality (10)	Current Level: 10	5,000 rp

Not too expensive at least, she thought. She went ahead and purchased all three upgrades and was going to upgrade them all again when she saw that their costs had tripled. Her intent all along was to increase the quality of the weapons and armor that was included in the loot dropped from her chests. With this in mind, she went ahead and spent first 6,000, then 18,000, and finally 56,000 resource points each to raise the Weapon and Armor Quality up to 50. She ended up spending

156,000 resource points to do so, but the benefits of having good quality loot would hopefully pay for itself.

With only about 60,000 resource points left to spend – and needing to keep some to improve the new floor once it had its walkthrough – Krista visited both the Alchemy Shack and the Enchanting Hut to improve the quality of potions/items and enchantments that she could use for her loot inside the dungeon and for players to purchase here in town. Another 52,000 points down and she was pretty much broke as far as her points went. She noticed that she had just received another 5,600 points in the last couple of minutes and figured that Devin was watching his friends die some more, providing her with additional resources and experience.

Looking around at her town, she instructed Sgt. Rucker to post lookouts at the top of the wall and continue training their new recruits to increase their levels. He agreed, and Krista turned her attention back to the latest room the beta-testers were making their way through, leaving the town in his – hopefully – capable hands. She was interested in seeing if they had any more suggestions on how to make it even deadlier.

Chapter 24

Domn3r picked himself up again after having to dodge *another* fireball coming from behind him. He blocked the next one with his shield and turned to the new mob that this room had introduced. The **"BWMYF"** had wiped the entire party previously after an unexpected onslaught of fiery fecal matter.

When they had entered this room following the showdown with the **Shroomba of Doomba**, they saw a long room with a "lavafall" facing them from about 75 feet away. To the right of the "lavafall" were stone steps leading to the top and what he assumed was a way past the lava. As they approached the pool of lava below the falls, he saw two **Lava Salamanders (Level 36)** emerge from it and head in their direction. As his group engaged, Max observed some **Fire Drakes** flying above the molten falls. They were accompanied by a something familiar but altogether new.

The **"BWMYF" (Level 36)** looked like a Harpy if you were to light it on fire for a couple of minutes and then put the corpse out. It was entirely black and charred-looking, had wings of fire, and was dripping sparks as it flew. Domn3r thought that the Harpies were ugly before this; the burnt-corpse-look didn't help any.

As they easily defended against the Salamanders and dodged fireballs from the Drakes, they readied themselves for some new attacks from this new mob. At first the hellish-looking Harpies didn't move and Domn3r figured they wouldn't be triggered until they arrived at the top of the falls. He couldn't have been more wrong.

Just as another two **Lava Salamanders** left the lava and joined the fight, the group was distracted enough to almost miss the attack. Mac and Ambrose saw the **"BWMYF"** fly toward Bolt3n, Max, and Domn3r and called out a warning. The charred Harpies swooped down and missed the Archer and Rogue who were able to dodge out of the way with the warning. Domn3r wasn't so lucky since he was hemmed in on all sides by the Salamanders. As he looked up with the warning, one of the Harpies landed on his head and squatted down. Expecting to be picked up and dropped somewhere – most likely in the lava – he bashed his shield into one of the legs on his shoulder hoping to weaken it enough.

If that had been the **"BWMYF's"** plan, it probably would have worked. Unfortunately, he instead got a face full of lava-filled pee as the Harpy relieved itself on his head. He survived the initial wave of molten rock due to being helmed, but as it flowed down his body it entered all the joints and creases in his armor, cooking him alive. Ambrose healed him as much as she could without acquiring massive amounts of aggro, but it wasn't enough; he fell dead within seconds as he was cooked alive from inside his armor.

The remaining group members still could have taken out the remaining monsters with a little luck – except for the new Harpy mob. Instead, just as Domn3r fell dead, the remaining two **"BWMYF"** Harpies that had missed Max and Bolt3n earlier in their swooping dive hovered over the party and started spinning in the air. As they spun, flaming balls of fecal matter erupted from their asses and covered the party. Max was able to dodge most of the fireballs but was overwhelmed by the remaining enemies when the rest of the party died.

After Devin *Resurrected* them, they tried again and had Bolt3n pull the new fire Harpies from extreme range, hoping to tackle them first. As his arrow hit one of them above the "Lavafall", all the flying mobs attacked as one. They had taken the chance that they would all come, but this way they were able to concentrate on them without having to worry about the Salamanders.

As they tried their swooping pee attack, Domn3r used his AOE taunt and then squatted while holding his shield above his head to prevent them from landing. With their attention on him, he sprinted ahead – nearly out of range of his own party – and crouched down, awaiting their AOE lava-poop attack. Instead, they started lobbing single "firepoops" at him, accompanied by the normal fireballs that the Drakes were sending his way. He was getting attacked on all sides and although he could block quite a few fire...things...with his shield, he had to attempt to dodge even more that came from behind.

He had taken quite a bit of damage from all the shots that he couldn't block or dodge and was in danger of dying.

Luckily, his group was nearby, and Ambrose started healing him as soon as she was in range. Bolt3n and Mac started hitting the Harpies while attempting to stay out of range in case more "stuff" came flying their way. An *Ice Arrow* from the Archer hit one of the **"BWMYF's"** flaming wings and put out the fire, causing it to plummet to the ground, landing on the other wings and breaking it with a large *crack*. The grounded Harpy screamed in horrific pain and Max quickly ran over and put it out of its misery.

Once they discovered a way to bring them down, Mac and Bolt3n started aiming for the wings of the remaining two. A lucky *Ice Shards* spell, followed up with an *Ice Arrow,* were enough to bring them down. Once they were dead, the **Fire Drakes** were even easier to take out.

"I wonder why they didn't use their AOE attack again," Domn3r asked.

Ambrose, as usual with her game knowledge, answered, "It was probably because there was only you in range and they felt it to be unnecessary. If another one of us had been in range, that would have been an entirely different matter."

Domn3r thought that was a good explanation as any, so they approached the lava pool and started taking out the remaining **Lava Salamanders** that emerged. After 10 of them, they stopped coming and they cautiously made their way up the stone steps, wary of any more surprises.

As they reached the top, Krista's voice surprised them, "How did you like that room? I just got back from an errand and Devin told me about his observations. Do you have any suggestions?"

Domn3r answered for the group, "The only suggestion is to put the flying mobs back farther to make it harder to pull them from across the room. I do have a question for you though – what does 'BWMYF' mean? Those were some disgusting new creatures – why were they throwing their shit at us?"

Krista sounded embarrassed as she responded, "I think the Main System AI has a sophomoric sense of humor and designed all of the different attacks to reflect that. 'BWMYF' stands for **'Bitch Will Melt Yo Face'** – see what I'm talking about? I wish I could change some of these names, but I'm stuck with them as soon as they are developed."

All of them started chuckling when she explained the meaning of the name, Devin included. Mac then regaled them with a story about how the **Pussy Master Orc** had such a funny name that they didn't take it seriously – which led to them getting wiped out. Krista remembered that and how they were making fun of the name at the time. She was glad they now learned to respect her mobs despite their names.

They made their way to the next area with Devin following behind and Krista observing. As they entered the huge, high-ceilinged, and lava-filled room, there didn't seem any way for them to reach the exit about 1,000 feet away on the north side. Suddenly, as if their mere presence elicited the movement, platforms with elevated pathways between them rose from the molten lake. As the lava streamed off the stone platforms, Domn3r could see the waves of heat still emanating from them. As he continued to watch them rise, he counted 25 different areas of safety that they would end up having to cross to get to the exit.

"Well, no time the present – let's see what this room has got for us," Domn3r told his party. Putting action to his words, he led them forward onto the pathway leading to the first platform. Normally he would have Max lead into unknown locales, but he wasn't expecting any traps from below. Logically, since they were raised above the lava, he was expecting more of an aerial assault.

When they were traveling to the second platform, his expectations came true in the form of two Fire Drakes – or what he thought were Fire Drakes. As he unslung his shield to deflect the fireballs he was expecting, he braced himself in front of the party and taunted them both. Instead of lobbing fireballs in his direction, the Drakes swooped down in close and started breathing fire at him from two sides. He was able to block one, but the other was just out of reach of his sword. As he started taking damage from the fire, he saw an arrow and *Ice Shard* strike – what he now could see was a **Fire Wyvern (Level 37)** –

through the flying creature's neck and chest. The flame stopped and as it tried to retreat, wounded, another arrow entered its eye and the Wyvern plummeted into the lava below.

Apparently realizing the futility of trying to burn the well-defended enemy, the remaining **Fire Wyvern** turned to the rest of the party and started quickly flying in circles. It was so fast that none of them – even Max with her significant Agility – could hit it as it passed by all of them for the briefest moment. As it flew, it emitted a gas that floated in the air like a noxious fog. As everyone started coughing at the fumes, the Wyvern ended up back where it started near Domn3r. Coming to a hovering stop, it turned to the trail of gas and breathed fire on it, instantly igniting the highly flammable vapor. An explosion of flame engulfed the entire party, damaging all of them and killing Mac.

Ambrose was standing a little further away from the others and didn't take enough damage to kill her – if she was standing any closer it would have done her in just as quickly as Mac. As it was, she was able to heal them quickly with a costly group heal – she didn't want anyone else to die. This led to her acquiring the aggro of the last **Fire Wyvern** and it headed in her direction. Bolt3n was ready for it and fired off an *Ice Arrow* that hit it mid-flight. It lodged in its wing, hampering its flight so that it could only move at a reduced speed. That was enough for Bolt3n to pepper it with three more arrows to take it down.

As Ambrose *Resurrected* Mac, Domn3r turned to him and Bolt3n, "I think you're going to be vital for this room – you're our only real ranged damage dealers. Whenever possible, try to take out their wings – if it doesn't make them fall in the lava it will hopefully slow them down enough to prevent what just happened. Max and I will do what we can to keep you alive because without you we'll be hosed."

They agreed, of course, and they traveled along the pathways and platforms while fighting off additional **Fire Wyverns**. They learned that if they were able to cripple them with some lucky shots right off the bat, they had a better chance to hit the slower ones as they tried to use their gas attack again.

Everything was going well until one of the Wyverns got fed up with being shot at and rushed at Bolt3n as he acquired too much aggro. Expecting to be blasted by flame, the Archer dodged out of the line of fire only to find that the Wyvern didn't stop. Instead, it got close and latched onto his arm, injecting molten fire into this bloodstream. He started screaming – he told them later it felt like he was boiling from the inside – and fell to the ground, taking massive periodic damage.

Ambrose was able to barely keep him alive and Mac got a fortunate hit in that killed the **Fire Wyvern** that bit their Archer. With the threat eliminated, Ambrose was able to continue healing Bolt3n until the DOT effect wore off. After that incident, they were a lot more careful when fighting the surprisingly-versatile enemies.

About halfway through their trek to the exit, a couple of **Fire Wyverns** were accompanied by another surprise. Domn3r saw what he thought was a Dragonkin riding on the back of a slightly larger than normal Drake. The Dragonkin was wielding a spear and as it stayed back behind the two Wyverns, the Drake started lobbing fireballs in their direction. To draw all their fire, he used his group taunt once again and saw the Wyverns head in his direction. As his party used their normal successful tactics to take down these two adversaries, Domn3r kept an eye on the new flying duo. With their fireballs being blocked, the Dragonkin-Drake combo flew closer and he was able to see that it was called a **Dragon Rider (Level 38)**.

He didn't have much time to think about that because he was quickly assaulted by sweeping lunges with its spear – almost as if it was jousting. Fortunately, his shield was fairly large, and it was relatively easy to block each pass. Domn3r watched as an arrow took down the last Wyvern and they then turned their attention to the new mob. A well-timed *Ice Shard* caught the **Dragon Rider** in the shoulder and seemed to infuriate the flying pair. With a sharp turn and furious flapping of wings, they lifted straight up into the air directly above Domn3r while dodging additional projectiles. Soon enough, they were out of range and they waited with patience to see what it would do.

Domn3r wasn't sure what had happened and only found out when he was brought back to life a couple of minutes later. While they all watched, ready to fling more spells and arrows at the **Dragon Rider**, said mob suddenly dropped straight down like it was shot out of a gun and impaled Domn3r through the eye slit in his helmet. The hit instantly killed him, breaking the spear in the process. Deprived of his main weapon, the **Dragon Rider** broke off and tried to attack from afar. The practice that Mac and Bolt3n had put in over the last couple of hours showed as they took the Drake down – and consequently, the Dragonkin.

That wasn't the only surprise in store for them during the journey through the rest of the room. As they approached the end of the pathways, they were attacked by four **Dragon Riders** at once. They were able to take one down from afar before the others converged on their position and blanketed them with rolling waves of fire. The massive firestorm killed everyone except Domn3r this time, but he was later overwhelmed by the "jousts" from multiple directions.

They were resurrected again by Devin, who looked on with sympathy as he brought them back to life. Noticing the change in his usual demeanor when he had to *Resurrect* them all, he asked Devin what the change was all about.

"Sometimes it's funny or silly how you guys die, but this time you were just overwhelmed and surprised by a massive unexpected attack. Nothing funny about that – I couldn't see any way to avoid dying," Devin told him.

He's right – I'm not sure how to defend against that. After asking his fellow party members, Ambrose suggested just running past them for the moment and hoping for the best since they were so close to the exit. What they really needed if they were to tackle this place again was some heavy fire-based magical resistance gear. That way they could take these blasts of fire without all of them dying so quickly.

Devin and Krista agreed, since time was running out on their "beta-test". While they had confidence that they could find a way to succeed even without resistance gear, they didn't have time to play around until they figured it out.

Once they decided on this plan, they implemented it by running full-out to the exit. Domn3r was slower than the rest, lagged behind, and got fireballed in his butt a couple of times. A final spear "joust" to his back propelled him forward into the exit, doing massive damage but not killing him. Ambrose healed him back to normal and they entered what Krista told them was the last "quote-unquote" room. Whatever that meant...

Chapter 25

After Krista told him that she was going to do something in the last room to prevent other groups of players from just running through, Devin watched as Domn3r and crew cautiously explored this new area. From where he could see it behind the group, it looked like a normal room with smooth, straight walls that ended about 50 feet ahead. In the floor was a hole in the ground that looked like it had exploded upward with scattered rocks strewn about. A hellish glow emanated from the crevice, signaling danger to anyone daring the journey down below.

Max was the first to reach the fissure after determining that there were no traps to surprise them all. She looked down the hole and reeled back in surprise, exclaiming, "What the fuck?!"

Not accustomed to her swearing like that, Devin was curious about what made her react that way. Krista whispered to him that it was safe for him to look. He squeezed past the frozen-in-shock party members as they surrounded the object of their attention. His initial sight of the view before him made him mirror the shock of Max when she reeled back in surprise. Instead of cursing, he said, "Holy hell, Krista, you really outdid yourself."

Leading below was a pathway of shattered rocks – which vaguely resembled a staircase – that led downward toward a jaggedly curved wall. This wall encompassed a giant tube sinking 1,000 feet down into the bowels of the earth, culminating in a massive lake of lava at the bottom. The pathway of jagged rocks eventually morphed into a staircase that wound its way down to the bottom, circling the entire room multiple times. It was only as Devin stood back and looked at the whole scene that he realized what he was looking at. As hard as it was to believe, Krista had designed and built the inside of volcano.

Flapping around the center of the volcano, Devin could see all kinds of flying monsters that were coasting along the currents of rising heat emanating from the lava below. He saw **Dragon Riders, Fire Wyverns, Fire Drakes, "BWMYFs",** and even a **Death's Roar** that was trying unsuccessfully to hide in the shadows along the rock wall. If he saw one, there were bound to me more *successfully* hiding somewhere in there.

"Uh...I don't think I want to even try that. If we were to fall all the way to the bottom, you wouldn't be able to get down quick enough to *Resurrect* us. I can tell you we aren't prepared enough to get through that and we really don't want to lose any experience from a permanent death – never mind the 3-hour lockout," Domn3r told him.

Devin scratched the back of his neck, considering, and said, "Yeah, I think you're right. I wouldn't be able to get to you in time and the last way I want to repay your help is to have you die without a *Resurrection*. Krista, what do you say?"

"I didn't even really think of that, but it makes sense. I got some good info and suggestions on how to improve this place already, so I think that this was a great success. I want to thank you all for your help evaluating my new dungeon floor. As a thank you, I have some news. While you were in here, I was able to break off and create something I want to show you. Normally, your presence would prevent me from making a teleporter to bring you back to the entrance. Fortunately for you, however, this floor isn't quite yet part of the dungeon and I'm able to make one for you now. Give me just a second."

True to her word, a second later a teleporter appeared in the room they were standing in. They all entered it one at a time, with Devin following the last of them. They appeared just outside the dungeon entrance and at first Devin thought Krista had somehow teleported them to a nearby town. Looking around, he was surrounded by buildings ranging in size from a hut to a larger Inn. All in all, they weren't that big compared to others that he had seen in Briarwood, but that was probably because they all had to be contained in a stone wall surrounding them all in a semi-circle shape. There was a gate in the middle of the wall that was closed, and Devin could see numerous guards patrolling in front of the gate and standing on the wall above.

"What the? Is this what you were doing earlier when you left for a bit? You did all this in what – fifteen minutes?" Devin asked Krista.

Instead of answering, she watched the members of Domn3rs' group look around in wonder at the new town that had just sprung up out of nowhere. They were talking excitedly and pointing at the various buildings, exploring the different locations with their eyes. Finally, Ambrose addressed Krista, "Did you do all of this while we were in the dungeon?"

"To answer all your questions – yes, I did just make this small town. It helps to provide additional resources that I can use to improve the dungeon and spend it on upgrades. Why don't you look around and see the various shops that I've constructed – I'm sure you can find somewhere to offload all that loot from your 'beta-test' of my dungeon floor," Krista answered them all.

She didn't have to tell them twice as they took off and started exploring the small town. It didn't take that long – since it wasn't overly large – and when they came back, they looked extraordinarily pleased. Max had a question though, "I was talking to the Blacksmith and he said that he can provide some better armor for a fairly good price. However, it being out of my price range, he told me about some sort of 'Death Conversion Contract' but wasn't able to explain it. What is that?"

Devin was as confused and curious as the rest of them, eager to find out the answer to this unusual question. Krista put off an explanation, instead asking for them to request the *Reckless* guild leadership to come to the dungeon so that she could explain it to everyone at once.

Domn3r had already let De4thfrmbeh1nd and the others know about their "beta-test" and were eagerly awaiting the results of their adventure. As they were waiting not too far away from the dungeon, they were able to travel there in less than a half hour. While they were waiting, Domn3r's group sold all their extra loot, shopped for additional potions, and used some of their hard-earned gold from the battle with the **Shroomba of Doomba** on some gear upgrades.

Not having anything else to do, Devin went along with them on their shopping excursion while Krista excused herself to finish the changes to the new floor. The party was just finishing up when De4thfrmbeh1nd, Sh1fty, EyesHlzU, and Stalw4rtShield arrived at the gate entrance. Krista, having kept an eye on the goings on up top, told the guards to open the door for them and invited them in herself.

Startled at the disembodied voice, they all pulled their weapons and readied themselves for a fight. This in turn made the guards anxious, which led to them readying their weapons as well. Devin thought that the situation might have gotten out of hand if Domn3r hadn't run over and calmed their leaders down. He was heard telling them about Krista and that it was her voice that they had heard from the air. Relaxing at this situation, they all apologized to Krista and offered various greetings while looking silly staring at random places in the air.

Devin walked over to them and introduced himself as Devin, which got him another couple of funny looks – though not as much as when he was Troll and met Domn3r's group for the first time. EyesHlzU was fascinated by his Healer build – she had never seen anyone put their skills together like he did. It wasn't practical in 99% of situations so it was quite the novelty – a Healer who couldn't heal very well.

After the introductions were over with, Krista gathered them all together and told them all about this town and what it means to both the dungeon and to them. Devin listened as she explained how the basic functions of the town worked. He learned how the buying and selling of items and services at the stores would provide a profit of dungeon resources. This sounded like an awesome way to increase the power of the dungeon without having to kill players for their resources. Of course, these additional resources didn't provide any experience – that was only acquired within the dungeon proper.

He also learned how a guild can take "ownership" of the town, getting bonuses that would increase/decrease the price of goods sold/bought by the players at the shops. Additionally, they would gain the Dungeon Core bonus while delving into the Altera Vita dungeon.

When the *Reckless* guild leaders heard this information, they all looked excitedly at each other. Devin could even hear Sh1fty giggling softly like a little schoolgirl. He could sense that they all had questions on their lips wanting to come out, but Krista wasn't done yet. She told them about the special "Death

Conversion Contract" only available to the guild that was in control of the town.

Apparently, the players could sacrifice themselves to help pay for goods or services as part of a contract with the dungeon. The dungeon would get the resources that would normally be gained from their death inside the dungeon and the player would get that equivalent in trade. The only caveat was that they could only do this once a week – which made sense to Devin. If they were able to do it anytime they wanted, they would be able to purchase an almost unlimited amount of anything.

"I want you all to know how much I appreciate your helping Devin retrieve and safely bring back the Dungeon Core. When it was stolen, I thought that was it for us – that this was end. I was out of my mind with disappointment, resentment, apathy, and depression when the Core was stolen, and your assistance has given me back both my mind and my life. As a token of my thanks, I would like you and your guild to control this town.

"You'll receive all the benefits from our association, in addition to little perks like 'beta-testing' new floors for the dungeon – as Domn3r and his crew can attest to being awesome. In exchange, we need help to defend this place from the other guilds. We need to keep the gates open so that players can come in and challenge the dungeon, as well as patronize the different shops here. If another guild were to take over control, there is an almost definite possibility that they would close the gates and potentially try to steal the Dungeon Core. I know that from your help retrieving the Core from before that you don't want that to happen almost as much as us. If you all agree, you can move in and base all your operations from here."

Krista concluded her "presentation" with the sight of the Guild House, which until Krista had chosen *Reckless* as the controlling guild was invisible. Shocked at the sudden turn of events, all of them – including Devin – just stopped and stared at the decently-sized house that appeared as if out of nowhere.

De4th was the first to speak and addressed Krista, "It would be our honor to defend this place. This is a unique opportunity that – if I can speak for my guild members – would be insane for us to pass up. This is all we've wanted since we've learned of your existence – to keep the Dungeon Core out of the hands of those who would abuse it. Although this would give us a hefty lift in our own power as a result, we will use it to help regulate the comings and goings from inside and outside of the dungeon. You can count on us." Everyone else present seemed to agree with that statement and there were smiles all around.

Even though they already had a larger guild house in the capital, this one meant so much more to them. This one was a representation of what they had been working towards for the last couple of months. All the members of *Reckless* rushed over to it, enthusiastic to check it out.

After spending some time checking it out, Domn3r and his group took the *Reckless* leaders on a tour of their new town. Krista answered all the questions they had to the best of her ability but had to ask Carl a couple of times when they had some specific inquiries she didn't have the answer to. She told them about the current NPC guard situation, and how they could acquire additional units. Krista could provide some resources for them, but ultimately it would be up to the guild to purchase what they needed. Until the dungeon had a surplus of new resources, they would have to use their own gold to get by.

Since the guild was still getting settled in and had things in hand for the moment, Devin heard Krista tell them that she needed to steal him away for some unfinished business. He was pretty sure he knew what she was talking about and said his goodbyes and thanks to Domn3r, Ambrose, Mac, Bolt3n, and Max. They sent him off with heartfelt thanks as well, making Devin glad that he met them and trusted them all in the first place.

Although he was looking forward to what was coming next, he dreaded it as well...

Chapter 26

Krista had finished up most of the improvements the "beta-testers" had suggested earlier while they were exploring the town, so she didn't have a lot that needed to be done to open the new floor. She adjusted the levels of the monsters to better suit the level cap – which she was going to set at 40. This meant that they would potentially see quite a few advanced classes, but that also enabled Devin to access them as well when he leveled up. She was nervous about seeing how the new advanced classes would fare against her dungeon, but she figured she needed to do it eventually to learn about how they operated.

She also changed the loot in all the chests, leaving a small amount of gold and adding more powerful weapons and armor that she had access to from the blacksmith in town. Having these advanced weapons and armor also allowed her to upgrade all the weaponry that her sentient mobs used – the Goblins, Orcs, and Dragonkin all got an upgrade. Although they stayed the same level, even the Goblins on the first floor were potentially twice as hard to kill now.

These changes used up all her additional resources that she had accumulated from the "beta-testers" when they died on this floor, and from their selling/purchasing in her town. She was also just a couple of players' deaths away from increasing her Dungeon Level to 14 – which hopefully would come soon since they were almost ready to open for business.

One thing that the beta-testers couldn't see was the recreated initial Guardian Room she had installed just after the volcano. This was to be Violette's new room, placed just before Bruce's final guardian room. Bruce wouldn't move down to the new floor until she connected the stairs down to it, but she still could place Violette there. She had been dreading this part, because she wasn't sure what was going to happen. *Will she be as crazy as she was before she died? Or will she be worse? And what really happened between Devin and Violette?* The only way she was going to find out was to just do it and damn the consequences.

She had respawned and placed Devin in the recreated Guardian Room, noticing that he had chosen to be a Brawler with insane amounts of allocated Strength in his build. She wondered what that was supposed to mean but stopped dithering and placed her volatile Guardian into the middle of the room.

Violette appeared collapsed on the ground, weeping, exactly the same way she was before she was killed by the *Guiding Light* guild all those weeks ago. It wasn't long before she became aware of her surroundings and looked up at Devin standing a distance away from her. Her sobbing stopped, and a smile appeared on her face as she picked herself up and started crossing the distance between them.

"STOP! Don't come any closer Violette. I know you'll still probably be able to snap me like a twig, but I won't hesitate to defend myself," Devin ordered her.

"Devin!! It warms my heart to see you here! I'm so sorry about our argument before, but you've obviously forgiven me if you are here now! Come and hug me like we used to, and everything can go back to the way it was before!" Violette said in her bubbly voice, as if she wasn't just crying her eyes out moments before.

Well, that answers that – she's still crazy. "What happened Violette? When we were attacked, you were inconsolable, collapsed on the floor complaining about Devin and what he did to you. When you were killed, our Dungeon Core was stolen and if it wasn't for Devin we wouldn't be here now. You only had one job and you failed – what do you have to say for yourself?"

Violette's face fell at the mention of the stolen Dungeon Core and for the first time she actually looked ashamed. Krista waited for her to speak and after a minute she finally told her, "We just had a little misunderstanding and Devin told me he never wanted to see me again. I was losing the person that I was in love with and I didn't know why. I kind of broke down completely after that. It's not my fault – if Devin hadn't said that I would have been fine."

Krista turned her attention on Devin and asked, "Is this true – did you tell her you didn't want to see her ever again? Why would you do that?"

Krista had never seen Devin so furious – he normally had an easy-going if shy attitude and the look on his face kind of scared her a little. His mouth kept opening like he was going to say something, but he seemed to be struggling to get out what he wanted to say. He finally seemed to get his thoughts in order and practically shouted, "You're forgetting about the part where you threw me on the ground, ripped off my clothes, and tried to take advantage of my inability to fight you off. Once you finally stopped and I was able to get away from you, I told you I didn't want to see you again because it was true – I didn't ever want to see you again after what you did. If it wasn't for the fact that I needed to prove to my true love, Krista, that it wasn't my fault that the Dungeon Core was stolen I wouldn't even be here now."

Krista's thoughts almost shut down after hearing what Violette did to her Devin. When she could finally form a coherent thought, she started yelling at her with the loudest voice she could project. If she had the physical ability to hurt her, she would have ripped her pretty little head off her shoulders. "YOU TRIED TO RAPE HIM? ARE YOU INSANE? WHAT AM I SAYING? OF COURSE YOU ARE! I CAN'T BELIEVE I LET YOU BACK IN HERE NOW KNOWING WHAT YOU DID TO HIM!"

Violette just stood there, looking more and more beaten-down until she collapsed to her knees and started bawling. Krista stopped when she saw this, unable to continue shouting at the already broken individual. She didn't have any sympathy for her, she just felt that whatever she said would've fallen on deaf ears.

Between sobs, Violette started asking Devin for forgiveness and for him to keep her company again since she was still lonely. She said that she would behave herself and nothing like that would happen again. Krista couldn't believe the gall of the woman, thinking that they would just brush off what she had done without any consequences. She wasn't surprised when Devin finally answered her pleas, "No, Violette, I will not be back after today. I can't trust you, I don't like you, and you hurt me more than you can probably comprehend in your twisted mind. I may eventually forgive you for what you did – but I'll never forget. Goodbye, Violette." He turned around and walked out of the room without looking back.

Violette just knelt there, uncontrollably sobbing, with – *damn that woman, ADORABLE* – hiccups occurring every couple of seconds. Krista just watched her with indifference, secretly glad that she was taking Devin's departure so hard. She didn't deserve pity, so Krista wasn't going to give her any. When her crying didn't look like it would be stopping anytime soon, she addressed Violette with an emotionless voice, "Despite your broken emotional state right now, I still need you to defend this place against the players coming to steal the Dungeon Core. Fortunately for us, you are not the final protection we have in place. If you aren't able to function properly, we have a backup Guardian that has a room just behind yours. He's been doing an awesome job on the previous floor and he'll be here to save us if they get that far. If you have any desire to meet him, you can see him through the exit doors at the top of the temple. If you need anything else – don't call me. Goodbye."

Krista found Devin angrily walking up the pathway that wound itself around the volcano. She followed him for a while, not sure what to say to him after the previous revelation. Finally, she decided to ask him, "Do you want me to respawn you somewhere?" She had to ask him twice, he was so entrenched in his own angry thoughts. He nodded in the affirmative, apparently not trusting himself to speak quite yet. She removed him from the floor and placed him back inside the dungeon entrance, trusting that he would respawn when he was ready.

She had a lot to think about as she made her way to the first room to finish the stairway leading down to the new floor. *Despite the uncomfortable situation back in that room, it certainly cleared up a lot of things. I should have trusted Devin when he said that it wasn't his fault that the Core was stolen. I should have known that he wouldn't do anything deliberately to jeopardize what we have here – our way of life. I should have known how he felt about me before all of this. I should have*

known a lot of things...

Chapter 27

Devin laughed as he watched as another **Goat Sucker** caused an unprepared group to start screaming and attacking each other as much as the goats around them. He cast another low-powered *Grasping Vines I* spell that caused vines to sprout from the ground, encircling the players' legs and trapping them in place. Since it was such a low level, the spell would only keep them immobilized for a couple of seconds but that was enough for the hallucinations and remaining goats to get their work done.

When they were freed from the vines, their tank was the only one still standing. Before the hallucination wore off, Devin used *Major Rot III* to inflict massive amounts of damage-over-time effects on his health points. He hid again before he was seen but was able to see the almost-dead Defender on his last legs as the hallucination dissipated. A couple of seconds passed as his spell continued to affect the player, until he finally collapsed in death, surrounded by the monstrous-looking mushroom goats.

He heard an almost imperceptible *ding*, and thought, *I did it! Finally, Level 40!* Since the new floor opened almost a day ago, he had been gaining experience and levels hand-over-fist. Their higher levels – coupled with their unfamiliarity of the new floor and monsters – allowed Devin to participate in their slaughter without too much danger on his part. Early on, when he was using a Rogue-Archer build, he got caught by an extra-sneaky Assassin when he ventured too far out of hiding. He ended up dropping back down to level 33 from 35.

After that, Devin started staying farther away and only appearing when there was very little danger of being snuck up on. He also created a Druid-Warlock build that focused on crowd-control spells as well as damage-over-time (DOT) spells that would allow him to stay out of combat. He discovered that even a simple paralyzing spell would give him experience from a player death – which meant he was able to cast and run away. It wasn't the most honorable way of fighting, but he was a doing it for a good cause. He needed the experience to level up and keep the Dungeon Core safe. He knew they still had Guardians (well, at least one good one), but he still considered himself the first line of defense.

The different groups of players that were entering the dungeon were having a hard time of it – the learning curve was steep. When compared to these others, Domn3r's group looked like experts. He was sure that higher quality groups would be incoming, but these first groups were a good enough judge on how challenging this floor was. It wasn't impossible, but it would be some time before they learned how to navigate their way through without dying around every corner. Hopefully by that time, they would have accumulated enough resources and the dungeon leveled up enough to build a new floor and the cycle would start again.

After watching the bodies of the dead players dissipate into thin air, he called out to the air around him, "Krista! I'm ready to respawn – I finally made it to level 40!" Krista offered her congratulations and within seconds his viewpoint changed, and the character selection window was in front of him. Now that he was finally able to choose some advanced classes, he was excited to see what he had available. He had learned earlier that if he had the base class unlocked, the advanced classes would be available to him.

Normally, each base class – such as Archer or Defender – had two possible advanced classes that were unlocked by the player through a lengthy quest that could involve days of preparation and traveling to accomplish. Since he was technically a monster, Devin lucked out because he wouldn't be able to do them. Therefore, the system automatically made these advanced classes available to him without all the trouble of completing each individual class quest. He could imagine De4th and his guild good-naturedly calling him a cheater and overpowered again – but there wasn't anything he could do about it. There were rumors that master classes were available after level 150, but as there was no one even close to that it wasn't something they had to worry about now.

Dungeon Upgradeable Mobile Boss
Character Creation

DUMB Level:	40

Available Races		
Human	Orc	Goblin
Elf	Troll	Ogre
Dwarf	Undead	Dragonkin
Gnome		

Available Classes	
Base Class	**Advanced Class**
Fighter	Warrior
	Knight
Brawler	Monk
	Berserker
Archer	Ranger
	Hunter
Rogue	Thief
	Assassin
Sorcerer	Conjurer
	Illusionist
Mage	Wizard
	Elementalist
Paladin	Crusader
	Holy Knight
Warlock	Necromancer
	Death Knight

Healer	Battle Priest
	Cleric
Druid	Witch Doctor
	Shaman
Defender	Barbarian
	Commander
Pet Trainer	Beastmaster
	Summoner

He dove into the details of each of the advanced classes, spending what seemed to him like hours learning about what the advantages and disadvantages were for each one. While he could specialize with one class and min/max his stats with more flexibility than a normal player, he had the advantage of being able to pick two classes with his dual class upgrade. He already knew that he wanted to choose the Dragonkin race – because, seriously, who doesn't want to be able to fly? The Dragonkin race only had a small additional bonus to fire-based magic resistance, but the other benefit was well worth it.

Based on his own experiences with what worked for him both inside and outside of the dungeon, he chose as his two classes a Necromancer and a Hunter. He loved being able to direct pets against his enemies as a Pet Trainer, but he was unable to do it in the dungeon because he couldn't "tame" the dungeon monsters. The Necromancer class didn't care where the monsters came from, just that they were dead. The disadvantage of this class was its lack of ranged attacks – it relied solely on its undead pets.

To get around this lack of ranged damage, the Hunter class would allow him to use a bow to attack from afar as well as set traps. He would be able to set additional traps in the dungeon, surprising the incoming players with unexpected obstacles that he could throw out on the fly. With his choices made, he spent another hour allocating his stat points and picking his skills and spells. There were massive amounts of skills to choose from since many of the base class options were still available. He ended up boosting his Agility and Wisdom scores based upon a couple of key skills/spells.

Raise Undead Scout IV			
Bring target back from the dead under the Necromancers' control for a limited time, increasing its speed and Agility while also decreasing its Constitution. Undead Scouts are best used for hit-and-run attacks and should be rarely used in stand-up fair fights.			
Undead Scout Limit:	5	Duration:	300.0 seconds
Casting Time:	1.5 seconds	Agility Increase:	30%
Constitution Decrease:	15%	Mana Cost:	200

Raise Undead Behemoth V			
Combine and raise from the dead multiple targets under the control of the Necromancer for a limited time. The resulting Behemoth has stats equal to a portion of every target combined but loses a portion of its Agility Stat due to its increased size. Because of the strain upon the Necromancer keeping the various body parts together, a sizable mana upkeep is necessary to maintain its structure.			
Targets Required (minimum):	3	Stat Point Portion:	75%
Agility Stat Decreased:	70%	Casting Time:	5.0 seconds
Mana Upkeep:	5 mana per	Initial Mana Cost:	800

	second but increases by 1 each second		

Snareshot III			
The Hunter fires an arrow that snares and pins the target to the ground for a limited time. Success is based upon the Agility stat compared to the target.			
Success Chance:	Hunter Agility > Target Agility	Duration:	20.0 seconds
Cooldown:	60.0 seconds		

Now that he had chosen his loadout, he appeared at the entrance of the dungeon and looked around. He needed some gear that would increase his Agility, Intelligence, and Wisdom. He almost had enough Wisdom now to keep a potential behemoth alive for almost five minutes based upon his mana regeneration. A little bit more would cover the upkeep while also allowing him to cast any additional spells that were needed. He took a couple of other Hunter-based utility skills to help deal some damage from range, but his main focus would be his undead pets.

After a couple of minutes, Krista found a decent bow and a combination of Archer and Warlock gear that made him look unique. He was a little worried at first whether he would be able to wear it, but Carl told him that any advanced class could wear the same gear as its base class. Just after he finished equipping the last piece of gear, Krista told him that there was a situation outside that he needed to look at.

He was still momentarily stunned every time he exited the dungeon as he took in all the buildings around him. Getting accustomed to the town being outside was going to take some getting used to. He rushed toward the closed gate – which had previously been open letting all players enter the town and dungeon as they wanted – and he saw De4thfrmbeh1nd and a couple of other guild members talking in a group.

As he got closer, he must have startled them because they almost pulled their weapons before they saw his name, **Dragonkin Hunter/Necromancer [Reckless]**. Now that he was in their guild, he found that he could choose to display his guild affiliation. This helped calm some of the new guild members that had seen him without having met them before.

"That's so not fair – *two* advanced classes? That is so OP – it took me days to unlock the Assassin class," De4th commented. "Hunter/Necromancer, huh? Well, I'm sure you have a good strategy in mind. Anyways, enough chitchat – we have a situation. Come up to the walls and take a look with me."

Devin followed De4th up the small staircase leading to the battlements atop the wall. As he looked over the edge, he saw what looked like hundreds of players arranged outside the wall in scattered camps. He looked closer at the individual players and found that they were a mixture of the *Divine Truth* and *Guiding Light* guilds camped outside. Worried, he looked over at De4th and saw the same sort of worry etched on his face. All Devin could think was, *this isn't good*.

"*Divine Truth* started arriving about an hour ago with *Guiding Light* following soon after. From what we can tell, they somehow learned about the properties of the town and how to go about capturing it. I would normally say that we have a mole somewhere in our organization, but I don't believe they counted on us already being here. When the Dungeon Core event first started, they were the first guild to become entrenched around the entrance and had to have been moving before it was announced. I have a friend that works for Wexendsoft and he let me know about it just moments before the patch notes were released – but he is just a lower-level coder. *Divine Truth* must have someone on the inside higher up in the organization to be able to take advantage of upcoming news. That's the only explanation that I have for this," De4th told him.

"My guess is that they are going to use most of *Guiding Light* to rush the walls and take out all of our defenders. Since PVP is disabled for anyone over level 40, there isn't much that *Divine Truth* can do other than provide gear and buff them up to the gills with high-level spells. I've counted at least 60 players there within the level range and they might have some hidden that I can't see. All our efforts to get closer to get an accurate count has ended in failure – they are watching for stealthers all over the place.

"As of this hour, we have 15 town guards that are all level 40 or above and are a range of different classes. The PVP restriction doesn't apply to NPCs, so the level 41 and 42 guards that have been training and leveling up can still participate. These extra levels probably won't affect that much, anyway, since they will be facing multiple parties of players. On our player side, we have 26 that can participate in the battle – we've never had a ton of players and those we have are generally a higher level. Your friends Domn3r and his party are included in this number, so we'll have to rely on them and the others to defend us. Of course, we have you as well, and if you're game you can help wherever we need you."

Devin agreed wholeheartedly – this was very similar to what he normally did: defending the dungeon. It didn't matter if it was alongside the mobs inside the dungeon or with his guild friends outside the dungeon. Fighting players was what he was created for and he would do it to the best of his ability no matter where it was. He was contemplating going back inside the dungeon to change his classes since there weren't any monsters to bring back from the dead, but his choice was taken away from him even as he thought about it.

The enemy at their gate finally decided to attack.

Chapter 28

They came slowly – there was no need to rush into danger. Instead of the 60 that De4th had estimated, there were exactly 80 players in 16 five-person groups heading their way. They all converged on the gate, being that it was weaker than the rest of the stone walls and the only obvious point of entry. Their tanks rushed ahead while the ranged fighters slung spells, arrows, and even throwing knives at the gate, steadily bringing its structure health down. As the tanks started beating on the stone gate, Devin could see the gate start to shake. Its health down to 75% already, the defenders started fighting back.

Mage and Archer guards, as well as all the defending players who had ranged attacks, began firing down on the attackers near the gate. Their combined attack did massive amounts of damage, but they were healed quickly by the waiting healers waiting back with the main group. Devin told the players and guards around him to concentrate on only one at a time, hopefully overwhelming any incoming healing with concentrated fire. It worked – as the first one fell, they target the next down the line until they had taken out three in a row. Unfortunately, their healers were close enough to cast *Resurrection* and after a couple of seconds the first of the bodies on the ground were brought back to the main group, ready for another round.

As he watched the revived tanks rush back into the fray, Devin couldn't help but see that the gate was down to 50% health. *If it keeps going like this, we'll never make it.* Looking around for a solution, he frantically searched the battlefield for an advantage they could use. Despairing, he watched as another tank went down and was promptly *Resurrected* about ten seconds later. Something about the time that it took them to revive the dead player stirred something in the back of his mind.

He couldn't completely concentrate on whatever it was, because some of the ranged attackers broke off from attacking the gate and fired toward the defenders on the wall. *I guess they don't like us killing their friends.* They quickly ducked down, but a couple of the NPC guards took some damage before they could hide. Ambrose and two other Healers were there to bring them back to full health, but they couldn't safely attack those outside anymore. Domn3r instructed all the guards and players down from the walls in order to defend the gate when it went down.

As he reached the bottom of the stairs leading down from the wall, he joined the rest of the defenders getting in position inside the gate. He could hear the pounding from the assault taking place outside the walls and as he looked around he saw resigned faces all around. With no other option, he got into position far away from the gate but still within range of his bow.

He nervously waited with his fellow ranged defenders; he suddenly wished he had time to run in and change his classes. *This Necromancer class is doing me no good here – there are no monsters to reanimate.* Looking through his skills again – hoping for miracle – he thought he may have found one.

Devin immediately jumped on guild chat and outlined a plan for both the remaining defenders and the rest of the waiting guild members. It was a longshot, but if it worked they might be able to salvage the situation. It would mean a great sacrifice for most of their guild members, but this was the only way he could see to pull it off. They reluctantly agreed to the plan, mainly because if they were overrun they were probably going to die anyway.

The health on the gate was down to 5% by this time and the defenders fell back to defend the guild house as per the plan. Devin retreated toward the Blacksmith where the rest of the higher-level guild members, including De4th and his lieutenants, were starting to file in. When they were all inside, Devin could hear an enormous crash of shattering stone emanating from the direction of the gate followed by a resounding cheer as the attackers took down the gate.

He looked out the window and saw all the enemy tanks rush inside and pause, confused at the absence of defenders. They moved farther in as the rest of their parties hurried inside, eager to wipe out the rest of the defending players and NPCs. As they approached the guild house, spells and arrows shot toward the attackers while the remaining melee defenders lined up in front. The last stand of the *Reckless* guild – or so they thought.

While they were distracted, all the higher-level guild members talked to Smythe, the blacksmith at the same time. While this sounds impossible, the system allows for more than one interaction via menu-based shopping screens. Within moments, each player inside the blacksmith dropped dead. *I hope they at least chose an awesome weapon or piece of armor.* Devin was lucky that no one had taken advantage of the "Death Conversion Contract" yet, as they were all concentrating on improving the defenses of the town first.

He walked outside, taking care to not pull attention to himself until he was hidden behind the Enchanting Hut with a full view inside the Blacksmith. Crossing his fingers, he used his *Raise Undead Behemoth V* spell and targeted every single dead player he could see – which amounted to over 50 of them. Inwardly thankful that the spell allowed him to target them (he wasn't entirely sure it would), he turned toward the middle of the town and directed the result of his spell to form there.

Out of the corner of his eye, he watched the bodies piled up in the Blacksmith start to rapidly deteriorate and disappear. In the center of their little town, a massive tornado of body parts and bones swirled around and around. They rotated faster and faster until they all flew together to coalesce in the middle of the eye of the tornado, revealing a 50-foot monstrous amalgamation of body parts.

It slightly resembled Bruce – as far as its size and undead status – but there the similarities ended. This was the mindless creation of a Necromancer and had no personality of its own, had two massive legs that could be mistaken for ancient Redwood trees, and two giant arms with fists the size of the Enchanting Hut that Devin was hiding behind. It didn't have a head, per se, because the two eyes located at the top of its chest was where the Behemoth ended.

Fighting on both sides of the battle paused as everyone stopped and stared as the **Undead Behemoth (Level ???)** appeared behind the attackers. Before anyone could move, Devin had his new pet attack the *Guiding Light* healers and casters near the rear of the attacking group. Two heavy, massive fists slammed into the ground, completely obliterating 22 of the grouped-up ranged players. As the shockwave expanded out from the impact, everyone within a 30-foot radius lost their footing and tumbled to the ground.

The Behemoth raised his fists a little bit off the ground and swept his arms to the sides, smacking into the remaining ranged players that were missed earlier. They were picked up from the ground where they were just getting to their feet and were thrown through the air at high speed, most of them splatting dead against the stone palisade.

The other tanks and melee fighters who were fighting the *Reckless* guild members turned toward the hulking monster and attacked in masse. Devin watched as his pets' health barely wavered as it took each of the attacks without even trying to defend itself. His Behemoth, whom he decided to call Happy (since that was what he was feeling right now), lifted his foot off the ground and quickly stomped forward, smashing a few of the armored figures into the ground. Seeing that their attacks were largely ineffective, the remaining attackers started to run for the entrance.

They were caught before they made it by the defending players and NPCs that blocked off their escape while they were trying to damage Happy. Their numbers were now evenly matched – with *Reckless* having a slight advantage – but *Guiding Light* didn't have any ranged attackers or healers left. They made short work of the attacking players without even needing any extra help from Happy. Once they were dead, instead of a resounding cheer which Devin had been expecting, they sternly marched over to the gate and lined up in front of it – as if daring someone to try to get past them. Devin backed up this look by having Happy fall in behind them and stare out at the *Divine Truth* players waiting in their camps.

After about 30 seconds of this, he had Happy retreat and lie down and curl up out of sight so that he couldn't be seen from outside the walls. His mana was dropping at an exponential rate and he needed to release his Undead

Behemoth from his spell. As soon as he was confident he couldn't be seen, Devin canceled the spell and watched as Happy fell apart into hundreds of different rotting body parts before disintegrating away.

He made his way over to the remaining defenders and sidled up next to Domn3r as he was watching the camp outside. "That was some fancy spell you had there, Devin. You know you're a cheat, don't you? I've looked into the Necromancer class before and their spells all say, 'target monster'. I've never heard about player corpses being used to create undead before – how did you do it?" Domn3r asked him quietly, but with a small smile threatening to emerge on his face.

Devin had seen that his spells all just said "target", and he got the idea that since he was a monster the rules might be a little different for him. He didn't know if it would work, but they needed to try something – and it had all worked out in the end. He didn't tell Domn3r about his uncertainty, however, "My mom always used to tell me that I was special – I guess she was right."

They had done it...but for how long?

Epilogue

After the attack two days ago, everything had pretty much gone back to normal. Or as normal as running both a dungeon and a town can get. *Guiding Light* and *Divine Truth* didn't attack again that day, or even the day after. The patch notes had announced the presence of the town and numerous players were flocking toward it to check it out. It started as a novelty for lower-level players, but they slowly found that they liked being able to run through a dungeon, leave when things started getting hard, and be able to sell all of their loot right outside the dungeon for more than they would get in town.

Krista had repaired the gate and improved their other defenses with the additional resources she acquired from the deaths of the attacking players. She was able to expand the capacity of the barracks so that it could accommodate even more guards – which were needed as they had an influx of players trying to damage buildings to get the monetary reward. They were all stopped before they did more than cosmetic damage, but it just meant they had to stay vigilant and watch everybody coming and going.

Despite the improved defenses, Devin was worried about another attack. He was sure that the *Guiding Light-Divine Truth* duo would attack again at some point, but they had shown no signs of it so far. They had gone away shortly after getting their asses handed to them by Happy and the town defenders. He figured they were looking for a way to get past Devin's **Undead Behemoth**, unaware that it was a once a week defense and only used in the direst emergencies.

The "sacrificial lambs" were for the most part happy. They were ecstatic when they learned about how the battle was won, stoked about whatever gear they had gotten in exchange for their deaths, and sad because they had all lost experience and, in some cases, a level. Levels and experience could be regained, but the town's existence and prosperity were worth their sacrifice.

Domn3r and his group had all gained multiple levels after the fight for the town. All of them were at least level 40 and were looking forward to going on their quests to gain their advanced classes. Domn3r wanted to be a Barbarian, which would switch his style from "all defense" to "a little defense plus a whole lot of attack". Devin wasn't sure how that would affect their group dynamic, but that was completely his decision. Ambrose was looking forward to becoming a Cleric, which would boost her healing spells and give her more helpful buffs.

As Devin figured he would, Bolt3n wanted to become a Ranger — allowing him to do even more damage with his precise shots. Max had her sights set on being a Thief way back in the beginning and had tailored her skills in trap detection and disarming to accommodate this.

Mac dithered back and forth between Wizard and Elementalist. As a Wizard he would be able to cast any spell but wouldn't have any specialty in any specific field. As an Elementalist, he would maximize his damage with elemental-based attacks. He was still deciding when he left with the rest of Domn3r's group to start their class quests. Devin figured he probably wouldn't decide until the last minute.

All in all, things were looking good. De4thfrmbeh1nd had really taken his town-building to heart and was steadily improving each building as their guild treasury steadily gained profits from their own dungeon-diving. Every building had at least a couple of upgrades and he wasn't neglecting their defenses either.

A new Mage Turret was unlocked when every building in town had been upgraded at least once. Krista bought this for them and was able to place it during the night when no one was around. It stood on top of the gatehouse and fired magical bolts toward any attackers outside or inside. De4th upgraded this as soon as he saw it, increasing its rate of fire and damage output.

De4th did have one more tidbit of information for Devin and Krista. He hadn't been able to tell them before this – it had been too crazy with everything going on. Shortly after hearing Devin's story, he had a hacker friend of his research both of their names and found a former address – but no current address.

From what he could piece together, after purchasing two one-way airline tickets to the Julius Nyerere International

Airport in Tanzania, they disappeared. Their bills and mortgage were paid for automatically from Krista's checking account for a couple of months before the house was sold to an anonymous buyer. There were no more records after that. Devin and Krista weren't sure how to respond to that – it was something that they would worry about later.

Violette...well, Violette was being Violette. Krista told Devin that hours had passed after he had left her crying before she got up and actually did something. She went through the motions of summoning her minions for her Guardian Room and dejectedly settled at the top of her temple. A few hours later – from what Violette had told her – she heard booming laughter coming from the room behind hers. Curious, she opened the door to the second Guardian Room to see where it was coming from. As she watched Bruce talking and laughing at himself, she felt new life invigorate her.

As it turns out, they had a lot in common and would talk for hours through the doorway between their two rooms. They couldn't leave their respective rooms, but they could at least see and talk to each other. Bruce later asked if there was any way that they could be in the same room together, but Krista had to shut him down. The system wouldn't allow them to guard the same room. However, after consulting with Carl, she took pity on Bruce since he had been such a good Guardian.

Krista was able to attach a large hidden room to both of the Guardian Rooms that was inaccessible to players but accessible to their Guardians. She made them promise to stay vigilant when it was busy in the dungeon, but they could use the room to relax together if they needed a break. Just a couple of hours ago they were finally able to meet in "person" for the first time. Although Krista wouldn't talk specifics about what happened next, Devin could hear the revulsion in her voice when she mentioned an "unnatural use of body parts". He thought he was probably better off not knowing.

As for Devin and Krista, things were just the same as they were before – but Devin secretly hoped that would change soon. They were both so busy with the all the various ongoing projects that they never got a chance to address his not-so-secret-anymore love for Krista. However, she was due to increase her Dungeon Level to 15 anytime now, which would give her access to her very own avatar. There were things that he wanted to tell her, but he wanted to be able to do it in person.

As it happened, Krista had gained enough experience to increase her Dungeon Level to 15 on a player that Devin dispatched in the dungeon. He was experimenting being a Dragonkin Assassin/Illusionist and had just surprised a Mage that was lagging behind the rest of her party. As soon as he heard the news, Krista respawned him in a little-visited room on the first floor. There was a Goblin Brawler in the room with him, but Devin ignored it.

Anxiously waiting, he was surprised at the sudden appearance of a High Elf Healer in the room with him. After a millisecond of confusion, he realized that it was Krista. She looked the same as she did when she first started the game with him, except that her hair had streaks of pink in it – similar to how she looked in real life. She looked as beautiful as he remembered – she really did look good as an Elf. She was wearing a simple white Healer robe, had a silver circlet resting on her head, and had a flashy sapphire necklace hanging around her neck. She had no weapon, but she didn't need any; she couldn't attack anything even if she wanted to.

"Hi," Devin said. *Smooth, moron.* "It's good to finally see you again. It's been hard only being able to talk to you without seeing you – it was like having a long-distance relationship."

Stuttering, he tried to correct himself, "Not that we're in a relationship, or anything. Unless you want to be...or something. You know the way I feel about you and you're free to choose what you want to do. No pressure – just as long as you know that you'll always be the one for me. Whether or not its reciprocated doesn't matter." Realizing he was rambling, he took a deep breath before continuing, "I love you Krista, and I want to stay near you whether or not you feel the same way. There, that's all I have to say."

Krista approached him and said, "I love you too, moron. I think I always have – I just never thought of you that way before we came here. You've changed so much over the last couple of months and I think it's been for the better. I'm proud of the person you've become – my friend, my champion, my hero.

Come here, you big lug." She slid into his arms and Devin felt complete for the first time in his life. They hugged for what seemed like forever but was more like a couple of minutes.

Devin, still in his Dragonkin body, looked down at Krista and said, "Wanna go watch me kill some people?"

"You know I do," she looked up at him with a mischievous grin on her face.

"It's a date," Devin responded happily.

Author's Note

Thanks for picking up the Glendaria Awakens Trilogy Compilation!

If you've already read this series and just wanted the entire trilogy in one book, then thank you for purchasing it!

If you are new to the world of Glendaria Awakens, I hope you enjoyed the journey of Devin and Krista! This was the first book – and first trilogy – I had ever written, and as I progressed along the trilogy my writing became a little better as a result. I have edited each of the books a little more (though Dungeon Player received a bit more than a little of attention) for grammar, fixed some formatting issues, and corrected a few mistakes that were pointed out to me by avid readers. It's not perfect (I wish it were :)), but without a complete rewrite it is still better than it used to be.

Following the next few pages are a few bonus items I included with this compilation, including some pictures of some of my notes and maps I made while I was writing. I'm not an artist, nor do I have great penmanship, so they are a bit elementary; nevertheless, they are what I used to keep track of the dungeon as I was describing them.

After those pictures is a very short story that I felt like writing to extend the Glendaria Awakens universe a little. I haven't decided yet whether I will write another whole story centered around the world I created, but if you enjoyed this book and the short story, let me know if you'd like more!

You can find me on facebook or email me at: jonathanbrooksauthor@gmail.com

And, as usual, if you liked my book – leave a review! Reviews help other readers know if a book it worth reading or not – every review helps. I personally love 4 or 5-star reviews, but if you didn't like it then I still invite you to review it. I appreciate constructive criticism!

If you enjoy dungeon core, dungeon corps, dungeon master, dungeon lord, dungeonlit or any other type of dungeon-themed stories and content, check out the Dungeon Corps Facebook group where you can find all sorts of dungeon content.

If you would like to learn more about the Gamelit genre, please join the Gamelit Society facebook group.

LitRPG is a growing subgenre of GameLit – if you are fond of LitRPG, Fantasy, Space Opera, and the Cyberpunk styles of books, please join the LitRPG Books Facebook group.

For another great Facebook group, visit LitRPG Rebels as well.

If you would like to contact me with any questions, comments, or suggestions for future books you would like to see, you can reach me at jonathanbrooksauthor@gmail.com

I will try to keep my blog updated on any new developments which you can find on my Author Page on Amazon.

To sign up for my mailing list, please visit: http://eepurl.com/dl0bK5

To learn more about LitRPG, talk to authors including myself, and just have an awesome time, please join the LitRPG Group

Books by Jonathan Brooks

Glendaria Awakens Trilogy

Dungeon Player

Dungeon Crisis

Dungeon Guild

Glendaria Awakens Trilogy Compilation w/bonus material

Uniworld Online Trilogy

The Song Maiden

The Song Mistress

The Song Matron (December 2018)

Station Cores Series

The Station Core

The Quizard Mountains

Book 3 (Early 2019)

Extras – Notes and Maps

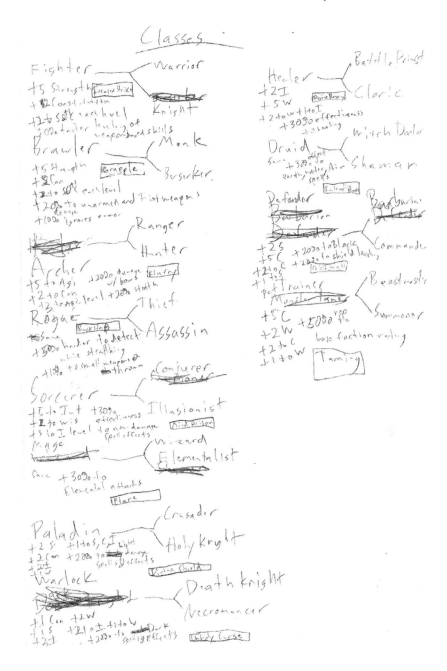

Classes

Fighter — Warrior
+5 Strength [Excused Strike]
+2 Constitution
+2 to 50% each level
+30% faster leveling of
  weapons and skills
Brawler — Knight
             — Monk
+5 Strength [Grapple]
+2 Con
+2 to 50% each level — Berserker
+20% to unarmed and Fist weapons
+10% ignores armor

— Ranger
— Hunter
Archer +20% damage [Flurry]
+5 to Agi w/ bows
+2 to Con
+2 to Agi level +30% stealth
Rogue — Thief
        — Assassin
+50% harder to detect [Back Stab]
  while stealthing
+10% to small weapons
            thrown

— Conjurer
Sorcerer
+5 + Int +30%
+2 to wis effectiveness Illusionist
+5 to I level to non-damage [Mild Poison]
            Spell effects
Mage — Wizard
       — Elementalist
Same +30% to
Elemental Attacks
[Flare]

— Crusader
Paladin
+2 S +1 to S, C if Light Holy knight
+2 Con +20% to damage
+2 I Shills & effects [Divine Shield]
Warlock
               — Death knight
               — Necromancer
+1 Con +2 W
+1 S +2 I + 1 +1 to W Dark
+2 I +20% to spelling effects [Unholy Curse]

— Battle Priest
Healer
+2 I [Divine Boon] Cleric
+5 W
+2 to W + HoT
+30% effectiveness
  to healing
Druid — Witch Doctor
same +30% to — Air Shaman
earth/nature
  spells [Entangle Roots]

Defender — Barbarian
           — Duelist
+2 S +20% to Block — Commander
+5 C +2% to shield leveling
+2 to C [Shield Wall]
+1 S
+1 W
Pet Trainer — Beastmaster
Monster Tamer
+5 C +50% to — Summoner
+2 W base faction rating
+2 to C [Taming]
+1 to W

655

Initial Goblin Cave

→ Treasure Chest

Goblin Chieftan
Goblin mage
Goblin Brawler

Teleporter to beginning at the entrance

Entrance

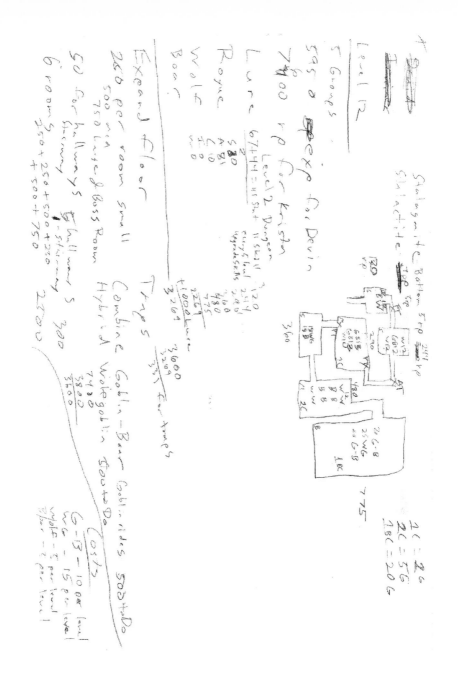

Start

Level 2

5 Groups
5050
7900 xp for Krista
Lure
Royne
Wolf
Bear

Level 2 Dragon
6744+4145a+11Sawl = 720
cityfield 240
upgrades 240
460
480
475
2265
+1000 Lure
3265
3265
351 for trops

5050 xp exp for Devin

Level 2
S3D
A81
L10
B0

Expand floor
250 per room small
500 min
750 Lure & Boss Room
50 for hallways
6 rooms

Traps
Combine Goblin — Bear
Hybrid Wolfgoblin
3600
3209

250+500+500+750 2300

Goblin rides 500+Do
Stout+Do

3600
7400
3800
3500

Costs
G-B — 10 per level
WG — 15 per level
Wolf — 5 per level
Bear — 8 per level

1C = 2G
2C = 5G
18C = 20G

775

360

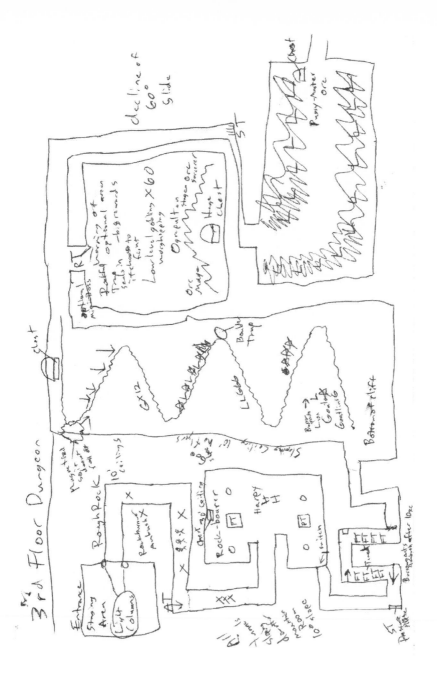

3rd Floor Dungeon

658

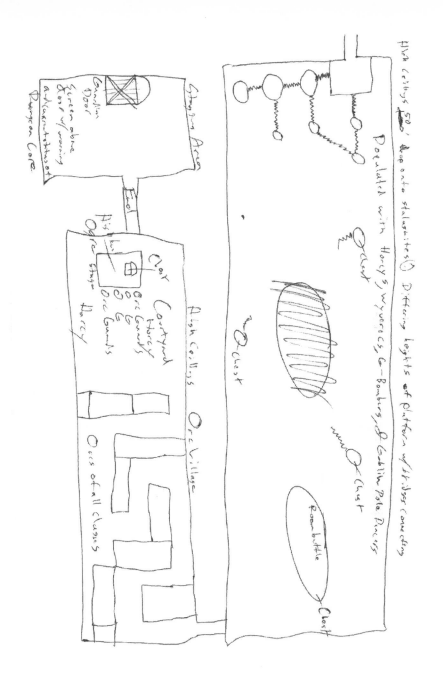

High ceilings 50' drop onto stalagmites() Differing heights of platform w/ 3+3ss connectors

Dotulated with Harey's Wyverns, Etc. ← Bombers, & Goblin Pole Racing

Chest

Chest

Chest

Raw battle

Chest

Common Door
Screen w/ wire door w/ warning
a slave with at
Dungeon Core

Dungeon Area

High Ceilings   Orc Village

Orcs of all classes

Clay   Courtyard   Harey
Orc Guards
Orc Guards
Orc Guards
High Ceiling   Harey
Ogre Stage

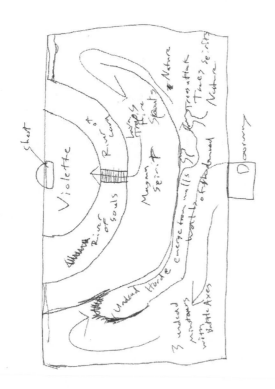

Violette

Shot

River of Souls

Magma Spirit

Wings Trees Spirits

Nature

Trees attack Nature

Trees sensing Nature

Undead Horde emerge from walls

Heart to of Redwood

3 undead minotaurs with Battle Axes

Doorway

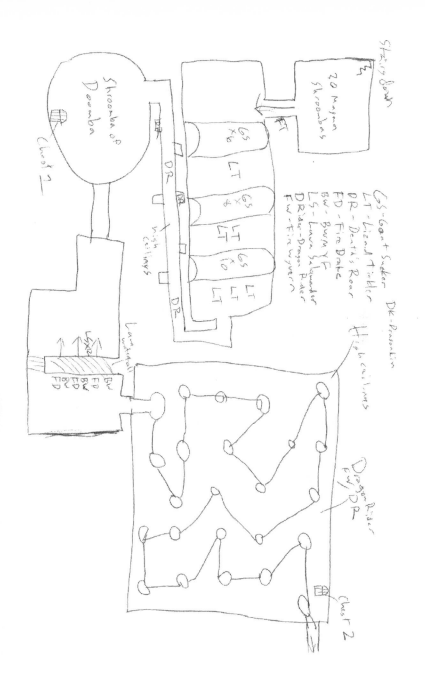

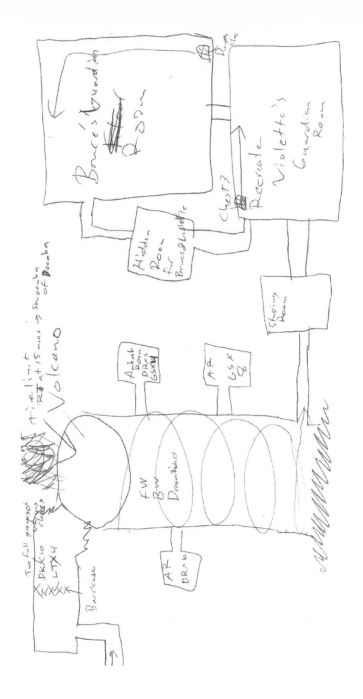

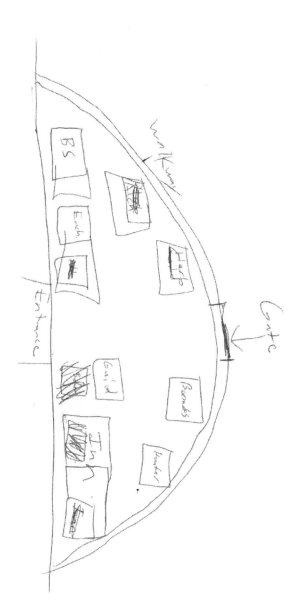

Extras – Short Story

*If you've read the trilogy, you'll perhaps notice that Devin is a bit of a cheater in terms of the game mechanics. He can change his class as well as respec his skills, change his race, and even go into battle with **two** classes. So, in honor of his OP status, here is a short story that showcases his abilities. By finding a way to combine two classes – which are decent in and of themselves – he takes advantage of their strengths while practically eliminating their weaknesses. This is just for fun; this is not necessarily how another addition to the series would go...but who knows? If I do decide to do another series set in this world, I may adopt a portion of this to enhance the story – though Devin's OP status would have to be toned down quite a bit to be "fair".*

"You want to go where?" Domn3r asked, a look of incredulity on his face. Devin could see him glance at the rest of his group, as if seeking some sort of confirmation of his disbelief.

"Sure, we need to add another dungeon territory – what better one than the Underwater Grotto? It's close by, so I don't see what the problem is," he responded, unsure why they were so hesitant.

"The *problem*," Ambrose replied, "is that nobody has ever defeated the Giant Squidler at the end. It keeps wiping even higher-level groups, even though the rest of the dungeon isn't hard; the mobs in there are only level 35 to 45. Easily done, especially since we're in our 60's now, but killing the boss at the end is a different matter."

"Damn right," Mac interjected, "we won't get any experience from killing anything in there, nor much in the way of loot drops, and you'd just wipe on the boss."

Devin couldn't understand why no one had ever finished this mid-level dungeon before. "How is it the boss has never been killed?"

Max uncharacteristically spoke up before anyone else could respond, "Because the most damage anyone has done to it is 50% before it uses an ability that confuses everyone in the room, causing them to inadvertently attack their party members – and even themselves when there was only one player left. No one had found a way to counter this; though, to be fair, there was one team I heard of that got it down to 45% because their pet was unaffected. Unfortunately, it didn't last long enough, and the party wiped. It's now kind of abandoned because the mob drops inside are not worth it, even for groups of the same level."

Hmmm...I think I have an idea.

"Hey Krista, can I get a respawn please?" he asked of the room in general, knowing that she could hear him.

"Sure, one respawn coming right up, my little cutie pie!" He blushed a little at her nickname, but he was fortunately transported to the Transition Room before he had to endure the looks from his guildmates.

Looking through his options, he thought he found a good combination of classes and skills that would allow him to survive the encounter at the end of the Underwater Grotto. Since he had to kill the boss by himself, he thought his selections would work exceptionally well. It would either work spectacularly...or it would waste almost two hours or more of their time.

He popped back into the entrance to their own dungeon within minutes, surprising them by appearing as a ghastly-looking Undead. He chose it for its extra Intelligence and Wisdom starting bonuses, as well as the extra bonuses from Dark-based spells and effects. From what he could tell, that *should* increase the effectiveness of...his main attacks.

"Ok, I think I have a solution. If you all can get me through the main part of the dungeon, I think I can defeat the boss."

Bolt3n looked at his name and his class selections and frowned, "I'm not sure how using those classes will help, but I'm game. Didn't have anything else to do for the next couple of hours, anyway. How about the rest of you?"

There were no objections, although most of them needed to log out after the dungeon dive, so Devin knew he probably only had one shot at this. If he died, they probably wouldn't want to waste another chunk of time again, meaning that he had to get this right the first go around.

It didn't take them long to get to the new dungeon after they left the blossoming town around their **own** dungeon entrance. It was a short 15-minute jog through a low-level area, which meant that they didn't have to fight off hordes of mobs along the way.

Eventually they arrived at the river where Devin had originally tried to lure a Giant Frog from — before their Dungeon Core had been stolen. There was still a plethora of new creatures there that would be an excellent addition to their burgeoning dungeon, but what he didn't know until earlier that day was the presence of a dungeon nearby.

Fortunately, he didn't have to locate it himself, he only had to follow Domn3r; the party leader and now long-time friend knew the locations of most of the dungeons around the world of Glendaria Awakens — even if he hadn't been there yet. He was always looking to conquer new and exciting things, so he researched constantly about where he wanted to strike next.

Before they entered the Underwater Grotto, Devin stopped them all and prepared himself for the coming fights. Although he wasn't going to participate in killing them — for the most part — his strategy involved benefitting from the deaths of the mobs inside.

As a Summoner, one of the Advanced classes a step up from a Pet Trainer, he could summon beings to his side to fight for him. They ranged from simple beasts to demons to elementals – it all depended on how you decided to specialize. For this dungeon, Devin specialized in creating elementals; the only thing was that he didn't want just one – he wanted a whole bunch.

Summoners were strong in the sense that they could summon something their level to fight their battles for them. Where they got weak was when they summoned more than one thing to fight by their side; the more summons, the weaker they became. So, when Devin summoned 8 Dark-based Shadow Elementals, the rest of the party was confused. At their size and power, they looked like little shadow children, with their levels ranging between 7 and 8.

"Trust me, I know what I'm doing," he told them.

The former Defender turned Barbarian led the way into the entrance and Devin could immediately feel the difference inside the enclosed space. The moisture was heavy in the air, and the lack of light made it difficult to see further than 25 feet in front of them. Ambrose, however, had the solution to that as she used one of her Cleric powers to create a bright light that hovered overhead, lighting up the entire first cave.

Which didn't help Max out, since as a Thief she was used to slinking through the shadows so that she could sneak up on her prey. Luckily, the mobs in there were far below all their respective levels – by nearly 20 or more. She didn't need to stealth to be able to put the hurt on the Giant Frogs (Level 36) they saw when the room was lit up.

Domn3r immediately attracted all their attention with a mighty Barbarian Shout, causing them to surround the lightly-armored but extremely deadly tank. Ambrose cast one of her divine protection spells on him, increasing his defense by such an amount that the lowly frogs 30 levels beneath his own did absolutely no damage.

When they were all gathered around Domn3r, Mac began casting one of his longer AOE spells as he intended to finish off the entire group all at once. As an Elementalist (he finally decided on the class because he really enjoyed blowing stuff up), his elemental attacks got a huge boost, at the sacrifice of some basic utility spells that he otherwise would've gotten if he had become a Wizard. Devin made sure to back up near the side wall, gathering his shadow children around him. He didn't want to accidentally get hurt, since he was still technically a dungeon mob to the others, despite being in the same guild.

A firestorm erupted above the ineffectually-attacking Giant Frogs, destroying the croaking amphibians in less than a second. Domn3r was unhurt, as friendly-fire was turned off for their own party. Bolt3n stood around, essentially twiddling his thumbs, as there was very little for the Archer-turned-Ranger to do.

Now, however, it was Devin's turn to get to work. As a Witch Doctor – who relied on a mysterious otherworld sight to see the spirits, or "souls", of the recently deceased – he could utilize the class's special powers to capture and convert the spirits to power different things. Most of the Witch Doctors he had seen – which, admittedly were not that many, as they weren't a popular class to play – used the spirits they captured on heavily destructive Dark-based spells. They weren't popular because they needed a steady stream of souls, which were consumed when they used their spells. Players were more inclined to use classes like Mages, who only had to rely on their mana to power their spells.

One under-utilized aspect of the Witch Doctor, however, was the ability to infuse those spirits it captured into themselves or their party members; in this case, however, it could also be used on his summons. The drawback to these "infusions" was that they only lasted for one battle before being consumed, leaving almost all players to ignore the benefits that the ability could impart.

If Devin were taking part in the battles through the dungeon, then he would have to agree with the majority of players. The small extra bonuses from the spirits he gathered after the Giant Frogs died would be wasted on the next fight, leaving them as puny and weak as they were before. In fact, dispersed between the 8 of them, their stats were raised just enough from the "infusion" of souls that they were the equivalent of only level 10 now – barely even a threat to a single frog, let alone the roomful that was just decimated.

Fortunately, Devin had his own group that took care of the mobs inside the dungeon; as a result, his Shadow Elementals weren't involved in a single battle. Players couldn't do that, because as soon as they or their group initiated combat, there went the bonuses to themselves or others afterward. Since he wasn't technically in their group, and he never actually participated in any battles, the bonuses he "infused" in his shadow children just kept adding up.

By the time they reached the bottom floor of the dungeon, Domn3r and his group had killed hundreds if not thousands of mobs, most of which were taken out without much effort. From Giant Frogs, Water Sprites, various water snakes, Armored Crabs, and Lizardmen that were similar to the Dragonkin they had fought before, they all fell to the over-leveled party of experienced dungeon dwellers.

Only once did they have any type of fight on their hands, when they were surprised by an ambush of Royal Naga Guards. The human-snake hybrids had burst out of a pool that Max had assured them was empty, catching Ambrose in the side and doing a bit of damage before Domn3r picked them up. Fortunately, the surprise attack was salvageable and easy once they got them away from their healer. Devin almost intervened and helped with his Shadow Elementals; however, things got better once she was able to heal herself and concentrate on killing the ambushing mobs. He was relieved – it would've sucked going down almost the entire dungeon without anything to show for it.

His elementals – they couldn't really be considered shadow **children** anymore – had grown both in size and level. Because of the Dark-based nature of the "infusions", his Undead class improved the bonuses they received. They towered over the party, nearly four times the height of Bolt3n who was the tallest of everyone there. When he looked at their levels, he was surprised to see that their stats were equivalent to players around level 90 or above. Even though individually the mobs they killed were weak, when you added up all the bonus stats they provided it because ridiculous.

When they reached the door leading to the final area, he could see the incredulous looks on his friends' faces as they took in his summoned elementals.

"I've never seen anything like that – but I shouldn't be surprised. You seem to break all the rules," Domn3r told him, as he prepared to head in.

"Yeah, if this worked here, we can use the same method for other dungeons, though this was easy because of the lower-level mobs. If they were higher level and lived long enough, there would be a possibility that their AOE attacks could hit you, resetting these guys back to nothing. I'm glad it didn't happen this time, at least," Mac told him, before shaking his hand, "Good luck, my friend."

The rest of the party wished him good luck as well, and Devin pushed the doors open, ready to face the Boss of the Underwater Grotto dungeon. He wasn't exactly sure what he was in store for, but he was as ready as he was going to get.

The doors slammed close behind him when he and his 8 summons walked inside. In front of them, a long stone pier stretched across the first half of the room; the rest of the room was filled with deep, nearly-black water. It was only now that it was so dark that he realized he couldn't rely on the light spell from Ambrose to see anymore. It wasn't pitch dark, as there was at least a little ambient illumination, seemingly coming from all around him. Either that, or his Undead race could see a little better in the dark than others.

Either way, he approached the edge of the pier and looked inside the water, trying to figure out where the boss was supposed to be. When nothing appeared, he stepped back and looked around – and that was when a massive tentacle emerged from the water with a huge splash and wrapped around the Shadow Elemental right next to him. It tried to lift it up but seeing that it was made of shadow...well...it was kind of slippery. As a result, although it could hold the elemental, it couldn't get enough grip to lift it into the air.

The tentacle, despite not being able to pick up his summons, was still able to do a little damage to it. Devin could see that instead of suction cups (or whatever they were called) like an octopus would have, the tentacles were lined in sharp spikes, which – if they ever got ahold of him – would tear him to shreds.

Luckily, the damage was minimal due to the difference in their "levels"; when Devin looked closer at the serrated arm sticking out of the water, he could see that it was called Giant Squidler (Level 50). Such a difference in their respective stats, even though this was a boss, was so great that the Shadow Elemental was in no danger of dying anytime soon.

But that didn't mean that **he** was in the same boat. Devin immediately retreated towards the entrance doors, putting as much distance between him and the water before ordering the rest of his summons to attack the grasping Squidler arm.

They literally tore into it; within seconds of their concentrated attack, the end of the tentacle broke off, torn to pieces. The rest of the arm was quickly sucked down in the water and silence reigned across the room as his Shadow Elementals paused as they waited for another target.

Which soon erupted from the center of the water, causing a huge wave to splash against and over the edge of the pier. Even from his "safe" position near the door, Devin was still drenched as the wave continued until it crashed against the wall behind him.

When he was able to clear the water from his eyes, he could see that a gigantic shape had emerged, where it somehow perched on the surface of the dark pool. Its humongous head seemed to comprise most of its body, with multiple eyes creating a ring that saw in every direction. It also had at least six mouths that he could see, beaked horrors that were filled with fangs larger than his arm.

It dwarfed everything in the room; Devin estimated that it was nearly 150 feet long from head to tentacles, give or take a few inches. Speaking of tentacles, he could see that despite the one they damaged, the Giant Squidler still had dozens of the deadly appendages.

Ranged attacks seemed to be the normal way to go when fighting this monstrosity; either that, or you'd have to wait until the tentacles tried to snatch someone and then destroy it before it could do to much damage. Once the tentacles had been pared down, it was most likely that the Squidler would get close and attack with its body.

Devin didn't want to wait and take the careful approach, however. Although he didn't have any ranged attacks, he didn't need them. His Shadow Elementals were made from "shadow" – they weren't exactly what you would call landbound. He sent them out over the water, and he watched as they floated above the tentacles that tried to snatch them out of the air.

When they were close enough, they started laying into the head, eyes, and even mouth of the Giant Squidler. A horrific noise came from it; something like a cross between a yelping dog, a screeching bird, and a wailing injured elephant emerged from multiple mouths. With 10 seconds, Devin could see that its health was already approaching 50%.

When it hit the threshold, the giant squid seemed to shrink into itself. It got smaller and smaller and Devin thought that, inexplicably, it was dying. Instead, once it reached a certain size, it seemed to explode ink out of every part of its body, thoroughly drenching everything in the room.

When Devin was able to clear the second liquid in less than a minute from his eyes, he felt strange. Even though he had never drunk alcohol excessively when he was "alive" and out in the real world, he felt like what he thought he would feel if he were heavily intoxicated. And maybe stoned...and on lots of pain-killers. It was to the point where it hurt to try to concentrate on anything for more than a moment.

Devin heard more screams of pain coming from the boss, but his vision was so impaired that he couldn't see far enough to make out what was happening. He sat down, worried that he would fall and hurt himself – or worse yet, stumble near the water and fall in.

It was only when he realized that his vision was clearing, and the sounds of battle were over, that he knew they had won. He looked toward the pool and saw the corpse of the Giant Squidler, black blood leaking out from multiple wounds as it floated on top of the water.

After standing up, Devin walked toward the edge of the pier and saw a floating tentacle near him. He concentrated on it and attempted to loot the boss, knowing that it was what he needed to do to finish the dungeon.

Congratulations!

You have successfully captured the dungeon: Underwater Grotto! The Dungeon Player now has access to this dungeon as well as:

- Expanded Dungeon Territory
- All monsters currently used by the dungeon: Underwater Grotto
- The ability to combine all dungeons together with further expansion

Further expansion from capturing additional dungeons will further add potential benefits.

Current Dungeon Total: 3

In addition, because this dungeon has not been fully defeated before, the Dungeon Upgradeable Mobile Boss will receive:

- +30 to available starting stat points
- The ability for the Dungeon Player to unlock access to a third class

---

Well, damn...looks like I'm even more OP now.

Thank you for reading my little short story!

Again, if you'd like me to write more in the world of Glendaria Awakens, let me know. If there is enough response and desire for more, I will give my adoring public what they want!

Made in the USA
Columbia, SC
23 December 2019